Few Blue Skies

ALSO BY CAROLINA IXTA

Shut Up, This Is Serious

few blue skies

CAROLINA IXTA

Quill Tree Books
An Imprint of HarperCollinsPublishers

HarperCollins Children's Books, a division of HarperCollins Publishers, 195 Broadway, New York, NY 10007

HarperCollins Publishers, Macken House, 39/40 Mayor Street Upper, Dublin 1, D01 C9W8, Ireland

Quill Tree Books is an imprint of HarperCollins Publishers.

Few Blue Skies

harpercollins.com
Library of Congress Control Number: 2025947623
ISBN 978-0-06-328791-4
Typography by Jenna Stempel-Lobell
25 26 27 28 29 LBC 5 4 3 2 1
First Edition

The children in the Inland Empire are like canaries singing in coal mines, but no one is listening.

—Elizabeth Sena, founding member of the South Fontana Concerned Citizens Coalition

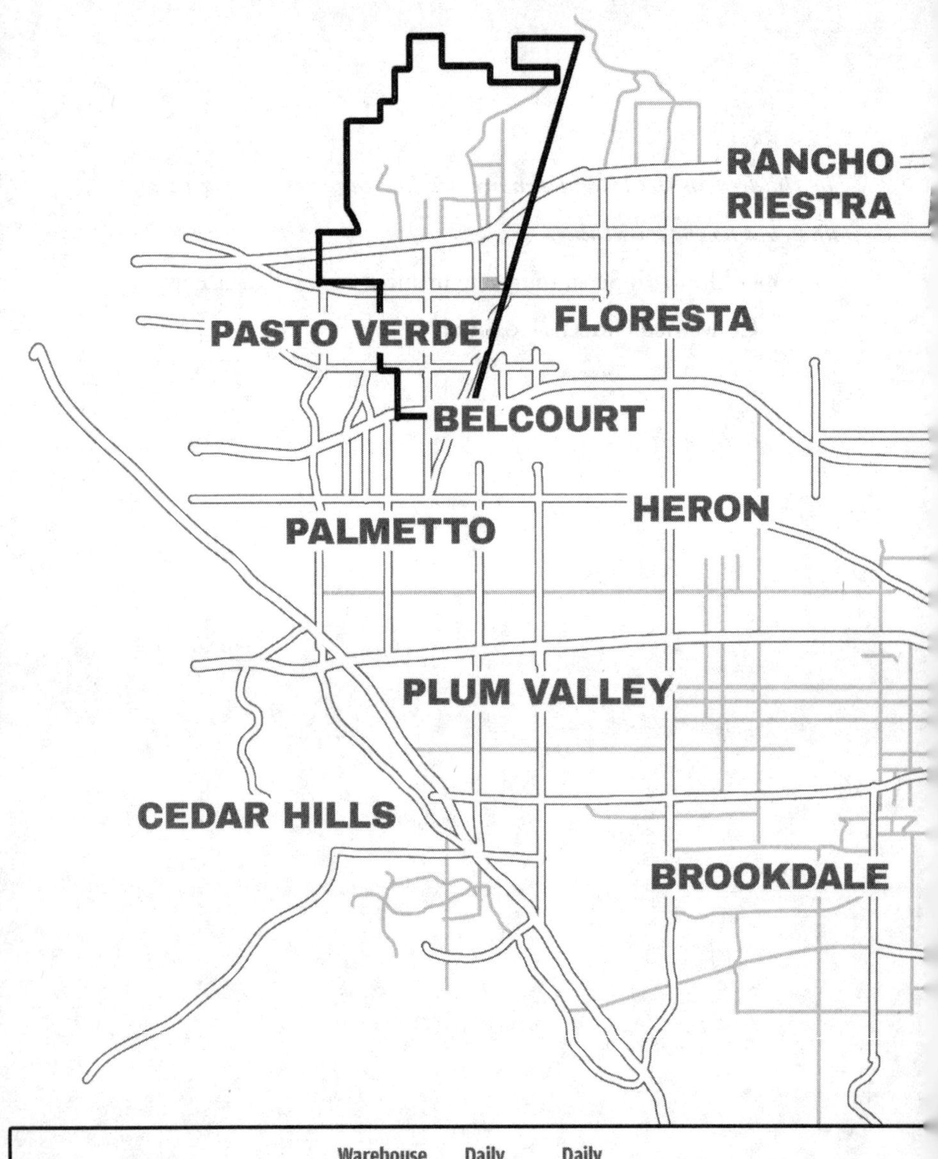

Category	Warehouse count	Acreage	Warehouse floor space (sq. ft.)	Daily truck trips	Daily diesel PM (pounds)	Daily NOx (pounds)	Daily CO2 (metric tons)	Jobs
Approved	12	630	15,100,000	10,000	13.8	1,558	420.6	5,040
Pending Construction	1	18	400,000	0	0	0	0	144
Existing	332	2,946	70,575,000	47,000	65	7,323	1976.7	23,568
Vacant	21	185	4,425,000					

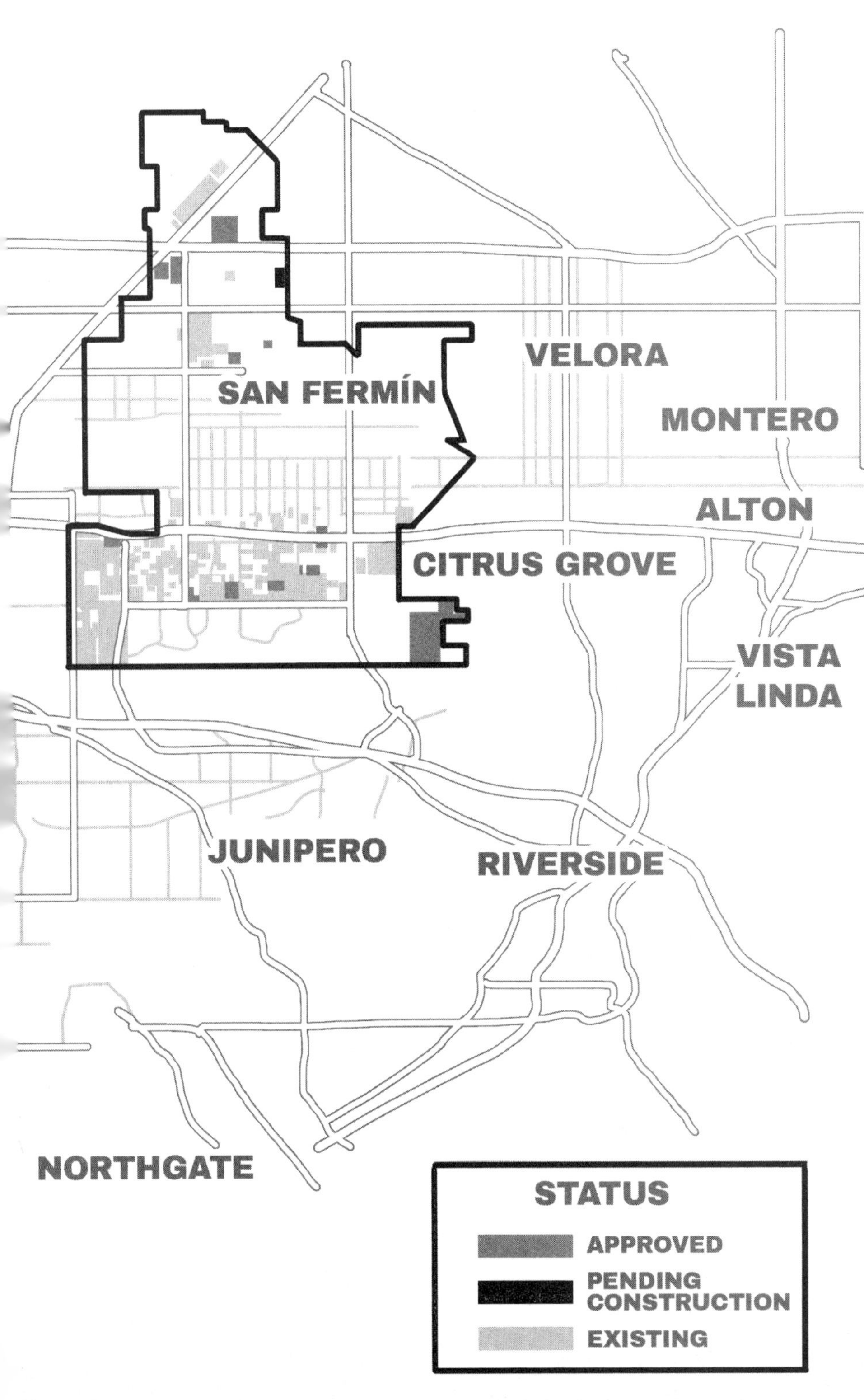
VELORA
SAN FERMÍN
MONTERO
ALTON
CITRUS GROVE
VISTA
LINDA
JUNIPERO
RIVERSIDE
NORTHGATE
STATUS
APPROVED
PENDING
CONSTRUCTION
EXISTING

Few Blue Skies

NO MATTER HOW HARD I TRY, I CAN'T SEE THE SKY. NOT even the line of the Jurupa mountains.

It used to be so easy—a clear view of the earth around me. But after Selva moved in, everything turned gray. Especially the air we're breathing.

I sit in a haze of exhaust on my way to school. It's hardly eight, but the semitrucks have already begun to bottleneck onto the road, slowing everyone's pace. I inch past their homes, a series of Selva warehouses, and peer through the smog to find my pa. He stands outside the parking lot, along with a hundred other Selva workers, picketing.

The strike was supposed to be simple. Demand better pay, better health insurance, better treatment, sign a contract, and get back to work within one week.

But nothing with Selva is simple.

One week turned to four and, for the last month, my pa has been on strike.

Before working for Selva, my pa and his best friend, Ernesto, were farmworkers, factory workers, painters.

When I was younger, I would tag along with them while they ran work errands. It was always the four of us—me and my pa, Julio and Señor Ramos. Because our fathers were best friends, Julio and I became best friends. While our fathers shopped, Julio and I sat in the heart of the hardware store, thumbing through paint swatches. We would come up with our own names for them: Eggshell, Rodeo Dust, Butter Pecan.

I thought with names like that, nothing could be bad about paint.

But its smell never matched the card descriptions. It was unforgiving, relentless, and always made my pa cough. No matter how many times my ma put my pa's clothes through the washer, no matter the brand of detergent she used, no matter the number of rinse cycles, the scent lingered in the fabric.

I later learned in science class that paint has toxins in it that can hurt the human body with enough exposure. I'd never known that before—that working could give you money but take your health.

And I never understood why my pa's cough got worse when he and Julio's pa quit their jobs as painters to work at the warehouses.

They'd been enticed by the large advertisement Selva put over the 10. It was in a premier location: after the giant In-N-Out Burger replica, before the billboard for Adriana's Insurance. A large, forest-green rectangle that promised an ease to commerce no one had ever experienced before. One click could get anything to your doorstep in a matter of hours.

But that ease needed workers to make it happen. And that employment came with its own risk—one that was never featured in those billboards.

The cough that started with painting worsened in the warehouses.

Even when I forced my pa to start wearing surgical masks for most of the workday, even when he would get annual checkups at the doctor, even when he brought his asthma inhaler everywhere he went.

But after Julio's pa died, I realized it wasn't the paint at all.

It was the air.

It was the mayor.

It was Selva.

Fall Semester

One

TODAY IS THE FIRST TIME JULIO SPEAKS TO ME IN OVER A year. Julio used to be my best friend. He used to be my boyfriend.

But nobody would know that. Because, since last August, Julio has acted as though I do not exist.

Things aren't like they used to be. Back in the spring, when he first touched my hand. Back in the summer, when we first kissed in my bedroom. Back before his pa died, before everything was different.

But today, Julio steps into science class, walks up to me, and gestures to the empty desk beside mine.

"Is anyone sitting there?" he asks.

This is the first thing he's said to me since the day I arrived at his front door. It was a week after his father's funeral, and I stood on his porch—a bag of Baker's in my hand and hope in my heart. He looked at me from the entryway, listening when I told him that I would be there for him, even if it was just to hold him.

But Julio said that he couldn't see me anymore, that he needed some space, that it would be better if I left him alone for a while.

Then he slammed the door in my face.

That while turned into a week, turned into a month, turned into a year, turned into today.

Hearing his voice blooms something inside of me. It's still familiar—a ring from a season nearly forgotten, like the birdsong of spring after a miserable winter. But it wilts quickly.

I stare at the whiteboard, shake my head, and say, "No."

And then Julio sits next to me—like all of this is normal, like nothing between us ever happened.

I pretend not to care, like I do every time Julio is close by. But my heart pounds at the base of my neck, thuds in my throat.

I breathe, trying to quiet it, and stare straight ahead. I only glimpse at Julio when he's distracted, pulling his notebook out of his backpack. Even from here, I can see the brown of his eyes. Deep like something else that's elapsed—the amber of a sunset, coffee granules at the bottom of a mug.

He looks at me just then.

And despite the year that has passed, his eyes blink in flickers that hopscotch time. That almost makes it feel like none has passed at all.

They still have it—his eyes are soaked in summer.

The entire season strikes in his stare.

He opens his mouth to say something, but I turn away again. Mr. Padilla is starting class, outstretching the homework tray on his desk toward us.

"Good morning," he says. "Please turn in your independent study packets from yesterday's AQA day."

Yesterday was an Air Quality Awareness day—it was the third one this month.

When the air quality index states that the air outside is too hazardous, regular school is canceled. Instead, we go to the school gym to pick up an independent study packet, finish it at home, and turn it in whenever the air is safe enough for us to come back to school. I spend every AQA day with my friend Ale. We sat in her apartment yesterday, HEPA filters on her windows, N95s on when we had to go to our shift at Nicho's.

I stand to turn mine in when I see Julio's palm extended in midair. "Paloma," he calls, "I can take yours up."

I hesitate, trying my best not to look at him again. I stare at his packet instead, at the perfect symmetry of his five-letter names written along the front page: Julio Ramos.

His handwriting is still the same, the *J* sloping lazy and low on the bottom. I haven't seen it since he wrote me letters when we were together. They're beneath my bed, buried and dusty-edged like all other memories of that summer.

I throw my packet on top of it just so I don't have to think about it anymore, so I don't have to remember. I avoid looking at him, but I can feel him smiling.

Julio turns it in and walks back to his seat. He scoots his chair a centimeter closer to mine, and I scoot mine away.

I try to ignore him when Mr. Padilla reads the morning announcements. But I can't focus. I can smell Julio from here, his perpetual blend of grass, sunshine, and soil from his pa's garden.

The only thing strong enough to pull me out of it is when Mr. Padilla begins talking about the college and career fair.

"After school on Friday," he says, pinning a flyer to a bulletin board, "in the school gym. I know college applications have already been turned in, but it might be good if you're looking for financial aid options."

Julio and I used to go to the college and career fair together every year. We had our futures all planned out: I'd go to UC Riverside for media studies, he'd go to UC Davis for plant sciences.

We mainly went to the fair to figure out how we could afford it. That's where we first discovered the Projects for Purpose scholarship—a scholarship based on science research. Winners got their work published in the *Young Scholars Journal* and won a ten-thousand-dollar prize.

It seemed perfect for us.

I'd been dreaming about getting a national publication since I started writing for our school's *Herald*.

I originally joined to help with my college applications, but I stayed when I saw what was happening to Julio's pa, saw that mine was getting sick, saw that so many people lived here, like we had, unaware of what was happening until it arrived embedded in a body or submerged in a grave. The paper helped bring some awareness to the warehouses sprouting on every corner, but not any national attention.

Even though I'd slowly worked my way from staff writer to editor in chief, a national publication was still out of my reach. Winning the scholarship would guarantee I would get the publication, and would guarantee Julio the money he needed to go to Davis.

We'd planned on applying together since we learned about the scholarship sophomore year. The only thing that complicated our plan was what would happen to our relationship when we went to schools on opposite sides of the state.

When we discussed it before, the horizon still always held the promise of each other—no matter how vague or improbable.

But today, there is no horizon. There is no future. There is only a foreground—a right now.

And right now, I am applying to this scholarship alone, because Julio is not part of my life anymore.

But maybe Julio doesn't know that. Because after Mr. Padilla announces the fair, I can feel Julio staring at me.

I keep my gaze straight, listening as Mr. Padilla begins class, starting the introduction to our daily lesson, flailing his hands in excitement about the new section in our anatomy unit.

My stomach turns.

In the previous lesson, we'd dissected cow eyes. Before that, pig fetuses.

Before each dissection, Mr. Padilla begins his spiel on the marvel of human anatomy, cracking the same joke about how we dissect parts of animals to understand the human body, because can you imagine how disgusting it would be if we had to dissect a real person? And we all haha and pretend it's funny, and we all can't wait to move on.

Mr. Padilla begins passing out the handouts, photocopies that are always blurred. Last week, when we studied cow eyes, the cornea was a blob of smudged ink.

But this time, for once, everything is sharp and clear.

So sharp that I feel my breath catch in my throat, that Julio winces beside me, that Pablo Pelayo begins laughing.

Pablo has disliked Julio since we were in middle school. It was a soccer rivalry that soured, curdling when Pablo claimed Julio stole his jersey number in the ninth grade. It continues today, completely one-sided—Julio quit the soccer team after his pa died.

Julio always joked around with me, saying, "Wouldn't you be upset if you were stuck with a name like Pablo Pelayo?"

But Julio is not joking today.

The warmth he had a second ago evaporates when he hears Pablo's laughter. Julio swivels in his chair, turning to face him.

"What's so funny?" he asks.

Pablo holds up the handout, the stark image of bull lungs spreading across the page, and shoves it against Julio's chest.

Everything else happens quickly.

The punches thrown, the crowd ringing around them, the blood on the floor.

Mr. Padilla is the slowest of all, breaking up the fight only after Pablo is on the ground, his eye raised and red.

"That's enough!" Mr. Padilla shouts. "What is the big deal?"

Mr. Padilla obviously doesn't know, but Pablo definitely did.

He wipes the blood sputtering from his mouth with his shirt collar. Julio whips around, grabs his backpack, and bolts to the door. I shake my head at Pablo—no matter how upset I am with Julio, it was a terrible thing to do.

"What?" Pablo asks me, a grid of red clenched between his teeth. "It was just a joke."

But it wasn't a joke.

Because Julio's pa died of lung cancer.

Two

"YOU DIDN'T FOLLOW HIM? TO ASK IF HE WAS OKAY?" Ale asks, stirring the elote in the electric pot. She's been doing this most of the time we've been at Nicho's, the antojería where we work, occasionally pausing to pick up a ladleful just to watch the kernels cascade back into their broth.

Our shift has been slow today.

I glimpse at the clock nailed to the lime walls of the shop. We still have an hour before we close.

"No," I say, leaning back against the counter. "He told me not to talk to him."

"Paloma," she scolds, stirring again. "He said that a *year* ago."

"It's been a year and three months," I correct.

"Okay?" She snorts. "Obviously, something has changed. You don't want to know what?"

"No."

"You're such a bad liar," she says, gently rolling her eyes at me.

I try to respond, but a customer walks in. He orders an esquite, and Ale does her routine: scoop, serve, smile. It's a winning smile, one she tried to teach me when I first got hired last year.

"If you flirt," she'd said, wide-mouthed as she readjusted her strip lashes in the reflection of the industrial fridge, "they tip."

It always works, even today. The pink sheen of her lips is enough to make this man fish a five from his wallet and feed it into the tip jar.

Ale reaches her hand into it after he's gone. She counts the bills, proudly fanning herself with them while leaning against the counter. "Why can't you just admit that you want to talk to Julio? It's obvious you do."

Ale would have never been able to say this when I first met her. Back then, she was just a girl who Julio would mention from soccer practice. He said she was the best striker he'd ever seen, so good that college recruiters were beginning their scouting process during our sophomore year.

But now, Ale may know me better than anyone.

We became closer after Julio and I broke up, when she offered me this job at one of the Selva union meetings our pas had dragged us to.

I used to go to every meeting with Julio. We'd sit in the back and do our homework together. After his pa died, I had to go alone.

I spent the first few sessions surveying the crowd for anyone else I knew. I didn't recognize a single person until I saw Ale sitting by the door. I thought it was a strange place to sit—the door was busy with people coming and going. But, I realized later, it wasn't strange at all. It was a strategy.

Ale sat with a faja catalog in her hand, offering people deals as they entered and exited meetings, usually making a sale by the end of the session. She seemed so focused that I was shocked she even noticed me the day I sat beside her. She darted her eyes at me and asked if I needed a job.

"Selling fajas?" I asked.

She shook her head. "No, the antojería I work at is hiring. It's easy."

I thought about it for a second, agreeing after I realized it would be a good way to escape my post-breakup routine: school, newspaper, cry.

She made a call and got me hired on the spot. Our manager, Maira, loved Ale. It was hard not to—Ale was the hardest-working person I knew.

Apart from being on the soccer team, she worked at Nicho's through the week, often took double shifts on the weekends, sold fajas for a swap meet stand in between, and took care of her siblings on the rare times she had off.

As I got to know her, I realized I'd never seen anybody, any family, work like hers did.

Her pa had been working on the floor of the Selva distribution center for years, and her ma split her work time. On weekdays, she was the custodian at our school. On the weekends, she sold raspados beneath a tent on the corner of Locust and High.

It was the only way they could manage with five kids.

All that time working at Nicho's is what led me and Ale to get so close. We started as just coworkers, standing in thick sheets of silence during shifts. Ale tried making conversation, but I didn't say much. I couldn't. I'd stand there, watching the water condense and drip on the panes of the dipping tubs, envying their release.

I spent many shifts holding back tears, excusing myself to privately cry in the walk-in freezer during my breaks. Its hum was the only thing loud enough to stifle my sobs. I sat on the industrial ice cream containers, crying and shivering until my fifteen was over. I had the system down until Ale walked in on me.

"Sorry," I said, jolting up and wiping my tears with the collar of my work apron. "I'll b-be out in a second," I stammered, teeth chattering. I wasn't sure what made me colder: the chill of the freezer or my loneliness.

I expected her to be irritated with me. I'd been working there for about two weeks, and this was the most I'd really said to her. I felt so pathetic, so embarrassed, so childish. I figured she thought the same.

But when I looked up, she looked worried. Her breath clouded, a mist of white before her glossed lips.

And then she hugged me.

She stood in the freezer, listening as I cried over the loss of Julio's pa, over the loss of Julio, and held me until I didn't feel cold anymore.

She had been listening most of the year. She never interrupted, she never looked disinterested, she never judged. Ale is a good listener—I figure it comes from being the oldest. But it also makes her good at giving advice. After a few months, she began urging me to move on.

"I know you're sad, but guys are kinda like gum," Ale said, mopping the floor as we closed the shop. "They lose flavor, you spit them out, you get another. Un clavo saca el otro clavo."

The comparison made sense for Ale. All her boyfriends were like gum—so stuck to her they'd pick her up from shifts, watch her at soccer practice, drive her to Victoria Gardens. She had a rhythm to her dating that I could never follow. Always someone to succeed the predecessor, a new flavor to try.

I knew she could only say that because she never had someone like Julio in her life. Someone she was really friends with, someone she was serious about, someone she loved enough to allow her to be this hurt.

That's why it's easy for her to suggest I move on—even now.

"There's a jaripeo this weekend. You should come," she says, stuffing her tips into the pocket of her jeans. "Maybe you can meet a new guy."

"I don't *need* to meet a new guy," I retort.

"Yes, you do," she says. "It'll help you get over it."

"But I *am* over it."

Ale stares at me for a second. Then she laughs.

I roll my eyes at her. "It's not funny."

"You just need to admit it," Ale says, running a hand through her flat-ironed hair. "You're still, like, in love with Julio."

I blink at her. I can't admit it—not to her, not even to myself.

"No, I'm not," I protest. "I'm mad at him."

"If you're mad at him, it means you care."

"How could I not care?" I scoff. "What he did was terrible."

"Paloma, I know he broke up with you and everything," Ale says, her voice softening. "But his dad *died*—it makes sense that he couldn't be with you."

"That's not why I'm upset with him," I say, turning to her. "He *ignored* me—like, acted like I was invisible until today. And I bet you he doesn't even want to talk to me, I bet you he needs a partner to do that stupid scholarship with."

"Don't *you* need a partner for that?" Ale asks.

I shake my head. "No. You can apply alone, and I'm doing it alone."

"But you two would do really well together," she urges. "It would be a nice way to reconcile."

I shrug, rolling my eyes. "There is no 'together' with Julio."

She sighs. "Fine, then. Let's just go to the jaripeo, it'll be fun."

I shake my head.

"Why not?" she whines.

Julio and I would go to jaripeos often as kids, tagging along with our fathers to watch the bull riding, the dancing, the drinking. We started going by ourselves when we were old enough, spent that whole summer in the arena, dancing in the sunbaked dirt until the day turned dark.

The memory stings just standing here in the antojería. I couldn't imagine how much more it would sting if I was back in the arena, face-to-face with it. When I tell Ale this, she smirks.

I roll my eyes and turn away from her, but she tugs at my uniform apron, cloaks an arm around my shoulders. "Come *on*, anímate."

"It doesn't even matter," I say. "I can't go. The college and career fair is Friday."

"So?" she asks, her lips smacking against the syllable. "Jaripeo isn't until Saturday."

"I have to start working on my scholarship application right after," I say. "If I win, it gets published in the *Young Scholars Journal*."

Ale teeters her head side to side, looking for a rebuttal.

It would be hard to find one. She spent most of last year with me, either here or in the school paper's production room. She'd frequently sit beside me as I wrote, spinning in a desk chair, watching as I submitted my articles to national papers in the hopes that they would be published.

But all of them were rejected.

Winning this scholarship is the only way to broadcast my work. The *Young Scholars Journal* is reputable—it's one of the only national science publications available for high school students.

Julio and I would read it all the time, bookmarking sections by previous winners who had researched water contamination, oil pipelines, or food deserts across the country, making waves for change in their communities.

I don't want to make a wave, I want to make the ocean itself.

I'm just not sure if that will be possible without Julio's help. We'd worked on science projects before, and it was always an easy exchange: Julio did the research, I did the writing.

I knew he would be the best person to help me with the application. But I had been mentally preparing to do it alone for months, and the time had finally arrived.

"Paloma, you will win and you will get published," Ale coaxes, encouraging me. "But you're never going to get over this thing with Julio if you keep avoiding every reminder of him."

I glare at her.

"Come on, my ma is selling raspados in the vendors' tents, so we can get in for free." She squeezes my hand.

"Fine," I relent, just so she'll stop pushing it.

She claps her hands together. "We'll pick you up at eight."

Three

THERE IS A TOMB WHERE THE TREES USED TO BE.

A massive block of gray where there had been pasture.

I haven't been to my grandparents' house since the summertime. And in those three months, a warehouse has erupted beside their backyard.

I press on my brakes when I approach it, slowing down to make sure I'm seeing it right. But it's unmistakable—the iron gate, semitrucks, and windows each swallowing the field and horses and citrus trees that had been here before.

Those pastures are a parking lot now, the roads leading up to it so new that the smell of tar hangs warmly in the air.

I grab the tub of ice cream I've brought from Nicho's. Helado de chicle, my pa's favorite. He always says it's two desserts in one—the ice cream and the marbles of bubble gum he gets to chew after.

When I walk to the backyard, I try to stare at the Nicho's label instead of looking up at the warehouse. But its gray paint permeates the building. It casts a shadow over my grandparents' house, and I'm forced to walk in its darkness. It's still hot out, but it's cold in the shade. It's a unique chill—one that is not felt along my skin, but in the depths of my bones.

I try to swallow the anger bobbing in my throat—for Julio, for Selva, for this warehouse. It's my pa's birthday today, and I can't be upset when we celebrate him.

I open the gate to the backyard, where I see my grandparents have kept some of the house's origin, some of its history. Despite their new neighbor, I still see the statue of San Isidro, the saint of farmworkers, on the back patio.

My pa sits beside the statue, a foldout table spread in front of him. His family gathers around it, arranging his birthday cake in the middle. They puncture the center with candles, one waxy cylinder dotting the *i* in his name: Jaime.

I move to help them, setting the tub of ice cream beside the gelatina, then face my pa. I haven't seen him all day today—he left earlier than normal this morning for a prestrike meeting, but he's replaced his Selva uniform cap with his vaquero hat.

I hug him, squeezing him tightly. "Happy birthday, Pa," I say.

He stands and kisses my forehead, then pulls out a chair for me. "Thank you. We were waiting for you."

I sit beside him, looking around. "Where's Ma?"

"Overtime," he says, brushing me off and gesturing to the candles. "Come on, before the winds blow them out."

We sing him "Sapo Verde," and my pa closes his eyes to make a wish. I know I'm not supposed to, but I make a wish when he does. Still, it doesn't come true. As soon as the smoke from the candles rises, he begins to cough.

His brothers, who were eagerly awaiting their opportunity to push his face into the cake, disperse to get him water.

My pa sits down, hacking into his elbow. The coughing continues even after the smoke has cleared, worsening as the winds sweep the exhaust from the semitrucks next door into the yard.

San Fermín is one of the windiest cities in Southern California, with gusts strong enough to knock down trees. Part valley, part desert, part suburb, it's about fifty miles east of Los Angeles, nestled just where the Santa Ana winds push through the Cajon Pass, bringing us both wild winds and the most polluted air in the entire state.

When I was younger, I thought it was somehow related to San Francisco. It sounded and looked similar enough to the photos I'd seen in textbooks. When I asked my pa, he'd laughed.

"That's *fog*," he said. "This is *smog*."

With the exhaust from the warehouses, it's only gotten worse.

I gesture to the shirt pocket where my pa keeps his asthma inhaler. He puffs it into his mouth, and I clap my hand on his back the way his doctor taught me to. The coughs usually dwindle after a puff or two, but today, they're relentless. He takes another, and when his breath finally steadies, I turn to check the expiration date.

"Pa," I say, squinting at the smeared ink. "This expired last month."

He shrugs and slips it back into his pocket. "It works."

I give him a look.

"I'm running low on them," he mutters. "I'll drive to Tijuana soon."

My pa crosses the border biannually. Sometimes he goes to visit extended family, but he usually goes to stock up on inhalers—they are a quarter of the cost there, the only way he can afford them. It frustrates me that he can't afford to go to the local pharmacy. But my pa is so grateful that he can legally cross the border that he often dismisses the sadness of why he needs to cross it to begin with.

My tío brings him a glass of water, and I get my pa a plate of cake. I sit beside him, supervising while he eats. It's a reversal of what he would do when I was younger, me looking after him when he's sick.

My grandma comes around with a plate for me, but I shake my head.

"Cómete algo," she insists.

"No, no," I say, "I'm not hungry."

Watching my pa have a flare-up destroyed my appetite, and it only worsens when I look up at the warehouse again.

From this angle, everything feels like a blend of the past and the present: the horses lined up before the semitrucks, the smell of manure mixed with gasoline, the gray where there once was green.

My pa catches me staring.

"I know," he says, clearing his throat.

"What happened?" I ask.

"They tore down those trees in a few weeks," he explains, pointing the tines of his fork to a few cropped trunks that remain. "Built the warehouse basically overnight."

I look at him. "Are you okay?"

He pushes the cake around his plate, icing smearing along the paper rim. Then he takes a deep breath. "We can't let them intimidate us. We just have to keep going—with the strike."

My pa has lived here his whole life—his family has been in San

Fermín for generations, a bloodline rooted somewhere beneath the soil.

His pa had come here during the Bracero Program, a temporary farmworking program established during the Second World War. Like my pa, my grandpa had been enticed to work by empty promises: days working on farms in exchange for remittances to be sent to his family in México.

Instead, he was forced to sleep in horse stables, eat spoiled food, and was sprayed with pesticides before going to pick the citrus that had ripened in the sunshine.

He coughs, too, but for different reasons. The microscopic remnants of those pesticide particles are still there, stuck to his lungs even now, like remnants of that history.

After my grandpa finishes coughing, he whistles at me from the end of the table. "Paloma, ándale," he says, passing me a bowl of sliced oranges confettied with Tajín. To this day, he serves oranges with everything—even dessert.

I turn to him. His thick hands, chapped and chafed from all those years working, look comical holding the small bowl.

I almost say no, I'm still not hungry. But I take a slice out of respect for him. Then we do what we always do when we eat oranges—suck the juice from the pulp and leave the rind against our teeth, laughing when we reveal leathery smiles to one another.

He walks over to me, plucking the peel from my mouth to feed it to the horses. He rubs a palm over their muzzles, and stares at the warehouses beyond their backs.

Despite the gray, he still looks at the land remaining with so much pride. Julio and I used to joke that our love for this city was hereditary—given to us by our fathers, given to them by theirs.

They taught us that this place, even with all of its changes, was not a home; it was a history. One my pa was trying to preserve. The death of his best friend and the slow death of the community as he knew it are the largest reasons my pa refuses to leave the strike, even with my ma trying to push him out of it.

At first, she said she was supportive. But my ma is practical to a fault—everything in her head had to make financial sense.

And a strike did not make financial sense.

When the strike first began, she sat at the kitchen table, poring over the bills, trying to find some stability in re-accommodating their budget since my pa wouldn't be working.

But there was an inverse to it: as the stability decreased, her stress increased.

I feel her tension now, even in her arrival. I can tell she's just come from work—all the clues are still there. She's in her uniform, her hair is in a bun, and exhaustion clings to her skin.

My ma waits tables at Casa Jimenez over on Foothill, where she's worked since she moved here. She usually brings leftover tortillas from her shift, but today, I don't see them in her hands. Instead, she carries a bright orange packet of paper, the color smearing in her movement.

My pa rises to greet her. But my ma does not say *hello*, does not say *happy birthday*. Instead, she looks him in the eye and says, "We need to move."

Four

IT WASN'T ALWAYS LIKE THIS.

My ma used to be happy here—at least, that's what my pa says.

But when Mayor Warner began her first term, my ma began dreaming of moving back home to Pasto Verde. Now, it's not a dream. It's a demand.

When the three of us finally get home, we sit in front of the TV in the living room. Our K-FER evening news reporter, Cristina Fajardo, stretches against the screen. The caption below her reads: *Notice of Filing Beside San Fermín High School.*

My ma slaps that orange packet of paper onto my thighs. "This is a renter's application," she explains. "There's a house for rent in Pasto Verde. I was late because I drove to tour it."

"Why?" I ask.

"Because," she says, gesturing to the TV, hand waving in exasperation, "they want to build a warehouse next to your *school.* I saw this on the news during work. We can't stay here."

I look at the screen. "It's just a notice of filing," I correct her, "not a guarantee."

"Paloma," she sighs. "Those signs are a death sentence."

I turn back to the TV. B-roll footage of the empty field beside my school stretches across the screen. Back when I thought we were falling in love, Julio and I would go there after school. We'd gaze at the sun curving behind the tips of the Jurupa mountain range, and watch the dusk dim.

Now the field has been boarded up.

A Rent-a-Fence laps around the entire perimeter, yellow caution tape tied to its posts. It billows and snaps in the breeze, bold in its announcement—like a siren, like a warning.

A fence is always the mayor's first step for a new warehouse. She moves swiftly after: voting at the next council meeting, approving its overnight construction, and endorsing its addition at a press conference.

At those, she'll stand behind a podium and boast about what this latest warehouse will provide for our community.

"This is not just a warehouse," she'll gloat. "This is a *job center.* This development has the ability to offer our community more jobs, more money, more growth."

She promises the same thing every time—all this warehouse could give. She never mentions all it could take.

But I'm reminded when my pa coughs beside me.

I go get him a glass of water, and my ma follows behind me.

"Paloma," she calls after me, "think about it."

"No, Ma," I start, reaching to grab a glass. "I don't want to move."

She leans against the sink, shaking her head and staring at the refrigerator across the way.

Where most people had family photos pinned to the fridge, my ma had newspaper clippings of houses for rent back in her hometown. They all looked the same: jaws of gates, stucco walls, terracotta tiles, an hour from here, away from all the warehouses, away from all the smog.

I could imagine her at work, sitting in a corner booth, poring over them in her break—a pair of scissors in her hand as she cut fantasy from paper.

"*How* can we stay here?" my ma asks, watching as my pa crosses into the kitchen. I hand him his water, and he ushers us to all sit at the table. My ma sets her elbows against the surface, presses her fingers tight against her temples. "She's putting them everywhere."

She tilts her head toward the living room, where the news is still on, where the mayor is still smiling. The volume is low, and I want so badly to get up and turn it off. To not know.

But not knowing feels worse than knowing.

I glimpse at the mayor, who has divided the city, the community, my family, in half. She began her term twelve years ago and has yet to be voted out, using her quiet Selva donations to bolster her reelection campaigns every cycle.

But what my ma is saying isn't true. The mayor isn't putting them everywhere.

On the north side, where Mayor Warner lives, there are no warehouses. There are parks, there are gardens, there are trees.

But on the south side, where most of the Latino and Black residents live, there are warehouses.

Here, everything natural is fleeting—even the street names.

They used to nod to nature: Mango and Maple and Poplar and Pine. Now, they've been renamed—Palmetto Place becoming Production Pathway.

Most of the gardens and trees here have been demolished, replaced by distribution centers. The only park left is Southside Park, and it doesn't even have real grass, but plastic Astroturf.

The division was marked by a house on Anastasia Street. It was rumored the Klan formerly congregated there, a plain reminder of the city's history as a sundown town.

My pa pauses for a long while, running a hand through his hair. "Karla, I know it's frustrating, but we can't just leave. I need to finish this strike."

"Finish?" She scoffs. "You need to *work*. I've been keeping us afloat with overtime for the last few weeks, but I don't think I can keep it up anymore."

"And where would I work?" my pa asks. "Jobs don't just appear out of thin air."

My ma sits up. "If we move, my parents said we can work at their restaurant—"

My pa shakes his head. "No."

"Why not?"

"I'm not taking any handouts."

My ma's parents own a restaurant, El Correcaminos, back in Pasto Verde. As one of the only Mexican restaurants nestled in the white college town, it is both incredibly popular and incredibly profitable.

It's actually where she'd met my pa.

The business at the restaurant slowed only once, during a recession.

Her family wanted to repaint the restaurant to attract more customers, and my pa volunteered to do it for free. It's what drew her to him then—his propensity to help others.

It's the same thing that keeps them apart today.

She blinks at him. "Why are you being so proud? We could both work there, and then we could enroll Paloma into that school."

"Ma," I cut in, "I'm not going to school there."

She sighs. "Why not?"

"I graduate in six months," I say. "It doesn't make sense. And I *like* living here."

"You like living next to all of this waste?"

"It's not waste." I scoff. "It's our home. Can't you just wait?"

"Wait for what?"

"For me to finish school—or for the strike to end?"

"That's not going to fix the problem," my ma says. "This is my last straw. I can't keep living like this—either something has to change here, or we have to leave."

"Change takes time," my pa interjects. "But it will come."

"You getting better health insurance and a pay raise is not enough change," my ma retorts. "I mean with these warehouses."

"You'd want to live here if they didn't build that one?" I ask.

"Maybe," my ma says, running a hand through her hair. "It would at least show some progress."

"I'll go to the city council meeting and see what she says," I blurt. "I'll—"

My ma sighs, arcs her arm across the table to squeeze my hand. "Paloma, this is too complicated to fix," she says. "It's time to move and to move on."

I pull my hand away. It's the same thing as always. My ma's solution when things became challenging was to leave.

She did this all the time when I was younger. A string of arguments with my pa, and she was suddenly an hour away, at home with her parents until she cooled off. When she'd go, my pa would keep me out of the house to be distracted from her absence—the only thing worse than an empty home was a half-empty one.

He'd take me to a jaripeo or a charrería tournament or to feed the cattle on his parents' land.

By the time we'd return home, her car would be there, as if nothing had happened.

I hated how it felt—holding my breath as we approached the driveway, wondering if she came back.

It happens less now, mainly because she's working so much. But that history is always hovering above me, dangled there just enough to remember it was a possibility. She could leave, and I needed her to stay here—for me and for my pa. The stress of the strike was already making him sick, I can't imagine what her absence would do.

"I need something *definite*," my ma continues. "I can't keep waiting forever." She turns back to my pa, and I slump in my seat. "Jaime, come on. You know the move would be good."

My pa shakes his head. He felt the same way I did about Pasto Verde. It didn't have warehouses and it didn't have pollution, but it also didn't have everything that he had been raised with—the remnants of citrus trees and the people riding horseback and the street vendors on the corners.

Pasto Verde was a copy-and-paste town: a collection of gated communities, subdivisions, and suburbs.

"I can't just leave," my pa says. "There are people relying on what we're doing with this strike."

My ma sighs, presses the heels of her hands against her forehead.

It's quiet.

I nervously look around our kitchen. At its low ceilings, at its yellow tiles, at its western sensibility—hollow horses carved into the cabinetry. I nervously push my tongue against the space in my front teeth, feeling the flesh wedge between the gap of bone.

I look at my pa. He stands up to take some space, peeling his uniform jacket off and walking to the laundry room just off the kitchen. I can hear him throw it into the drum of the washer, the buttons clinking against the steel.

Then he walks out, carrying a box of powdered Sun detergent in his hands. It's nested in a larger Selva box, the twined tape ripped open against the cardboard.

"Did you order this from them?" my pa asks.

My ma looks up, then buries her face in her hands again.

"We're in a boycott," he reminds her.

My ma's head snaps up. "What am I supposed to do?" she asks. "*I'm* the only one working here, and they sell it the cheapest."

"The only reason they can sell it the cheapest is because they're abusing the people who work to deliver it," my pa reminds her, gesturing to himself.

"I'm just trying my best," my ma says. "It's not easy handling everything."

My pa rolls his eyes, scoffs. "Trying your best? You can't even respect our strike." He rattles the box with accusation, soap cascading through the air, powdering his feet. "You're trying to get us to move before it's even over."

"If we just moved, everything would be fixed."

"Would it?" my pa asks.

"What do you mean 'would it'? Of *course* it would. Living here made you sick," my ma says. "All those fumes you're breathing in—it already happened to Ernesto. You want to live in a place that's going to kill you?"

"No, I want us to work to prevent that from happening to me and to other people." He pauses, presses. "You cannot fix the things you abandon."

I know that "us" doesn't mean all of us.

I know it means "you"—it means her.

And I know he doesn't just mean something. He means here, the community. Here, our home. Here, our family.

She shakes her head and says, "Sometimes that's the only way to fix them."

And that's when I need to take my own space, to leave before my ma has the chance to.

"I'm gonna go for a drive," I call from over my shoulder.

I try to make eye contact with my ma, but she doesn't look at me. She's gazing at her hands, studying the pleats in her palms. As if the seams of her skin will give her the answer for why she and my pa have created an expected geometry for each of their conversations—moving in so many circles, they've turned to cycles.

I grab my keys and head for the door.

Despite the sun curving west, it's still hot out. I cross the front yard, bounding for the driveway. My favorite smell is still in the air—baked dirt, cypress trees, and the lapse of sunshine that scents everything sweet.

When my parents would argue like this, I used to call Julio. He'd pick me up and drive me around the city reminding me of everything we both loved about being from here—the palm trees, the sunsets, the few fields left that were ripe for growth, ripe for greed.

But I can't call Julio anymore.

Instead, I get into my car and peel out of the driveway, heading to Tom's. Tom's is a dine-in drive-through on the corner of Sierra and Randall. They're open late enough that I can sit inside and finish my homework while I wait out my parents' arguments.

I slump into a booth, blinking at the ocean scape printed on the vinyl back—a tiny dorsal fin peeking from the froth of a wave.

I look down at the Projects for Purpose scholarship application I'd printed in the journalism room after school, papers spread out along the table. Then I gaze out the window, at the shopping plaza in the parking lot, and think of my ma.

Despite the distance between us, I see her everywhere.

In the lacquered brick of the restaurant—a cherry red that matches her acrylics. In the Coin Laundry at the corner of the shopping plaza, washing my pa's uniforms the summer our laundry room flooded. In the 99 Cent Store where I helped her pick the best bag of beans from the cardboard bins in the back.

And I even see her in the sign in the parking lot beside it, half of it bordered by the chain-link of a new fence where a new warehouse would be in a matter of weeks.

I know this is not what my ma wanted—a home where the land was slowly becoming a series of boxes. I wish I could give her my perspective, one that still saw beyond the signage. Because when I look beyond the fencing, I see the western sunlight, the rays warmer in the cradle of polluted air. And even when the sky is bruised this shade of purple, I think there is something hopeful about it, a healing that's promised to come.

The dark leans into the sky, and I look down at my scholarship application. Maybe if I won, she wouldn't want to move. That would be the largest prize—not the money or the publication, but a change in my ma's perspective to want to stay here at home, to stay here with me.

Five

JULIO HASN'T BEEN AT SCHOOL SINCE THE FIGHT.

I keep looking for him during our lunch period, trying to find his Dodgers hat in the mill of students walking along the soccer field. Lots of people wear them, but his is a specific blue, one that had softened from its year-round use.

Rumors had been circling that he and Pablo had been suspended, and they might actually be true. I can't find Julio anywhere.

Ale catches me staring. She's sitting beside me in our usual spot—toward the front of campus, under the shade of the school marquee. She grabs some of the Japanese peanuts from the bag we'd stolen from Nicho's.

"I think you should go to Julio's place to see if he's okay," she suggests, chin up as she funnels a fistful of peanuts into her mouth.

I turn to her. "He broke up with me, he ignored me, and you want me to go to his *house*?"

"I mean, you're clearly worried." She shrugs. "You keep looking for him."

"I am not looking for him." I scoff.

"Yes, you are. Even if you think you're playing cool, you're not," she says, turning her palm to study the curve of her cuticles. "Maybe you can drop off the work he's missed for Padilla's class."

"No," I say. "If he wanted to talk to me, he would talk to me."

"He *did* talk to you."

"Whatever," I say. "Are you coming to the fair tomorrow? We can walk together after sixth."

"Wouldn't matter for me," Ale says, shrugging.

"Why not?" I ask. "Aren't you still picking schools for soccer?"

"I quit," she says, matter-of-factly.

"You *quit*?" I echo. "Why?"

She shrugs again. "Just don't feel like playing anymore."

I blink at her. "But you were gonna get a scholarship."

"I don't want to play anymore," she repeats. "I'm going to Chaffey Community. I'll work and I'll transfer at some point, I guess." She throws her hair over her shoulder, dismissively.

Her tone is so cold that I don't want to push it. I lean back a little, wondering if this has to do with her family. For years, it was just Ale and her younger brother, Alex.

The triplets had been a surprise to everyone.

Alyssa, Alberto, and Álvaro were three, and spent most of the day with their grandma so that their ma could continue her job as our custodian.

I look around. She's usually taking out the cafeteria garbage at this time of day, but I don't see her anywhere.

I turn to the screen of the marquee instead, watching the daily message flicker on a loop:

SAN FERMÍN HIGH SCHOOL, THURSDAY, NOVEMBER 17, 12:17 PM, 87 DEGREES FAHRENHEIT, AIR QUALITY INDEX: 23 (SAFE), GO FARMERS!

I wonder how much the air quality index would change if a warehouse went up. The new Rent-A-Fence is just across from us, the posts behind the statue of our mascot, Phil the Farmer. He carries a barrel of hay over the bulk of his biceps, juts his jaw, and squints his eyes into a wink.

Ale always hated our mascot. "Everyone at tournaments gets to be something cool," she'd complain. "It's so embarrassing."

But I never thought it was embarrassing at all. I thought it was an homage to the city's history, a place full of people who worked on farms, in fields, and now, in factories.

People like my pa.

Someone had tied grosgrain ribbons into the chain-link behind him—in celebration or memoriam, I'm not sure.

Either way, the fence blocked our view, our entire reason for sitting in this spot in the first place.

From here, the empty field allowed us to see every detail of the mountain range—down to the weeds pushing through the pores of earth. The view was already blocked by the silver links, and if a warehouse did go up, it would be blocked completely by a row of semitrucks.

Ale pulls her backpack onto her lap, and I do a double take. It's a shade of gray I could recognize anywhere, the background for the forest-green logo that had been patterned across the city for the last year. A Selva backpack.

Mayor Warner and a handful of Selva representatives had come to the school to give them away early this morning. It was part of her usual antics when she was approving a warehouse—donating their merchandise. I always thought the people who took it were kind of stupid, walking around like free advertisements.

I never figured Ale would do the same, especially since she knew how bad it was working there because of her pa.

Ale catches me staring, quickly pulls her makeup bag from the small pocket, then slides the backpack down onto the grass.

"Did you see?" I ask, gesturing across the way. "They're probably putting one here."

"It's hard to miss," she says, but she doesn't look. She opens a compact mirror and reapplies her lip gloss. I wait for her to say more, but she doesn't. Just grabs another fistful of peanuts and rolls them around in her palm like marbles.

The wind pushes against us, tangling my long hair in its gusts. "Well, what do you think?"

"About what?"

"About them potentially putting one here," I say. "Right by the school."

"I don't know," she says, shrugging.

"You don't know?" I echo. "What do you mean you don't know?"

"I haven't thought about it too much."

The bell rings, and Ale looks relieved.

She stands up. "I have to go," she calls, slinging her new backpack over her shoulder.

And then she leaves.

I watch her go, the Selva logo bobbing rhythmically with her footsteps. I sit there for a moment, jostled by her quickness, and look ahead at the field. It lies empty, for now, unsuspecting of what may come.

I watch the breeze gently bend the blades of grass, wondering why every time I tried to talk to Ale about the warehouses, she shrugged me off. At times, I was grateful—it left room to talk about everything else.

But looking at that fence, I wonder what Julio thinks. He was the first person I wanted to call when my ma showed me the news segment last night, when my parents argued, when I sat at Tom's, staring at my scholarship application, unsure of where to begin.

I knew he could help me.

He understood it all: the research, the application, the desire to win to keep my ma at home. Since his pa passed, I knew he got what it was like to have someone who belonged at home always missing.

But I didn't call him.

I sat at Tom's until it closed, drove home, and saw the evidence of an unresolved argument there, with my pa asleep on the living room couch.

I rise now, wiping the grass from the back of my jeans, and walk to class. I look for Julio's hat amid the rush of students funneling into the hallway. The same routine since we broke up: dragging my eyes lazily enough that it wouldn't be obvious if he caught me, but widening them enough to see beyond the boundaries of my periphery.

Despite my denial, Ale was right. I'd spent over a year looking for Julio everywhere—every truck on the road, every hat in a crowd.

It was usually a relief when I couldn't find either. But today, as my eyes peel in search of that soft shade of blue, I feel nothing but disappointment when I don't see it, when I know Julio is not around.

Six

I WAKE UP IN A PUDDLE OF MY OWN BLOOD.

This happens every now and then—the thick heat of the day mixes with the poor air quality, and my nose bleeds while I sleep. It's usually the worst in the summer, when I have to sleep with towels lining my pillowcases.

But this morning, I feel the blood rolling down my face, pooling beneath my cheeks.

I jolt up. The viscous liquid sputters onto my upper lip. I pinch my nose shut and scramble to the bathroom. There, I bunch toilet paper in my palms and shove it up my nostrils. I look in the mirror—my sleep shirt bloodstained, my long hair matted—and sigh.

I strip the sheets from my mattress.

I cross through the kitchen, where I see my ma. When she turns to glimpse my way, she does a double take. She looks at the bloody sheets in my hands and crosses herself.

I walk around her and into the laundry room, so bright white it makes my head hurt. I shove the bedding into the machine, then pick up the powdered detergent from my parents' argument the other night.

I stare at it.

Things between them haven't gotten any better. I don't know what happened after I went to Tom's, only that they haven't said a word to each other since.

I slam the washing machine shut, listening as water fills the drum, and step into the kitchen. My ma leans against the counter, examining the stains on my shirt. "I'll send your pa to get new HEPA filters for the windows. This is your fourth one in a few months."

"I know," I say, my voice adenoidal and whiny.

I feel more blood drip down my chin. My ma rushes to get paper towels from the dispenser, but I run to the kitchen sink. I remove the wadded paper from my nostrils, completely red and soaked through, and lean forward, allowing the blood to freely drip into the basin.

She moves toward me to hold my hair, but I pull away from her.

"I'll call to excuse you from school." She can't be more than a few feet from me, but her voice feels farther, as if she's not really there at all. "You should stay inside as much as you can," she advises.

"I can't," I say, gritting my teeth to avoid tasting the blood. "I have to go to school. The college and career fair is today." It'd been on my calendar since Mr. Padilla spoke about it earlier this week. I quietly hoped that Julio would be there, too.

But I know I won't even have the chance to look for him. Because when my pa sees me bleeding into the sink, my ma looks at him.

"She can't go to school like this," she says.

And, for the first time since their argument, they're finally in agreement.

The warm blood slows to its last drips, and I wipe my face with a damp towel. Over the mound of paper, I look at my pa. He's in his uniform, headed to the picket line.

He looks different when he's wearing it.

He never looked different when he was painting houses. Back then, his skin was bright against the palette of colors that smeared against his clothes. Reflections of himself found in reflections of his work.

But now, it's like all the brown of his skin is sucked out in his Selva uniform, washed into a matching gray.

He hooks an arm around my shoulder.

"Are you okay?" he asks.

I nod.

My ma gestures to the renter's application she stuck to the refrigerator. It's there behind a magnet, right beside the clippings of houses that look nothing like ours. "Paloma, you wouldn't have to worry about this if we just moved."

"Come on," my pa says, deflating. "Not right now."

"But it's true," my ma protests. "Can we at least just tour the house when we're there for Thanksgiving? See if you like it?"

I almost roll my eyes. I know she's wrong—even if we got a tour, I know I won't want to move. But if it means delaying her decision and preventing another argument between them, I'll do it.

"Fine," I say.

My pa nods at me, mercifully, and hugs me goodbye. "Call me if you need anything."

He heads outside for another strike day, leaving me and my ma alone in the kitchen.

She surveys my shirt again, pinching the hem with the tips of two fingers.

"This will stain soon," she notes. "Put it in the laundry room. I can get the blood out."

I look down at the fabric, the red turning rust, and remember the nosebleeds I would get as a child.

Before the warehouses, it was the true mark of the summer, the promise of a heat wave for the day.

They used to scare me when I was younger.

I'd walk to the center of the house, blood-soaked and fearful. My ma would usher me to the bathtub, holding my hair and watching the blood bead against the ceramic. When it finally stopped, she'd run the water and shampoo my hair.

I'd sit in the center of the tub while she knelt on the bath mat, her hands working at my scalp until the lather formed, thick suds lapping against her elbows. The metallic smell of my blood mixed with the scent of her jasmine shampoo, the odor circling in the steam.

Then she'd wrap me in a towel and hold me until I slept, even if we both awoke in my blood the next morning.

But I can't imagine being that close to my ma now.

I feel such a safety with my pa that I no longer know with my ma—it was lost every time she would leave.

Since then, I've never been able to fully trust her in moments like this, when she's offering her help. I am always waiting for her to decide this is too hard to fix, to drive off, to disappear. Instead, I retreat into myself, my body my only company as I prepare for her to walk away.

Even now.

I look at her briefly before walking to the bathroom, staring at the wrinkles between her brows. There are other lines on her face—parentheses around her mouth, the phantom proof of laughter folded into her skin.

But these lines are new.

I wonder what expressions she must be making to create those lines there between her brows. I try to understand where they've come from—puppeteering my face in different directions, only feeling the short lines bending in my skin when I am scowling.

I fling the shirt into the hamper on the washing machine.

I avoid her the rest of the time she's home, showering and lying in my room. When I hear her leave for work, I feel relieved that I can change the laundry without needing to talk to her again.

But when I go to open the washer, it's empty.

I step back, looking through the brightness beaming through the window, a galaxy of dust dancing in the pillars of sunlight.

I see then that my ma has already washed them, the sheets dried and folded, stacked in the hamper.

Beside them is my T-shirt, all evidence of blood bleached and forgotten, as white as it had been.

I'm forced to spend another day inside.

I thought I'd be used to it, with the AQA days. But without Ale here to keep me company, I feel an uneasiness pulse through me. In lieu of attending the college fair, I'm sitting in the living room, blankly staring at my Projects for Purpose scholarship application, with the TV on low.

"When you work for Selva, you are responsible for the rise of employment opportunities in this city." Mayor Warner stands in front of a gray building, hard hat on as she walks down a tarmac. "Where other places will offer you a minimum-wage starting salary," she continues, "they pay ten dollars over."

I blink at the screen. This ad runs so often that I have it memorized, down to her scripted pauses.

Still, I wait for her to mention all the money they donate to her reelection campaign—that the inflated paycheck may lead you to illness.

That once you work in the warehouses, you may cough.

You may even die.

That June, when they found the cancer in Julio's father, it was already advanced. Malignant spores all over his pulmonary tract, like mold blooming on his lungs.

Julio and I would drive around town late at night, where he would explain everything to me through a sigh. "Selva doesn't give medical insurance, so we can't afford treatment," he said, winding down the roads we'd known our whole childhood, the summer slick around us. "It's debt or death—and the doctor keeps saying that, at this point, the latter is inevitable."

And it was.

Two months later, my pa, ma, and I went to the funeral.

I sat beside them, sweating in the thick tweed of my black dress, feeling the toe of my flats bend as I knelt down to pray. I listened to the service—a pastor speaking about his pa's kindness, his love, his work ethic. The last one stuck with me the most.

Even after he'd died, we were talking about how hard he'd worked.

At the funeral, everyone pointed to God to explain the loss. Nobody pointed to Selva, to the mayor, to the warehouses.

As we read from the Bible, I imagined all of the national newspaper headlines that could be published about what was happening here: *Warehouse Way—diesel death zones.*

Every article could describe how respiratory illness had risen since the warehouses began to move in. And to some, like my pa, it was just asthma, just allergies, just nosebleeds.

But to others, to Julio's family, it was lung cancer.

It was death.

Julio sat stoic in his suit the entire mass. It was the first time in my entire life I'd seen him without a hat on and that, somehow, made me the saddest.

His ma took it hard, her head leaned against his shoulder, her hands counting rosary beads. But nobody took it harder than Yvette.

Yvette has always been the most serious in the family.

Where Julio was soft, Yvette was authoritative.

She wears the eldest daughter well. Because I didn't have any siblings, I was always in awe of her. I loved watching her style her hair into a bun before work, smooth her hospital scrubs, gloss her lips. There was so much mysticism about her demeanor. She's twelve years older than me and Julio, so I never saw her as my peer—I always saw her as an adult.

But that day, she cried like a child.

Chin pointed heavenward, as if maybe then her pa could hear her.

After the final bit of soil was spooned over Señor Ramos's casket, my family joined the assembly line of funeral attendees, shaking hands with the family to express condolences. It felt like such a cold, robotic way to wish someone well. But my pa, ma, and I waited in the line, hands extended for taking.

Julio shook everyone's hand, thanked them for coming.

I expected, after everything, for it to be different with me.

But when I approached, he offered me his hand like he'd done to everyone else.

That's when I should have known things would change between us. I looked at his hand, just hovering there, and walked around to try to hug him.

But he shook his head.

I stepped back, curling into myself. It was humiliating, our families watching us dance around each other after having spent an entire season so close.

I tried not to feel hurt, but I did. I do.

It was the last time I touched him, and despite its brevity, despite my anger, sometimes I can still feel it. His hand melding into mine, my fingers running over the lines in his palms that mirrored a map of this city.

Even though I've lived here my entire life, since Julio and I stopped speaking, nothing about being here felt the same. The mountains felt flatter, the sky farther. Something within me ached with homesickness—not for a place, but for what it was like when we were together, when we were friends.

And commercials like this reminded me of how much things have changed since we'd stopped talking—so much grief, so much gray.

I reach for the remote and turn it off, pulling my application closer.

I try to focus, try to stop thinking about Julio. But I can't. The thought of him returns the moment I look back at the requirements printed on the application. I know he's the only person who could help me with the research.

I bury my face into my hands, looking up when I see headlights curve over the yard. It's early, but I grab a new inhaler for my pa from the last of his supply, ready to get the door and hand it to him.

But when I open it, I peer through the slits of the iron security screen, blinking a few times to make sure I'm seeing right.

It's not my pa who's at the door.

It's Julio.

Seven

THE LAST TIME JULIO WAS HERE WAS IN THE BEGINNING breaths of August.

We'd gone to the San Fermín summer carnival at Memorial Park together. When we got back to my house, we sat on the pavers in the yard and split a Slurpee—our hands held, our tongues blue.

Today he stands on those same pavers. They slant unevenly beneath him as he rocks back and forth on his heels, wide-eyed and quiet.

"What?" I ask, trying to give my voice an edge. I'm trying to conceal the ring of surprise, the excitement in it.

I'm grateful, for a moment, that he isn't replying. I wouldn't be able to hear him over the sound of my heartbeat thumping in my ears.

He parts his lips to speak, but nothing comes out.

Instead, he lingers there, both the door and his jaw ajar. I count the beats of silence until I get to twenty.

"Yes?" I push.

Still nothing.

I wonder if maybe he's considering that coming here was a

mistake. Maybe it's going to be a repetition of the past year—where he sees me and is silent.

And as quickly as it came, that excitement from earlier spins into the same embarrassment I felt when I tried to hug him and he shook my hand, when I offered him my help and he slammed the door in my face.

Maybe this time, it's my turn. I reach for the metal security door to shut it closed. But Julio wedges his foot between the frame.

He draws a breath.

"Hey," he finally says. "Can I talk to you?"

Julio looks around my room.

I wonder if he notices anything different about it.

It hasn't changed much—the walls are still white, the desk is still beside my bed, my collection of *Young Scholars Journals* is still stacked on my bookshelf. It's the same as it was when he'd come here late at night, sliding through the window frame to see me.

Before Julio could inherit his pa's truck, he would bike to my house. When I'd hear the click of his gears, the yanking of the bike brake, I'd quietly pull the window open to let him in. We'd sit where we're sitting now—Julio by the bed frame, me by the wingback chair.

We had our first kiss here.

We were sitting beside one another, watching the uneven orbit of the ceiling fan twirling above us, until Julio pointed to the walls.

"What color would that be?" he asked me.

We'd been doing this for weeks, the same game we'd played as kids, finding the names for the colors of the sunset splaying across the walls. It was one of my favorite things about spending time with him—the colors threaded through the season, sewn into memory.

Sometimes the light was orange, other times pink, but that night, it was shades of blue.

We began trading ideas, eventually agreeing that it was the color of few blue skies here—a rare blue that happened when the air smelled sweet and the smog lifted. So perfect and pale, we called it "Cloudless."

The light traveled, painting over both of us. And in it, I saw Julio look at my lips. Even in the indigo of the night, I could see his face turning red. When he finally leaned into me, I felt like all the color we'd described was dissipating. Like that cloudless sky around us was falling—crashing onto my body, then cradling me as we floated through the rest of the summertime.

I glimpse at his lips now, wondering if he's remembering, too. But when he turns toward me, he doesn't look nostalgic. He looks worried.

"Are you okay?" he asks me.

"Am *I* okay?"

He gestures to my nose. When I reach up and touch it, dried blood flakes from the folds of my skin. I wipe it away with my hands, embarrassed. Julio gets up and hands me a tissue from the box on my desk. He extends it to me, a white flag hanging from his fingertips.

I take it and run it over my face.

"Is that why you didn't come to the fair?" he asks, tapping his nostrils. "I was looking for you there, but I couldn't find you."

"You were looking for me?" I ask.

After months of searching for him in crowds, it's the first time I ever think about him doing the same. I wonder, for a moment, what he remembered most about me that was worth widening his eyes for.

He sits beside me again. "Of course I was." He fishes his hand into his backpack and pulls out a notebook. "I took notes for you," he says, sliding the notebook over to me.

I blink at him.

"For scholarships that are available," he explains. "I thought you might need them."

I don't say anything, not even thank you. I don't even reach for the notebook in his hands. It hovers between us until Julio sighs, opens it to the bookmarked page, and slides it onto my lap. In the exchange, I feel the smooth moonstone of his nails, the hair sprouting from his knuckles rough against my thighs.

I look at his notes. Julio has bullet-pointed the information, highlighted due dates, flagged important suggestions. I don't read any of it—I'm too distracted by the bracket he's drawn along the perimeter. He's written my name around the border, the letters so light and minuscule, it's as if he's whispered them onto the page.

I press the notebook against my knees, running my fingers against the spiral. The metal rattles beneath my nails in a perfect scale, ascending and descending with every pass. It's the only thing I can do to ease the warmth of my blood pulsing beneath my skin, rushing hot to my cheeks.

I look at Julio, expecting him to say more. But he doesn't. He's looking at the window—maybe for an echo of the summer, maybe for an escape from today.

I clear my throat. "I didn't ask you to do this," I say.

"I know. I just felt like it was the right thing to do."

"Well, I don't need them," I say, pushing the notebook back toward him. "Is that it?"

"No," he says, lifting his gaze from the window, then looking right at me.

I always imagined what this would be like—if Julio ever spoke to me again.

If he'd apologize or if he'd yell or if he'd cry.

But my imagination could never conjure this scenario—Julio arriving at my doorstep, coming to my bedroom, bringing me his notes. Sitting here, nervous.

I raise my eyebrows in surprise. I never thought Julio would be nervous around me. But he's wringing his hands in his lap, pressing the heels together tightly. Part of me wants to reach into the space between us to unwind them, to hold them. But out of pride, I force myself to sit here, as still and quiet as he'd been all year.

"Did you see the fence by the school?" he asks. "What are we going to do?"

It was the same question I'd asked Ale yesterday, when I knew Julio would be the only person who I could talk about it with. And somehow, I feel upset he's brought it up. Because, when most people say "we" with this question, they usually mean the community—what is the community going to do?

But by the way Julio is looking at me, I know he means we, the two of us.

And the idea of that no longer exists.

"Yes," I say. "I saw it."

He looks at me for a long while, probably expecting me to say more. When I don't, he sighs again. "I'm sorry, I just don't know who else to talk to about this who would care."

I wonder if that's why he came here—for understanding. And I don't even want to offer him that. There had been so many moments through the last year when I needed someone, and he wasn't there.

But then he says the thing I knew he'd been wanting to say since he sat next to me in class the other day.

"I've been meaning to talk about this with you, I know we had this plan—"

I shake my head immediately. "No."

"You haven't even heard what I'm going to say," he presses.

"Because I *know* what you're going to say," I scoff. "You need a partner for that project."

He blinks at me. "Okay, yes, I do. But—"

"I'm not going to do it with you."

"Paloma, listen—"

"No," I say. "You cannot just come back into my life when you need something. I'm doing it alone."

"You can't do it alone," he says.

"I *can't*?" I scoff. "I can and I will."

"No, you literally can't," he says, picking up his notebook. "They changed everything. The requirements, the name, the prize money amount."

"What?" I ask. "When?"

Julio shrugs. "I don't know. But now you need a partner to apply."

I blink at him.

He puffs his cheeks out, rests his wrists on the knobs of his knees. "I didn't want to ask you to partner with me without apologizing to you first."

The word echoes in my mind: apology. In all those daydreams about this moment, I never knew what I would do if I ever received one. I was beginning to settle with the fact that I'd never get one at all. "And what are you apologizing for?" I sneer.

"For when we stopped talking," he starts, then pauses. He runs his hands back and forth on the carpet beneath us, watching the fabric flip dark to light, light to dark. "Sorry." He corrects himself. "For when *I* stopped talking to *you*."

His eyes are still fixed to the floor, his head slightly bowed. I study him, the blue of his Dodgers cap lightly faded, the bill frayed, and I see them. The ER embroidered on the side.

Julio and his pa collected Dodgers hats. They'd get them at Ontario Mills, the outlet mall down the highway, then take the hats to the swap meet to get them embroidered with each other's initials. It was a tradition his pa began—a piece of his son stitched into the seams.

Every time I passed Julio in the hall, saw the blur of blue on his head, I wondered if he still did it. But today is the first day I've been close enough to him to know.

He adjusts it now. Three times, until the bill is high enough, a nervous habit he's had since we were kids. When he looks up at me again, I can see his eyes. They're glassy, like a layer of resin is coated over his pupils.

Despite how angry I am at him, seeing him cry makes things different, serious. I feel something inside of me release. I rise to grab a tissue and hand it to him. My own white flag now waved.

He takes a breath, his cheeks deflating as he puffs it out. "After my dad died, things got really hard. I know you tried to help, but I couldn't do it." He hesitates. "I was put into grief counseling."

"Really?" I ask. "Since when?"

"For about a year." He pauses. "It was hard at first—like, embarrassing to be there. But it was helpful after a while. For a long time, I thought I didn't owe anyone an explanation for keeping to myself. I was really angry," he admits.

"At me?"

"No. It wasn't about you." He looks ahead. "But I think I could've told you I needed more time. I'm sorry. And it's okay if you don't, like, forgive me. I get it if you're upset—you'd be kind of right to be."

It was hard to decide how I felt about it.

I was angry at him for just disappearing; sometimes I was worried about him, often I was sad. But when I lay here in my room over all of those letters he'd written me, looking at the window where he'd sneak in, staring at the carpet where we first kissed, no feeling was more buoyant than loss.

I missed him.

He was one of the few people I knew who talked about this community the way our fathers did—with a blooming imagination that saw something beyond the warehouses, saw the possibility of something bigger in this city.

And I want to tell him that, that I missed him.

But I don't. Because despite him being beside me, things aren't how they used to be. Not when I could tell him everything. And though I can't trust him yet, I can at least be honest.

"I thought you were upset with *me*," I explain.

He cocks his head back. "Why would I be upset with you?"

"I don't know," I admit. "It felt like you hated me."

"I could never hate you," he says, shaking his head. "Not at all."

He looks away, and I'm grateful. A windmill moves in my chest, cycling all the air from my lungs.

He sighs. "I came here to ask to work together, and to tell you I was sorry."

"Julio, it feels like you're here to say you're sorry *so* that we can work together." I look at him, skepticism seeping through my gaze.

"No." He shakes his head. "I can ask someone else. But I don't think there's anyone better to do this with." He looks at me for a long while. "I understand if you don't believe me. I do think we'd work well together, though."

I know he's right. It's what I'd been thinking before he arrived. But that was all an idea, a yearning daydream rooted in the past.

This is real—and it feels so sudden.

Nothing about our relationship had ever felt so rushed. It took him ten years to try to hold my hand. Three weeks of him sneaking into my room before we kissed. Over a year of not speaking before he arrived again. And suddenly, he was here, apologizing and willing to work as my partner for this project.

He looks at me so hopefully that I almost wish I could say yes. But I don't think I can. I don't trust him. And, despite this apology, I'm still so mad at him.

After a while of being quiet, Julio lets out a long breath.

"You don't have to decide right now," he says. "I understand it's a lot. But I do have some ideas to run by you, if you'd be open to listening."

I tilt my head at him. He mirrors me, which almost makes me crack a smile. "Sure."

He nods and stands up, extending a hand to help me to my feet. I take it—his hands still feel like a map of this city, like a homecoming.

Once I'm up, he looks at me.

"You wanna go to Baker's?"

Eight

JULIO FIRST HELD MY HAND HERE.

It was July—his namesake.

We were waiting in the line of the Baker's drive-through, Julio pointing to parts of the city around us—the light migrating from the moon, the sensor of a stoplight, oil puddled in a parking lot—and we named their colors together to pass the time.

Afterward, he pulled forward and paid for our shakes. They were so thick we could never drink them from a straw, so I spooned ice cream into his mouth while he drove, cookies and cream batter melting on his tongue. When I set the shake into the cup holder, he buried his hand beneath mine.

The drive back to the south side took seven stoplights. But after he held my hand, time passed so quickly—had it been measured by my body, it would've passed in a handful of heartbeats.

We boarded the overpass, and Julio turned into the parking lot of the San Fermín Equestrian Arena. It's where the jaripeos of our childhood were hosted, what we looked forward to every June.

But that summer, the arena was shut down.

The horses were gone, herded into carriages and hauled down the interstate. In their place were different animals: a series of cranes.

Beside them there were large piles of rubble, the planks of the hangar heaped into small mountains. The only solid remnant that had been left intact was a mechanical bull positioned a few yards away from the fence posts, its spotted body still visible among the tall stalks of grass.

We sat in the truck bed and stared at it, watching it slowly disappear into the dark. Julio leaned back and cocked his head across the way. "What do you think they're gonna put there?" he asked, passing me the shake.

I knew he was only asking to indulge in imagination—with that notice of filing staked into the grass, we both knew what was coming.

Still, I shrugged, taking the drink from his hand. I spooned it into my mouth, then set it between my thighs, the Styrofoam cold against my bare legs. "I don't know," I said. "What would you put?"

He looked ahead, deep in thought. "Maybe, like, a community garden." He turned to me. "You?"

A strong gust of wind blew, the bull's body rocking gently in the breeze. I looked at the grass beneath it, beaten brown beneath the sun. After a moment, I said, "I don't think I'd put anything there."

"Why not?"

I shrugged again and looked at the row of houses just beyond the expanse of grass. All short and ranch-style, each with a variation of a palm tree in the yard. I figured it must be beautiful to be able to wake up and see a mountain range from your window, the sun sliding above the summit, the moon crest beneath its peaks.

I told Julio this, and he held my hand again. I felt the itch of his nails at the center of my palm, in the center of my chest. We sat there for hours, talking about everything and nothing until the dark and the quiet came.

Today, the equestrian arena is a warehouse.

We pass by it on the way to Baker's. Julio drives too quickly for me to check if the bull is still there—all I can see is a smear of gray.

We keep a measured distance inside of the restaurant, a gap between our bodies while we wait for our food. It grows wider when we sit down—each of us on opposite sides of a booth near a window, the length of a table between us.

I take a bite of a fry, feeling grateful to be eating solely to have something to do with my mouth. The silence mimics the crooked quiet from the car ride here. But I refuse to be the one who breaks it.

And Julio knows this, too. So, he perks up and asks, "How's your dad doing?"

I stop for a second, holding a fry midair, wondering what to say. I hardly know what to share about me, let alone about my pa. And not even because of what was happening to him—but more because of what had happened to Julio's.

"He's actually not great," I admit. "His asthma got worse."

That wasn't even the full truth, but a half-truth. His asthma had gotten worse, but it was also *getting* worse. The other day, I heard him coughing so hard that he vomited into the bathroom sink.

I don't tell Julio this, though—the first comment alone was enough to make his face fall.

"I'm sorry," I blurt. "We don't have to talk about this. I know it's sensitive."

He shakes his head. "No, it's okay. Is he using an inhaler?"

I nod. "Yeah, it's hardly working, though. And they're expensive."

He nods. "I know." He pauses. "I was actually hoping to see him at your place. I wanted to thank him for what he's doing with the strike. It's really important. I know it would've meant a lot to my pa."

I nod again, unsure what to say next. It's so odd. We've known each other our entire lives, and somehow it feels like we're on a first date. But maybe I'm the only one measuring the pauses in conversation, because Julio naturally falls into step. He sips his soda and asks me about school.

"Did you apply to Riverside?" he asks, a fry dangling from the corner of his mouth, limp like a cigarette.

"I did."

"Journalism?"

"Media studies," I correct him. "But yes."

"Your articles are good," he says.

"You still read the paper?"

He shakes his head. "Not really. Just your articles."

I blink at him, feeling my cheeks redden.

"They're very informative," he adds, nodding.

I clear my throat. "Did you apply?"

"To Davis?" he asks.

I nod.

"Yeah—plant sciences. For a second, I thought I wanted to be premed, maybe be a doctor. I thought they saved lives." He pauses and takes a long sip of his drink again. "But I think studying plants feels more like my pa. More like me."

"You'll get in," I say.

"So will you."

It seemed we both had stuck with our original plans, the only thing that was different was us. Before, we'd wondered if we'd stay together through school. Now, I wondered if we could even work on this project together.

Julio looks right at me. "Paloma, you're the smartest person I know. And you're the only person I want to do this project with."

I sigh. "Julio—"

"No, please let me finish."

I look at him, a little annoyed. But when he sits up, his body is erect with urgency. I nod for him to go on.

"Getting this scholarship is the only way I'm going to be able to afford school," he explains, "and I know you will probably get other scholarships and I know you don't owe me anything, but I *really*, really need this money."

I swallow.

This was another moment I daydreamed about in the year of silence—the day he would need a favor, and I would have the power to make him feel as small as he'd made me feel all those times I passed him in the hall and he wouldn't even look at me.

I never thought it would actually happen.

But here it is—the scale finally tipped in my favor. And it doesn't feel nearly as good as I imagined it would. It doesn't feel good at all.

I try to skirt away from the responsibility. "But it's not even enough to cover much of anything. It's ten thousand dollars—that's, like, one quarter at Davis."

He turns to his backpack, pulls out his notebook again. "No, it's not ten thousand anymore." He flips it open to his notes, pointing a finger at the number on the bottom. "It's one hundred thousand dollars, each."

I blink at the page. "That has to be a mistake."

"It's not," he says, shaking his head. "Trust me, I asked. I told you, they changed everything about it—the name, the requirements, the prize money amount. They even moved the office somewhere around here."

"*Here*?" I ask. "Why?"

He shrugs. "The woman at the table said they wanted to focus on health-related research on local communities. That's why they renamed it—it's called the Communities Care scholarship now. So, we need to present on a local issue affecting our community to get it published in the *Young Scholars Journal* and the one hundred thousand dollars."

I want to respond to him, but my eyes are fixed on the number, every zero looping into my brain, winding into a spiral. I mentally calculate—even if Julio was offered no additional aid, no other scholarship, no other grant, this would be almost enough money to pay for university for four years, in full.

"I know how badly you wanted to get published nationally," he coaxes.

I blush, embarrassed that he remembers that.

"I can help you with the research part," he pushes. "But it's this for me." He points to his notebook. "Or it's nothing."

"That's not true," I respond, my eyes still fixed to his notebook. "There are other scholarships—did you apply to those?"

"Yeah, but they don't offer this amount. Plus, they're just essay- and transcript-based. I'm no writer."

"But you're a *great* student."

"I guess," he mumbles. "I was kind of able to keep my grades up after my pa died. But the rest of my transcript isn't strong—I had to quit the soccer team. And then I got suspended for the fight with Pablo." He sighs. "But this one isn't about that. It's about research, and I *know* I can do well with that. Maybe *we* can do well with it."

I swallow. "What about your family? Can they help?"

He shakes his head. "My mom isn't working right now—she can't. Yvette's doing doubles at the hospital and I'm mowing lawns on the weekends. But it's not enough."

I blink at him. I still needed the money, but not the way he did. I wouldn't be moving across the state—Riverside was only a half hour away. Since I'd be staying local, I'd be living at home and commuting, cutting the costs significantly. I had applied to a handful of other scholarships, and I knew I had the essays and the grades to get them.

I needed this scholarship so my ma would decide to stay. I was hoping that if my research was published nationally, the mayor would receive enough bad publicity that she'd reverse her decision to build the warehouse beside the school. If that domino fell, it might be enough to keep my ma at home. To keep her with me.

When I explain this to Julio, his eyes soften. Julio knew all about my parents. He was there that summer, hanging out with me in my bedroom while my parents argued in theirs. He'd take me to jaripeos or Baker's to get out of the house. When we'd return, my ma's car was almost always missing from the driveway.

"Things are still bad?" Julio asks.

"Worse now, with the strike. And then the potential of the warehouses by the school was her tipping point, I guess. She just feels really hopeless about living here. She wants us to tour a house in Pasto Verde during Thanksgiving break."

"You think if you win, she'll stay?"

I shrug, study the granules of salt stuck to the pads of my fingers. "I don't know, maybe it'll give her some hope about living here."

I pause. I've never said it aloud before, and I realize now how stupid that sounds. Like David versus Goliath, some ridiculous pipe dream. "It's not *all* about her, though," I blurt.

He nods. "It's okay if it is, though," he says. "I get it."

That sentence enough reminds me of one of the things I loved most about Julio—he was so easily affirming, so naturally kind.

"It's a big part," I admit. "But I also want to get my writing published so people understand what's happening here."

"I think research about the warehouses is a really good idea," he says. "If we do this together, we can both get what we need out of it."

I know it would make the most sense to partner with him.

And even though it's the most logical thing to do, even with all of his understanding, the barrier of my resistance rises again.

"Julio." I sigh. "Applying isn't the problem. I'm going to apply."

Julio blinks. "It's just applying with me?"

"Of *course* it is. We didn't talk for over a year."

"I know," he says, nodding. "I'm sorry."

"This stuff with my ma is too much for me to risk if you're just going to disappear like you did."

"I'm not going to," he says, looking at me firmly. His gaze is heavy with the weight of tension—a sentence, a season, left unpunctuated, unfinished.

I shake my head. "But what if you do? My application has to go into the garbage because you don't want to talk to me again?"

"I always wanted to talk to you," Julio says. "I just . . . couldn't." He looks down at the table, his reflection distorted in a ring of water his drink has left along the tabletop. He drags his finger around it, pressing the edges into the lacquered surface.

"I understand." He pauses. "The preliminary proposals for the projects aren't due until the end of the month. Can you at least think about it? It would mean a lot to me."

He looks at me, and I know he means it. His eyes always reveal his truth.

But going through the loss of Julio was something I didn't know I could do again. It had already been enough back-and-forth with my ma. The sound of his silence was easier than the sound of his heels turning again.

But his gaze is pleading enough that I give in. "I'll think about it," I say, even though I'm sure my mind has already been made up.

He nods again, somewhat relieved, and then looks out the window. Citrus Plaza is across the street, a Subway and the Superstar Donuts housed beneath the palm trees. The view is blocked by a semitruck carrying its freight, idling in the intersection.

A rusted rectangle of cargo sits on its bed, and in its ridges is Mayor Warner's face. Dented and accordion-like against the metal, her slogan shining above her—*San Fermín, Forward.*

It passes just as quickly as it came, her face distorted in a blur in its departure, leaving nothing but a cloud of exhaust in its wake.

Nine

"JUST *PULL*, PALOMA," ALE INSTRUCTS. "THEY PUT straps on them for a reason."

"They don't fit," I protest, lying flat on my back, trying to pull the boots over my ankles. "I'll just wear sneakers."

"You *can't* wear sneakers to a jaripeo," she scolds. "That's why I brought these."

We've been sitting in my room for the last fifteen minutes, trying to get her cowboy boots onto my feet. She brought them over as soon as I mentioned I'd outgrown mine and has been trying to squeeze me into them since she arrived.

I sigh and gather myself, trying, unsuccessfully, to get her boots on.

Ale rolls her eyes with impatience. "Let me do it."

She kneels on the carpet and uses the heel of her hand to push against the heel of my foot.

"Hold still," she grunts, "and pull them up while I push."

Though one slides on, when she helps with the other, the force sends her stumbling backward, her back thudding against my dresser.

I scramble to help her up. "Are you okay?"

"Yeah," she says, rising and adjusting her dress. Then she squints her eyes, examining me. "They look great—you did good with the outfit."

I look in the mirror. Though Ale lent me her boots, the rest of the outfit is mine. A regurgitation of what I'd wear to jaripeos with Julio: a blouse thin as tissue and a pair of jeans that flare at the knee. So different from what Ale is wearing—the second skin of a denim dress and cowhide boots.

I look into the mirror, adjusting my hair. Waves so long that they spill past my waist, threatening to tangle into my concho belt. I consider putting it up, but Ale shakes her head.

"Your hair is one of your best assets," she says. "Guys love long hair."

I give her a look.

"And make sure you smile a lot," she advises, glossing her lips in the vanity mirror. She leans in so closely that her breath gently fogs the glass. "You have a good smile—the gapped teeth and the deep dimples. Guys love dimples."

"I'm not there to meet a guy," I remind her, adjusting the part in my hair so that it's perfectly centered. "I'm going there because you're forcing me to go."

Ale shakes her head. "Yes, you are there to meet a guy." She faces me, pointing her lip gloss wand toward me with accusation. "Do *not* get sidetracked just because you talked to Julio. Do *not* narrow your options."

I sit on the edge of my bed and roll my eyes at her. "Isn't that what you wanted, though?"

"No," she says, capping her lip gloss and grabbing her vaquera hat. "It's what *you* wanted, you just won't admit it."

"I wanted him to apologize to me."

"He *did* apologize to you."

"Doesn't count. He only apologized because he needed something," I say, "like I said he would."

Ale rolls her eyes and fishes her perfume from her purse. She spritzes it against her pulse points, then arcs her wrists out to fan them dry. The potent smell of artificial vanilla itches inside my nostrils, makes me sneeze. "But don't *you* need something, too, though? You don't need a partner for that project?"

"Yes," I start. "I was actually going to ask you if you—"

"You're ridiculous," she dismisses.

I sigh, lying flat against my mattress. I knew she would say that.

After Julio dropped me off yesterday, I'd spent all night wondering what to do. I lay here just like I was doing now, staring at the ceiling fan the way I had before we first kissed.

I tried to find a solution, especially when I joined my parents in the living room, where they were watching the evening news. Broadcasters stood near the school, teasing the importance of the city council meeting this Tuesday, where the fate of the lot would be decided.

It was odd.

Mayor Warner was usually the one to announce city council meetings. But since the fence had risen, she had retreated.

My ma was beginning to do the same.

When the news segment ended, she and my pa started their same cycle as always, beginning with my ma wanting to move, ending with her leaving. She spent the night in Pasto Verde with her parents. She had been there since, the house loud with silence.

I needed this scholarship badly, and now there was the additional obstacle of finding a partner. I thought about asking some of the staff writers on the paper, but I didn't know anyone else who cared about this the way I did—nobody would get it like Julio.

I roll my eyes back to look at Ale.

"I don't know why you're stressed." She snorts. "There's a very clear solution here."

"No, there isn't," I whine. "I can't work with him."

"Ay, Paloma," she sighs, exasperated. "Te gusta la mala vida."

I shake my head at her, but Ale doesn't notice. She pins on her hoops and looks at her phone. "We should go, my ma says we need to leave now if we want to beat traffic."

This jaripeo was on the very edge of Rancho Riestra, about a half hour from here, where there was still enough land left intact for arenas. I hadn't seen a jaripeo here since the equestrian center had been demolished two summers ago.

I gather my things and follow Ale out to the living room, where her pa has been waiting for us. Señor Cardenas always comes in when they pick me up. Since he and my pa work together, they catch up while playing darts on the board nailed to the entryway.

But this time, when we step into the living room, they're silent.

My pa is sitting forward in his recliner, his elbows pressed to his knees, shaking his head. Ale's pa is sitting on the single step separating our living room from our dining room, a sour look on his face.

Not a word between them.

The air is so thick with tension, I reflexively hold my breath, straighten my spine. Ale and I step onto the brown shag carpeting of the room together, separating to stand beside our respective fathers. I purse my lips and dart my eyes between them, waiting for either of them to break the silence. But they sit there, tense and quiet, until I clear my throat.

"Is everything okay?"

My pa rises quickly, then nods. He stands in front of me and cautiously assesses my face. "No more bleeding?"

I shake my head. "Not since yesterday."

"Okay," he says. "Well, call me if it starts again and I'll go pick you up." He reaches into his pocket, pulling out his wallet to hand me some money.

I shake my head. "No, Pa, it's fine. I have some from work."

But he insists. "Eat something," he says, handing me a twenty-dollar bill. "And be back before midnight."

I nod, slipping the money into my pocket, and wait for Ale's pa to tell us he's ready to go.

"Alejandra," he calls. He gives Ale a look, adjusts his vaquero hat, then drags his eyes over my pa. "I'll meet you at the car in a minute."

I look at Ale for an explanation, but she rushes me out the door.

It's still warm outside. The gentle heat insulates us as we cross through the yard and onto the driveway. Stars reveal themselves against the dark, the winds around us soft but sonorous. "What's going on?" I ask her.

She shrugs. "I dunno."

We approach Ale's parents' van, where banda sounds through the speakers, the warm-up before the real thing. Ale's mom is sitting in the passenger's side. It's the first time I've seen her in days. She hasn't been at school, taking out the garbage at lunch or sweeping past my locker after sixth period.

"Paloma," she calls, "good to see you."

"Igual," I say. I turn to Ale. "Is everything okay with your mom?" I whisper. "I haven't seen her at school in a while."

"Oh," Ale says, dismissively. "She quit."

"Really?" I ask, eyebrows raised. "Why?"

Ale slides the van door open. "Don't worry about it."

We duck inside and scoot into the middle bench beside Alex, the triplets in the back behind us. Every seat of their eight-seater van is fully occupied.

A moment later, her pa rushes out the front door, that same sour look still spread across his face.

He settles into the car, then begins slowly reversing out of the driveway. As he turns around to check traffic, he looks at me for a moment, then glimpses at Ale.

His face softens—less sour, more sullen.

As if, maybe, there's a lot for me to be worried about.

Diego offers me his hand.

I look at it, then look at Ale.

I'm trying to signal to her that I don't want to take it, that I don't want to dance with him, that I don't want to be here anymore.

But the banda onstage strikes their cymbals and begins their next song. Luis, who had eyed Ale the second the bull riding finished and the dancing began, pulls her toward him. Their boots kick up a cloud of dust as they move across the field, their bodies swallowed by the swirl.

Diego looks at me, his hand still hovering midair. He waves it with impatience, but I shake my head and sit down.

I'd relented for one song, but I hated the way he led. I hated how he grabbed my waist, I hated how he dragged me across the floor, I hated how he touched me like he owned me.

But, more than anything, I hated how much being around him reminded me why I didn't want to come to this to begin with: it only made me think about Julio.

Where Diego grabbed, Julio held. Everything was a suggestion with Julio—he was always soft, always gentle, and always understanding of when I wanted to stop.

So, when Diego smacks his lips and says, "Come on," I ignore him.

He slumps beside me in the foldout chairs arranged beneath the canopy. The scent of cologne sticks to his skin, sticky and heavy even over the smell of birria in the air.

He eyes the other girls standing around. I wait, hoping he'll ask one of them to dance instead, but he doesn't. He just sits there, staring at me.

I look away from him to avoid making eye contact, watching Luis and Ale instead.

Luis flings her in the hollow spaces of his body—her legs passing in the open crook of his arms, moving over his shoulders, her entire body flung beneath the bridge of his legs. She twists and tumbles over his back, then spins back into position against his chest. It's acrobatic and exhausting and dizzying just to watch for one song, let alone the five they dance back-to-back.

When they're finished, they walk toward us, Ale panting and adjusting the hem of her dress. Luis offers to buy us drinks, flashing us the neon 21+ bracelet strapped to his wrist.

I look at Ale, shaking my head.

"Tragué tierra," she says, melodramatically coughing for emphasis. "I need a drink."

She pulls me through the crowd before I can protest, tightly gripping my hand while weaving me through the mass of people. She quickens her pace so that we're a few feet ahead of Luis and Diego. When they're just barely out of earshot, she turns to me.

"Paloma," she hisses. "Can you *please* be nice to Diego?"

"Why?" I moan.

"I'm trying to hang out with Luis. They're best friends."

"Ale," I whine. "He smells bad."

"He doesn't smell bad," she says, rolling her eyes. "Look at him, he's cute."

We round the corner toward the vendors' stands on the edge of the fence, where I catch another glimpse at Diego, his face illuminated in the wide bulbs of the string lights. He adjusts his vaquero hat, a ring of sweat where his hair had lain against the satin.

I turn back to Ale. "He's gross," I say, "and old."

"He's not old, he's our age. They have fake IDs—they go to high school around here," Ale explains.

I turn away from her, looking for her family among the crowd. I find her ma at the opposite end of the vendors' tents. Two of the triplets are beside her, asleep in foldout chairs. She balances Alyssa in one arm and scoops spheres of ice with the other. And then they're gone, blurred into the sea of bodies milling around the arena, lining up to buy drinks.

Luis and Diego stop at the last tent, a broad booth with vinyl windows. Ale and I stand back, waiting for them by the rows of portable toilets near the horse stables. Diego turns around and smiles at me. I blink at him in response.

Ale nudges me, her elbow piercing my side. "Come *on*." She sighs. "You don't need to be in love with him or whatever, but please just talk to him."

"There is nothing for us to talk about," I deadpan. "I promise."

"Okay, then don't talk," she says. "Dance with him."

"I *did* dance with him," I protest. "But he's bad at it. He just grabbed me and dragged me around."

"He wasn't bad at it—that's how you're supposed to dance. They're supposed to lead."

I shake my head. "That's not true, when Julio and I—"

Ale looks at me, expectantly. I don't finish my sentence. I don't want to give her the satisfaction. She leans forward, pulls my phone from the pocket of my jeans, and shoves it toward me. "Paloma. Just call him."

I stare at my reflection framed in its dark screen. It's the smallest I'd ever seen it, and somehow the most accusatory.

The most complicated part about seeing Julio yesterday was that I still missed him, even though I didn't want to. And worse, I knew that I didn't have to. I *could* just call him.

But it wasn't as simple as Ale made it sound.

There was a gap of distance—time, trust—that keeps my hand hovering the way Diego's had a few moments ago. Close, but still unable to reach.

I shake my head at her, cross my arms. "No."

She rolls her eyes, hard. "Fine," she says, slipping my phone back into my pocket. "Then please, for *me*, try to be nice to Diego. I really like Luis."

And I do try.

But Diego makes it impossible.

When he and Luis return from buying us drinks, he shoves a plastic cup at me.

"Drink it," he says. "It's named after you—a *Paloma*."

The way he says it is less of an offer, more a command. So, when his back is turned, I pour the cup out, watching the dirt below us clump into mud.

We wander around the grounds for a while, looping around until Luis and Diego lead us back to the arena where we'd watched the show. The bleachers surrounding the perimeter gleam silver with vacantness. Couples duck beneath them, kissing in the shadows of the aluminum slats.

Luis pulls Ale under, and she follows him into the darkness. Diego cocks his head for me to join him, but I stay put, my back against the entryway of the performance ring.

He follows me, hoisting himself to sit atop the wooden rail of the fence. I can see a pen a few yards from us, the performance bull circling its enclosure. It looks at me for a moment, his brown eyes wet, then moves toward its trough to drink from its depths. The rhythmic lapping of his tongue is almost loud enough to conceal the click of the lighter beside me.

I look at Diego, who has a cigarette between his teeth, the end burning orange as he inhales. I roll my eyes.

"I don't think you're allowed to smoke here," I say, gesturing to the barrels of hay stacked beside us. "It could start a fire."

He scoffs. "We've been hanging out all night, and the first thing you say to me is that I'm not allowed to smoke here?"

I feel the impulse to correct him—to tell him we haven't been hanging out all night. He's been hanging around *me*, unable to catch a hint. But instead, he flicks ashes onto the floor, jumps off the fence rail, and stomps them out with the toe of his crocodile-skin boots, as if to prove a point.

"Come on. Talk to me," he says.

I want to laugh, but I remember what Ale said in line. I take a breath instead. "About what?"

"I don't know—tell me something about yourself," he says, exhaling a thin stream of smoke from the side of his mouth. "What do you like to do?"

I blink at him, shrug. "I like to write, I guess. I write for my school paper."

"What's that job called?" He snaps the thick pads of his fingers, trying to provoke his memory.

I gently clear my throat. "A journalist."

"Right," he says. Then he shrugs. "I don't really like to read."

I nod, as though that didn't already seem obvious to me, and watch while he inhales from his cigarette. His face illuminates in the soft glow of the ember, an appraising look in his eye. "Where are you from?"

"San Fermín."

"San Fermín?" he guffaws, his tone incredulous. The corners of his mouth curl up, teasing laughter.

"Yes," I say, slowly. "What about it?"

"Nothing," he says, pulling the cigarette from his teeth. "Don't you guys just walk around like this?" He lifts the hem of his shirt to cover his nose and mouth, the fabric imitating a mask.

He coughs and wheezes behind the collar, laughing stupidly to himself. After he steadies, he looks at me for a beat—as if waiting for me to laugh, too, to understand the punch line.

Instead, I take the cigarette from his hand and flick it against his face. It skips over his nose, ashes cascading onto his lips. Diego winces and swats them away—he begins to shout something, but I walk away before I can listen.

He calls after me, but I don't turn around. I keep walking until his voice is distant and far, becoming smaller with every step forward I take. By the time I'm on the floor of the arena, I can't hear him at all.

I stand in the center of the ring, where the umber dirt beneath me has been milled to powder, ground small from the boots and bulls that preceded me. I sit in the middle, where the bull rider had knelt during the oración, feeling anger burst through my body. It's similar to how I've felt every time I see that fence in front of the field by my school. An anger I know only Julio would understand.

I think about calling him, but I don't. I can't.

Instead, I feel the warmth from the overhead floodlights that burn bright. The shadow strung to my body widens beneath it, its shape larger than my reality. It makes me forget that I'm alone for a moment.

But when I look at the bull in his pen, I remember.

I see my face reflected in the dampness of his eyes, in the sheen of his roan.

He moves back to his trough, staring into the mirrored surface of the water. I wonder who herded him inside, enclosed him only with himself. I wish, for a moment, I could blame my own loneliness on someone else. But, as I sit on the rusted dirt, I know this is of my own making. And that somehow feels worse than one I know anyone else could have fabricated for me.

I finally pull my phone from my pocket—the release after resistance.

The bull bucks gently, his hooves like my heartbeat. I dial one of the few numbers I have memorized. The one to the only person I know who would understand this feeling: being homesick while being so close to home, missing someone you know will pick up the phone.

And he does.

Julio picks up on the first ring.

Ten

JULIO PICKS ME UP FROM THE JARIPEO.

I see his headlights curve into the parking lot, where I've been waiting for him for the last half hour.

Behind me, the dance floor is still pulsing. I'm sitting on the top of the wooden fence bordering the parking lot, the posts vibrating with the bass and boots a few yards away. I turn around to look, trying to find Ale among the crowd, but I can't see her.

When I told her that I'd be leaving, that Julio would be picking me up, her eyes widened with excitement. I was under the bleachers with her and Luis, our faces striped in their shadows.

"Where are you guys going?" she asked. The three of us hunched low, backs grazing the benches while we walked back to the arena.

"I don't know," I said, my head brushing the stands above us.

"You don't know?" She turned toward me, licking a finger and adjusting the flyaways that had sprung along my hairline.

"We're just going to talk about our project."

She scoffed. "How boring. Come on."

"It's not boring," I protested. "It's about the warehouses—we know a lot about that."

After that, Ale was quiet.

It was hard to make out her expression in the shade of the bleachers. But when we moved into a strip of light, I saw it. She looked irritated, she looked disappointed, she looked sad.

"Are you okay?" I asked.

"Yeah," she said quickly, stepping away from me, out toward the exit.

Ale was silent the entire time we walked back to the main festival grounds. I couldn't tell if it was me or Luis who was third-wheeling, especially with Ale in the middle. We approached a fork in the road, one side leading to carnival games and the dance floor, the other leading to the exit.

"See you Monday," Ale finally offered, veering away.

Her voice was so quiet that I could just barely hear it over the music. It was so quiet that I'd been sitting here on the fence, waiting for Julio, wondering if I'd been imagining it—if she'd even said goodbye at all.

Julio's headlights slice against the darkness, striking the fence in two luminous pupils. I hop off the railing when he's close enough, sweeping the dirt from the back of my jeans. I expect him to idle, but Julio pulls into a parking spot instead. I stand by the ticket booth, watching as he walks toward me, feeling my heart gallop in my chest.

His sneakers and Dodgers cap are out of place in the sea of western wear, and the people tailgating in the lot double-take at him. But

Julio doesn't seem to mind. He walks forward, standing under the floodlights, his face shaded beneath the bill of his hat.

"Are you okay?" he asks.

It's what he'd asked when I called, when I could hardly say hello after he answered so quickly.

"Yeah," I say. "Thanks for picking me up."

The first few minutes of the drive are completely silent, and it makes me so angry with myself. I called him, I told him I wanted to talk, I took up his offer to pick me up, and here I was, staring at his profile, unsure of what to say.

And there was a lot to say.

I could tell him that I'd been dragged here with the purpose of forgetting about him, but that all it made me realize was that few people like him existed. That he was the only person who understood how I felt about our home, about the warehouse, about this project. And that I knew that was the largest reason why working with him would be the best thing to do, and that I was afraid to admit it.

Because the problem wasn't about work at all.

It was our past that made me hesitate.

After his year of silence and my ma's constant threats to leave, I wanted everything around me to be stable, solid. It was the entire reason I was doing this project to begin with—to align the dominoes to fall in a way that would make my ma want to stay. I couldn't stomach the idea of working with him if that was just going to lead to more abandonment. The idea of hers had been more than enough.

I try to say this, but the explanation lodges itself in my throat. A tight, narrow pressure funneling inside my neck, making me unable to speak at all.

So I sit there, instead, looking around his truck.

It's mostly the same—a rosary dangling from the rearview mirror. A picture of Julio's pa in the visor. A Styrofoam Baker's cup in the holder. Julio catches me staring at it.

"That's from yesterday," he explains. "I didn't go without you."

I look at him. "You can go to Baker's without me. It's not, like, a rule."

"I actually haven't gone since we stopped talking," he admits.

I gawk at him. "You haven't eaten Baker's in over a *year*?"

He shakes his head. "Nope. Not once. It never felt right."

I fiddle with the straw poking from the lid, plastic squeaking against plastic. "You have a lot to catch up on," I say.

He turns toward me. "Yeah," he says, "I do."

We look ahead at the road, at the billboards that spread against the sky. Julio juts his chin toward one, a wide rectangle advertising Citrus Grove Radio, and begins naming the expanse of its blue.

"I feel like that one would be, like, 'Fountain.'"

I shake my head at him. "No—that's, like, 'Azure.'"

We go back and forth for a while, and then we're silent again. But this time, it doesn't feel tense. It feels like it used to, the reward of years of knowing one another—a shared, companionable quiet.

The farther east we drive, the fewer billboards there are. They are replaced by rolling fields of pasture that blend into the dark, the border of earth imperceptible against the night sky.

The nothingness is brief. Once we're close to home, that blankness is interrupted, replaced by a relentless maze of white boxes, one warehouse after another.

But when Julio veers off the highway, I am reminded that our home is not just this. Home is also the people riding horseback, the hands of palm trees, and the pattern of tents lining the road—all the street vendors making their nightly sales. Julio pulls up to one beside a 76 gas station, where a squat man sweats behind a black stone.

We walk toward his canopy. It's similar to the one Ale's mom has—mismatched, but practical, its sides covered with a blue painter's tarp to ward the winds away. I wonder if she's working at her post full-time now that she's quit her job as our night custodian.

I wonder why Ale has never mentioned it.

Julio orders us a plate and a Coke to share. We watch the taquero fry tortillas in lard, expertly flipping them without flinching once. There is something magical about street vendors—the heat of his grill making even the dull air shimmer.

Julio and I sit at a plastic table a few yards away, our arms sticking to the vinyl tablecloth while we eat. I look to my left, where a fence borders a vacant lot, construction workers doing overtime on its opposite side.

They drive tractors over the soil, their tires swirling dark figure eights against the earth. Julio's eyes flick to the notice filing sign near the fence—it looks identical to the one near our school. Then he turns to me. We both know what will be here soon.

And that's when I say it.

“I called you because I kept thinking about the project,” I say.

Julio blinks at me. “And what do you think?” he asks. I can tell he’s trying to be cool, sipping his Coke slowly. But his grip around the bottle is white-knuckle tight.

I hesitate for a moment, watching a bulldozer trek onto the field. It moves a pile of silt away from the site, the remnants of whatever was here before pushed to the periphery, soon to be the new bones beneath soil.

I take a deep breath, the air dense with gasoline and heat. “I want to do it with you,” I say.

Julio exhales with relief. His shoulders roll away from his ears and his spine curves, as if his lungs held his posture up by a string.

“But,” I start, “Julio, you cannot just disappear in the middle of this.”

“I won’t,” he says. “I *promise*.”

“I don’t mean just about the project, though,” I admit, looking at the food in front of me. The steam curls around Julio’s face, white swirls along the brown rounds of his cheeks. “I can’t do this project with you if we’re just going to stop talking. Like, if we lose, are things just going to go back to how they were? You just ignoring me?”

“Of course not,” Julio reassures me. “It’s probably hard to believe with the timing, but I really missed you.”

I breathe for a moment, feeling that funnel in my throat loosen, releasing the crux of what I had been stifling for the entire car ride. “I missed you, too.”

Julio tilts his head at me. “And I’m really sorry about that summer.”

And though he’d said it just yesterday, today I believe him.

Because his look holds the gravity of that season that I know anchors us here, today.

We're quiet for a long while. In the silence, I listen to the noise from the construction site—it pounds rhythmically, the hammers like heartbeats against the earth.

It's all I hear when I finally extend my arm across the table, my hand a bridge between us. Julio takes it, the halves of our palms forming a whole, and shakes it firmly. He stares at me the entire time, squeezing my hand gently before pulling away.

"Let's get started, then," he says.

The last time we worked on anything together was sophomore year, when we were partnered in biology class for a project on plant propagation.

I spent the semester sitting on the steps of Julio's backyard, writing our lab report while he trimmed clippings of plants from his pa's garden. We continued watering them, even after the class was finished. They began sprouting that summer we spent together, but we never got the chance to see anything fully grow. Because when that summer ended, everything between us stopped.

And, despite everything else that's happened since then, tonight, we fall into step.

Julio grabs his backpack from his truck. He pulls out his notebook and skims over his notes from the college fair. "We need to submit our thesis in a preliminary proposal by the end of the month," he says. "If our thesis is approved, we advance to the next round."

I nod, rolling a pen between my palms. "Well, my thesis idea was about the warehouses."

"But what about them specifically?" he asks. "It has to be a health-related issue in the community."

I look beyond the fence, watching an excavator claw at the earth, a cloud of brown dust powdering the air around us. "Probably how it's negatively impacting the health of the residents," I say, "with the pollution."

Julio looks at me, quizzically. "We'd have to talk about Selva, then."

I nod.

"You don't think they'll come after us in some way?" he asks. "Won't that be bad for your pa?"

"They won't care about this," I say. "My pa says they're pretty caught up with the strike. If we need it to be a health-related issue in *this* community, there is nothing more immediate than that."

Julio nods, writes in his notebook. He looks up at the night sky, musing for a moment. "I can get some air quality monitors from the library," he suggests. "Track the hazardous air beside the warehouses. Maybe make a map to keep track of specific places that are affected. We should go to the city council meeting on Tuesday—that's where they pass the zoning ordinances for them."

Zones decided what was allowed to be built in specific areas of the city—it's likely how they chose to put one beside our school, zoning it into obsolescence.

"We do need to go to the city council meeting," I agree, then teeter my head. "But a map alone won't *prove* anything. It would just state facts," I say. "We'd need something that proves that people's actual health is being impacted. Something more quantitative. Maybe, like, people's oxygen levels—you remember the Breathmobile?"

Julio nods, somewhat solemnly.

When we were in elementary school, the Breathmobile would stop by a few times a year.

It was as routine as the school district's dentist, optometrist, and lice exams. A large RV would park in the back of the campus, right by the drying garden, and shuttle kids in two at a time.

We'd sit in the trailer, where a doctor would use a gloved hand to press a stethoscope onto our chests and backs, guiding us through deep inhales and exhales. Then he'd turn to the nurses, giving them knowing looks—students with asthma got an apologetic smile, but kids without it, kids like me and Julio, got a simple nod.

Because our checkups were always quick, Julio and I would stand off to the side of the RV with our teacher, waiting for the rest of the class to be finished.

Nurses would teach them how to properly use an inhaler or a nebulizer, miming the movements on baby dolls. But on really bad air quality days, there would be no need for dolls. Our classmates would stay in the RV, plugged into nebulizers and ventilators until their asthma flare-ups settled.

Regardless of how long they stayed, they'd exit the car with a smile on their face, holding their Breathmobile tokens—sugar-free lollipops and stickers on their T-shirts that read: *Asthma help on the go, helping kids grow!*

Julio tilts his head at me now. "How would we do that, though?" he asks. "We don't have any medical equipment."

I pause for a moment. "I mean, Yvette would be good—she has a lot of inside perspective from working at the hospital. She could help us with, like, oximeters."

Julio releases a breath, his cheeks puffed out in exasperation. "I don't know," he says. "Yvette is . . . busy."

I knew that was half-true—I frequently saw Yvette at the hospital when I'd go to appointments with my pa. She was usually darting down the hallways, too busy to stop and greet us. But when I saw her, I didn't think she looked busy.

She looked gutted—empty.

I worried for her. Yvette and I used to be really close. She often treated me like I was her own sister, braiding my hair and giving me her hand-me-downs. After losing Julio in the breakup, it was hardest to lose Yvette.

She had disappeared, like Julio had, like my ma was beginning to.

"Is she okay?" I ask.

"I don't think so," he says, pausing. "We're all different after my pa passed, but she's really changed. She didn't want to join grief counseling with me," Julio admits. "I kept asking her to, but she wouldn't."

"Did your mom?"

He shakes his head. "No, we couldn't find anyone who spoke Spanish. But church helps—when she goes, anyway. She's better than she was before." He pauses. I study him, the deep curve of his lashes, the fullness of his mouth, the blotch of a birthmark near his neck.

"But Yvette is different. She won't talk about my pa at *all*, or anything related to him. They were really close—she had twelve extra years with him." He pauses. "He was such a good dad."

The statement was so simple, so short—the past tense of it making it so sad.

"He was," I agree, nodding.

"I keep telling her she needs to do something to process," Julio continues. "Yvette's just . . . I don't know."

"We don't have to ask her," I say, "if it's too sensitive."

He cups his chin into his palm, thinking. "No." He sighs. "You're right. Let me think of how to approach her." He looks down at his notebook. "What else, though?"

"Probably something qualitative—interviews, questionnaires. It's what we use for the paper."

"Well, who do you want to interview?"

"I think we could ask people who work in the warehouses about their health."

"Your pa?"

"Might be too biased," I say. "I can ask Ale if her dad will do it."

Julio and I plan for another hour, only realizing it's time to head home when the taquero begins cooling the grill and disassembling his tent. We pack up our things and sit for a moment, looking at one another as if in disbelief the other is really there, before walking back to Julio's truck.

We say goodbye to the taquero on the way. I wonder, briefly, where he will go when this selling site is gone, replaced by another tomb of a parking lot.

Julio drives me home. As he pulls away, I stare at the construction site, at that notice of filing sign. He drives forward and into the night. He turns the radio up, but the worksite is loud enough that I can still hear it. For once, I don't mind it too much. It's proof that everything around Julio and me is simultaneously being destroyed and simultaneously being built.

Eleven

SUNDAYS AT THE SWAP MEET USED TO BE SOMETHING sacred. They were the one thing I had with my ma.

My pa and I had charrería tournaments and evenings on his parents' ranch and the love for the land he had raised me on, and my ma and I had our Sunday morning routine at Los Ninos Plaza, in the indoor swap meet.

We used to make an entire day of it—winding through the aisles, polishing her wedding ring, stopping somewhere in the plaza to eat after.

She used to love it here.

Though, with my ma's face now, you wouldn't think so.

"Is this his size?" she asks, holding up a pair of slacks. I shake my head.

We've been running errands for my pa all morning. We picked up more masks from the pharmacy up the street, dropped off his work boots at the cobbler to be resoled, and now we're at the Frank's Collection stand, looking for a new pair of work slacks.

I offered him help—he looked too tired to do anything himself.

This Sunday was his first day away from the picket line in weeks, and he spent it driving down to Tijuana for more inhalers. After hours inching through the traffic to cross the border, he lay on his recliner, repositioning it again and again to support the soreness of his body.

I sat beside him, rising every few hours to dig my hand into the freezer and grab him some ice. I wrapped it in a kitchen towel and placed it onto his skin, watching it melt against the bulk of his muscles.

It didn't seem to help, though. He still winced every time he moved.

"Get some rest, Pa," I advised.

It was one of the things you say when there's nothing left to say—filler advice. Because, truthfully, I knew that wouldn't help either. Since his cough had worsened, he'd frequently wake up in the middle of the night to vomit in the bathroom. It happened again this morning, and I lay there, bleary-eyed in my bedroom, wondering what to do.

All I could think to offer was running errands for him. I looked at my ma—she'd just returned from Pasto Verde a few hours prior, and though her homecomings were always uncomfortable, I thought inviting her to come with me would ease the tension. Maybe even remind her of all the things she loved about being here, about spending time with me.

I didn't think she'd agree. But when she did, excitement soared within me—we hadn't been to the swap meet together in years. It made things feel solid enough for a moment that I almost forgot she had left to begin with.

But it was short-lived.

When we arrived, I tried following the normalcy of before. I lingered at the Hat Kraze stand near the entrance, the shop where Julio got his hats embroidered. But when I paused to look, my ma grabbed my hand and pulled me past it.

I stumbled into the aisles, walking over the duct-taped arrows on the cement floor. I released her hand, stopping reflexively when we reached the Gold Rush jewelry stand. I nodded at Kim, the owner, who always polished my ma's ring. But my ma stepped past her, beelining for Frank's.

"Ma," I called after her. "You're not cleaning your ring?"

She looked at me for a moment, her body leaning left, ready to leave. "We should really hurry before the rush starts."

Kim waved a gloved hand at her, gesturing for my ma to approach the counter. My ma sighed and reluctantly walked over. She twisted her wedding ring from her finger, a thin tan line where the band had been, handed it to Kim, and left.

I looked at Kim apologetically, then followed my ma. She rushed through the maze of stands with determination, walking so fast that the swap meet passed in blurs—bits of the piñatas hung from the ceilings, imitation designer perfume bottles, the airbrushed T-shirt stand.

I thought, at first, that my ma was just being efficient—ready to be in and out so that we could go get something to eat, spend some time together. But now, as we look through the clothes at Frank's, I realize she was disapproving of being here, if not disgusted.

She riffles through the clothes with pinched fingers, as if the brand-new items are dirty. We've been picking over the clearance racks for the last few minutes, trying to find a pair of pants in my pa's size that are reasonably priced. The stress of the strike, on top of being sick, had made him lose weight.

"I don't understand." She scoffs, turning toward a clothing rack. "Can't he just use a belt?"

"I don't know," I mumble.

"Why do I have to do everything?" she asks, pushing a row of hangers. The metal scrapes against the rack, a piercing sound ringing between us.

I finally find a pair of slacks my pa's size and hand them to my ma. She double-checks their price on the neon green cardboard sign taped to the stand. The handwriting on the display is scrawled thin and sloppy, so she strains her eyes and squints.

"They're forty-five dollars," I say.

My ma sighs and walks to the counter. I wait for her, leaning against a stand of Pro Club T-shirts, staring at the fitting room in the corner of the booth. A slender rectangle partitioned by a navy-blue curtain, the mirror inside etched with graffiti.

My ma pays, but when we try to exit the booth, there's a crowd congesting the pathway.

Up ahead, a girl in a quinceañera gown tries to squeeze into the photo studio booth. Her court is suited beside her, attempting to fit the hoop of her dress through the narrow entranceway. It's the kind of scene my ma would've enjoyed: a girl in a gown, men at her feet. But instead of admiring, my ma leans against the Frank's stand, her impatience palpable.

As much as I'd wanted it to be like before, it wasn't. We weren't coming together—she was coming with me, and that was enough to make all the difference.

All my excitement from earlier plummets, knocking the wind from my lungs in its descent and landing in the pit of my stomach.

I look around, trying to find something else to do to entertain her, to extend our time together. "You want to get something to eat?" I ask.

My ma shakes her head, looking at the pet shop booth beside us. A pair of parakeets peck against the wires of their cages, their beady eyes staring back at her. "I need to get home."

"But we just got here," I say, gesturing to the stands in front of us, at everything she once had loved. "We used to spend the whole day here."

"I didn't come for that," she says. "I came because of your pa, like always. I am always doing things for him. I wish he would do something for me."

The quinceañera crowd clears and disperses into the studio, and my ma and I finally elbow our way through the aisles.

"Well, let me do something, Ma," I say. "We can eat or get our nails done or something—I'll pay. I have tips from Nicho's."

"Paloma," she sighs. "I want to go home."

I wonder where she is talking about—what home she now considers hers.

We walk through the aisles wordlessly. "Fine," I say. "I need to meet up with Julio anyway."

Julio and I are meeting at the library later today to work on our project. We needed to make a map that tracked the areas where the warehouses were most populated—color-coding their patterns along street lines. It was the first phase of many to come.

"Julio?" she asks, doing a double take.

I nod.

"Since when are you two talking again?"

"Since this weekend," I say, rounding the corner.

Had she been around, she would have seen him dropping me off last night. It's so strange giving her the recap to my own life. She hadn't really even checked up on me since the strike began.

I almost want to tell her that Julio and I are working on the scholarship together, but she's been so dismissive that I don't even mention it.

I just imagine the look on her face when we win, the glow of hope that comes with new perspective.

That daydream carries me all the way to the Gold Rush stand, where Kim is waiting.

But it fades quickly, reality right in front of me taking its place.

Kim pulls the wedding ring out of a cleaning solution, a soapy liquid that foams blue, and hands the ring to my ma. Kim stands there, waiting for her to marvel at it like usual. It's a modest ring, a pinpoint of a diamond so small it hardly glimmers.

My pa says, at some point, it cost him all the money he had.

Still, my ma always did the theatrics after Kim cleaned it. Put it on and held it to the light until the diamond reflected its prism.

But today, she puts it on and throws Kim a five.

She tells me it's time to go, and I don't look up to see Kim's face. I can feel the shock and disappointment permeating from her body.

On the way home, my ma and I idle at an intersection. She looks at the mountains in the distance. She stargazes at the range, at its promise of another side. There is so much to tell her, and still, I am silent. The only noise is the sound of her turn signal. Its steady metronome suddenly sounds urgent, ticking between us like the impatient hand of a clock.

Twelve

MONDAY IS ANOTHER AQA DAY.

But it's the first AQA day Ale comes to my house.

Because she usually has to take care of her siblings, I normally go to her place. Her family lives about ten minutes from me, deep in the south side, in a neighborhood where the streetlights are swallowed. The overpass leading to her apartment complex descends in height, but also in light. I counted the streetlights every time I drove there—there were six, then four, then two, then none at all.

I'd usually arrive at her place so early that I'd have to route around with my high beams on, passing through a series of dilapidated apartment complexes. Eventually, my headlights would strike against her building, illuminating the chicken coop her neighbors kept in the front yard, the roosters crowing at the artificial break of dawn.

After, I'd help Ale arrange the living room—it doubled as her bedroom, tripled as our workstation. We'd fold the sheets, store the pillows, and push in the futon so we could start our work for the day. In between subjects, I'd help Ale tend to her siblings—making their lunch, doing their laundry, running their baths.

But I wasn't sure if we'd see each other today. Ale and I hadn't talked since the jaripeo, which was strange. I texted her last night about what had happened with Julio, but she never responded. So when she called while I was lying in bed, rereading the school district's email announcing our school's cancellation, I was surprised.

"Can we work at your place?" she asked loudly. I could hear the AQA day packet distribution chaos behind her: teachers and administrators handing out assignments to swarms of impatient students. "I'm at the gym already—I can grab your packet for today."

"My place?" I asked, rubbing my eyes. "Who's taking care of your siblings?"

"My ma."

I propped myself up on my elbows. "I thought she was working today—doesn't she sell on Mondays?"

"She's not," Ale replied, quick.

"Is she not working right now?" I yawned. "Not even at the stand?"

"No. Should I pick up your packet, or not?"

There was a snap in her tone. I waited for her to apologize for being short, but she didn't. Instead, I agreed to her coming over. So now, we're sitting in my living room, a plastic bowl of presliced watermelon from Stater Bros. between us.

It's hardly noon, but we're already done with our assignments. We almost always finish early—the packets are full of remedial work. It's usually better this way, so we can help with Ale's siblings after. But at my place, there is no one to help.

Ale bites another cube of watermelon, the pink flesh whispering against her teeth, then spits the seeds into her palm. She looks around, surveying the house. It's so still compared to hers, where there is always movement, always sound. There's nothing else to do, and I almost wish there were.

It's been awkward all morning with Ale.

She was cold on the phone, and has avoided looking at me since she got here. Even now, she leans back in her recliner, her flip-flopped feet on top of the ottoman, watching the wind pick up outside. "I wonder if snow days are like this," she muses.

I nod half-heartedly, knowing deep inside me that snow days can't be anything like this at all. That somewhere across the country, children are staring outside, marveling at the miracles the sky can create. But here, we stare out the living room windows, watching the air sift through HEPA screens like a sieve.

With nothing else to occupy us, I pull my backpack onto my lap and grab the materials for my project with Julio. I fan out the books and articles and binders on the TV tray, topping it with the draft of the map we began making yesterday.

While I organize, Ale reaches for the remote and turns on the TV.

Mayor Warner's face fills the screen.

It's the segment that runs every Monday—Mayor Monday. It broadcasts on K-FER between major news programs, and is later syndicated on other local networks throughout the week. Ten minutes of Mayor Warner positioned at her desk, an American flag to her left, the city seal to her right. She begins with a number of city updates, her eyes centered on the camera, occasionally moving left to glance at her cue cards.

Ale moves to change it, but I ask her to stop.

"Why? It's boring," she whines.

"I need to watch for my project with Julio," I say. "She usually gives updates about warehouses that are being built."

Ale is silent, listening as Mayor Warner announces a Thanksgiving food drive scheduled next week.

"I'd like to thank the sponsor for this event, Selva, for all they are doing to nourish our community," she says.

I roll my eyes. She segues seamlessly into a new segment—something she's calling a "warehouse walkthrough."

"For transparency in our community, I'd like everyone to see and hear the updates of our growing warehouse industry."

We watch as she enters the fenced worksite where Julio and I had just been over the weekend. A construction crew lays tar along the road where the taquero had stood, his vending post gone. I wonder where he's working now. The camera pans to the skeletal building already in his place—the mountain range just hardly visible through the planks of wood lined against the sky.

"I am here to answer some of the misconceptions about the warehouse development in our community," she begins, the work tarps behind her blowing against the breeze, whipping like sails. "The largest is the belief that they're creating a lot of pollution in our community. Fortunately for us, we live in one of the windiest cities in Southern California. Most of that pollution just blows away!"

"God," I say, turning the TV off when the segment ends. "She's such a liar."

"Is she?" Ale asks, flat. She twists her wrists and studies her nails.

"We're in a valley. The air just circulates." I gesture to the windows, where the winds blow so hard that the panes rattle. "If the pollution just blew away, we could go outside right now."

"Crazy," Ale deadpans.

I dramatically crane my neck so she can feel me looking at her. Still, she doesn't budge. "Are you okay? Are *we* okay?" I ask, a hand gesturing between the two of us.

"Uh-huh," she responds, short.

"Really?" I ask. "You haven't looked at me since you got here."

She's quiet for a while. "You just ditched me," she says, "at the jaripeo."

I blink at her. I can't tell if she's kidding or not, but by the way she still hasn't turned to look at me, I know she's serious.

"*That's* what you're upset about?" I ask. "Weren't you the one who was convincing me to see Julio?"

"It was still rude of you," she mutters.

I turn away from her. Her tone is unconvincing, like there's something she's still not telling me.

I fidget in my seat, the binder in my lap suddenly feeling like a stone, waiting for her to explain. When she doesn't, I sigh.

"I'm sorry," I say. "I just really needed to talk to him."

She looks ahead, studying the walls of my house. The wood paneling, the family photos, my pa's dartboard by the entrance. "So, what? Are you two dating again?" she asks, which eases the tension enough. Both of us laugh.

I shake my head. "No. Just partners for the project."

"For now." She snorts. "Give it until spring semester."

"I don't think so," I say, trying to contain my smile.

"What?" she says. "It's overdue. Plus, this project is kind of bigger than that. Don't they give you a lot of money if you win?" she asks.

I nod.

"You trust him like that?"

"Yes," I say, "I do."

"Damn," she says, "you really like him."

"I really *trust* him," I correct.

Ale shrugs, rocks in the recliner. "Just be careful."

I roll my eyes at her. "Careful with what? You wanted me to see him, now you don't?"

"No, no," she says, "I like Julio. He's really nice. I mean, be careful with the project. People get really weird about money." She looks at me for a few beats.

"What do you mean?" I ask.

She looks away, shaking her head gently. "Nothing." She pauses. "How is the project going?"

"Fine," I say. "We just started. I was actually going to ask you if you'd ask your pa if he could participate in some of the interviews we're doing."

"Interview about what?"

"The project is about the negative health impacts caused by warehouses in the area," I explain. "I thought he may be a good person to talk to, since he's part of the strike."

"Oh," she says. The brief ease between us fades. Ale turns away from me again. I try to read her expression, but she looks toward the window, her reflection clouded in the commotion outside. The jacaranda tree in the front yard slants in the winds, Ale's face lost in the mass of moving branches.

She's quiet. In her silence, all that is audible is the ring of the neighbor's wind chime. It's usually gentle, serene, but the gusts of air make the tubes strike violently, their trills like a siren.

"So—are you down?" I ask. "Can you ask him?"

"Yeah," she says, still not turning to meet my gaze. "That sounds fine."

Thirteen

JULIO BOUGHT ME A BURRITO.

He hands it to me, warm and wrapped in butcher paper, from the driver's side. We're sitting in his truck, shaded beneath the solar panels in the city hall parking lot, eating before the city council meeting starts.

"You didn't have to do that," I say, looking down at my food.

Despite my protests in the Miguel's Jr. drive-through, Julio bought it for me. There, he craned his neck out the window, reciting my order perfectly into the speaker box. I was shocked he still remembered it.

He nods. "I did. This meeting is going to be long," he says, looking at the cars steadily streaming through the entrance, the lot now almost at its maximum capacity.

It's surprising.

Recently, city council meetings were empty—not because people didn't want to attend, but because Mayor Warner had made it so that they couldn't.

She changed their weekly times from starting at six to four, landing right during work hours. Her goal to diminish attendance has worked—hardly anyone can get time off to come to a meeting. Even I had to barter with Ale to close Nicho's today without me.

But this meeting is different. At this meeting, the mayor would be voting on zoning ordinances for new warehouses, including the one by our school. Local activist organizations were stationed near the fence for the last few days, handing out flyers to encourage people to attend.

Cristina Fajardo from K-FER interviewed a group of them during last night's news segment, their pleas to get people to attend the meeting broadcasted on screens across town.

It seems to have worked.

By the time we're finished eating and head inside, the lobby is packed with people.

Most of them are in line to get a public comment card, the human current bending beyond the bathroom, around the drinking fountains, and stopping near the vending machines.

I blink at them, amazed at the immediate ripple effect. One local segment resulted in hundreds of people showing up—if our research was published nationally, I wonder what waves that might provoke.

Julio inches forward to join the line.

"You're gonna speak?" I ask.

"I always speak at meetings," he says, shuffling forward.

When we finally get to the front, he folds the card into his pocket and turns to me. He sweeps me through the thickness of the crowd, his palm pressed to my back, making my spine straighten. His touch is familiar and unfamiliar all at once.

We wait by the double doors that lead to the chamber, where Julio begins to fill out his comment card. "Do you want to speak, too? I can fill it out for both of us." He asks, peering at me from over his shoulder.

I don't even have time to respond.

The doorknobs begin to jimmy, and the crowd behind us pushes forward. I look over my shoulder—they gaze toward the door expectantly, most of them still wearing work uniforms. I wonder how many of them requested to leave their shifts early to attend—they look as if they've been waiting all day for the opportunity to be here.

Right when the doors burst open, the crowd propels forward, rushing inside.

I panic for a second, wondering how we'll make it through the stampede. But then I feel Julio grab my hand, his fingers lacing through mine, pulling me inside with him.

"Hey," Julio whispers to me, "you should speak."

We're seated right at the front of the chamber. The stage is directly across from us, our council members sitting in the five lecterns positioned in a semicircle, Mayor Warner in the center. The new San Fermín city seal is behind them, a factory nestled between a citrus grove.

I look at Julio—we'd agreed to come to the council meeting to get more information about zoning for our project's map, not to make a statement.

"I can't," I respond.

"Why not?"

Truthfully, the first thing in my mind is my ma. She watches the news coverage of meetings while at work. If she heard me speak, I know it would wedge the gap between her and my pa, her and me, even further.

I skirt around the question. "You're definitely gonna do it?" I ask him.

He nods. "Yeah. Especially since my mom and Yvette aren't here."

"Where's Yvette?"

"She wanted to come," he says, "but she has a shift soon."

"And your mom?"

He looks at me, but right then, Mayor Warner calls the meeting to order. At that, Julio grabs his binder, pulls out the draft of the map we'd made over the weekend, awaiting to hear where we'd have to draw in new warehouses. I balance my notebook to do the same, listening to the roll call, when Julio leans close to me again.

"You should think about it. I can still add your name to the card."

I give him a look, and he smiles at me.

"I've read your articles—you know a lot about this stuff," he whispers. "I bet you'd say something good."

He shifts beside me, laying his wrists onto the armrest, the mountain range of his knuckles grazing against my skin.

The meeting begins with a brief list of city amendments, the updates unremarkable, the crowd unmoved. But when the conversation about zoning begins, heckles break through the audience.

"Excuse me," Mayor Warner scolds, peering at us from over the frames of her glasses. "Please remain respectful."

We listen to the mayor present a proposal for three new distribution centers on Oleander Street. She regurgitates her same silver linings—more jobs, more money, more mobility. More, more, more.

They vote shortly thereafter, the council unanimously deciding on its approval with the slam of a gavel.

Mayor Warner looks down at her notes. "We will now move on to the notice of filing beside San Fermín High School."

The urgency I'd seen getting into the main chamber pales in comparison to the urgency I feel now. The room feels tight, inflated with all of us holding our breath—me especially.

All I keep thinking about is my ma, how this construction would demolish life as I know it if she decided we need to move. I close my eyes, remind myself that this decision could be reversed if we win the scholarship and our research is published.

Still, a drum beats in my chest. Mayor Warner shuffles the papers on her lectern, stacking and restacking them before folding her hands together and leaning close to the microphone. "The decision about this project is under indefinite postponement. The site remains pending until further notice."

The crowd, once restless, grows quiet.

Nothing like this has ever happened before. I'm relieved, for a moment, that it may also postpone my ma's decision to move. But something unfulfilled remains, lingering over the crowd like the haze of smog in our sky.

Mayor Warner tries to breeze past the announcement and move on to public comments. But the first public comment asks about it directly.

A short man approaches the podium set in front of the council, a doubtful look on his face. "Why has the city council postponed the decision about the lot beside San Fermín High School?" he asks. "The agenda said the decision would be made today."

Julio and I crane our necks around the people in line to get a better look.

"That information is confidential," Mayor Warner says, not even bothering to look up.

I turn to Julio, who shakes his head in confusion.

The comments afterward address the new warehouse approvals on Oleander Street. They move back and forth, one opinion opposed by another.

Employment opportunities.

Environmental impacts.

Economic expansion.

Health crisis.

Tax revenue.

Cancer rates.

Profit.

People.

Money.

Death.

Almost an hour into the public comment session, a pregnant woman waddles toward the podium. She wears a postal service uniform, the buttons on her blouse nearly bursting against her stomach. She pulls a sheet of paper from the pocket of her pants, and reads into the microphone.

"I have been a proud resident of this community my entire life, and I'm saddened to say I'm not sure how much longer I can live here," she begins. "I know these frequent school cancellations will only worsen when a warehouse is built beside my future daughter's high school—"

"I repeat, no decisions about the property beside San Fermín High School have been made," Mayor Warner interrupts, manicured fingers pressed to her temples.

"Mayor Warner, I believe there are no interruptions during public comments," the woman retorts.

"It was not so much an interruption as a correction," Mayor Warner deadpans. "Please avoid spreading misinformation."

The woman points a finger at Mayor Warner, posed in blame—but, somehow, I feel like she's pointing directly at me. She continues speaking, begins crying, but I can't listen.

All I can think about is my ma.

Everything this woman is saying are things my ma has already said to me. She moves a hand over the moon of her stomach, cradling her daughter, reminding me that I was once also cradled this way: curled inside of my mother's body, physically tethered to her.

I watch the rest of the interaction as if I am not really there, as though it's all the blur of a dream. The only thing grounding me is the draft of the map in my hand, the main reason I came to the meeting to begin with.

And then, the dull ring of a bell sounds through the chamber.

"I'm sorry," Mayor Warner says, removing her glasses and folding the plastic stems. "Our time for public comment has finished."

The woman wipes her eyes, checks the time. "I thought we were allotted two minutes per speaker. Only one minute has passed."

"We've limited public comments to one hour tonight. The hour has elapsed," Mayor Warner responds. She rises and waves a dismissive hand. "Thank you for your comment."

"You can't at least let me finish?" she asks.

Mayor Warner shakes her head. When the woman continues speaking, Mayor Warner doesn't react—she doesn't turn around, she doesn't even look at her.

It's as if the woman does not exist.

Instead, Mayor Warner adjourns the meeting and leaves.

The other council members follow suit, exiting the chamber one by one, leaving the entire community behind.

Fourteen

THE LAST TIME I WAS IN JULIO'S HOUSE WAS THE TIME I was sure he was going to say that he loved me.

He'd invited me to help him water the plants in his pa's garden. His ma was at work and his pa was at a doctor's appointment with Yvette, so it was just the two of us at the house. I filled a watering can in the kitchen, staring at the Dodgers calendar pinned to the wall. The starting lineup stood in a perfect row, August in a neat grid beneath them.

Outside, Julio pruned the orange tree in the center of the yard. I circled around him, watering the plants in the pathway. We sat together when we finished, watching the wetness of the asphalt steam beneath the sunlight.

It was a rare moment of stillness in the chaos of Julio's life.

By then, his pa's face was sunken and sallow, his body succumbing. It was hard for Julio to find pockets of peace, but we both cherished them when they came.

We lay down, our hair tangling into the teeth of grass, our faces turned toward one another. The sun struck midair, its rays warming the orange blossoms on the tree, the smell fragrant and sweet between us. Julio tugged on a strand of my long hair, wrapped it around his finger like a ring. We were quiet for a moment, listening to the leaves overhead shaking in the wind, like they were applauding this arrival.

Julio looked at me then.

I could feel it—something heavy sitting on his tongue, ripe fruit slung low on a branch after months, years, of harvesting. Something easy, something natural, something earned.

It would have been perfect.

And then his phone rang.

It was Yvette. She was calling him from the hospital, and she was crying. Julio shot up, pressed the phone to his ear. Despite its closeness, I could still hear her. I couldn't make out what exactly she was saying through her screams. They were jagged and uneven, like the rhythm of my heartbeat.

Everything else happened in a haze—Julio rushing to his truck, pulling out his keys, starting the ignition. I called after him, but he sped off into the distance.

I drove myself home, looking at the blue beyond the mountain range, thinking of how quickly it had changed in a matter of minutes. It was a gradient in the garden, holding the hope of many colors, like it had been in my bedroom the first time we kissed.

But as the night came, it had turned into the kind of blue that was one-note, flat—nothing but sad.

I sat in my driveway for a while, my headlights striking against my house like yolks. I was still for a moment, looking at our white security door illuminated against the light.

I wondered what to name that shade of white—so evasive and empty, so full of nothing. When I couldn't come up with a name, I thought about what Julio would think.

Sorrow overcame me.

I turned off the headlights and sat in the dark.

I knew.

I went inside and sat in the living room with my pa, thinking Julio would never have such a simple privilege again in his life. I put my phone in my lap, the plastic warm against my skin, and waited for the message.

It never came.

The next time I spoke to Julio was at the funeral, the space between then and now stunted with silence.

And yet, despite the passing of time, I still know the route to his house by heart.

Off of Merrill, onto Mango, six palm trees, one church, two lefts, and there was Julio's house.

After the city council meeting, Julio pulls into his driveway, the sun setting behind the slant of the roof. I shield my eyes with my palm, taking in the house with a squint.

They've repainted it since his pa's passing.

Before, it was the blue of denim washed one time too many, faded and pale against the sunlight. Now, it's sapphire, deep and true. The white fence his pa built a few summers ago stands uneven in the grass, like teeth crooked in a jaw. I can see bits of plants from around its bend, pieces of the garden his pa spent his entire life building. Blooming and evergreen, despite it all.

We enter the house through the side door, stepping into the kitchen. There, Yvette clamors around in her scrubs, frantically preparing a thermos of coffee before her shift.

It's been so long since I've seen her outside of the hospital. I had often wondered what it would be like if we ever spent time together again, occasionally indulging in the daydream that Julio and I would reconnect.

Now that the moment has arrived, I'm shocked to be reintroduced to her this way.

She's nothing like she used to be.

She gives us a cold once-over when we enter. Her hair is slicked into a bun, revealing her unwavering expression—solid and still, even when I smile and greet her.

"Good to see you," she says, her tone militant and clipped. I recoil a bit, mentally replaying her greeting in my head, wondering if I've offended her somehow. But then she turns to Julio, speaking to him with the same cadence. "I have to go. I have a double. She hasn't eaten."

Julio nods, and I'm not sure what she's talking about until I look at the living room.

Julio's ma is sleeping on the couch, hardly perceptible beneath the blankets bundled over her body.

Yvette steps toward me, trying to reach the refrigerator to finish packing her lunch. I veer out of her way.

"Yvette," Julio calls, "would you be open to helping Paloma and me with something?"

I look at him, wide-eyed. We hadn't spoken about asking Yvette for help since I brought it up at the taquero stand, and now, I regret even suggesting it.

It was worse than what I had imagined when Julio described how Yvette had changed—she was more than different, she was unrecognizable. Nothing about her demeanor said she wanted to talk, but especially not about her pa.

"Helping with what?" she asks, distracted.

"Our scholarship project," Julio explains. "We need to get numbers on people's real health metrics."

"What is that about again?" she asks, peering into the refrigerator and reaching for the coffee creamer. She pops the top open, then looks at us. "What are you two researching?"

Julio rocks gently on his heels. "Warehouses," he says, "and their negative effect on the health of the community."

Her face falls when he says that, the stable, solid look fading into something different. It was an expression I was growing to recognize, one Julio made any time I asked him a question that was too specific to his pa—like someone picking at a scab, the skin still too tender to get tough.

Yvette stares into her thermos, her face reflecting against her coffee. She douses it with cream until her mirror is gone, clouded in milk.

"What do you need me to do?" she asks.

"Mainly help us with some medical equipment, if you'd be open to it," Julio explains. "We're hoping to use oximeters to track how people's oxygen levels have been impacted depending on their proximity to the warehouses, comparing the south side residents to the north side—"

"Fine," she interrupts, exasperated. "Let's talk about this later. I'm late."

"Thank you, I know—" Julio begins, but Yvette turns away from him. She twists the lid onto her thermos, grabs her car keys, and leaves, the side door slamming behind her.

I take a breath and look at Julio, waiting for his reaction. But he doesn't seem rattled by the interaction at all. Instead, he walks to the refrigerator, pulls half an onion from a Ziploc bag, and begins making dinner, as if all of this had been normal.

"Are you okay?" I ask him, "Is *she* okay?"

"She was actually a lot better today," he muses. "Probably because you were here."

I scoff. "No way."

"Yeah," he replies, grabbing a pot from a cabinet. "That's why I asked her in front of you. She wouldn't have agreed if it were just me."

I give him a look.

"Come on. She loves you—even if it doesn't seem like it. She asked about you a lot when we weren't talking."

"Really? What would you say?"

He shrugs. "That I missed you."

My face gets hot. I clear my throat, gesturing to the stove. "You need help?"

Julio shakes his head.

Julio makes soup, toasting fideo in a pot with oil, blending tomato with garlic and onion, and pouring in canned chicken broth. There is no recipe, just the measurements of memory. While the soup simmers along the stove, he washes dishes in the sink, the air around us fragrant with Palmolive.

"You make dinner a lot?" I ask him.

"Yeah," he says, setting the blender on the drying rack. "My ma can't really do much right now."

I nod, watching as he ladles fideo into a bowl, douses it with Tapatío, and arranges it onto a tray with tortillas and wedges of lime. He carries the tray to the living room, where he sets it on the coffee table.

I look around, absorbing it all. There's a staleness to the space, the windows closed, the curtains shut. My eyes are drawn to the potted plants in the corners of the room. I tilt my head at them, wondering if any of them are those clippings Julio and I propagated as sophomores. They seem to be the only life in a room completely committed to grief.

There's an altar to the left, positioned right over the space where Julio's pa's recliner used to be. It holds a framed photo of him, enclosed by a collection of saint candles, their flames swaying when Julio rubs a hand on his ma's shoulder.

"Ma," he calls.

Señora Ramos grunts, the sound muffled in the blankets absorbing her body.

"*Ma,*" Julio repeats. "It's dinner. You have to eat."

His ma sits up a bit, supporting the weight of her body on her elbows. Julio helps her up, smoothing over the back of her head, where her coarse black hair is dented. He pushes the blanket off her torso so it sits just at her waist, then stands the legs of the tray upright.

"Paloma," she says, her voice crooked with sleep. "I haven't seen you since last year."

"Hola, señora," I respond.

Julio gestures to the tray on the table. "Cómete algo, Ma."

She ignores him. "¿Y tu apá?" she asks me, looking straight at my face. Her eyes still hold her tiredness, the boundaries of her pupils blurred.

I smile at her. "He's good," I lie.

"Good?" she echoes. "Even with that cough?"

The sentence hangs between us.

I blink at her, unsure of what to say. Luckily, Julio cuts through the tension. He pulls the coffee table forward with importance, gesturing to the tray of food again. She doesn't budge.

He grabs the spoon from his ma's hand, and for a moment, I think he might spoon-feed her. I look at the floor, the carpet depressed with the weight of my body, embarrassed at being here for such a private moment. But I listen as he stirs the spoon into the soup, and supervises, hovering patiently, until she takes her first bite.

He stands then, adjusts his hat, and gestures for me to join him in the kitchen.

"Nice seeing you," I say to his ma, who is moving toward her food slowly, like every motion of her body boggles her with pain.

As we leave, I wonder what the city council members and their supporters would think if they saw this—Señora Ramos's face stamped with the lines of the couch, crust caked at the corners of her eyes, shoulders slumped with exhaustion. How a warehouse was not the way to work, but rather the weight of grief.

* * *

Julio and I sit at the kitchen table. We spent many elementary afternoons here with Yvette, who would help us with our homework.

It's almost like it used to be back then—Julio and I still sit at our assigned seats, beside each other at one end of the table. Books and articles and papers spread between us, our map among them.

I pick it up, studying the boxes shaded along the graph paper. We'd be submitting it with our preliminary proposal at the end of the month—proposals that were accepted would receive an email by mid-December to prepare for the presentation given in April.

"This is due soon," I note. "Two weeks from now."

Julio plucks it from my hand and adjusts his glasses—thick, plastic frames sitting over his nose. He's farsighted, so he wears them to read. I've always liked when he wore them; the lenses distort his eyes and make them look even larger, like fish swimming in a bowl. He catches me staring, and I look away.

"We'll get it done. We have all Thanksgiving break to work," he assures me. "I'll get the air quality monitors from the library this week. We can use them around town, compare the results from the north and south sides, prove the people on this side have it worse."

He sets the map down, points to the shaded area around us that was boxed in by warehouses. "Should be easy here."

"We can't prove that without their oxygen levels." I sigh. "You think Yvette can help us that fast?"

He nods. "Yeah. We'll need participants, though."

"Do you know anyone?"

"I'll ask people at my ma's church if they want to participate," Julio says. "If she goes."

He looks ahead, where his ma is still asleep on the couch, her food not even half-finished. His shoulders slump.

"Are you okay?" I ask.

He puffs his cheeks out. "I just really need to win this money," he says. "For me, and my pa, but also for her. It'd be nice to give her something to celebrate."

I blink at his ma, then look at Julio. Maybe, in some ways, winning this for him was about his ma, too.

I reach over the table and squeeze his hand. "Let's take a break."

Julio nods and stands, looking toward the kitchen window, where the sun is beginning to sink behind the garden. "I have to water the plants on Tuesdays. You wanna help?"

"Sure," I say, smiling.

Some of the garden is the same—the orange tree still outstretches in the center, its limbs littering ripe fruit along the ground. But a lot of it is different. The grass is gone, replaced by a fresh patch of soil, and a series of plants are lined against new risers pushed near the driveway.

"You got rid of the grass," I observe, gesturing to the dirt. He looks at it for a moment, then looks back at me. Like he, too, is remembering what almost happened there. He glances away quickly, crouching down to examine the soil.

He swallows. "Yeah. My pa had planned to fill it with his propagations—he started a little before he passed. I'm trying to finish it for him."

"How long have you been working on it?" I ask.

"About a year," Julio says. He stands, wipes the sod from his jeans, and grabs a plant from one of the risers. He pulls a trowel from beneath the structure, then kneels against the soil again, digging into the earth. "The goal is to finish before I go to Davis," he says, transferring the plant from a pot into the dirt, cupping soil around its base.

I uncoil the hose from the side of the house, then water the new addition.

"Well, actually, the goal is bigger," Julio continues, reaching to plant the next one. "I'm trying to use some of my pa's clippings in a garden I want to start."

"You want to start a garden?" I ask.

He nods. "Yeah. I have the whole thing planned out—I think I even picked a lot for it." He pauses for a moment. "I'll take you there sometime."

"Is it close by?" I ask, watching as the downpour catches in the light, a curved rainbow forming against the shower.

"Yeah," he says. "I want to study botany at Davis, move back, and plant it here."

"I didn't know you wanted to move back," I say, watching as he plants a set of flowers.

"Of course I do." He looks out at the horizon. "I love it here."

Julio was one of the only people I knew who talked about San Fermín this way. It was so different from what I'd heard my ma say my whole life. In Julio's eyes, it was never a stop along the way, but a place to literally plant roots, a home to habitat.

"Honestly, it's hard enough to move," he admits. "Especially with the way things are with my ma."

I nod. "I never realized things were so bad. It must be hard for you," I add, watering his next plant. "I'm sorry."

He shrugs. "They're honestly better than they used to be. This helped a lot," he explains, gesturing to the soil.

"Gardening?"

"Yeah," he says. "I talk to them. It was good for me, and good for them, too."

"You talk to the *plants*?"

"Yeah, talking to them helps them grow," he explains with a smile, blushing a little. "What about you? You think you'll ever move?"

"Not if I can help it."

"Your ma is still making you take that tour?"

I nod. "Next week, during Thanksgiving."

He turns to me. "How come she wants to move so bad?"

I look at him. It's a question I wish I could still answer even for myself.

"I don't know," I say. "She just keeps saying she's tired. But I think my pa is tired. He's the one on strike, he's the one who's sick."

"Does your ma help?" Julio asks, reaching for another plant to dig into the dirt.

"With my pa?"

Julio nods.

"Not really."

"Not at all?" he asks, surprised.

"I mean—I guess." I sigh. "She's just working."

"She's the *only* one working?" Julio clarifies.

I push loose hair behind my ears. "Yeah."

"That's hard—I can't imagine. Right now it's me *and* Yvette. But if it was only her, I don't know." He pauses, shrugs. "That would be a lot on her."

I look down. I was standing here, watering flowers, while my ma was working another overtime shift. I feel a sudden pang of guilt, but it evaporates when Julio says, "Well, I hope you don't move. I'd miss you."

He rises again, reaching for the hose. I hand it to him, watching him water his finished work. Then I sit on the steps near the back door, observing while Julio circles the yard, searching for the best orange the tree has offered us. He grabs one, rinses it off, and moves to sit beside me, knocking his knee against mine.

He peels the fruit, the pith powdering in the sunlight. Then he portions it, the segments sitting like lips or lungs cupped against his palms.

I take one from his hand and pop it into my mouth. Julio laughs a little, gesturing at the gap in my front teeth where some fibers have stuck. I get embarrassed, picking them out with the tip of my nail, and Julio looks at me.

Today, the brown of his eyes is less prismatic, more decided. He leans back onto the heels of his hand, layering one casually over mine.

My first instinct is to move my hand away, but I leave it there, letting the warmth of his skin spread onto my own.

The sun has been setting for what feels like an eternity, rust with color and with time. Orange light peeks through the leaves of the trees above us, painting Julio's face in blotches of sunlit watercolor, until it finally turns blue, then black.

For a moment, it feels like that summer. When we would sit back here together, kissing in the shadows of the escaping daylight. Especially now, when Julio squeezes my hand after I tell him I should get home.

"Wait," he blurts, hopping off the steps and bending toward the soil. He roots his hand around, plucking one of the flowers he'd just planted and extending it to me. My heart slingshots against my chest.

I take it, gently spinning the stem between pinched fingers, the petals fluttering like a skirt in the wind. I'm grateful for the night around us, the deep of the darkness hiding the blush on my cheeks.

"Thanks for your help," he says. "Let me drive you home."

Fifteen

"HE GAVE YOU A FLOWER," ALE SAYS, SWAYING IN HER seat. "Come *on,* Paloma."

"But he didn't say anything," I protest. I reach over to take a handful of Rancheritos from the bag we're sharing. I lean back in my chair and look out the window of the journalism room, where we are obligated to spend our lunch today.

Selva is hosting their annual career fair near the front of campus. Every year, they convince wide-eyed seniors to take a job with them right after graduation, pipelining them into a warehouse on the first day of summer.

I usually saw those same students shortly thereafter—kids at union meetings who had been lured in by the fair, only to have grievances and labor disputes within their first few months as employees.

I couldn't bear to watch it happen, so we walked here instead. I turn away from the window, back to Ale, who is rolling her eyes at me.

"He doesn't *have* to say anything," Ale says. "He's, like, in love with you."

I shake my head. "You're being dramatic."

"No, I'm not. You saw how he looked at you. It's crazy."

We had bumped into Julio on our way here. It was the opposite of before, where I'd pass him in the hallway and try to figure out how to ignore him. Now I wondered if we should say hi or hug—what our new normal was.

"What is that?" Ale asked, pointing at his hands, where he was holding a plastic container full of dirt.

"Soil," he said. "It's for gardening club—we're testing different soils today."

"What do you garden?" Ale asked. "Flowers?" She drew her eyes over to me, blinking slowly. My face flushed.

"Sometimes," Julio replied, coolly. But when he adjusted his hat, I could see it there, even in its shadow. He was blushing, too. "Where are you guys headed?"

"The journalism room," I said.

Julio nodded, looked at Ale. "What about you?"

"I'm going with her," she said, arcing her thumb toward me.

"You're not going to the field?" he asked. "I thought the girls' team played during lunch."

"I quit the team," Ale explained, quickly.

"You quit, too?" Julio asked, incredulous. "Why? I thought you were being scouted."

She shrugged, lifted the ends of her hair to study the split ends punctuating the tips. "Busy."

Julio nodded again, slower this time. "I should go—our meeting starts soon. We're working today after school, right?" he asked me. "At the library?"

I nodded, angling my body to allow him to get by. As he passed, he squeezed my hand, his fingers gently pulling around my nails. "I'll see you later."

And then he looked at me like he had the night before, like he did all that summer. With something luminous, something lucid, something like love.

Ale pops another chip into her mouth. "If someone looked at me like that, *I'd* think they were in love with me."

"Don't say that," I say, pushing her. My force is gentle, but still she rolls back in her computer chair.

"Don't say that?" she mocks, arcing her legs to propel forward, scooting closer to me. "He's a guy—they don't know how to use their words, so they use their face."

"Julio's different," I counter.

"Julio *is* different," she agrees. "But he likes you. And you like him." She pushes the heel of her hand against the edge of the table, spinning slowly. When I don't immediately respond, she stops mid-swivel to look at me. "Right?"

I don't say anything.

"Paloma," she scolds. "Why can't you just say it? It's obvious."

"Fine," I say, my teeth slightly gritted. "Yes."

"So, *what*, then?" she asks. "He's clearly interested in you. Why don't you two just date again?"

"Because we already broke up once." I sigh. "I don't want to go through that again if it doesn't work out."

She flicks her wrist at me, dismissively. "That's *boring*."

I blink at her. It was hard not to entertain the thought, especially with all the time we'd been spending together lately. But I never imagined it would actually happen. Things with my ma had taught me to never count on anything as promised—to always prepare for the worst.

"I'm just saying, I've dated a bunch of guys," Ale says, tipping the corner of the bag of chips into her mouth. She taps it gently, getting every last crumb. "None of them have ever looked at me like that. Please just tell him you like him—I need something exciting to happen in my life."

"You *do* have excitement in your life. What happened with Luis?" I ask. "From the jaripeo?"

"Nothing."

"Really?" I ask. "After all that, you guys aren't even talking?"

"Nope."

"Anyone else?" I ask.

She looks away. "No. I don't really have time for all that anymore."

I cock my head back. "How come?"

"I'm busy," she says, echoing what she'd said to Julio in the hallway. I blink at her, waiting for her to explain, but she twirls in her chair again. "So, when are you telling Julio?"

I watch the blur of her body, feeling dizzy. "I don't think I can. I can't risk it," I say. "Especially with this project."

She groans. "What *about* the project?"

"I don't think it's a good idea for us to date if we're working on that together," I tell her. "We both need to win this."

"And you'll get it," she says. "All you've been doing is writing and applying for things," she says, gesturing to the computer in front of me.

November had been a busy month—along with the regular stream of classwork and college applications, it was scholarship season. Apart from the Communities Care scholarship, I applied to a handful of other scholarships—some for writing, some for Latina students, some in general.

"It's not that simple," I explain. "If we don't get it, I can't get my work published. That's all I've been working toward." I gesture around us, to the journalism room.

"Your work *has* been published," she notes, jutting her chin toward the wall.

It was a wall of fame—the best of the *Herald*'s articles framed and on display. A handful of them were mine.

"But *nationally*," I correct her. "People need to know what's happening here. And Julio won't be able to go to Davis without it."

"That shit is so unfair." Ale snorts, gently shaking her head. "I'm glad I don't have to do it."

"Not yet," I say. "But I can help you when it's your time to transfer."

Ale takes a breath. "I don't know if I'm gonna go anymore."

I widen my eyes. "You're not gonna go to *Chaffey*?"

Ale teeters her head from side to side. "Maybe not."

"Why? It's free. You can join the soccer team and get scouted from there, too."

She runs the bag of chips on the edge of the desk, pulling it back and forth until it's ironed completely flat. "Triplets won't be in school for, like, two more years. My parents will probably need help until then."

"But what about you? What are you gonna do until they go to school?" I ask.

"Work," she responds, simply. "Like always."

I blink at her, waiting for her to look at me. But she doesn't, just folds the bag of chips again and again, as small as she can make it. With her head down, all I can see is the part in her hair, a perfect seam splitting her dark hair in two. When she catches me looking, she swivels in her seat, her face lost in the movement.

"But I thought your mom wasn't working anymore," I say. "She can't take care of them while you go to school?"

"She's not working for *now*," Ale explains. "That can change, depending."

"Depending on what?"

She doesn't answer me, just sucks the orange Rancheritos powder from her fingers, twisting each one against her teeth to get all the seasoning off. "Are you seeing him during break?"

"Who?" I ask, confused.

"Julio."

"Oh," I say. "Yeah, to work on the project."

"You can just hang out with him, you know," Ale says. "Not only work on this project."

"It's important we get it done soon—the preliminary proposals are due at the end of the month. Did you ask your dad if it's okay if we interview him?"

"Not yet," she says, short.

"Well, can you? Maybe Julio and I can come by during break when they have extra time off."

"What extra time?"

I blink at her again—it's the first Thanksgiving where our pas won't be forced to work overtime to fulfill Black Friday and Cyber

Monday deals. When I mention this, she spins away from me in her chair, using the toe of her sneakers to steady herself to a stop. She rises, her back toward me, and walks to the garbage can by the door to throw away her empty bag of chips.

"Right. I'll ask him," she says, reaching for her backpack. "I should go—the bell is gonna ring soon."

I check the time—there's still fifteen minutes left in our lunch period. I turn to tell her this, but when I look, Ale is gone. All that is left of her is her seat, its casters squeaking slightly, still swaying in the invisible force of her absence.

Sixteen

ON THANKSGIVING, MY PA DRIVES US TO PASTO VERDE.

We idle at a stoplight by Memorial Park, watching wordlessly as Selva representatives arrange the food drive Mayor Warner publicized during her Mayor Monday segment last week.

Cristina Fajardo and a handful of other news anchors border the perimeter of the receding grass. They're preparing their evening report to promote the event. I wish they were preparing to tell people the truth instead—how Black Friday and Cyber Monday deals often left Selva workers in shambles. Last year, it took a day to erect the hunch in my pa's spine, a week to heal the blisters on his hand that had burst and bled.

Instead, their scripts will probably discuss how Selva was bringing families together, unaware of how they were one of the main reasons my family was apart.

But maybe not for much longer.

The strike has been going on for nearly two months and the *LA Times* finally published an article about it last week.

When people all over the country read about how their same-day delivery packages came with the cost of many workers' lives, the Selva human resources department called my pa to ask if they could meet and negotiate.

The immediacy of their reaction reminded me how impactful national news coverage was, and it made the weight of me and Julio's research feel heavier.

I slump back in my seat, wondering why we're even touring this house. With negotiations on the rise and the mayor's indefinite postponement about the warehouse beside the school, I thought maybe my ma would feel appeased.

I lean forward to ask her, when I see my pa glimpse at me in the rearview mirror. It's a look he's begun to reserve for my ma—one that says he's just trying to keep the peace, and one that suggests that maybe I should do the same.

I fall back and stare at my ma's hands instead. The left one lingers on the center console, her polished wedding ring a few centimeters away from my pa's hand. For a second, it makes me forget the duality of the right one, which is nested in her lap above the renter's application.

We board the ramp to the 10, heading east. I look out the window, watching the clouds transform, the canvas of the sky changing with it. Close to home, ads pattern across its expanse in a steady rhythm: Adriana's Insurance, Selva. Jacoby & Meyers legal representation, Selva. Morongo Casino, Selva.

As we approach Pasto Verde, there are hardly any billboards. The sky is continuous—boundless and blue.

And though it would be a hopeful sight for anyone else, it fills me with dread. I know this is exactly the sight my ma wants. When she sees it, the yearning expression she had last week at the swap meet is gone. It's replaced by something I can't identify until she reaches up to open the sunroof, fingers tangling through the clean mass of wind.

She's happy.

Her expression seems so foreign because she's smiling, something I haven't seen her do in weeks.

I expect it to dissipate when my pa closes the sunroof and pulls into the driveway of the rental home, but it doesn't—it widens.

I look at the house—it mirrors the style of the other homes that had been pinned to our refrigerator for months. The only distinguishing factor about this one was that it was right beside Pasto Verde High School.

I stare at it the entire time my parents talk to the landlord.

It holds all the markers of my own school: the marquee and soccer field and mascot statue. But so much of it is different.

The marquee on this lawn doesn't mention anything about air quality, just features a cycling pixelated image of autumnal leaves floating into darkness. And the field behind it upholds the city's namesake—verdant pastures rolling everywhere. The greener grass my ma desired.

I blink at the windows, wondering what the students here look at while they do their work. My daydreams at school depend on the air quality of the day. When it's clear out, I can look outside my classroom window and doodle the loose curves of the Jurupas. And when it isn't, I can lay my pencil flat and sketch the whisper of the smog.

I look to my right to see what's visible from here, wondering what the students at Pasto Verde High doodle during the lulls of their classes, what symbolic promise of their future looms across the street. But here, it's not the same thing at all. Because across from Pasto Verde High School, there is no promise of warehouse work. Across from this school, there is a library.

My ma's good mood ended the moment we finished the tour.

Truly, it ended the moment I answered her question.

"What do you think?" she asked.

We stood beneath the shade of a tree canopy arcing over the house. Even in the shadows, I could see the hope in her eyes. Her smile was so broad that the skin around her eyes folded into the dainty footprints of a bird.

I blinked at her, unsure of whether or not my answer mattered.

It seemed my ma had already made up her mind—as we'd toured the house, I had this unshakable feeling that she was beside me, but wouldn't be for much longer. Her excitement made it seem like she was already gone.

She walked through the house with the ease of someone who already lived there, imagining where everything would fit into her new home, her new life.

I looked at my pa, who was nervously biting the cuticles around his nails. He shot me the same look he'd given me in the car, trying to stop me before things could escalate.

"Come on," he said, gently tugging the sleeve of my sweater. "Let's just go."

"What?" my ma asked, looking between us. "You didn't like it?"

"It's nice, Ma." I looked at my pa apologetically. "But I don't know. Things seem to be changing back at home—don't you want to wait to see if things get better?"

After that, her face fell.

The expression I'd seen since the strike began had returned, and I knew then that the brief moment of joy she'd had in the car ride here was over. I waited there in front of her for her to answer my question, but she never did.

Not when she walked ahead of me, not when she slammed the car door shut, not when my pa started driving. The tension spread through the car as we drove and persisted indignantly through dinner.

We've spent every Thanksgiving at my grandparents' restaurant since I could remember. But this year, things are different. When we arrive, it feels like even time is holding its breath, everything at a standstill.

When my family sees us, they stop arranging the restaurant furniture and swarm toward us, buzzing with the excitement of moths to flames.

It's the warmest welcome we've ever had.

But it's not really for us.

As soon as everyone turns to ask my ma how the tour of the house went, I realize that this holiday isn't really a holiday, but the potential for her homecoming.

They're so excited to hear about it that they pull her toward the head of the table, seating us right next to my grandparents. It's an eagerness I recognize, one I feel every time my ma returns after being away.

As food is passed down the length of the table, my pa and I begin a performance, pretending that what had just happened at the rental house, what had been happening at home, what had been happening for months, was not happening at all.

It's easy to put the charade on, swallowing mouthful after mouthful of food, until my grandpa looks at my pa.

"How are things at work?" he asks. "I read something in the paper that mentioned a strike."

My ma, who was eating beside me, stops abruptly.

She glances at my pa for the first time since we arrived—a brief, pleading look.

My pa looks at her, confused, before turning back to her father. "Yeah, I've been on strike for two months."

"*You've* been on strike?" my grandpa asks, accusingly pointing the tines of his fork at him. "What have you been doing for work the last few months?"

"Organizing has been the priority, so I haven't been working," my pa explains.

My grandpa blinks at him. "You haven't been working?" he echoes, incredulously. "Who's working then—just Karla?" he asks, eyes flicking to my ma.

My pa and I look at her. She sits with her face hidden in her hands. My pa turns back to my grandpa. "I'm sorry, I thought you knew."

"*Is* she the only one working?" he asks.

And then it's not my pa turning back toward my ma, but everyone else at the table. They draw long looks and pick quietly around their plates. After a few beats of silence, my ma eventually lifts her head, like she's coming up for air. But still, she doesn't answer.

My grandpa asks again. "Karla," he says, "are you the only one working?"

"Yes," she says through her teeth. "But it's temporary."

"I'm searching for something part-time," my pa clarifies. "And we're in negotiations."

I look at my ma. Her face does not brighten at the reminder, and it's the first time mine doesn't either. Her embarrassment is contagious.

My grandpa lets out an exasperated breath. "What happens if you can't negotiate? Then what?"

My pa repeats what he's been telling us for months. "Then we keep striking."

My ma sighs—it's so long and winding, it sounds like it's been simmering in her lungs for days.

"But for how long?" she asks.

"Until we have a good contract," my pa says. "We can't rush this."

"Well, if the negotiations don't pan out, maybe it's time to quit," my grandpa says, simply.

"I *can't* quit," my pa explains. He pauses for a moment, clears his throat. "My best friend died doing this type of work—I feel a responsibility to see this through for him."

"I'm sorry to hear about your friend," my grandpa says, shaking his head. "But this is unfair—to both my daughter and yours." He gestures toward me. "There are other things that can be done about this. If you need work, we always need people here. You and Karla can help manage."

My pa is silent.

My ma turns to him, waiting for him to respond. But my pa says nothing.

That nothing carries through the rest of dinner, follows us into our car ride home. It's dense and decided—a nothing ripe to turn into something.

Inside, my pa sits in his recliner. He leans back, looking at the ceiling, as though preparing for what's coming next. I sit on the step between the living room and the dining room, staring at the carpet, my ma pacing above it.

It used to be lush and thick, but after years of her pacing, years of their arguing, it offers little support. The brown shag now lies flat against the ground—the crosshatched backing revealed in spots with the most recession and wear, the near exact outline of her feet.

"I can't *believe* you told them," she says, moving from one side of the room to the other.

"I didn't know you were keeping it from them," my pa says.

"Of *course* I was."

"Why?"

She stops for a moment, hands locked on her hips. "*Why?*" she spits. "Do you think I'm proud of what's happening here? Do you think I want my parents to know that I am the only one working to provide for our family? Don't you think I'd be embarrassed by that? Aren't *you*?"

"I'm not embarrassed by it. I'm working in a different way—" my pa starts, but my ma holds a hand up, cutting him off.

"Are *you* getting a paycheck?" she asks.

My pa stops, shakes his head. I try to interrupt, but they keep going.

"I didn't tell them because I knew they'd be worried for me," my ma continues. "I knew they'd offer us help and I can't *believe* you're not taking it. Do you ever stop to think about anybody but yourself?"

"Of course I do," he retorts. "It's why I'm doing this strike to begin with. I am thinking of an entire community, of people's families, of people's health."

"I mean, what about *your* family? *Your* health? Not *their* families and *their* health—but what about *you*? And *us*?" she asks, her hand weaving between the three of us, then smacking directly on her chest.

My pa is quiet.

I sit there, between my parents.

It's the first time I feel like I'm really between them, not beside my pa. I remember the woman at the city council meeting, cradling her stomach. I remember Julio's ma, lying on the couch, grieving her husband. I remember Yvette, frantically working to cover the person who couldn't.

And I look at my ma and I understand why she didn't answer my question after we finished touring. She had been patient.

Though I understand it, somehow, I still didn't want her to go. "Ma," I say. "I'm sorry. I know it's hard. I just feel like there's something else we can do—"

I stand up and wrap an arm around her, squeezing gently, expecting her to lean into the embrace. But she shakes her head and does the thing I'd been fearing most: she steps away from me.

I stand there for a moment, my arm still outstretched and stiff, like a ballerina in a perfect third position. The kickback of her rejection is so strong that I feel like the wind has been knocked out of me, a bloated pain piercing my side. I force myself to sit down again.

My ma stands near the credenza and takes a breath. "I don't know how much longer I can keep doing this. I don't want to have another holiday dealing with this in front of my family," she says, wiping her eyes. "This strike needs to end soon or—I don't know."

But it seems like she does know. The answer is in the thud of the door slamming, the hum of the car reversing out of the driveway, the quiet of her absence.

A feeling of emptiness settles into the room, one I had been trying to avoid by working on this project that, now, I don't think will be enough. Despite the work I'd been doing with Julio, the echo of the past had still arrived. Sitting with my pa, wondering what to do while my ma was away. Looking at the door, wondering if she'd ever return at all.

Seventeen

"WHAT'S WRONG?" JULIO ASKS.

We're sitting on the edge of his truck bed, waiting for the results of the air quality monitor a few yards away. We spent most of the afternoon driving around the city, tracking the air quality neighborhood by neighborhood for the preliminary proposal of our project that's due next week.

I don't answer his question. I stare at the monitor instead, waiting for it to finalize its results. It sits on the driveway of a house not too far off from my pa's family's house, where my pa and I eventually went last night. It was the only thing my pa would think of doing other than sitting around, waiting for my ma.

Anytime anyone would ask where my ma was, I said the only thing I could say that wasn't fully a lie. "She's tired."

I'd spent all morning trying to forget about last night. But the memory of her always returned—she hadn't come home yet, and the house felt crowded with her absence.

Spending the day with Julio had worked to distract me for a few hours, but it didn't seem to be working anymore. Especially not now, looking at the distribution center neighboring the house where we've placed the monitor. It beeps, and I rise to read its result: hazardous.

It was a reminder of what being at home felt like—like there was nothing left of what used to be, like there was no room to breathe.

I sit beside Julio again, writing the result in my notebook.

Julio slides closer to me, his hand nearly touching mine, and asks again, "What's going on?"

I look up, the sun is misted in a veil of gray, the pollution of the day so thick that it appears to have been hole-punched into the sky, hollow in the atmosphere.

"My parents," I say. "They got into this huge argument last night about the strike. My pa is at negotiations today, but I don't know how long that's going to take. My ma says it needs to be fixed soon."

"It needs to be fixed soon, or what?"

"She didn't say." I pause. "But I feel like she's going to leave."

I've avoided saying the words aloud since my ma presented us with the renter's application a few weeks ago. They felt stained with something superstitious, like a jinx. Truthfully, it's the first time I've even admitted it to myself.

I'm quiet after, staring down at our legs dangling from the edge of the truck bed, our sneakered feet hovering midair. "I just don't know how to convince her to stay."

"Have you told her about the project?"

I shake my head. I didn't want to.

If I did, it opened me up to the possibility of double rejection—first of me, then of this project. After last night, I wasn't sure how much more of that I could take.

I explain this to Julio, but he doesn't say anything after. He takes my hand, squeezes it, and hops off the ledge of the truck. "Let's go for a drive."

Julio plays Bobby Pulido while he drives, the sweeping accordion guiding us down roads neither of us have seen before, looping through cul-de-sacs and weaving around gated communities. It's what we used to do when we were together that summer, wandering without any specific destination in sight.

It would probably be boring with anyone else, but with Julio, it always felt like enough. Not because it was, but because we were together. I glimpse at him from the passenger's side.

Julio looks the best when he drives.

The long lean of his body folds against his seat, hand hung over the steering wheel, pulse pressed to the plastic.

Looking at him is nearly enough to lift the anxiety looming over me, which tightens every mile we get closer to my house. It's like it used to be—wondering, hoping, my ma's car would be there when we returned.

But Julio doesn't take me home. A few blocks before my street, he turns into the parking lot of the Save-a-Minit liquor store on the corner of Arrow and Alder.

"My dad played the lotto here every Friday," he says, lifting the parking brake. "I started doing it for him as soon as I turned eighteen."

We go inside, where I wait for Julio to purchase his ticket. But he walks into the snack aisle instead. He reaches for a narrow bag of peanuts clipped to the edge of a stand and turns the bag my way.

"Are these still your favorite?" he asks.

I look at them—Sabritas sal y limón peanuts. I nod, watching Julio grab a pack of Gansitos for himself. He walks to the cashier, places the snacks along the glass countertop, and asks for a lotto ticket. The cashier hands him a slip and gestures to the pen chained to the counter. Julio fills it out quickly, not pausing to consider what numbers to pick.

"Do you just pick random numbers?" I ask, peering over his shoulder.

"No," he says, "I play my pa's birthday every time."

"What about the other ones?"

Julio turns to face me, flashing me his circled selections.

I study them, squinting. He's circled a five and a ten. "That's *my* birthday," I say, pointing to the digits.

"I know—that's why I picked them. Two really good days."

Something somersaults inside of me.

"Then what's the last number?" I ask, trying not to stutter.

"You pick," he says, handing me the slip.

"What if it doesn't win?" I ask.

"Doesn't matter." He shrugs. "Our bigger prize comes later, anyway. When we win the scholarship." I soften. Everything about Julio is so tender—even, especially, his optimism.

I look at the row of numbers, then circle an eleven. He studies it for a second, nodding curiously.

"Your old jersey number," I explain.

He smiles at me, taking the slip. He pays, folds the ticket into quarters, and shoves it into the pocket of his jeans.

Back outside, I begin walking toward Julio's truck. But then I feel him take my hand. He pulls me gently, guiding me to the empty field beside the parking lot. He tilts his head to its expanse, as if there's something I should be looking at. But all I see is garbage.

The uneven grass is covered by flattened cardboard boxes and broken liquor bottles, the shards gleaming in the late afternoon sun.

When I don't say anything, Julio says, "This is where I want to put my garden."

"Here?" I ask.

"Yeah," he says, smiling. "What do you think?"

I look around the lot. Julio has a perspective I've never encountered before. One I wish I could give to my ma. She could look at the possibility of the sky and still see it as a ceiling, as a limit. Julio saw this field beside a liquor store and didn't see dirt—he saw soil, a place where things could still grow.

I blink at him, standing on the grass with his arms outspread, the field wide against his wingspan.

"It's beautiful, right?" he asks, standing amid the trash.

"It's perfect," I agree.

He pulls me forward to the center of the field, where two deflated tires sag in the heat of the day. He crouches down, touching a few green buds sprouting around the rubber treads. "I planted some seeds here a few weeks ago," he says. "They're finally growing."

"You can do that?" I ask. "What did you plant?"

He shakes his head. "You're not supposed to, but my pa and I used to. He taught me how." He cocks his head to invite me closer, and I kneel beside him.

He twirls the stem slightly, his pressure soft. "This will be bee balm in a few months. Good for pollinators and air purification—blooms all year."

He stands and points a finger, drawing midair. He plans his entire imagined layout for the lot: sunflowers there, citrus trees here, and plants propagated from his pa's garden in the center of it all.

"So that he can be part of it, too," Julio says. "He would love this."

He walks toward the fence, broken glass crunching beneath the soles of his sneakers. "Maybe over there," he calls to me, "we could do like an educational center, to teach people how to grow their own things at home."

I look at him, turning the word over in my head, savoring it: *we*.

He grabs a few scattered milk crates and pulls them together to form a makeshift bench. We sit on the netted plastic, looking at the sunset over the field.

I lift my hand to shield my face from the rays, but Julio takes off his hat, sets it onto my head, and adjusts it so that the bill shades my eyes.

We're silent for a moment, watching the trash blow against the gusts of wind.

"The first time I came here after my pa died, this field looked like a wasteland. I felt like you do—kinda hopeless." He pauses, swallows. "But I don't know. I started planting things here, and it reminded me that things grow when you let them."

I look ahead, at the small buds worming their way through the soil.

"You should give your ma a chance," he suggests. "Tell her about the project."

"I don't know," I say, shrugging. "I don't think she'd change her mind."

"If there's still room *here* for things to change, there is room for you and your ma."

He gestures at the space in front of us. And I hope, for a second, he may gesture to the space between us as well.

Because Julio looks at me and I think it might happen. I think he might kiss me.

Despite the arrival of the darkness, I can still see him looking at my mouth, at the hollow space between my front teeth.

My lungs flutter in my chest, like wings humming against my bones. I can't place if it's excitement or fear—maybe both combined into one. But as Julio looks at me, I realize that it is memory.

It was a feeling I had all that summer.

A lightness that felt atmospheric. I figured for a while that maybe it was specific to it—to that summer. That season.

But so much of it was cycling back to me—the tension of not knowing what will happen next, despite him leaning close.

The feeling sticks to me even as the streetlights interrupt us, even when Julio stands up, even when we finally have to go.

I realize then that the feeling around Julio wasn't specific to the summertime at all—it was unavoidable, it was perennial.

Eighteen

IT'S STRANGE SEEING YVETTE OUT OF SCRUBS.

It's odd even seeing her sit down.

Every time I've been around her, she's always up, always working. But today, on Sunday, she's sitting beside Julio in the St. Elizabeth's staff room. It's their family church, the one where Julio gathered the majority of the participants for our oximeter study today.

After mass this afternoon, participating attendees line up near the break room doors to have their vitals taken.

Yvette trained us on how to use the oximeters yesterday. She's next to Julio, supervising to ensure that he uses the equipment correctly. I'm sitting at a table across the room, waiting to interview the participants when he's finished. But even from here, I can see the similarities of siblinghood shared in whispers—the angle of their smile and the bend of their front teeth and the brown of their skin.

And similarities apart from siblinghood, shared in loss—the same tone when they speak about their father.

I hear it when a participant enters and sits across from Julio. Julio had been warm and conversational all morning, up until now, when this woman's eyes narrow with recognition.

"Aren't you Ernesto's son?" she asks.

His Adam's apple bobs in his throat, his jaw clenches. "Yes," he says, motioning for her to extend her hand toward him. He sets the monitor on the tip of her index finger and waits. When he's finished, she arcs her arm over and squeezes his hand.

"I'm sorry about your loss," she says. "Your father was a good man."

"Yeah," he says, looking up at her, "he was."

He smiles at her, but when he looks over at me, his expression falls. He tilts his head, gesturing for me to give the woman one of the flyers stacked near my notebook. It's the system Yvette trained us on last night.

"No matter their results," she advised, pacing the living room floor, "do not be reactive—good or bad. You're not medical professionals, just students doing research. But if their results are bad, hand them one of these."

She gave us a stack of flyers that listed free clinics in the area. We didn't hand out any of them earlier this morning when we conducted the same study at the north side's community center. The results there hardly varied. Some were better, some were worse, but overall, they were normal.

Here on the south side, results also hardly varied—most were bad.

Our pile of flyers has steadily grown smaller in the hour we've been here, even smaller now when I have to hand one to this woman after interviewing her. I look down at my notebook—a simple series of questions, similar to the ones I've prepared for Ale's pa if we ever get to talk to him. I kept calling Ale all weekend to ask if we could interview him, but she hasn't answered once.

"I'm Paloma," I say, extending to shake the participant's hand. "I'm just going to ask you a couple of quick questions."

She nods, gently raking her fingers through her hair.

"What is your name?" I ask.

"Maria Danna."

"How old are you?"

"Thirty-seven."

"What do you do for work?"

"I work at a factory," she says, "loading orders onto cargo beds."

I ask for her zip code, then turn to the map beside me. We finally finished it yesterday, our drafts on chart paper now a mosaic of coded colors. A thick red line bisects the north and south sides, orange lines over city streets on the north side, yellow lines over the ones here. Julio drew green rectangles to represent the few parks left, and blue boxes to represent the warehouses.

On the north side of San Fermín, the boxes skipped in uneven patterns. On the south side, where we were, where I lived, where my pa worked, they were everywhere.

I try to find my house among the color-coded streets. Trying to see if my ma could maybe still find a home here.

It would be hard, though, amid all of the gray encompassing the city.

We'd used an air quality map to help us represent the pollution in the area, shading a light layer of gray over the county, more sheer in the areas with less pollution, more opaque in the areas with more of it.

The farther I looked away from the south side, the more the pollution became a gradient. In Rancho Riestra, dark gray. In Floresta, light gray. In Pasto Verde, nothing.

But here, there is a pattern of color bruised over the city: black and blue, black and blue, black and blue.

I add a red thumbtack to Maria Danna's zip code area, one of many pins in the sea of darkness.

"Thank you," I say, turning back to my notebook. "This is for you," I say, handing her a flyer as she rises to leave.

We finish the study in about an hour. It's the last piece we need for the preliminary proposal that's due next week, and I want to feel relieved that it's nearly finished. But as Julio packs up the equipment, I don't feel relief. I stare at the map, feeling my stomach tighten into knots. Most of the pins representing residents with health complications were amassed on the south side. Most of them lived near a warehouse. Most of them were either Latino or Black.

I tell Julio that I need to use the bathroom, but just stand in front of the sink instead. I watch the faucet drip against a ceramic basin, the edge as chipped as my pride.

I began this project with the hope of helping the community—but, for many, the damage has already been done. And for some, like Julio's family, it was irrevocable.

The knots snake up to my chest, twisting my lungs until my breath is tangled in their grip. I feel so guilty that there was nothing else I could do for any of the participants, that all I could offer them was a piece of paper.

Back outside, I see Yvette at the end of the hallway. She irons a dollar bill along the edge of the coffee vending machine before slowly feeding it into the pay slot.

"Julio's posting the leftover flyers around. I told him we'd wait here," she says, gesturing to a bench near the windows. "You want a coffee? Might be good in this weather."

Outside, the day was dim, the mountains hidden against the gray breadth of the sky. I could feel something teeming and palpable pulsing through the church windows—the imminent roll of rain.

"Sure."

I sit beside her on the bench, trying my best to be casual, even when the coffee scalds my tongue. But Yvette's demeanor pulls a string in my spine. She'd kept the same attitude she'd had in the kitchen both yesterday and this morning, the relentless firmness I'd come to recognize as her new self. So I sit up straight, my shoulders squared, my mind searching for the right thing to say.

"Thank you for your help with this," I start, gently clearing my throat. "It'll be really useful for our project."

I don't expect Yvette to respond. She doesn't for a while, stares at the large crucifix hung over the entrance doors. Last summer, Julio had walked beneath it with the rest of the pallbearers. "Of course," she says, looking away. "I used to help you guys with homework all the time."

She smiles at the memory. I'm shocked to see a different expression on her face, but I try not to show it. I shift my weight and scoot farther up on the bench, closer to her.

"It's really nice seeing you back at the house," Yvette adds. "I know it's not what it used to be, but my ma enjoyed seeing you. She missed you—we all did."

"Did she come to mass today?" I ask.

Yvette shakes her head. "No. She had a tough morning—some days better, some days worse. It's hard."

"How do you deal with it?" I ask, gesturing to the break room. "I feel so guilty that I wasn't able to offer any of those people more help."

In the past, Yvette always gave me the best advice, pulling wisdom from thin air. It's why I expect her to have an answer now—I figured she would have one, she always did.

Instead, she shrugs, her brief smile slackening.

"I don't know," she says, matter-of-factly. "I don't know how to deal with it."

I curl my toes, immediately feeling like I've overstepped. "I'm sorry, we don't have to talk about this."

Yvette blinks a few times, the hood of her false lashes drooping slightly. "It's okay. I just don't know how I'd be helpful—I don't really feel like I've ever helped anybody."

"What?" I ask. "Of course you're helpful—you're a medical assistant, you work at a hospital."

"Doesn't mean much. I feel guilty, too," she admits.

"Guilty about what?"

"The same thing—that I can't do more for these people. I'm just constantly taking them to the lab or the pharmacy or handing out stupid flyers." She pauses. "I couldn't even do more for my own dad."

"But that's different," I say. "You did all you could—"

She shakes her head. "No, I don't think I did." She pauses again. "I feel like I should've known."

"Should've known what?" Julio asks.

He's crossed into the hall to pin the last flyer onto a bulletin board by the front doors.

He turns around after and looks at his sister, who sits with her palms flattened against her knees. Her lips are pressed together tightly, a dam bending before it bursts. "I should've known our pa was sick," she explains.

Julio's brows curve inward.

"Yvette, how could you have known that?" Julio asks. He steps into the reflection of the stained glass, his face Technicolor. "He didn't have any symptoms until it was too late."

"But I took all those classes. What was the point of taking them and doing all of that schoolwork if my own dad was sick and I couldn't even see it?" she asks. "I feel like it's all my fault."

Julio looks at her. It's the first time I see their gazes reversed. Usually, as the eldest, Yvette watches over Julio. But today, it's Julio who looks at her this way. And when she looks up, their gazes mirror, twin tears falling from both of their eyes.

"Yvette, that's not your fau—" he starts.

Yvette rises quickly, wiping her face with the sleeve of her sweatshirt.

"I should go," she says, tucking her purse under her arm and moving toward the front door. "I have another shift soon."

Julio reaches out for her, but Yvette pulls away. She walks out of the church doors and into her car, the echo of her footsteps as quick as my heartbeat.

After Yvette erupted, the sky did, too.

Rain released through ruptured clouds, falling around us as Julio drove me home.

He's been quiet since Yvette left church. The only sound the entire car ride was the windshield wipers rhythmically swiping the raindrops jeweling the glass.

I look out at the palm trees.

True to their name, their fronds sit wide and outstretched against the sky, like hands attempting to cup water. I peer beyond them, trying to find the mountain range, but it's muddled against the thick sheets of rain.

Julio parks in my driveway. We sit quietly together for a while. It's so different from the last time we were together, when we almost kissed. Somehow, we feel closer now, bound by something different.

"I didn't know she felt like that," Julio finally says, staring out the windshield. The rain is steady around us, like a tap left running. A Selva truck parks farther down the street, idling as the deliveryman drops off a package at my neighbor's house. "Why would she tell you and not me?"

"She probably doesn't want to worry you." I turn to him, rest my cheek against the headrest. "You've been through a lot."

"Yeah, but so has she. After she didn't want to go to grief counseling, I never knew how to talk to her—she's never really home, she's always working."

"I know you're working when you can, but without your mom working, Yvette's the only person with a full-time job. It's probably really stressful for her."

I hear it then—the echo to the conversation Julio and I had in his pa's garden, when he had said the same thing about my ma. She pulls into the driveway now, parks right beside my pa's car, returning from an overtime shift.

"I have to go," I say, turning to Julio. "But you should talk to Yvette. I think this project really helped her open up."

He nods, then looks at my ma. "Did you tell her about it?" Julio asks. "It could help you, too."

I shake my head. She had just returned home yesterday—I didn't want to rock the boat. She steps out of her car, an arm arced overhead as she shields herself from the torrent. She squints at Julio's truck, sees me, and gestures for me to come inside with her.

I move to head outside, but Julio is already at the passenger-side door, holding it open for me. I step down, breathing in the smell of damp asphalt. Julio walks me to the porch.

"Julio," my ma calls to him, pulling him into a hug, wet hair matted against her forehead. "It's good to see you again. Paloma is always so happy when she comes home from hanging out with you."

I blush, embarrassed that she's said that, surprised that she even noticed.

"It's good to see you, too," he calls, over the sound of the downpour. "I just wanted to say hi. I know it's been a long time."

I look at Julio, the rain dripping from the bill of his hat. He hugs me goodbye. Halfway up the steps, he honks lightly. I turn around and see he's extended over the center console, where he's used the tip of his finger to draw my name on the steamy windowpane.

Instead of writing my last name, he draws a soft zigzag beneath it. Undulating hills that nod at its origin. And then he wipes it away. Beaming at me from the clear space of the glass, he drives off into the rain, the memory of the mountain range held in his hands.

Nineteen

THE MONDAY AFTER THANKSGIVING BREAK IS ANOTHER AQA day.

I look for Ale in the lines of students filed in the gym who are waiting to receive their independent study packets for the day. She's usually easy to find in her AQA day uniform: sweatpants and an N95 mask.

But today, I can't find her anywhere.

I even look for her car in the student parking lot, but it's not there either. When I call to ask if we'll be working at my place or hers, she doesn't answer.

I start to worry that something is wrong.

She hadn't picked up the phone all day yesterday, when I called again to ask about interviewing her pa.

I drive to her place to check on her.

On the way, I pass by the warehouse—the picketing is still going on, now a couple of members short. My pa is somewhere inside of the building with a few of his teammates, still negotiating.

I cross the overpass to Ale's apartment complex, reflexively turning on my high beams in the dark of the early morning. But I flick them off when I notice new streetlights on the side of the bridge. I double-take at them. They're so new that the poles look wet with shine, gleaming beneath the cool light of their bulbs.

They turn out to be the smallest change that awaits me.

Because when my car is back on Ale's street, I have to blink a few times to make sure I'm in the right place. I check the signs and the map on my phone. But this is it. This is where Ale lives—though maybe not anymore.

Her apartment complex is gone.

All of the complexes on the street are.

Everything has been demolished. Crumbled brick, shards of drywall, planks of wood are enclosed within the frame of a fence, littered around the notice of filing that is newly staked into the middle of the dirt.

It announces that new Selva self-service delivery lockers will be here in the next few months, over the remnants of other people's histories, of other people's homes.

The only evidence that life was once here are the chickens from the neighbors' coop. They flit behind the fence, wings wide beneath the new streetlights, beaks pecking at the remaining earth that has yet to be taken.

Ale's family moved two weeks ago.

At least, that's what she explains when she finally picks up the phone.

"Why didn't you tell me?" I ask. I'm still parked near her old complex, watching as construction workers arrive for their shift, heads dotted in hard hats.

She doesn't respond, but I can hear her breath against the receiver, soft and tentative.

"Okay," I say, dragging the word out. "Well, I have your AQA work packet—should I drop it off?"

She hesitates for a while. But eventually, she sighs. "Sure."

Ale's family now lives a few streets down from their old apartment complex. It's a ranch-style house that's painted pale yellow with a blue trim, like a waxy stick of butter. They have a small front yard with balding grass, and a backyard with just enough space for a plastic play kitchen.

I park near the driveway, staring at a deflated soccer ball drooping against the pavement, when I see one of the triplets burst out the front door. Álvaro runs past the front yard and onto the street. I rush out of my car to grab him, but Ale is faster. She pushes off the porch and swoops toward him, her long nails hooking under his armpits.

Álvaro begins crying, wails piercing against the slow sunrise. She shushes him and positions him onto her hip, nuzzling him against her chest.

She's walking back into the house when she sees me standing against my car.

We stare at one another for a while.

She looks tired—her hair is looped into a bun and yesterday's mascara is folded beneath her eyes.

I wait for her to greet me, but she doesn't.

I don't know what else to do but step forward and give her the packet of work for the day. She takes it from me—her brother in one hand, her schoolwork in the other.

Then she walks into her new house. I stand in the driveway, unsure whether I'm invited in, and watch the cabinets in the play kitchen peek open in the breeze. When Ale notices I'm not following, she leans against the threshold, looking right at me. "Are you coming, or not?"

Ale stands beneath the hood of the stove, preparing her siblings' breakfast. The triplets and Alex are sitting around the kitchen table, so new that the wood still smells like polish. Ale spoons scrambled eggs onto their plates, portioning them evenly.

"Can I help you with anything?" I ask, gesturing to the stacks of recycled Selva boxes heaped around the house.

Ale shakes her head.

After she's done cooking, she puts the stopper into the sink drain and fills the basin with water. She adds a scoopful of powdered Foca detergent, then softly glides her hand into the mixture until it suds.

"The washing machine is still being installed," she explains, turning to a hamper nearby. "So, I have to wash this by hand."

"Why didn't you tell me?" I ask again. "That you moved."

She grabs a shirt from the pile. The fabric is a gray I could recognize anywhere. She dunks her pa's Selva uniform shirt into the water, letting it steep for a moment before wringing it out. "I didn't know how you'd react."

"React to you moving? This seems great for you guys," I say, gesturing to the house.

"It is," she agrees.

"So, what, then?" I ask, slowly. "Why would I react badly?"

Ale sighs and pulls her hands out of the water, the pads of her fingers just barely pruned. One of her press-ons has come off, the bright green bit of plastic floating along the water's surface like a paper boat.

"This was part of a deal," she says, gesturing to the space around her, drops of water flicking onto the countertops. "With Selva."

I blink at her. "What do you mean?"

She sets her hands onto her hips. "My pa isn't striking. They promoted him to floor manager."

We stare at one another for a while, stuck in a stalemate.

I don't know what to say.

I look around the house instead, at the furniture spread around the room. The only piece I recognize is the papasan chair the triplets constantly fought over at the old apartment—the rest of the furniture is new, unrecognizable, just like Ale is becoming to me.

I finally clear my throat. "When?"

"Two months ago."

"But that's when the strike began," I say. I rack my brain to remember the last time I saw her pa. It was just before the jaripeo, when he and my pa were sitting in the living room in a tense silence. "Has he *ever* been on strike?"

"No," she admits. "They offered my pa a lot of money if he didn't strike and took a job as a manager instead. He wasn't going to take it, but then Selva bought out our entire block and evicted everyone. So, he signed a contract and bought this house."

I scoff. "And you guys took that deal?"

"Wouldn't you?" she snaps, shoving the shirt back into the sink. The water rises and laps over the rim of the basin. I stand back, just hardly saving myself from the splash, and stare at the small puddle it leaves along the tile.

Then I look at her.

It feels like she doesn't know me at all.

She had spent months listening to what that company had done to Julio's pa, what it had done to my parents' relationship, and what it had done to me and my ma. She had seen me research and write articles and op-eds about how this city had changed since the mayor allowed Selva into the community.

"No, I wouldn't," I say, definitively, twining my arms over my chest.

Ale shakes her head and continues washing, scrubbing the fabric aggressively. "Paloma, it was between not having a place to live and getting enough money to live somewhere nicer."

"Ale," I sigh, "it's *wrong*. They basically bought your dad out. He's okay with that?"

"It's wrong?" she echoes, ignoring my question. "Paloma, this is *survival*. Look, it's not like I'm happy about it. My childhood home was just demolished." She pauses. I can see her eyes getting wet, but she blinks fast, turns away from me. "But we were finally able to move. With that money and my pa's promotion, we finally have some flexibility. That's why my ma quit working—she could afford to, for a while," she explains. "But she can't anymore, which is why I'm here, doing this."

"What do you mean she can't afford to now? Your pa got promoted." The last word cuts through my mouth.

"Because now my pa might lose his job—because of the strike."

I sigh. As part of the potential negotiations, it was rumored that Selva was downsizing other departments to pay the workers on the floor the wages they were striking for. I hadn't realized Ale's pa might be one of them until she stood across from me, washing a uniform he may no longer need.

"My pa can't lose that job. It's done a lot for me and my family," she continues, her voice breaking a bit. "It got us this house."

I look around. I want to be happy for her. This place is so much larger than their old apartment. I can imagine Ale no longer has to sleep on the futon, that she finally has a room of her own.

But I can't stop comparing it to Julio's house—his ma asleep on their couch, too weak to get up and sleep in the bed she once shared with her husband. What had Selva given his family apart from a funeral?

I shake my head. "Just because you guys were able to get something out of his job doesn't mean that everyone else is. Some people aren't given anything—some people have things taken from them."

"I *know*," she says, loudly. "I don't agree with everything they do, Paloma. I'm not stupid."

I hold my hands up in defense. "I'm not saying you are, it's just that—"

"But I feel like that's what you think of me," she accuses. "Like I'm dumb just because I don't care about this stuff the way that you do. I *knew* you were judging me for getting that backpack."

I roll my eyes a little. "Ale, you were wearing a backpack promoting their company."

"It was the first new backpack I'd gotten in years," she says, blinking at me. "When have you ever needed a donation to get school supplies?"

I look at the floor. I feel my face flushing, ashamed I hadn't noticed. "I'm sorry," I say.

Ale continues. "It's not that I don't care. I *can't* care about things the way you do, Paloma. The second my pa got his promotion, I had to work *more.* Because instead of being relieved about it, all I could do was worry about what would happen if he lost it, how we'd survive. That's why I quit the team."

"*That's* why you quit?" I ask. "Why wouldn't your mom just keep working so you could stay on? You were about to be scouted."

"My ma has never taken a break in her life. It was nice to see her have it while she could. If my pa loses this job, I don't know what we're going to do."

I look up at the ceiling, trying to find the right words. I know her family is in a corner, but I can't help but feel they've painted themselves into it. "Ale, I know your parents work hard. I know this makes things easier," I reply, sighing. "I just think there are other things you guys could have done before resorting to *that.*"

Ale shakes her head. "It's not that simple. God, Paloma, you're so removed sometimes."

"*I'm* removed?" I ask, a finger pointed toward myself.

"Yes," Ale says. "Just because you read the paper and watch the news and write your articles doesn't mean you know everything. You know a lot—but this is real life." She sweeps an arm toward her siblings, who are throwing bits of egg across the table. "My pa needs this job to support us. *I* need to support us. You don't even realize how easy you have it."

I scoff. "Easy? My pa is striking and my ma is working overtime at a restaurant—"

She flicks her wrist at me, a trace of water dripping onto my cheeks. "You don't know what it's like to live like this. I'm the *oldest* of five, and you're an *only* child. You have your mom's family's restaurant to fall back on. We don't have that. Our plan B is my ma selling food, and the city is putting warehouses on every street where that would even be possible for her. My pa needed this promotion, so he took it."

The triplets finish eating, and Alex carts their plates to the kitchen. Ale wipes her hands on her sweatpants, leaving a trail of wet fingerprints against her thighs like cat whiskers. She leads all four kids to the living room, where she pulls coloring books and blocks out of one of the moving boxes, splaying them out onto the carpet.

When she returns to the kitchen, she rounds the table, collecting the bits of egg scattered atop the surface.

"I'm not helping you with that project," she says. She looks at me, but I can't look back at her. My eyes are focused on her hands instead, at that one finger with the nail missing. "If that wasn't already clear. I don't think my pa would have anything to contribute. It's not like you'd agree with anything we'd have to say, anyway."

I stand there for a while, my feet cemented to the ground, searching for the right response. But she's right. I don't agree with her.

So, I leave.

I drive away from Ale's house for the first and potentially the last time, my AQA packet in the seat beside me. It'll be the first day I spend it at home, alone.

Her voice follows me, stretching behind me like an elastic band, even as I move away from her house. I think about what she's said. I know I don't understand her life, and I feel embarrassed that I judged her for getting the backpack, that I never considered her perspective.

But when I drive past the remnants of her old apartment complex, I can't help but wonder if every other family that lived here got the deal her pa did. If they were offered new places to live, or if their new homes were similar to Julio's, where the grief was palpable in the air.

I stop at a red light before the overpass, where I see Ale's mom sitting beneath her vendor's canopy.

She sees me, and I lean back in my seat, feeling almost caught. I figure she's probably angry at my pa for planning the strike that compromised her lifestyle, that forced her to sit out in this air today, trying to make a sale. Maybe she's even mad at me.

But when I look up again, she rises from her foldout chair, her smile visible even through her N95 mask. She waves an arm for me to park, gestures for me to get a free cone.

I shake my head and drive onto the overpass, watching her smile grow smaller in the soft glow of the new streetlights.

Twenty

MY PA IS COUGHING UP BLOOD.

On Sunday morning, his hacks knocked me awake.

I heard the wheeze tearing through his body, the phlegm rising in his throat. He stumbled into the bathroom and turned on the shower, the steam successfully steadying his breath. Relief swept through me, brief and deceitful.

Because when I stumbled into the bathroom to shower, I saw it.

I squinted in the harsh light of the bulbs and rubbed the sleep from my eyes. When I set my hands down, everything was blurry but the red.

I blinked a few times, hard enough I heard a *whoosh* in my ears, just to be sure I was seeing it right. But there, in the trash bin, were blood-soaked tissues.

I pushed my way into the kitchen, where my pa was in his uniform. Sunday, God's proclaimed day of rest, and he was going to negotiate so that he could return to work.

A cough fumbled from his lips, the sound ragged in his throat. Instead of coughing into his elbow like normal, he coughed into paper towels bunched over his mouth. The paper was wet with fresh blood.

"Pa," I said. "Are you coughing up blood?"

He waved me off. "Just a little bit—don't worry." He started for the door.

"Pa," I repeated, weaving in front of him, "that's not normal."

"Happens every once in a while." He shrugged.

"Does it?"

He nodded at me, but there was something unconvincing about it.

"You have to go to the doctor," I urged.

He flicked his wrist at me, rummaging through a drawer in our entryway table for a mask. "It'll be better by tomorrow."

The iron security door rattled, almost as if in response. Through the blinds of the living room, I saw the winds had knocked over our neighbor's tree. It was December, the windiest part of the year, and the gusts were unforgiving—the howl of them like a warning.

Regardless, he turned toward the door, ready to go. I stepped in front of him. My ma was out, already at work, so it was just my body between him and the door.

I grabbed my car keys off the hook.

"Where are you going?" he asked.

I grabbed his hand. "We're going to the hospital."

Yvette is the main reason why I'm here.

While my pa insisted that he was fine, all I could hear were her gasps for air on the phone the day her pa died. Then they turned to something else—the confession she'd shared last weekend, the guilt she felt that she had not done all she could have.

I sit in the hospital waiting room, staring at my phone. I've been trying to call my ma the entire time we've been here, but she hasn't picked up. I consider calling Ale instead, but we hadn't spoken since the last AQA day on Monday.

For the past week, she's dodged me in the hallway and switched her schedule at Nicho's. During lunch, I sat in the journalism room, peering through the windows at the school marquee where we normally sat. It was empty. Just a few yards beside it, I saw Ale sharing a bag of chips with some of her old soccer teammates.

At first, it hurt. In our days apart, I'd felt so angry that she didn't understand how unfair her pa's deal was. And somehow, I still missed her. I hoped that maybe we could talk things through.

But sitting in this waiting room, I'm confronted with the line drawn between the two of us: she and her pa were comfortably tucked away in their new home, while me and mine were in the hospital—both because of Selva.

So, I don't call her—she would never understand. I call the only person who would. I don't expect Julio to answer—he's spending his morning mowing lawns on the north side—but he picks up immediately, listening intently when I explain what's going on.

"It's going to be okay," he assures me. "The winds are really bad right now. I'm sure it's just a flare-up."

I pace the hallway. "What if it's not, though?"

"Then the doctor will handle it. Don't panic until you find out."

I smack my lips. That's what I had been telling him since we submitted our preliminary proposal on Friday. We weren't supposed to hear back about whether we'd advanced to the next round until late December, but Julio began refreshing his email the moment we submitted.

I could sense his smile on the line. "Text me when you're home," he says. "I'll come over."

I hang up and look at my pa, another tactile reminder of the research Julio and I had finished, when I hear my pa's name being called. Yvette waits by the threshold of the examination hall, waving for us to join her.

I swallow, expecting things to be uncomfortable after the oximeter study last week. But Yvette doesn't miss a beat. Her ponytail swings as she leads us to an examination room, her scrubs swishing in each step. She takes my pa's vitals the way she'd trained us to just last week, then sits in a computer chair, reading his medical chart on the monitor's screen.

She leans back, the casters squeaking slightly, and goes through the routine questions about my pa's health: diet and exercise, health habits, family history. It's one of the first times I don't see her as the oldest sister or a third parent, but as a professional.

"What brought you in today?" she asks.

He shrugs. "Just a little coughing."

She tilts her head, eyes scanning her computer screen. "How severe is the cough? Your medical chart says you have asthma."

"Not too bad," my pa says.

I give him a look. Yvette waits, her hands hovering over the keyboard. I turn to her. "He was coughing up blood this morning." Yvette nods and begins typing, her keystrokes urgent.

She peers over at my pa and asks, "Do you smoke?"

"Never," my pa says, readjusting himself along the examination table, the tissue paper crinkling beneath the weight of his body.

"Are you exposed to secondhand smoke?"

"Not often."

"Are you exposed to other harmful inhalants?"

My pa gestures to his Selva uniform, which still smells like the distribution floor—a mixture of new paint, dust, and gasoline. "I work at a warehouse."

Yvette's professionalism fades to personhood, her eyes downturned in the thickness of her fake lashes. She gives us a wan smile before standing up. The lanyard looped around her neck jingles with passes, fobs, keys. She collects the clipboard with the questionnaire I filled out for my pa in the waiting room. "I'll go get Dr. Fisher."

The doctor arrives after a minute, Yvette lingering behind him, the clipboard from earlier pressed against her chest.

He's kind enough—making small talk about the Dodgers, about the traffic, about the winds. But Yvette cuts through the pleasantries, explaining the blood I saw this morning.

Dr. Fisher grows serious.

"It's a rough time of the year, with the winds," he says. "I can write a stronger prescription for your inhaler. You can get it downstairs, at the pharmacy."

My pa sighs. "I need it today?" I can see the wheels of his mind turning, trying to find a time to travel to Tijuana.

I squeeze his shoulder. "Pa, this is urgent."

Dr. Fisher gives me the same look those nurses gave us in the

Breathmobile, one pained with pity. He clears his throat. "I'd also recommend getting a nebulizer while you're there."

"How much do those cost?" my pa asks.

Dr. Fisher pauses. "I'd say less than a hundred dollars, insured. A few hundred, uninsured."

He reaches for the clipboard in Yvette's hands, then pulls a pen from the pocket of his lab coat. He scribbles in large loops while looking at my pa.

"What do you do for work?" he asks.

"Warehouse."

Dr. Fisher nods. "Tough job. Do they ever bring in any mobile clinics?"

My pa shakes his head.

The doctor doesn't respond—what is there to say to that? He sends us off with prescriptions and promises: the windy season will pass, the stronger inhaler will work, the nebulizer will help, things will be okay, stay inside, go Dodgers—such optimistic praise for a hospital room. He gives an airy goodbye, then ducks into the hallway.

All I can think when he leaves is: *That's it?*

My pa and I sat in the waiting room for almost an hour, all for a visit that lasted less than five minutes.

I sit there, mentally calculating how much this visit has cost him per second, when Yvette steps toward me.

"Do you have any questions? I can help," she offers.

"How is my pa supposed to just stay inside?" I ask. "He has to work."

Yvette nods. "I know that's not realistic advice for everyone—are you wearing a mask when you're outside?" she asks my pa.

My pa nods, pulling the one he'd had on this morning from his pocket, as if for proof.

"That's a surgical mask," Yvette says. "Do you have any N95 masks?"

He nods, taking a deep breath. "Yes, they're just more expensive."

"They don't provide them for you at work?" Yvette asks.

My pa shakes his head.

Yvette sighs. "We have some at home. We also have a nebulizer—it used to be my pa's. I'll ask Julio to drop them off."

"Thank you," I say. "Is there anything else we can do?"

Yvette gives me an empathetic smile. "Not really, unfortunately. Asthma is chronic—and as long as the air is the way it is, we can only manage symptoms, not cure anything." She takes a breath. "I'm sorry—I can have someone demo the new inhaler for him, if that's helpful," Yvette offers, gesturing to the door.

My pa nods. After Yvette returns with another medical assistant, he's swept down the hall for a demo, leaving Yvette and me alone in the examination room.

"Thank you for all of your help," I tell her.

"Of course," she says. "Are you okay?"

It was the question I'd been wanting to ask her, especially after last Sunday.

The truth was, none of it was okay—my pa's job was deteriorating his health, my ma hadn't picked up the phone, the air quality was only getting worse, Ale was on her side, I was on mine, and I felt as though there was nothing I could really do about it.

But Yvette isn't the person to tell any of this to. Not with that cancer ribbon pin pierced through the fabric of her lanyard.

I thumb through the trifold, reading the bullet-pointed list of advice. But it's all the same as always—all things we'd been doing.

"I don't know—I know all the stuff in here already," I admit, shaking the pamphlet. "It's hard to feel like there isn't more I could be doing."

"You're doing a lot," she assures me, squeezing my shoulder. "Don't be so hard on yourself."

I look at her. "I guess so. It's hard not to be."

"Yeah." She pauses. "I know."

She's quiet for a moment, looking at the posters and diagrams on the wall. Up by the sink are drawings of systems: the cardiovascular system, the digestive system, and the pulmonary system. Just above us, spread like two butterfly wings, are lungs.

"Thank you for listening the other day," she says. "And thank you for talking to Julio. We talked about my pa for the first time that night—it helped."

I blink at her, surprised. More surprised when she hugs me. She wraps her arms around my body, squeezing me so tightly that it's hard to breathe.

We hold each other for a moment, then Yvette returns to work.

It's a tender moment, one that is interrupted when I walk down the hall and look at my phone, checking if my ma has returned my messages.

She hasn't.

I find my pa near the elevator, and we ride down to the pharmacy together. There, the line is long with people who look like iterations of him: middle-aged, brown, tired.

My pa lines up behind them, another piece of the pattern. I stand beside him, trying to keep calm.

There is so much happening.

To my left, a woman files her nails, the tips shaping beneath the grit of an emery board. To my right, children loop through the legs of their parents, looking at them with shared impatience.

But worst of all, there is the ubiquity I'm growing painfully familiar with.

So many people bending into their elbows, pressing tissues against their mouths, lifting their shirt collars over their noses—coughs cacophonous, harmonizing, echoing through the pharmacy line.

Twenty-One

JULIO CAME OVER AFTER MY PA AND I RETURNED FROM the hospital.

My pa was lying on his recliner, a warm, wet cloth pressed over his nose and mouth to help open his sinuses. Every few minutes, I would remove it from his face and redampen it. I was standing to take it to the kitchen sink when I heard my phone ring.

It was finally my ma.

"Paloma?" she asked. She sounded worried. "Are you okay?"

"I'm fine, but Pa had to go to the hospital," I explained. "I called you in the waiting room—why didn't you pick up?"

"I'm still at work," she said. I could hear people around her, buzzing like bees. "Let me talk to your pa."

My pa tried to get up, but I shook my head. I set my phone on speaker mode and laid it beside him.

"Are you okay?" my ma asked.

"I'm fine. Just a little blood."

"*Blood?*" She balked.

"I'm fine," he repeated. "I got a stronger prescription and a nebulizer."

"Okay. I'll be home in an hour. I can call you out from work—do you still need to do that if you're negotiating?"

My pa cleared his throat. "No need to call in. I'm going to negotiate tomorrow."

There was a long pause on the line.

"Jaime," she warned, her tone forceful but even, "that job is the reason you're sick and you're not even going to take a break? Are you ever going to know when to stop?"

"I need to get this contract settled." He sighed. "I know it's been a long time—please, be patient."

My ma was quiet. The subtle buzz was gone, replaced by the clatter of dishes. And then, it was silent. She'd hung up.

I sat beside my pa after, wondering what would happen when she arrived home. Now, when I hear a car door slam, I flinch. But it's not her—it's Julio.

He stands by the security door in the balmy heat of the evening, Dodgers hat on, masks and nebulizer held in his hands like boxed breath.

He hands them to me, mouth curved into a half-moon smile. He comes inside, grass stains stretching across the knees of his jeans. When he slips past me, he squeezes my hand.

Without any hesitation, he crouches down and begins setting up the nebulizer. He shows my pa and me how to assemble it, and teaches us how to comfortably set the mask onto his face.

"If you adjust it here," he explains, pulling at the string around the plastic mouthpiece, "you can make it a little looser. You don't want it too loose, or the medicine will seep out into the air. And you don't want it too tight, or it'll press against your skin and leave an outline."

He positions the plastic over my pa's mouth, winding the bright blue strap around his head.

"That okay?" he asks my pa.

My pa gives him a thumbs-up, and we watch the vapor in the nebulizer begin, a thin veil of medicine frosting the mouthpiece white.

Julio waits around for the treatment to finish. When it sputters out the last of my pa's medicine, he kneels beside the machine to show us how to disassemble it, taking each piece to the kitchen sink to rinse them off before storing them away.

He hangs around afterward, watching a soccer tournament on TV with my pa the way he used to with his. He stands up when the game ends, reaching for a dart near the board, offering my pa a round.

My pa agrees, but when we see my ma's headlights curve in through the living room windows, he glances at me. "You know what? Why don't you two go out and do something? You don't need to supervise me. I'll be okay."

"But, Pa—" I start. Then I feel Julio's hand on my shoulder. He whisks me outside before I can continue. Both of us know my pa is just making an excuse—nobody knows what is going to happen when my ma comes inside, if she even comes inside at all.

Out in the driveway, I see her sitting in the darkness of her car, staring at the house, as if she's willing herself to enter.

Julio catches me looking. He arcs his fingers around my wrist, pulling me gently toward his truck. "Come on," he says. "Let them handle it."

The streetlights flicker on Alder. Their dim light suffuses in hazy yellow funnels against the sidewalks. I lean my head against the passenger-side window, the glass cool beneath my skin.

"You okay?" Julio asks.

"No." I blink. "My ma probably thought my pa was finally going to quit."

"Is he going to?"

"No," I repeat. "And she's probably going to be so angry that he's not." I pause. "I wish we knew about the stupid scholarship already."

"Have you told her about it yet?" he asks, turning left onto Sierra.

I shake my head. "We haven't won," I say. "We won't even know if we made it past the preliminaries until a few weeks from now."

Julio shrugs. "Your ma loves you—I think just hearing that you did all of this for her to consider staying would mean a lot to her. Potentially enough for her to reconsider moving."

"Julio, she won't even go into the house when she's parked outside of it. I don't think *maybe* winning a scholarship is going to matter to her," I say. "We *need* to win."

Julio is quiet the rest of the drive.

He pulls into the Ontario Mills parking lot. We used to come here together often, especially as kids. Despite it being an outlet mall, we could hardly afford much of anything. We'd window-shop and spend the loose change in our pockets on the claw machine near the entrance.

It was impossible to win, the joystick mainly for show. Despite any strategy, the claw moved at its own randomized and omnipotent pace, like the hand of God. We played for over a decade and only ever won twice.

When we enter, I routinely begin walking toward it, but Julio leads me in the opposite direction. He weaves around the few stray shoppers wandering the halls, passes the Rainforest Cafe, and guides me to the food court, where he buys me a soft pretzel right before the stand closes.

It's late in the evening, so the mall is nearly empty. We're the only people sitting in the food court, a large holiday wreath hung above us. Our faces are bulbous against the ornaments, closer together in the mirage of plastic.

I study my pretzel, its doughy limbs as tangled as I feel inside. Julio finishes his food then squeezes my hand, a look of concern on his face.

"Have you tried talking to Ale?" he asks.

"No," I say, "I don't want to."

"How come? She's your best friend, right?"

I turn the words over in my head: *best friend*. For my entire life, those were words that were reserved exclusively for Julio, until they were replaced by *boyfriend*.

But the thrum of loss, the pang of anger, makes me realize that's exactly what Ale had become to me. Only someone you loved could betray you that much.

"Yeah," I mumble, "I guess she was."

"Was?" He blinks. "Talk to her."

I shake my head.

"Paloma." He sighs. "You're being stubborn—and proud."

"I don't know," I respond, slumping forward. "Pride can save you sometimes."

"Save you from what?"

"Embarrassment, I guess. Like, what if she doesn't want to talk to *me*?"

"So, first, you won't tell your ma about the project because you're afraid of her rejection." He pauses. "Now, you don't want to talk to Ale because of the same thing?"

I don't answer him. I look away instead, staring at the window dressing in a sports shop. A pair of faceless mannequins are arranged in a sprinting position behind the glass. I can't tell if they are running toward something or away from something. I can't tell if it matters.

Julio sighs. "It doesn't have to be that way—what if you reach out to her and you two fix things? It worked with me and Yvette. You got me to really think and to talk to her. And things aren't perfect, but they're somewhere."

"She's your sister," I argue. "That's different."

"She's your *mom*," Julio retorts, "and she's your best friend. You won't know if you don't try."

"It wouldn't make a difference—Ale made her choice."

"Did she?" Julio asks, stealing a bite from my pretzel, his lips brushing close to my hand. "Or did her dad make a choice?" he continues.

"Same thing," I say. Julio chews, teetering his head from left to right. I'm not sure if he agrees with me—if he doesn't, he doesn't say so.

I sit up defensively. "I just don't get how she can be sitting in her new house with her dad while my dad was in the hospital and when your dad is—"

Julio stops chewing, blinks at me. I blush and take a bite of my pretzel, just to do something, but the dough suddenly feels dense in my mouth, like chewing cement. "Sorry," I say.

He swallows. "It's fine—I mean, it's not fine. But it's true."

"Thank you for dropping everything off," I tell him. "I'm sure it's not easy."

He inhales, his shoulders rising with his breath. "It isn't. I hadn't seen that machine in over a year. Kinda bittersweet that it found more use."

"Yeah," I agree. "If it's too much to be at my house with my dad and everything, I understand."

"It's hard, definitely." He pauses. "But I like spending time with you. Even if we're just doing this."

He gestures across the way, the mall empty except for a custodian wheeling a cleaning cart down the hallway.

After I finish eating, Julio and I do a lap around the mall. On the way out, he lingers in front of the last store before the exit. It's a Men's Wearhouse, and it's closed. But Julio stands there, looking at the mannequins as if they were a museum display.

"That's the suit I'm gonna wear," he says. He points to a navy ensemble with a pocket square and pearlescent buttons.

"The suit you're going to wear when what?"

"After we win the scholarship," he says. "I read online that winners get to do this huge press conference and have news segments and television interviews. I only own one suit, and I wore it to my pa's funeral. I know I have to wear that one when we present, but after we get that check, I'm buying that suit."

I blink at him. "How do you know we're going to win?"

"Because you're my partner," he says easily, with a knowing shrug.

Then he looks at me the way he had in the hallway a few weeks ago, and when he looked at me like that, it made me forget everything that happened today.

The memory only returns when he drops me off at home. We both stare at my ma's car, empty now, then at the front door. He walks me to the porch and embraces me tightly. His face curves against the slope of my neck, his voice muffled against my shoulder. "Everything's gonna be okay," he assures me, "and if it's not, just call me."

I breathe. His skin smells clean—like soil and sunset and summertime. It separates me from the reality of December around us, the air finally cold. It's enough to make hope spark within my body. There's something atmospheric about being around Julio, like I'm allowed to live levitating.

But something is always quick to ground me.

The summer Julio and I were dating, it was Julio's house. We'd spend a beautiful day together and open the door to see his pa, to be reminded that anything, especially life, could end at any time.

This time, it's my house that ropes me back into reality, that sobers the sunshine.

But it's bigger than my feet finding their footing back on the ground. It feels like the ground is cracking beneath the soles of my sneakers, rupturing wide to swallow me whole.

Because when I step into the living room, I see my pa is sitting in the love seat by the window, his face buried in his palms.

And I see my ma weaving from her bedroom to the living room, her makeup streaked onto her cheeks, her bags stacked by the door.

Twenty-Two

MY MA TRIES TO EXPLAIN WHAT'S HAPPENING.

"It's your pa," she says, wiping the wetness from her eyes. "I just can't wait around for him to know when to stop. I can't keep doing everything alone." She breathes. "I'm so sorry."

It's what she has been repeating the entire hour she's sat with me in the living room. That she'd be moving to Pasto Verde that night, that she loved me, that she was so sorry. That she'd live with my grandparents, that she missed them, that she was so sorry. That she loved my dad, that it was complicated, so complicated, that she was so sorry.

It was the focal point she always cycles back to.

She looks sad. Like she really doesn't want to be doing this. Like this is really her last resort. Like the weight of every word leaving her mouth is moving out into the air, boomeranging back against her body.

It's hard to listen to her. The more she talks, the less any of it makes sense. It's as though she is speaking in a different language—all of her words tangling together, simmering like static.

I look through the thresholds of the house. From the openings of the living room to the dining room, the dining room to the kitchen, the kitchen to the laundry room.

There, I can see my pa. He looks so tired. All he had been doing recently was negotiating—first at work, then at home. He begged my ma to stay, said he'd call out tomorrow, said he'd take a break from working completely. But my ma shook her head.

"It's too late," she said. "I need to go."

Now, he takes old Selva boxes and stacks them atop the washing machine for my ma to pack the rest of her things. The cardboard towers like it had at Ale's new house.

I can't bear to look.

Instead, I stare at the cabinets in the kitchen, at the horses carved into the wood. When I tilt my head just right, it looks like they are moving, too, galloping hooves heavy in my mind.

I know this would be the moment to take Julio's advice. To admit to her how hard I had been working on this project to prevent the warehouse construction, to help the community—but, more than anything, to keep her here.

But none of that feels like it matters anymore.

Because I just want her to stay—with or without a project—because she wants to be with me.

Which is why, when she says, "This has nothing to do with you," I stare at her, agape.

"What?" I spit.

"My choice to move. It has nothing to do with you," she repeats. "Your pa—"

"He's sick, Ma. And even though he's sick, he's working to help other people."

She steeples her hands. "Paloma, I *know* he's sick and I *know* he's helping people. But he is still making a choice—and it's a little selfish."

"*He*'s selfish?" I scoff.

Her lips flatten into a line. She rests her chin along her fingertips, rocking her hands slightly. "I know you and everyone else will see what he is doing as selfless. And some of it is. But I need *help*. Your pa isn't going to quit and I can't do everything around here anymore. *That's* what this is about. It doesn't mean I love you any less—it has *nothing* to do with you," she repeats.

"Ma, of course it has something to do with me," I say. "You're leaving me, too."

"Paloma, I am not leaving you. I am *moving*," she says. "And I think it would be a really good idea for you to come with me."

We're still for a moment.

As she awaits my response, I study her. She looks like she did after the swap meet, like she did before we toured the rental property—yearning, hopeful. Like I would really consider moving.

And for a moment, I do.

I fantasize what it would be like to have the certainty that she would be home when I returned from school, to spend time with her, to see her happy, not for a moment, but for a lifetime.

But then I look out the living room windows, where the winds gust, where the palm trees sway. The street vendor who sells flowers near the Memorial Park dugout is walking down the road, heading home. He walks against a rush of wind, as many people here do, pushing against the force of invisible obstacles and somehow always moving forward.

It embodies everything my pa taught me to love about living here: all of the resiliency amid the imperfections.

I look at my ma, wondering how she could be too shortsighted to find the beauty in this. Then I think of what Julio had said, standing amid the garbage in a place he would eventually find plants. Things grow when you let them.

I inhale, bracing myself to explain it all to her. It feels like those cabinet horses have invaded my body, like they are treading through my chest, stampeding within my heart.

But then, my ma continues.

"Paloma, I'm not forcing you to come with me. But I *do* think it would be really good for you. I was wrong to think this was a good place to raise a family."

And that's what makes me the saddest.

That she is committed to seeing this community as it is. Committed to seeing my pa, this family, as it is. As something stagnant, not capable of change, or hope, or betterment. She can't wait for the strike to be negotiated, for my pa to get better, for my project to be finished. She is giving up on everything—my city, my father, and me.

After a prolonged period of quiet, she urges me to say something.

But I don't say anything.

Not even goodbye.

I stand up to get the door, kicking the bags out of the entryway to clear my path.

When she reaches out to touch me, I pull away. I watch her slip through the door, a gust of wind slamming it shut behind her.

Twenty-Three

MY MA CALLS RIGHT AT SEVEN THIRTY.

It's our new routine since she moved two weeks ago: every night, she calls me. And every night, I don't answer.

I sit up in the love seat in the living room, my phone clutched in my hand. I look at her face, mockingly wide within the screen, and send the call to voicemail. She's left to speak only to herself, and I figure it's only right—it's exactly what she had left me with.

Since she moved, a persistent echo rang through the house.

Sometimes, when I thought about picking up one of her calls, I'd force myself to say something loudly, just to hear my own voice bounce back against me. To remind me that she was not there to answer, that her vacancy had left room for my voice to only respond to itself, like the unreciprocated call of a bird.

After a few minutes, I read the start of the poor voicemail transcription: *Paloma, please—*

And then I close it and open my email.

I refresh it to see if there's any updates from the Communities Care organization. Julio and I still haven't heard back about our preliminary proposal, and we were both worried—Julio especially.

Every other scholarship he had applied to had rejected him.

His optimism about winning, so strong a few weeks ago, was beginning to fade.

I'd gotten two scholarships earlier this week. They weren't a lot of money, a few thousand dollars, but combined they were enough to cover the first quarter of tuition.

But I didn't care about the money.

When the waves of anger settled after each one of my ma's calls, they were replaced with the magnitude of the sea: loss.

I missed her.

So many small moments had arisen through the last few weeks that made me wish she were here—getting the top of a zipper up, securing the clasp of a bracelet, untangling the chain of a necklace. Things my pa could do, and did, but that always felt better between her hands.

Now, instead of winning this project to keep her here, I wanted to win for her to return. If this project could work as a parallel—fix the community, fix the family—maybe she'd move back.

This one email held the future at its crux. For my ma to return home, and for Julio to afford school.

And still, it hadn't come.

I exhale and put my phone down, then sink in my seat. I turn to my pa. It's the Friday before winter break begins, and we usually celebrate the vacation by seeing his family. But tonight, he's playing a round of darts before leaving for his graveyard shift at his new job.

Right after my ma left, he was able to get a job loading shipment boxes at a tortilla factory on Slover. He'd called my ma as soon as he got the news, conciliatory hope ringing in his voice.

"It'll hold us over," he said eagerly, "until negotiations settle."

I thought of that word—*us*. I couldn't hear what my ma said, but by the way my pa hung his head after he hung up the phone, I figured she was no longer interested in it.

Despite all of the recent changes, my pa was still trying to keep some remnants of our life the same. He took the Christmas tree out of the storage shed in the backyard, pushed it into the corner of the living room. My elementary school ornament projects anchor against the branches, imprints of my hands dried against salt dough.

His last dart skims past it, arcing toward the floor. He sighs, picks it up, and grabs his work boots.

"How long is your shift?" I ask.

"Until four," my pa says, "and then negotiations begin at ten."

"Pa," I say, "when are you sleeping?"

"Between four and nine thirty," he says, forcing a smile.

He rises, kisses me on the forehead, and leaves for his shift.

I know he's working for the money, but I also think work helps him keep his mind off my ma. With both jobs, it's easier to hide his heartbreak—he's usually too busy to show it.

But after he's left, I can see it. The living room walls have become perforated from the tips of darts. Proof that he'd been there, proof that he'd taken a shot, proof that he'd missed.

I peer at them—pores so small, they could go unnoticed. But I saw them there, the mark of hurt, like even the wood had been wounded.

In the last two weeks, I slowly began to realize the other things my ma had done around the house that I hadn't noticed until she was no longer around to do them. Refilling soap dispensers and sweeping the crumbs from counters and, especially, going to the grocery store.

I'd stared at the heels of a bread loaf all week, wondering when my pa would think to do the shopping. Then I realized my pa never did the shopping—it was always my ma, always after work.

I'm in the rice aisle at Stater Bros., staring at the different bags and brands, overwhelmed by choice.

I never thought of my pa as lazy.

I still don't.

But standing here, I'm beginning to understand all the other small things that my ma had been balancing that he never had to, like picking a brand of rice.

Julio is behind me, absentmindedly leaning his body against the handles of a shopping cart, sending the basket forward.

We've been spending a lot of time together. Julio says it's good to keep me out of the house when my pa is at a graveyard shift, away from its emptiness.

But really, I know he also needs a distraction.

Julio is usually good about keeping calm, but when he's nervous, it consumes him. And since we still haven't gotten an email back, all he does is what I had been doing an hour ago—refreshing his inbox, waiting for any updates about our project.

I've been trying to keep cool around him, to be a voice of reason, even though I'm also panicking. I know I want my ma home—but this scholarship was the only way Julio was going to be able to get to school, and without an email, he's spiraling. Literally. He walks in circles in the grocery aisle, his phone close to his face.

I pluck it from his hand. He smiles at me, embarrassed, then looks up at the selection. He scans it briefly, then grabs a box of instant rice. He shakes it, the grains rattling within the cardboard, the sound like a rain stick.

"Instant?" I ask him.

"Grief meals," he explains. "You need something easy to prepare. It's all Yvette and I ate once the funeral food ran out."

I nod and toss it into the cart. No matter how different it was, Julio was the only person I knew who understood what life was like when you had to transition to only living with one parent.

We load the cart with Julio's other shelf-stable suggestions: canned tomato sauce, Knorr cubes, fideo.

At the checkout line, I arrange the groceries onto the conveyor belt. Julio continues checking his inbox.

"It's almost midnight," he notes, panic in his voice.

I look at him. "Okay?"

He drags his finger down the screen, refreshing. "So, it's almost the eighteenth of December. They said that people who advanced past the preliminary evaluations would get an email by mid-December. It's the seventeenth right now, and in a half hour it'll be the eighteenth."

"Julio, that still counts as mid."

He shakes his head. "No, the *fifteenth* is mid. The sixteenth is kind of mid, because December has thirty-one days. The seventeenth is past mid, but the eighteenth is *definitely* past mid." He inhales, presses the heels of his hands against his forehead, the bill of his hat rising gently. He turns around and begins pacing the narrow aisle between the register, darting back and forth between the racks of magazines and breath mints. "What if we didn't make it?"

"Julio." I set a hand on his shoulder. "They would send us an email with a rejection as well. And, even if we didn't make it, there are other scholarships you can still get."

Julio stops pacing and shrugs my hand from his shoulder. "That's easy for you to say. You got two." He snorts.

I blink at him. His tone is short, clipped—the only other time he's ever spoken to me this way was when he broke up with me and slammed a door in my face.

It's quiet for a moment; all we hear is the beeps of the clerk scanning the groceries. I wait for Julio to say something, but he doesn't—he turns away from me and bags the food quietly, his head hung low.

Out in the parking lot, we sit in his truck amid a bloated silence. I watch the coin-operated mechanical horse beside the entrance buck gently in the night winds. Then I look up at the Stater Bros. sign. I think of my ma.

In Pasto Verde, there are no Stater Bros.

There are a bunch of Vons or Ralphs or other grocery stores so foreign to me that I can't even name them—such a small but major mark of distance.

"I know this scholarship is make it or break it for you to go to Davis," I say, quietly. "But I'm still doing this to hopefully bring my ma back." I pause. "I know it's different, but it matters to me."

Julio nods, then clears his throat. "I'm sorry."

I sigh. "It's okay."

He shakes his head. "No, it isn't. You really, really deserved those scholarships. I'm just so nervous."

I look over at him. "But, Julio, I'm nervous, too. I miss my ma."

He squeezes my hand.

I look out the window, at the desolate parking lot, while he turns the ignition. "Have you answered her calls?"

I watch as he veers onto the road. "No. I don't even know what I'd say."

He nods. Since she moved, he doesn't push. He had tried his best to be preemptively conciliatory, but this was out of his realm. "I'm sorry. What're you gonna do for Christmas? You guys can always come to our house."

We usually spend Noche Buena with my ma's family. I enjoyed it—my pa and I always joined the assembly line to help make tamales for dinner. After we ate, the adults sat around playing lotería and dominoes, while my cousins and I played cards in the guest room. At eleven thirty, everyone gathered in the living room and waited for midnight to strike to open gifts.

Despite her moving, I knew it was something we'd have to continue.

"We're going to see my ma's family," I say. "It'll be awkward with the three of us, but better than nothing."

He nods.

Julio is hungry, so before we head home, we pull into the only drive-through that's open: Baker's. We inch toward the speaker box, where Julio orders fries and a shake.

"Why'd you get a *shake*?" I ask. "It's cold outside."

"You're gonna have some."

"I'll have, like, one sip."

"You'll drink half," he snorts, pulling forward to the window, paying for the order. "You always drink half of my drinks."

"That's not true, when—"

And then, our phones chime.

At exactly midnight, we both receive an email from the Communities Care organization.

Julio flings the shake into a cup holder and presses on the gas, lurching us to the end of the drive-through.

He blinks at his phone, open-mouthed. "Do we read it now?" he asks, his voice trembling.

"I don't know," I say. I can feel my heart kicking at the base of my throat. "Maybe we should wait until we're at my house."

"You're right," he agrees, pulling onto the street. "A private place to cry."

"Or celebrate," I counter.

Julio nods. But while he drives, I keep staring at my phone. It rests in a cup holder, my face mirrored against the dark screen. I'm tempted to reach for it, but I drum my fingers along my knees instead.

But at a stoplight, I can't take it.

"Maybe we should just read it now," I blurt. "Rip it off like a Band-Aid."

"Now?" Julio asks.

I nod.

He pulls over to the closest available place to park, an ancient semitruck distribution center that's been desolate for years. Kids come here sometimes to smoke and play chicken, jumping from the height of the towers of empty freight containers.

We pull in slowly, the driveway narrow and flanked by stacks of cargo. Julio parks between them. His headlights illuminate the freight in steady columns of light, revealing rust and graffiti. I can hardly understand any of it: *909 - NENE/ SPIT.* But it stands there like a cave painting, hieroglyphics from a time before us.

He pulls up his parking brake, then takes out his phone. He stares at the screen for a while, then swallows.

"On three," he says, voice still shaky.

I extend my hand over the center console, cupping it against his knee. He reaches for it, his skin already damp with sweat.

He counts us down, and I open the email, a congratulatory message against the screen.

Our research had made it past the preliminary evaluations and onto the final round. We were slated to present in April, with a handful of other applicants. We have about four months to prepare. In that time, we need to organize our research, write our final paper, and prepare a presentation.

I look over at Julio, waiting for him to look back at me, but his elbows are pressed against his thighs. He's released my hand, his face hidden behind the wall of his fingers.

He's crying.

Julio gets out of the truck, opens my door, and pulls me out. We hug there, between the rows and rows of freight behind us, everything in transit.

He wipes his face and looks toward the beds of cargo. "Let's find one so we can sit," he says.

I follow behind him, stray cats peeking from the back of abandoned 18-wheelers. Julio points to one. I turn to see its side—it's a Selva semi.

I had never liked anything Selva had done, not since Julio's pa died, or since my pa got sick, or since the strike began.

But my ma moving was the thing that fully broke me.

I couldn't stand to see anything related to them. I changed the channel when their ads came on, I drove down different streets to avoid their billboards, I couldn't even sit on one of their discarded trucks. Everything about them disgusted me.

I hated them for what they did to Julio's pa and family, and now, for what they had done to me and mine. I hated the mayor for allowing them to ravage a community. I hated anything involved with them.

So, as soon as I see that logo, I shake my head. "Let's find another."

Julio walks farther down, his sneakers crunching over the gravel. He looks at the next one, a nameless flatbed with shallow cargo atop it. He climbs the rickety ladder nailed to its backside, sets his food on the roof, then extends a hand to help me up.

Once we're both at the top, Julio climbs onto the cab, scooting down the windshield like it's a miniature slide. He helps me down, and we both sit along the pane, legs dangling over the front bumper, my shoelaces tangling into the headlights.

We split the shake between us, trying to savor the last night we have left before we have to get back to work on this project.

When we're finished, he moves the Baker's cup away, sliding to sit closer to me.

Every time he's close like this it feels like time has stretched in a different direction, moving faster when he's beside me, slowing when he's gone.

Julio holds my hand, and I feel an archer in my body, rhythmically snapping a bowstring in my chest.

We look up at the stars, persistent through the pollution of the day. This sky would probably be a pathetic sight to anyone else, but Julio and I bounce ideas back and forth, naming the shade of darkness—Raven, Rutile, Onyx, Ox.

Julio traces his finger down my hand, draws circles in the center of my palm. We lean back against the windshield, the glass cold behind us, and look up at the dark of the night above us, while everything between us slowly becomes brighter.

Twenty-Four

"PALOMA." MY PA SIGHS. "YOU CANNOT SPEND TONIGHT alone. It's Christmas Eve."

"Pa, I *can't* go there without you."

My pa looks up at me. He's sitting across from me in the living room, suiting up for his graveyard shift, pulling his socks high over his ankles. "Why not? I'm working. Your ma wants you to spend the holiday with her."

"Why not?" I echo. "Pa, we always go together."

He inhales. "Your ma thinks it's best that I stay behind."

I give him a look.

"*I* think it's best, too. We can't be around each other right now, and you both need some time to reconnect."

I shake my head. "Reconnect? She could have connected with me here—but she left."

He steps into his steel-toed boots. The soles thump against the ground, like a single, dull heartbeat. "She did not leave," he corrects me, tying his laces. "Parents who leave usually abandon their kids, don't want a relationship with them. She *moved*." He rubs a hand down his face. "I know you're angry, but she's your mother."

I look away from him.

I wish I could tell him that I was angry. But I wasn't—I was hurt. And exactly for the reason he'd just said: she *was* my mother, and I couldn't understand how, as my mother, she could just go.

Why couldn't the inverse be true: don't move away—she's your daughter?

The hurt was the main reason I didn't want to go for Noche Buena. Especially without my pa. Seeing her happy away from us, away from me, after all the struggle to keep her here, would be such a betrayal. But I don't admit this to him. Instead, I hold my anger tight to my body—an impenetrable shield that would never let the truth out.

"Why are you defending her?" I scoff. "She left you when you were sick."

My pa winces, like I've pressed on a bruise. He releases a long breath, finishes lacing his boots, and looks at me.

"It's not that simple," he says.

"Pa, call it whatever you want. At the end of the day, she's not here."

My pa shakes his head at me. "She's not here, you're right. But she's here in other ways. She calls you, she sends money—"

"But she's not *here*," I repeat, gesturing around the room.

My pa rises. "This is the best compromise we could come to. Noche Buena with her, Christmas Day with me."

I want to roll my eyes—he, who was still in the thick of negotiations because he refused to compromise on anything, suddenly was able to compromise with her. But I know better.

I sit up on the love seat instead, the posture of protest. "Pa—"

"Paloma," my pa says, his tone a warning. "Please."

He holds up a hand, pressing it against the atmosphere with finality. I shake my head, but know not to push it further. This new job left him with hardly any sleep, gave him bags beneath his eyes. I couldn't add any more stress to that than this conversation already had.

So, while my pa gets ready for work, I get ready to spend Noche Buena with my ma. I rake through my closet, trying to find something to wear. I land on a dress I'd gotten with Ale at the Goodwill beside the Stater Bros. sometime last year. I was hesitant to buy it, but Ale forced me to try it on.

"I like the seams on the chest," she said, pointing toward the neckline. "Makes you look like you have boobs."

I smacked my lips at her before looking in the mirror, turning side to side. She was right—it did look good. Ale usually had a way of seeing things before I did.

The memory of her makes me hesitate to wear it, but I pull it on anyway. I smooth the hem over my thighs and pull on a pair of tights, but find a run near the base of my shin. I sit on the edge of my bed, wondering what to do. It was another one of those small moments where I needed my ma, and she wasn't here.

In the past, I'd usually call out to her to steal a pair from her. She always had an extra, even when I figured she wouldn't. She was always prepared, easily able to produce anything, as if from hammerspace—elastics, bobby pins, pantyhose.

I force myself into her old bedroom in search of a pair. My pa has left for work, so it's just the door separating me from their space.

When I step inside, I hold my breath and close my eyes, like I'm jumping into the deep end of a pool.

After I open my eyes, I see most of it is the same. Sheer pink curtains along the window. A wooden crucifix above the light switch. The half-wooden wainscoting on the walls.

The smell is what's different.

The shag of the carpet used to be scented with the whisper of her perfume, as if it had been applied in a rush. Now, it smells stale. Like a house before it's lived in, or after it's been left.

I turn to the black chest of drawers to the right of the room. The bottom set are my pa's. They're tightly packed, edges spilling out with old T-shirts and sweatpants. He hasn't moved them to the top portion, my ma's section, yet. I open those drawers, and they lie sacredly empty, as if he's still waiting for her to return.

I don't see anything and nearly give up, opening the top drawer only for good measure. I figure it will also be empty until I pull out the full length of the wood. A cardboard container of pantyhose, just my color, slides out toward the handle.

It rebounds against my force, then lands smack in the center, staring up at me like she left them for me, like she knew I'd need them.

My palms are slippery with lard, so slick I can almost see my reflection against them. To sidestep the discomfort after I arrived at Noche Buena, my ma's family immediately gave me something to do. They thrusted me into the tamale assembly line in the kitchen, where I stepped into my annual job of spackling masa onto corn husks.

I'm usually good at it.

In previous years, I pretended the dough was a mound of clay, smoothing and sculpting it until it lay flat enough for my pa to scoop on the filling. But this year, my abuela peers over my shoulder, clucking her tongue disapprovingly.

"Paloma," she scolds, "todo malhecho."

All of my tamales are wrong—too thick in some places, too thin in others. I can't focus.

I keep staring at my ma's hands, thinking about the book she used to read to me during the Noche Buenas of my childhood, *Too Many Tamales*. There, a girl tries on her mother's wedding ring while they prepare the tamales for Christmas dinner, loses it amid the dough, and searches for it by gorging herself with tamales.

Here, there is nothing for my ma to lose.

Her wedding ring is not on her finger.

I study the bareness of her hands every time she pulls the husks from my palms, gently correcting my work by spreading the masa with restaurant expertise.

Her hands look unrecognizable to me. I keep telling myself that maybe the ring is in her pocket or her bedroom for safekeeping, but the pervasive image of her at the Gold Rush stand, asking Kim to polish it before taking it to the pawnshop on the corner of Arrow and Sierra, deducing, bartering, what its history was worth, spins through my mind.

I wish I hadn't come.

All I am doing is comparing this home to my own. Here, there is no echo. The space is filled with people talking and laughing and shouting, my ma among them.

My ma notices my silence and tries to loop me into the conversation, but I have nothing to say. Her happiness feels worse than betrayal—it feels like the knife itself.

After the tamales are set to steam, the adults pool into the living room and spread out against the sectional couch. I stand near the hallway, ready to go to the guest room with my cousins. But they sit down with everyone else. I look at the guest room door at the end of the hall, where we normally spend the evening. It's closed.

My ma had moved in there.

My cousins give me sympathetic smiles, and I stand there, embarrassed and grateful to have a reason to leave when my ma ushers me inside to show me around.

I expect the room to look sterile, like it often did when she stayed with her parents—bound to the limits of luggage for her temporary stay. Instead, it looks lived in—more lived in than the room she shared with my pa.

The artifacts of her old life are here, rehoused. A bullet of lipstick on her vanity. A jewelry dish on the dresser. My senior portrait on her nightstand.

The longer I look, the more I panic.

Julio and I had spent the first week of winter break relentlessly working on this project. I'd been writing draft after draft of our paper, perfecting it in hopes of publication. If a national news report had led my pa to a negotiations table, I wondered what it could do for all of us, especially me and my ma.

But standing here, I begin to fear that it won't be enough to bring her home—if it ever was.

I turn back to my ma, who pulls something from beneath her bed. She rises, holding a large rubber square against her chest.

"What is that?" I ask. It's the first direct thing I've said to her all evening.

"An inflatable mattress," she explains, unfolding it in her wingspan. "I'll sleep on it, and you can take my bed." She spreads it along the floor, then attaches it to a pump plugged into the wall.

I blink at her. "But I'm not staying," I say. "I'm just here for dinner."

"I thought you could spend the night," she suggests, turning toward her drawers, where she pulls out an extra set of sheets.

"I didn't pack any clothes," I reply.

"You can use mine."

It was strange.

After I'd found the tights back home, I stared at them for several minutes, feeling a gnawing guilt for every one of her calls I'd ignored. But now, she was offering me her wardrobe and, suddenly, all of my anger had returned.

I had tried so hard to get her to fit in my life, and she didn't want that. Now, she somehow wanted me to fit into hers.

"Ma," I say, slowly. "I'm not staying here."

"Paloma." She sighs. "We haven't really seen each other since I moved."

"And whose fault is that?" I scoff.

"I've called you every day," she shoots back. "How do you think it makes me feel when you don't pick up the phone?"

"You wouldn't need to call if you hadn't left," I say. "How do you think it makes me feel that you're gone?"

We're silent.

All I can hear is the inflatable mattress's compressor whirring.

I look at it—the rubber rises and stretches taut against its seams. It mirrors the feeling that is beginning to swell through my body, an overwhelming sensation that warns I might burst.

She looks at me. “I'm not gone. I'm just *here*. I still want to spend time with you.” She pauses. “Please just stay. Maybe tomorrow we can get up early and you can see more of the town. I think you'll like it if you give it a shot—”

“Are you being serious?” I ask. “That's all I wanted *you* to do. You want to spend time with *me*?” I point a finger between us. “Ma, I wanted to spend time with *you*. I tried to do the things we used to do together with you and you hated it.”

“Paloma, I'm sorry. But I *had* to leave that place,” she says, her tone urgent. “I don't expect you to understand my decision—”

“You're right. I don't understand. I would never do what you did, it's so *selfish*,” I spit.

I try to walk toward the door, but the bed is a border between us, ballooning with every passing second. I almost trip over it as I try to yank at the doorknob, but my ma stops me before I can leave.

“What did you want me to do? I *tried*. I tried my best to be happy there, but I couldn't be. It was so hard to leave because you're there, but I had to.” She pauses again, looking up at the ceiling. The fan twirls above us, cyclically slicing the air. “I don't expect you to understand that,” she continues, looking back at me. Her eyes are so wet they've become mirrors. I can see myself reflected against them, against her. “But don't you at least understand that I love you?” she croaks.

Tears begin to fall. She adjusts the neckline of her sweater, pulling the collar up to wipe her face. She looks embarrassed. "And I love your pa, too. I know you both love it there, and I know you're old enough now that you can make your own choices. Including choosing to stay there. But tonight, I would like you to at least be here with me."

She blinks at me, her face inflated with hope.

I wish I could. I imagine us, briefly, relishing in the traditions of years past, even without my pa. Maybe forming new ones. And then, I feel that shield of anger return, that same eye-for-an-eye desire I felt every time I ignored her calls.

"Well, I wanted you to stay at home," I say. "I guess we're both not getting what we want."

I pull the door open, the wedge of wood pushing into the mattress. My ma's shoulders, risen to her ears in nervousness, fall. I slam the door, a gust of wind wafting out, the entire room deflating behind me.

Twenty-Five

I DRIVE IN CIRCLES.

My original plan to spend the rest of the evening at Tom's had been ruined. I'd gone there with the hopes of forgetting the fight with my ma. But even when I pulled into the drive-through, the whir of the air mattress pump persisted in my head, whispering against the folds of my memory.

I rolled my window down, ready to order, until I saw a piece of paper taped over the speaker. A note written in faded blue marker, crumpled from being wind-whipped: CLOSED. HAPPY HOLIDAYS!

I leaned forward, my chest pressing against the horn, and listened to its blare echo through the vacant parking lot.

Now, I loop around town, feeling humiliated that I am looking for someplace, any place, that's open to avoid going home. But everywhere is just as empty as home would be.

I finally feel some hope when I see cars in the Ontario Mills parking lot. I pull in, thinking the mall might be open, but it isn't.

Instead, the parking lot is crowded with people attending a Selva toy drive.

To the left, families form serpentine lines around rows of metal containers full of donated toys. To the right, a Selva ice rink spreads over the parking lot.

This is the largest community event they've coordinated yet, bigger than Thanksgiving. The timing was convenient—since the *LA Times* article, they were reaching for anything to mend their perception in the public's eye. Judging by the smiles of the families skating around the rink, it seems to be working.

The whirring in my mind continues.

No matter how much I try to quiet it, it grows louder and louder.

Then I look up and see new air compressors wedged between the limbs of palm trees. They wheeze out masses of fake snow that rains above the rink—polymer and plastic falling through the atmosphere.

It sprinkles over the families who glide over the ice in slow circles. I blink at them, all bound together—a unity that has become a memory for me and my family.

I sit there, my fists wrapping tightly around my steering wheel. I'm afraid to release my grip because I know what will happen the moment I allow myself to. And as hard as I try to hold it in, they still come.

Tears stream down my cheeks.

I wipe my face and pull out of the parking lot. I drive south on the 10, trying to get Selva out of my brain. But they're everywhere. Their warehouses beside every exit, their trucks beside me on the highway, their advertisements like visual pollution against the sky.

I feel like there is nothing left in the city that is not smeared with their fingerprints—not my community, not my friendships, not my family.

I look out at the mazes of distribution centers and, for the first time, I feel like maybe my ma was right to leave.

Because maybe this is it.

This is the reality I just had to accept—that company had ruined Julio's family, my pa's health, my parents' marriage. My ma would never come home. Why would she want to? This is really what it is becoming, no matter what I tried.

I slump against the steering wheel, mirroring the posture my pa had when he argued with my ma before he conceded, before he gave up.

And then Julio calls me.

"Hey," he says, "are you home yet?"

I wipe my nose and clear my throat, trying my best to sound casual. "Um." I sniff. "I will be in, like, two minutes."

"Oh. Okay." I can hear the imitation in his voice, the same attempt to keep cool.

"Where are you?" I ask.

"I'm already here, at your house." He breathes, laughing nervously. "I came to drop off your gift."

When I pull in, I see him sitting along the porch steps. Despite being dressed up from his Christmas Eve dinner, he still wears his hat. He adjusts it, smooths the creases in his slacks, and wipes dirt off his dress shoes. There's a large box in his hands. He moves to offer it to me until he sees my face.

"Are you okay?" he asks, setting the box back into the truck bed.

"Yeah," I reply, as if saying it would somehow make it true.

But I know he can see the way the evening has clung relentlessly to me—my eyes swollen, my cheeks red.

Julio offers me his hand. "Let's go on a walk."

"So, what's the point?" I ask.

We had been walking for nearly five minutes, and the tears had stopped for a bit. But now they start again, salty rivers running down my cheeks. "I decided to do this stupid project hoping my ma would come home, but it seems like that's not going to happen. And even if she *did*, it will never be the same."

"It won't be the same, you're right," Julio agrees, nodding softly. "Even if she does return, it'll take some time to adjust. But it will get easier. You just have to give it time."

"How much time?" I ask. We approach the end of my block and turn right, onto Locust.

A gust of wind blows, my skin prickling beneath my sweater. This is the most surprising thing about being near the desert—the wave of heat through a winter day, and then the dramatic decline into the evening. It's so cold that my teeth begin to chatter. Julio peels off his suit jacket.

"It's different for every situation," he says, carefully cloaking it over my shoulders. "But it *will* get easier."

"I don't think so," I say.

"Things in my family weren't great after my pa died," he begins. "This holiday wasn't like when my pa was alive. But it also wasn't like last year, where my ma cried all night. This year, she ate." He pauses. "And that's worth celebrating."

I'm quiet, unsure of what to say. I look down, the sidewalk shadowed with our silhouettes.

"I'm sorry. How was your dinner?" I ask.

"Not great, but it was better. Things are getting easier with my ma. She might be ready to get back to working soon," he says. "They'll get easier with yours, too. You just have to give it time," he repeats.

I look ahead, the palm trees rustling above us. "Sometimes it just feels hopeless."

"Stuff with your ma?"

I shake my head. "No, stuff here," I admit, gesturing to the street around us. "Did you see that Selva had a toy drive at the mall? The parking lot was *full*. What is the point of doing anything we're doing with this project? There's a *strike* happening and people are still at their events. They do whatever they want because the mayor lets them, and they just plan some events to distract people, and it always works."

"Some people *have* to go to those events—they can't afford toys for their kids," Julio counters. "But that doesn't mean they support what they're doing."

I think about Ale, about that stupid backpack. Her family went to donation drives often—usually at their church for gifts for the triplets. I wonder if they were at the Selva drive tonight, or if her pa was finally making enough money working for them that they could avoid it.

"But it doesn't even *matter* if they agree. That's all this place is becoming," I push.

Julio stops walking. He looks across the street, at the house on Locust that does an elaborate Christmas display every season.

Inflatable figures towering into the sky, a train looping around the grass, a Ferris wheel cycling beside the driveway.

My parents and I used to come at the start of every December to gather with people in the neighborhood.

The crowd around it is the biggest I've ever seen, so massive that people puddle into the length of the street, children drawing hopscotch tiles along the traffic lines.

He tucks his hands into the pockets of his jeans, rocks once on his heels. "When my pa first got sick, I asked him why we didn't just move a long time ago. He said there are places where things grow and places where you grow things. And he liked to grow things, and the challenge of growing them here."

He clears his throat gently. "After he died, I realized that there are also places where things die and places where things are killed." He pauses. "Selva has killed so many things here—my pa, the environment, the land. But it hasn't killed all of the community," he says, gesturing to the crowd. "And you cannot let them kill your hope."

I look at the crowd—some people are still suited up for work, like they had been at the city council meeting. Back when they were forced to disperse amid a thick defeatedness, like watching a team lose at a home game.

But tonight, there is no defeat. There is joy: everyone marveling at something the community had created, gathered around the only house haloed in light in the dimly lit portion of town.

Julio smiles at me, squeezes my hand, and pulls me through the crowd, toward the display.

We stand beneath the palm trees. Lights are strung around their trunks, braided between branches. They flicker and fade against the fronds.

The winds are persistent, and my hair flies across my face. It layers over my eyes, striping my vision. And even in the obscurity, even beneath the shade of the bill of his hat, I can see how soft Julio's eyes get when he looks at me.

He leans forward, pulling the hair from my eyes. He's so close that I can feel his breath along my skin, the only warmth in this atmosphere tonight, and it still makes me shiver.

It feels hard to breathe the entire time we're there, the entire walk back to my house, as if the air is thick with something other than our clouded breath.

And it's harder to breathe when Julio approaches his truck, pulling a large box wrapped in butcher paper from the bed.

"This is for you," he says.

I take it from him. It's so heavy that he has to help me set it onto the roof of my car. "I'm sorry," I say, embarrassed. "I didn't buy you anything."

"That's okay." He shrugs. "I didn't spend any money."

I carefully unpeel the wrapping paper and pull back the cardboard flaps. My hand roots inside until my fingers touch something wet. I peer into the box, where I see a potted plant.

Julio helps me lift it up and out of the box, the terracotta planter rough against my skin. We set it on the hood of the car, where some of the soil spills onto the side.

I stare at it.

I tilt my head, trying to recognize where it had been in his pa's garden—whether it was on the risers or on the ground. But I can't remember, because this one looks different. Those plants had leaves that were long and green, these petals are soft and white. I lean to touch one, as silky as powder.

"Was this one on the risers?" I ask.

Julio tilts his head now. "What risers?"

"The ones in your dad's garden."

He shakes his head. "This isn't from my dad's garden. It's from a few years ago."

"A few years ago?"

"From our project in science class sophomore year," he clarifies. "The one we watered that summer." I can hear his tongue soften when he says that season. Like he, too, knows the weight of it.

I think of that time, when he taught me how to propagate plant trimmings. I look at it now; the roots have blossomed into full leaves. They spread wide, like wings against the atmosphere.

"You kept it?" I ask Julio.

Julio nods, walking around the car. He sweeps the soil that's spilled from the hood into his palm, shakes it into the planter, and gently presses it back into the pot. "I know we didn't talk for a while, but I watered it for you the whole time. It really grew."

I can picture it. Him taking the spout of a watering can to the pot, observing the growth along the sill. I imagine him, even in the thick of grief and silence, wading in patience, watering something for me, watching it grow when I thought everything else had been stunted.

I look at the stems and think of everything that had

bloomed—even in the time of our separation—and think of what can bloom today. It would be January soon, but it felt like June.

The seasons begin to blend, muddling into each other. So when I reach up and kiss him, I know we are here, in the stillness of winter, but have held each other through our summer, through the distance of spring and the shedding of autumn, somehow blooming through it all.

Spring Semester

Twenty-Six

I'VE NEVER BEEN IN LOVE BEFORE.

I had no idea it would be like this.

That it would pull the past into the present and amplify it. In the last four months, Julio and I did all the things we used to do together: going to Baker's and walking around the mall and, what we were doing tonight, which was working on our project. But now, everything feels saturated, vivid.

Julio and I are in his living room, Yvette on the couch across from us, practicing our presentation.

"The findings from our oximeter study show a discrepancy in the health of residents on the south side compared to those on the north side," Julio says, reading from his index cards.

I'm trying to focus, but I keep staring at him—at the peaks of his shoulder blades, at the slope of his mouth, at the length of his hands.

Yvette clears her throat. "Paloma?"

I jolt up, glimpse at my notes. I clear my throat and point to our trifold set on the coffee table. "In conclusion, our results show that warehouses are disproportionately placed in areas with higher concentrations of Black and Latino residents. These community members generally displayed significantly higher rates of respiratory illness."

Yvette nods, claps. She's our only mock audience member tonight, and our most consistent participant. Sometimes it's her, sometimes it's her and my pa, and sometimes it's even her and Julio's ma. But tonight, she's at work.

Over the last few months, Señora Ramos has slowly returned to herself. It began with small things at first, like making a pot of coffee. Some bigger ones, like going to church. Then the largest—she returned to work at the Stater Bros. deli department a few weeks ago.

Yvette beams at us. "That was great. The best one you've done so far."

"Better than yesterday?" Julio coaxes.

She nods. "Yes. Better than yesterday."

"You're not just saying that?" Julio asks, pacing against the carpet. "It has to be perfect."

She rises and adjusts her scrubs. "No, I'm not just saying that," she says. "It's very detailed and very researched and very, very rehearsed."

Julio gives her a look.

She squeezes his shoulders. "It's a great project—it's taught me a lot," she says, gesturing to our materials strewn around the living room. "People are going to learn so much when it's published."

I brighten a bit when she says that. After months of working on it, our research paper had become the best thing I'd ever written. It was objective enough to be expository, and personal enough to have some narrative.

But we'd regurgitated it so often during these rehearsals that I was growing numb to it. Part of me was beginning to wonder if it was good enough.

"Thank you," I say.

She picks up her lunch box and thermos from the floor. Her night shift at urgent care starts in fifteen minutes. "You still want me to watch it again tomorrow?" she asks.

"I want you to watch every day until we present," Julio says. "Next Friday. So, seven more rehearsals."

"You got it."

After Yvette is gone, Julio and I are left home alone. We do our post-rehearsal routine in the garden. Julio tries to till the soil, I try to water the plants, but we end up with our lips pressed, our tongues tangled. We sit on the grass, kissing against the sunset.

With us pinned against the earth this way, it feels like something other than gravity is holding us in place.

Julio nestles against my side. We look up at the sky—the clouds skip over the blue expanse unevenly, like cold butter on toast. We lie here the way we'd lain that day in the summer, when he almost told me he loved me.

That feels like a bookmarked moment, three dog-eared words—*I love you.*

I turn toward him, touch his lips with the tip of my fingernail, gently tugging at the fullness of the flesh. I want to tell him—that I love him.

Because I do.

But I don't want to be the one to say it first, there's still so much to figure out.

Earlier this week, I had gotten into Riverside and Julio had gotten into Davis. We hardly celebrated—we were too busy mourning. The bubble we'd lived in these last few months had burst and the question we had spent years dodging had finally arisen: What was going to happen to our relationship when he moved away?

Every time I asked Julio, he'd remind me that he couldn't go to Davis if he didn't win this scholarship. It was enough to appease things for a while—but fear was buoyant. Always swimming to the surface, no matter how many times I thought it had sunk. Because, even now, when Julio is right next to me, all I can do is worry about him disappearing.

I never knew that about love—that it could simultaneously fill me with so much desire and so much fear.

But then Julio looks at me and his pupils dilate. He's so close to me that I feel his lashes grazing against my cheeks when he blinks. He traces the crest of my cheekbone, the edge of my jawline, and I can sense it. Something simmering in his throat. The words that would cement our relationship as something bulletproof, as something permanent.

His eyes are full, ripe as a moon in the height of the dark.

I swallow, preparing myself.

And then he turns away, distracted by a bird fluttering into the garden. It perches on a bough of the orange tree above us. Julio pauses, blinks at it.

"That's a desert dove," he notes.

I look up, watching its red talons grip against the branch.

"Do you remember?" Julio asks. "In fourth grade, when Ms. Turner made us do a presentation on what our names meant?"

I squint a little. "Yours means, like, youth?"

He nods, his hat pushing against the grass. "Something like that. But I liked yours. I see these desert doves all the time and think of you. It's, like, perfect. That's how it feels to be with you," he says, pointing to the bird's wingspan as it soars into the sky. "Like I'm flying."

Maybe we wouldn't say it today—maybe we would say it that way, in other words. I lean against his chest, the trill of his heartbeat muffled beneath his skin, and point to parts of the garden. We name its colors, note its growth from when I first helped him transfer the plants a few months ago. Proof that things, even us, still need time to grow.

Twenty-Seven

THE STRIKE ENDS ON A MONDAY.

After over four months of negotiating, my pa and his union are able to ratify a new agreement. He sends me a photo of him signing his contract—a pen in one hand, a picture of Julio's pa in the other. He has his first Selva work shift in months, and asks me how we should celebrate.

I almost want to wait until after Julio and I present. It's only a handful of days away, and if we win, it could harmonize with this moment: all of my work and my pa's work finally coming to fruition.

But I stop at Nicho's anyway. I buy a pint of bubble gum ice cream and a bag of oranges from the street vendor at Memorial Park, for sentimentality's sake.

But when I get home, I don't think we'll need them.

Inside, my pa is watching the evening news. He's spread against his recliner, a dull, aimless look in his eyes and his nebulizer mask cupped over his mouth.

Cristina Fajardo is on the TV screen, the caption beneath her reading: *The End of the Six-Month Saga of Selva Strikers.* She stands by the gate of my pa's warehouse, interviewing some of the participants I recognize from union meetings.

I linger next to my pa, waiting for him to appear beside them.

"Did they interview you, too?" I ask.

He shakes his head.

"Why not?" I tilt my head. "You led the whole thing."

He pauses for a long while. The nebulizer beeps, finishing his treatment. He reaches over to disassemble it, his eyes on the floor.

"I got fired."

There's a pause. I take a breath, the air around us suddenly stale.

I blink at him slowly, wondering if I've heard him correctly. But judging by the way he won't look at me, I know I have. He stares at the TV, the news segment ending, replaced by a rerun of yesterday's Mayor Monday segment. I reach for the remote and turn it off, blanketing us in silence.

"Why?" I finally ask.

"They said I took too many bathroom breaks today," he explains. "It's retaliatory. A few of the other lead organizers got fired, too."

I sit on the edge of a recliner, setting the ice cream and oranges on a TV tray. My pa doesn't touch them. He goes to the kitchen and rinses off the nebulizer, then returns to open the shutters of the dartboard.

I watch him wink and aim, thinking of all those times I saw him play a round with Ale's pa. I wince. The memory of Ale is like the memory of my ma—floating amid a purgatory that wavered between anger and loss.

For the last few weeks, it had been loss.

My lunch periods were now the opposite of what they were the year before—instead of sitting beside Ale and looking for Julio, I was sitting beside Julio and looking for Ale.

He and I would sit in the journalism room, working on our project after we finished eating. When the bell rang, I couldn't help but look out the window to see if she was sitting in the shadow of the school marquee. It was a magnetic pull toward pain, the desire to pick a wound before it's scabbed.

Julio kept encouraging me to talk to her, but I felt like I couldn't. I just looked out the window, somehow satisfied and disappointed every time she wasn't there.

But today, she sat on the grass alone, looking around for me with some discouragement, as if I'd stood her up.

Seeing her there, I felt the same twinge of guilt I had when I ignored all of my ma's calls. I almost ran down to talk to her.

But now, looking at my pa in front of me, I'm glad I didn't go. All of that longing is replaced by anger. Especially when I see the outline of the nebulizer mask pressed around my pa's mouth, his hands calloused from work, his spirit broken from sacrifice.

"Who fired you?" I ask.

He throws a dart toward the board, but misses. "One of the managers."

"Which one?"

"Doesn't matter," he says, squinting his eyes to aim another fletch at the board, his elbow parallel to the floor. It lands against the outer rings, a short *thunk* of the dart piercing into the cork.

"Was it Alejandra's dad?"

My pa sighs, but doesn't respond. His silence is enough of an answer for me.

"How could she do that?" I ask, sitting up in the recliner.

"*She?*" he asks, turning around to face me. "It's not her fault, Paloma. That's why I didn't even want to tell you he wasn't on strike. Your friendship shouldn't be compromised because of this."

"Pa, it already has been," I admit.

"Since when?"

"Since, like, Thanksgiving."

"You haven't spoken to her since Thanksgiving?" he asks, incredulous. "Why?"

"Because she told me her pa took this deal to be a manager so he wouldn't have to strike," I explain. "I can't be friends with her—she's his daughter."

"Paloma, you *can* be friends with her. She has nothing to do with this." He throws his last dart. This one lands, a perfect bull's-eye.

"But her pa does," I argue. "And he fired you."

"It doesn't matter. I didn't do this strike to keep my job. I did it so the people who needed it, like Ernesto needed it, could work in better conditions." He pauses. "And, honestly, it's not even her pa's fault. He has to respond to people above him. It's complicated," he says.

I sigh, feeling the impasse build between us. "So, what are we going to do?"

My pa pretends not to be worried. He walks toward the board, plucks the darts from the cork, and cups them into his hand. "I have my night job," he says. "I'll go back to painting in between."

But I don't buy that, and neither does my ma.

He calls her later that night. I overhear their conversation when I lie in bed, my legs tangled in the sheets I'd kicked off in the nighttime heat wave.

I haven't spoken to her since Christmas, despite her attempts.

She still calls every evening at seven thirty, like clockwork, and always leaves a voicemail that remains unlistened.

I wondered if, after these few months, she remembered my face. Or if it had become a memory mottled by time, the way hers was when I closed my eyes and tried to remember the slope of her smile. As hard as I tried, I couldn't even imagine that anymore.

I couldn't imagine her at all.

But her voice, thick through the receiver, creates the angles of her face from the abstraction of my memory.

I expect her tone to be smug, an I-told-you-so gloat that was used in every argument. But it doesn't sound like that at all. Instead, she sounds concerned.

And that, somehow, makes me feel terrible.

After she asks if my pa is okay, her next question is, "What are we going to do about Paloma?"

I'm surprised to hear her say that word—*we*.

I don't listen to his answer. I get up and walk to the kitchen to get some water.

I gulp down the glass, staring at the refrigerator doors. They had remained the same, even after my ma had gone. Those same pictures of houses beside the last grocery list she had written, months old, pinned beside it.

I miss her.

I stand there, eyes closed, trying to will the feeling to turn into anger, like it had with Ale. But tonight, I can't shake it. I open my eyes and study her handwriting in the dim refrigerator light, the loose wane of her cursive like the undulating mountainsides behind us.

I lean back against the kitchen counter, thinking of my project with Julio. If we could win, she could still return home, and all of this could be fixed.

I wonder what that celebration would look like if we got to have it—or if it would turn into consolation, like the end of this strike had been.

I glimpse at the living room, where I realize my pa and I had forgotten the ice cream out on the TV tray. It's been defeated by the thickness of the heat wave, a pool of melted fluorescent blue dripping onto the carpet like a puddle of tears.

Twenty-Eight

THIS IS MY FIRST WORK SHIFT WITH ALE IN MONTHS.

Since our fight, I had worked most afternoons at Nicho's by myself. It was lonely—there was no one to mop the floor with, no one to take out the trash with, no one to make the extra tips that I couldn't.

But after my pa was fired yesterday, I was okay with working by myself. It was better than seeing Ale.

I'm standing by the entrance, taping promotional flyers onto the wall, when she barges through the doors.

I double-take at her. "What are you doing here?" I ask. "You're not on the schedule."

"I had a last-minute change," she explains, pulling the length of her hair into a high ponytail, then threading it through her uniform visor. "I asked Maira if I could come in today, and she said it was fine."

I look at her, shake my head, and begin unpinning my name tag.

"What are you doing?" she asks.

"I'm leaving," I say.

"Paloma," she whines, "don't do that—it's your only shift this week."

I unknot my apron, ignoring her.

She sighs. "I'm sorry," she says, "about your pa's job."

I look at her.

"It was unfair, but my pa had nothing to do with it," she says, smoothing her hands over her thighs, her hot-pink press-ons bright against her jeans. "I was looking for you to talk to you about it. But I couldn't find you at lunch."

"I didn't want to talk to you," I lie.

She looks at me for a long while, her strip lashes drooping with disappointment. I know she doesn't believe me—I don't even believe me.

I stand there in our silence, remembering what my pa had said yesterday. I know, somewhere in my gut, that he's right. Her pa was just doing his job. I didn't choose to work this shift with Ale, someone else had made that choice for me.

But I can't tell her the truth: that I had missed her, that I do miss her, that I'm trying to cling to my anger to stop missing her.

"Fine," she finally says, palms up in surrender. "I just wanted to tell you that I'm sorry. Your pa worked really hard on the strike for a long time, and he didn't deserve that." She pauses, presses her lips into a flat line. "I'm only here for a few hours. Do you think we can do this together?"

I sigh, releasing my grip on my apron. If I hadn't promised Maira I'd close today, I really would leave. I tell Ale this as I walk to the opposite end of the dipping cabinets. She nods gently, standing behind the register.

Our shift moves from personal to professional, dancing around each other in complete silence, even when a few customers enter. It's almost like it had been when I first began working here, like we didn't know one another at all.

After almost an hour of silence, Ale attempts to make conversation.

"So, you and Julio are finally together, right?" she asks, refilling the napkin dispenser on the counter. "I see you guys holding hands in the hallway."

I stand there for a moment, relieved she had been looking for me at school the way I had been looking for her. Then I nod.

She smiles. "How's it going?"

"Good."

She tilts her head. "Just good?"

She looks at me expectantly.

I know she can tell that I want to talk to her.

And it would be the greatest relief to let it out—to tell her that I was in love with him but too afraid to tell him first, and that I didn't know what would happen to our relationship if he moved to Davis.

I swallow the words creeping up my throat. "Yes," I say.

"Well, I'm happy for you. You two were really meant to be." She pushes the last of the napkins in, then leans against the counter. "How is the scholarship going?"

"Fine."

"Are you ready to present?"

I inhale. Then I lie again. "Yup."

Our presentation was this weekend, and though I thought we were ready, Julio didn't. I thought the more we practiced, the more we'd be prepared. But it was working in an inverse: the more we practiced, the more Julio panicked.

After every one of our rehearsals, Julio spent hours looking up any additional information about the Communities Care organization—its presentation rubric, the juror panel, the previous winners. But because it was new, there was nothing. Everything about it, apart from our presentation date and the winner's prize, was vague.

Last night when he drove me home, he took the long route that passed by Save-a-Minit, checking if the lot for his garden was still open.

I squeezed his shoulder. "Hey," I said. "If you can't build it here, you can build it somewhere else."

He turned toward me, worry welling in his eyes. "But what if there's nowhere left?"

I gave him a sorry smile. Mayor Warner had approved six more warehouses at the last city council meeting. Construction began quickly, walls rising overnight, a strip of gray lining the mountainsides by the regional park.

And, despite their approval, Mayor Warner still hadn't said anything about the lot beside our school. She never brought it up at press conferences or during her Mayor Monday segment. It sat there, wide and vacant, indefinitely pending.

"Maybe that'll change," I said to Julio, "after we present."

I look at Ale now. The presentation was open to the public. I almost want to invite her so she could hear our research and understand why her family's choice felt like such a betrayal. Maybe even to wave a white flag between us.

"It's this weekend, right?" she asks, hopefully. I can hear her trying to coax the invitation out of me.

But I don't take the bait. I grab the rest of the flyers Maira had left for me to post. "Yes."

"Well, I hope you get it," she says, a quiet disappointment in her voice. "I bet you will."

Her reassurance means a lot, but I don't show it. I turn my back and tape a flyer onto the glass panes of the front door.

"I wouldn't put those there," Ale calls.

"Why?" I argue, ripping a piece of tape with my teeth.

"The glass gets humid and the tape will unstick. I'd put it over there." She juts her chin to the bulletin board beside the exit sign.

I ignore her and stare at the paper for most of the shift, watching as it stays put, as if to prove a point. Ale doesn't notice, not even as she shuts the door behind her when she finishes her shift.

I close alone, locking the register and mopping the floor until I can see my single reflection. I take the trash out for the evening, waving at Erin, the bookshop owner across the street, who is similarly closing her store for the night.

I turn off the lights and shut the front door, pulling my store keys from my pocket to bolt it, when I see the adhesive on the tape failing, the flyer fluttering to the floor.

Twenty-Nine

THE LAST TIME I SAW JULIO IN A SUIT, WE WERE AT HIS pa's funeral.

Today, when he arrives at the Steelworkers Auditorium, I still recognize that black polyester, so pressed and pleated I can tell he recently had it dry-cleaned.

He's parked in front of me, Yvette in the passenger's seat beside him. He adjusts his lapel and removes his hat. He examines it for a while, turning it toward the side panel, running his fingers over the embroidered initials. He stares at them for a beat—probably wishing he could take it into the auditorium for our presentation.

He sets it on the dash with disappointment. His best good luck charm, forcibly left behind. He leans forward, his eyes closed, his forehead pressed on the steering wheel.

Yvette flips down the overhead visor, pulls the photo of their pa from the CD sleeve, then gently tucks it into Julio's pocket. He looks up at her, smiling with some relief.

But the relief is brief.

Once he's out in the parking lot, Julio looks toward the auditorium.

Communities Care organizers are carrying banquet tables and linens through the side doors. The other participants stand out on the front steps, waiting to be let in. He bites his nails and peels off his suit jacket, revealing the wide rings of sweat curled around his armpits, then starts pacing the parking lot.

I walk to meet him. "Are you okay?" I ask.

He shakes his head. "No," he mutters. "We need to win."

Yvette approaches us, her arms full of our poster materials and maps. I take them from her, then turn to Julio. "You're going to do great—you've rehearsed so much," she assures him.

"There's a lot on the line," Julio huffs. "The money and stuff with Pa."

"What stuff with Pa?" Yvette asks.

Julio shrugs. "I just feel like I owe it to him to win."

"Julio." Yvette cups a hand over his shoulder. "Even if you don't win, I know Pa would be proud of you."

"He would be," I agree, pulling at Julio's shirtsleeve. He finally stops pacing, stands in front of me. "We're going to try our best."

"You're not nervous?" he asks, incredulous.

"I am nervous," I admit. "But we're going to be okay."

Before Julio and Yvette arrived, I sat in my car and read the city council meeting agenda for next week. Five months after its initial announcement, Mayor Warner had added a motion for the lot beside our school. By next Tuesday, a decision was going to be made.

I looked up. The slow trek of students had begun—each of them carrying poster boards and other materials for presentations that rivaled ours. Doing my best on this presentation was the only thing

I could control—the one thing that could lead to the city council's decision and my ma coming home.

A mix of anticipation and fear stirred in my stomach. I felt like I did when I was a child—when my nose would bleed and I could call out for my ma. She was always there, always ready to help.

I wondered if she'd come today. I hadn't invited her, but I'd overheard my pa mentioning it to her on the phone the other night.

I looked at my phone. My thumb hovered over the screen, tempted to call and ask her. But I scrolled through the voicemail inbox instead. I counted them—over a hundred messages I hadn't listened to, over a hundred days since she'd moved. I closed my eyes and picked one.

"Hi, Paloma," she said. It sounded like she was driving, the blur of white noise transient behind her. "I'm just leaving work. I wanted to tell you that I miss you." She paused for a long moment. "I love you."

It was enough to soothe me.

I look at Julio and pull him into a hug, holding him the way my ma once held me, and saying the words I wish she was around to tell me right now. "We're going to be okay," I repeat.

Finally, he exhales. His spine curves, his shoulders round. "You're right."

I step away from him and look back at the auditorium, where the doors have swung open. The event is starting, and the crowd that had amassed begins trickling inside. Julio takes a deep breath.

Out of habit, he reaches upward to adjust the bill of a hat that isn't there, his fingers in search of a phantom limb. Instead, they graze his hair, cropped close to his scalp, cut just this morning. Then he palms the pocket of his pants, feeling for the photo of his pa.

He nods. "We're going to be okay."

He repeats this to himself, mumbles it beneath his breath like a prayer as we walk to the auditorium, as we check in, as we set up our presentation materials.

And for a moment, I think we might be.

But when Julio and I make our rounds along the auditorium floor, my hope dwindles. We weave through the maze of banquet tables, staring at the other participants' projects, their presentation materials just as impressive as ours.

Julio notices my worry and squeezes my hand. "We're going to be okay," he repeats.

But now, I don't believe him.

The small ember of hope I'd carried is snuffed out when I look up at the stage, at the jurors table.

Julio says something else, but I can't hear him. All I can do is stare at the center judge, smiling in that same practiced way I've seen hundreds of times before, and let loss fall over me. Let the acceptance of losing settle in my stomach. Mayor Warner sits at the center of the table, the chair of the jurors panel for this year's prize.

Thirty

JULIO STARED AT THE JUDGES THE ENTIRE TIME WE presented.

He stared at them while he read from his index cards, when he referred to our map, and when he gave the list of potential harm-reduction strategies for the community. The largest being the most obvious—the removal of warehouses.

He didn't blink once.

Not even now, when all of the presenters are brought to the stage for the winners to be announced. He looks directly at Mayor Warner, eyes wide.

He clenches and unclenches his fists in the pockets of his suit jacket. It's what he did the entire time we waited during deliberations. While the judges made their decisions, they pushed all the participants into a banquet room down the hall.

Most of the other attendees sat around, probably equally as nervous, but they did a better job at hiding it. Julio, instead, paced the length of the room.

"Why is she here?" he asked. "Why is *she* the *chair* of jurors?"

I sighed. "I don't know," I said. "The scholarship is under new management, right? Maybe that's it."

"It still doesn't make any sense," he said. He kept trying to reach up for his hat. "It's not *her* scholarship. The other judges are professors and businesspeople and teachers and philanthropists. She's a *mayor.* And a terrible one, at that."

I urged him to sit beside me. He slumped into one of the chairs, defeated. And even after he sat, his legs kept moving, rhythmically bouncing up and down.

I tried offering him my hand, but he shook his head. He leaned forward, resting his elbows along his knees.

"We're going to lose," Julio said, definitively.

"We don't know that," I reassured him, resting my hand on his back. I moved it in slow circles, trying to give myself something to do.

Julio shook his head again. "She won't let us win. She loves Selva, she loves the money they give her. The winners have their work published nationally and get massive publicity. That would be terrible press—for *both* of them." He shoved his hands into the pockets of his jacket. I could see their outline through the fabric, the mounds of his knuckles squeezing into fists. He squeezed, released. Squeezed, released. "How are you not panicking?" Julio asked me.

I gave him a weak smile. To me, it was clear—we were going to lose.

But this loss just snowballed with every other loss I'd experienced the last few months—my ma moving, my pa getting fired, Ale and me not speaking. Seeing Mayor Warner almost made me numb. To me, there was nothing left to do but to accept it.

"At this point, it may be better to think about what comes next," I admitted.

"But *nothing* comes next for me," Julio said. His spiral from waiting for the preliminaries has returned. He rose from his chair and circled around me, his body in orbit. "If I don't get this money, I can't go to school. If I can't go to school, I can't get a degree. If I can't get a degree, I can't come back and open this garden. If I can't open this garden, I can't plant my dad's plants there. And if I can't plant my dad's plants there—" He paused, gasping for air, as though mid-swim. "Then, what was the point?"

"The point of what?" I asked.

He gestured to the hall, back to the auditorium where we'd presented. "Of any of this? Of researching, of presenting, of him even dying? If I can't do something to honor him, he died for nothing—"

"Julio," I said, standing to grab his hand, "stop."

He shook his head again. "No, it's true. And it's true even if we do win—he died for nothing. He didn't deserve that. But at least this would soften the blow a little. Might make it so somebody else doesn't have to die."

"*Stop*," I repeated, and pulled him to sit beside me. "It wasn't for nothing. It's only April—we still have time to figure it out. No matter what, though, *we* are going to be okay." I gestured between us.

He was quiet after, staring at the swirling pattern on the carpet. Then he rose and paced again, his panic ballooning through the room.

It grew as I sat there, it grew as the organizers called us back to the auditorium, it grew as they lined us up on the stage.

I looked out at the crowd. Julio's ma and my pa had arrived. They stood left of the stage, beside Yvette. My pa saw me looking and waved eagerly. I pretended not to notice, sinking inside.

I felt like such a failure compared to him.

He had worked for months, sacrificing his health and his paycheck and his marriage to ratify a new contract for his community. I had worked so hard and had hardly sacrificed anything, and I would have nothing to show for it.

And then I saw her—my ma.

She stood beside my pa, her face hidden in the blooms of flowers she held against her chest, an assortment of balloons tied to the stems. I blinked at her, waiting to feel the relief I'd felt earlier, listening to her voicemail in the car. But when our names weren't called in the runners-up section, it finally sunk in.

We were really going to lose.

And seeing her in the crowd cemented it for me. This was going to be the dynamic with my ma—her there, me here, separated by a sea of distance. I would never be able to bridge that gap. My one chance to convince her to move home was gone.

My eyes dampened.

We would lose, Julio would defer his admission, my ma would permanently stay in Pasto Verde, and that warehouse would spring up beside our school, then another school, then a park, then a senior center, then a hospital, then the lot beside Save-a-Minit.

And the same reason we were losing was the same reason any of this had begun.

I turned to Mayor Warner.

I felt so stupid to have even hoped—she would have the last word. She always did.

I rolled my eyes up to the ceiling, forcing the tears back behind my lids. I didn't want her to see me cry.

Now, I turn to Julio. I tug his sleeve, coaxing his hand out from his suit pocket. I try to get him to look at me, but his gaze is steady, still. It's then that I realize he isn't necessarily staring at the jurors—he's pleading with them.

When the organizers begin their preamble to announce the final winners, Julio's knees wobble, his hands shake. Applause pulses through the crowd, preliminary in its celebration.

The other participants onstage clap, too, but I don't.

I am too busy reaching for Julio's hand. It trembles, the dampness along his palms streaming into sweat.

"Just breathe," I whisper to him.

It's what I hear instead of the judges calling the winners' names: his attempt to inhale, his push to exhale.

The sound of his breathing is so loud that when he releases my hand and drops to the floor, I feel terrible. Like I could have held him steady through this newfound grief.

I kneel beside him while the crowd erupts in applause. I feel the other participants step up toward the front of the stage.

I turn my back to them, unable to bring myself to watch them receive the prize. I lean in close to Julio instead.

"Julio," I whisper, "get up. Let's go, we can do this backstage."

But Julio doesn't move.

I watch as the announcer extends his hand toward Julio, like his palm is a consolation prize. Julio doesn't take it. He just pulls his knees to his face, weeps into his legs.

But then the presenter extends his hand to me. My palm hovers over his hesitantly, and he yanks me up and pulls me toward the front of the stage. There, he drapes a medal around my neck, pins a ribbon to my blouse. I realize then that Julio is not crying of despair. He's crying in disbelief.

The participants from earlier descend the stairs just off the stage, heads hung in disappointment.

Two organizers breeze past them, a massive cardboard winners' check in their hands. They set it onto the floor and help Julio up, asking him to hold it instead.

So, Julio stands. He wipes his face. He looks at the check and cries again, his tuition payment held firmly in his hands.

Thirty-One

CELEBRATION IS THE BANDAGE THAT TEMPORARILY mends the past, even if only briefly. It is what allows everything else to be forgotten for a moment. As we sit in the vinyl booths at Casa Jimenez, it's like Julio's pa never died, like my ma never left, like my pa was never fired, like none of us at this table have ever known grief.

I look around—me, Julio, and my ma on one side, my pa, Yvette, and Señora Ramos on the other. This is the fullest table I've sat at in months, and still, I keep looking at the empty space near its end, wishing Ale were here.

I look over at my ma, grateful, at least, that we're finally together. I lean into her embrace now the way I did the moment I got offstage.

She was the first person to approach me after we'd won—she was crying, and somehow, that made me cry, too. As we wept into one another, I imagined our tears watering the soil of all that could finally grow because of this prize.

She held me in a way that she never had before, her arms the best frames to capture the victory.

I pulled her in tight, afraid she would disappear again if I let her go.

When she released, she began announcing my win to everyone who could listen. Calling my family, calling her friends, and now, flagging down her old coworkers.

"Paloma just won a scholarship," she says to each of them, so quickly the words all trip over themselves, like she can't say them fast enough.

They nod and congratulate me, passing sweaty glasses of water to everyone at the table.

"The interview is tomorrow, right?" Yvette asks, taking a sip from her cup.

Julio nods. "On K-FER. We're on live at seven."

"We should watch it together," Señora Ramos suggests. "I'll cook."

Julio smiles at her—I haven't eaten Señora Ramos's food in years, but by the look on his face, I don't think he has either. It was one of his many hopes fulfilled: his ma finally had something to celebrate after years of mourning.

"You should wear this," Yvette says, grabbing a gift bag from her feet.

Julio opens it, plucking away the tissue paper to reveal a brand-new hat. It's not Dodgers blue, but deep blue. He turns it to the front, where the UC Davis logo is sewn tight against the canvas. He looks up at her. "When did you get this?"

"Back when you first asked me for help with the project," she says. "I knew you'd win. Turn it to the side."

Julio twists the hat and sees them there—his pa's initials. Julio gets up and hugs her and Yvette wipes her eyes. "He would be so proud of you."

When Julio is beside me again, I pick up the hat, brush my fingers along the bill. "It'll match your suit."

He smiles. "I have to buy it before next Tuesday."

I hold his hand beneath the table, squeezing the length of his fingers.

"What's on Tuesday?" Yvette asks.

"The larger press conference," Julio explains. "When we have to give thank-you statements. It's nationally televised."

Señora Ramos pulls Julio into her chest, the way she would when he was younger, plucks off his new hat, and kisses his forehead. "I'll take the day off," she says. "I have to enjoy every moment with you before you go."

It's the first reminder since we've won that we will be apart soon. There are many decisions that still need to be made—the city council and the warehouse, my ma and moving home, and the conversation that Julio and I have been postponing for years: What was going to happen now that he was moving to Davis?

He squeezes my knee beneath the table, then nestles his palm back into his lap. I immediately miss it—his hand already feels miles away.

After dinner, Julio and I drive to the field by the old equestrian center. We sit in his truck bed, passing a shake from Baker's between us, looking at the mechanical bull. It had remained after all this time, just like we had.

I look ahead at the warehouse behind it, remembering that time when we sat here this exact way, wondering what would be built here. Back then, imagining a different future for this land felt like an indulgence.

Now, hope holds in the air for something different.

"You think they'll still keep the warehouse on the agenda for next Tuesday?" I ask. "They can't build it after our interview tomorrow."

"I don't know," Julio says. He pauses for a long while, watching as the semitrucks from the distribution center circle the lot. "I can't believe she let us win. Why would she do that?"

"Maybe she was outnumbered." I shrug. "It doesn't matter—we signed the contract, it's done."

He squeezes my hand, gestures for me to lie with him. On our backs, we look up at the sky. It had rained recently, so the expanse of the stars is clear. Julio points to Orion, its arms flared like a flamenco dancer.

I point to the constellation beside it. "Isn't that your new mascot?" I ask.

He squints at it. "That wishbone?"

I turn to him. "That's not a wishbone—that's the Taurus constellation. It's a bull."

"A bull?" he echoes.

"Those are the horns," I explain, gesturing.

"It looks like a wishbone," he repeats. "Or, like, one big fork in the road."

I tilt my head. "I can see that."

"But, no," he says. "Davis's, like, visual mascot is a mustang. But the real mascot is an aggie."

"An aggie is a horse?" I ask.

He shakes his head. "It actually stands for agriculture. I like it—farmers to an aggie. Lots of history there. My pa would've loved it, he would've loved all of this. I wish he could see it."

"He'll be alive," I say, "in your garden."

Julio nods. "And in the paper. You're about to get published nationally. You've been talking about that for forever."

I smile. The winners' contract we'd signed said that the research would be reviewed and fact-checked before it went into production. Publication was planned for May, a few weeks before graduation.

I think back to all of the framed newspaper articles in the journalism room, how the words would burst through the barrier of the frames and move into the hands of thousands of people across the country.

"I'm going to take a bunch of copies up to Davis," Julio adds. "I'm gonna brag about you to everyone up there."

I'm quiet after, so silent that I can hear the gentle flute of the night winds. I swallow, wondering if this is the time to ask. The question had been sitting on the tip of my tongue since his acceptance email had arrived. I finally force myself to spit it out.

"Julio," I say, "what are we going to do about us?"

"What do you mean?"

"You're moving," I explain.

He looks at me, squeezes my hand. "We'll be okay—we'll call each other, visit during weekends and breaks."

I turn toward him, resting my cheek against the flatness of my palm. He does the same.

"But it's far," I say to him. "It's *hundreds* of miles."

"It's a one-hour plane ride," he counters.

"How are we going to take *plane* rides?" I scoff. "They're expensive."

"We both just won one hundred thousand dollars, each. I think that'll be covered."

I shake my head at him, unconvinced. "We can't spend tuition money on plane rides, that's not how it works."

It's quiet again, and Julio counts on his fingers.

"Well, Davis and Riverside are only, like, seven hours away driving," he says, laughing gently. I love when Julio laughs; it lets me see the soft crookedness of his teeth, his two butterflied incisors.

"Only? How am I going to drive seven hours?" I ask.

He moves closer to me, so close that I can feel his breath against my lips. "*I'll* drive," he retorts. "You don't have to do anything."

"You'll *drive*?" I mimic. "We're going to be busy with school and work and you would drive seven hours to see me?"

"Of course I would," he responds with a shrug. "I love you."

I stare at him. He says it so matter-of-factly, so easily, that I think it might have been an accident.

But then he repeats it. "I love you."

The words roll off his tongue, rattle in my head.

I freeze. In my stillness, the movement of everything else is amplified: the winds blowing, the grass bending, the bull bucking.

I blink at him, reading his expression—it's dark, but I can see the width of his eyes, the whites like milk. His gaze is not expectant or impatient. It's even, soft, sincere.

"You don't have to say it back," Julio says, gently. "But I do."

My heart double-Dutches in my chest. "I love you, too."

He smiles, and I feel an apiary buried beneath the tent of my skin, a buzz in my blood. He's right beside me, but somehow I wish he were closer. I want to keep a space for him in the empty spaces of my body: a nest in my head, a crawl space in my heart.

He leans into me, and I wonder if he can hear it—the percussive pounding in my chest, a drumbeat in the desert. If he can feel the nothing of my breath, gone every time we kiss.

I open my eyes. We stare at one another, like we are both aware this is the type of moment that needs to be absorbed, too sacred to ever be replicated.

Everything about him becomes magnified. I can see all the things I couldn't before. The slope of his shoulders, the birthmark along his neck, the shadow bending against his elbow.

The earth tilts beneath us. I know we will be forced to shift against its axis, but when Julio looks at me, I am stable. Everything can change, will change, but I know I am certain that this is love, tender and true.

Thirty-Two

I KEEP STARING AT JULIO'S SHIRT. THE WESTERN embroidery swirls across his chest, the fabric loose around his shoulders. It's his pa's old vaquero button-down, the one he always reserved for special events, like this one. We're sitting in the lobby of the Steelworkers Auditorium, waiting for our K-FER interview to begin.

I squint at the stitching, umber ant trails creeping around the collar. It's the only thing I can focus on when I try to settle my heartbeat. It had trembled all morning, ready to leap out of my throat. First for the interview, then to see Julio.

I gripped the width of my steering wheel as I drove to his house, nervous that things would be different between us after yesterday. But the moment I saw him, everything felt as solid as it had been when we were in the field last night.

Maybe even more so.

We kept repeating "I love you" the entire drive here, as though we were breaking the words in. They still felt like a novelty, new against my tongue.

It's what he repeats now, when he can sense the nerves knotting inside of me.

"You got it," he says, squeezing my knee. "This is your part, the thing you wanted."

"I know." I sigh. "*That's* why I'm nervous."

He clicks his tongue. "C'mon. There's no way you can mess this up."

I turn to him. "But what if I do?" I ask. "The publication won't come out until May, but the city council meeting is on Tuesday. This segment is the only thing we have before then that can swing the vote."

"And we'll swing it. Once people watch the segment, they'll be cornered." He adjusts his hat, the new Davis one Yvette had given him yesterday. "You'll be great, I promise."

I nod, looking ahead. A woman approaches us—long and lean and paper-pale. Her blond hair bobs against her chin when she crosses the lobby. She extends her hand. Julio and I take it. "Sorry for the wait. My name is Carrie, I'll be handling your publicity for the prize."

We rise and stand beside her, watching a camera crew wheel their way into the auditorium. Cristina Fajardo trails behind them. It's bizarre—I've spent so many evenings watching her on-screen. Now she had morphed into more than someone two-dimensional, flat. She was real, flesh and bone and in front of me. She skirts around us, swallowed by the double doors of the auditorium.

"Thank you for signing your winnings' package contract," Carrie says. "Here's a copy for your records."

She hands us each a thick packet of paper. I take them both and stuff them into my bag. When I turn back to her, I see she's holding two gift bags, forest-green tissue paper bursting from their tops. "These are for you."

"Thank you," Julio says, taking one and pushing the tissue paper away.

Carrie stops him. "No, not yet. Our sponsor requested that you open them live. Cristina will prompt you."

Carrie leads us back to the stage, where we had stood just yesterday, to a set of armchairs set along the floor. Twin box lights are across from them, so luminous that they radiate heat. It's gentle at first, but soon, it consumes me. It feels like a summer day when the winds are still and the sun is at its peak, uniquely smothering. And it's worse when I look up.

Mayor Warner is standing left of the stage, in the bends of the curtains. Her eyes are deep and dark, striking me like two bullets.

I tug at Julio's hand. "Why is she here?" I whisper, feeling salty beads of sweat on the curve of my upper lip.

He looks up, pauses. "I don't know."

I want to say something else, but members from the crew begin pinning microphones onto us like boutonnieres. Cristina is beside them, pressing powder against her nose with a small sponge.

Carrie approaches us again. "Okay, we're about to begin rolling." She glimpses at her clipboard. "We'll need to meet in the lobby after this to discuss your press conference next Tuesday. We'll be hosting it at your city hall, and there are a few things we'll need you to prepare."

There's a turn in the air—heavy, then dense, then bitter. I swallow a mouthful of it, a pressure building within my throat. I want to ask Carrie about the mayor, but Cristina walks toward us then, and warmly shakes our hands. "Congratulations to both of you. I know being on air is nerve-racking, but just try your best, okay?"

I nod, unconvincingly. Julio can still feel my nerves, the knots loosening and then tightening in my stomach. "It's gonna be okay," he whispers.

I look at him, worry in my eyes.

"They're cornered," he reminds me, flicking his eyes to Mayor Warner. "We got it."

I nod, sit up, and square my shoulders—reminding myself that this is my opportunity to speak about everything that was happening here, the way my pa never got to when the strikers were interviewed and he'd been fired. This, I figured, was for the both of us.

"Let's go," Cristina says, clapping her hands together. "On three."

The cameraman counts us down and Cristina begins her introduction. I'm trying to focus, but I keep staring at Mayor Warner. She walks off the stage and across the auditorium floor, then sits directly across from us, arms laced over her chest.

She stares at us. Her expression is smug, glib. Like she knows something we don't.

Cristina continues. "Paloma and Julio have each won a one-hundred-thousand-dollar inaugural scholarship through the Communities Care organization. Julio, tell me a little bit about your reaction to winning. I heard it was a very heartfelt moment for you."

"It was," Julio starts. "This scholarship was the one way I could afford university. I feel really privileged to have gotten it."

She nods. "Paloma, how did it feel for you?"

"Great," I say, dragging my eyes back to Cristina. "I know this will be really impactful for our community."

Cristina nods, glimpses at the teleprompter ahead. "And how do you both feel, knowing what a beneficial opportunity Selva has provided you?"

We're still.

I sit up, closer to her, figuring I must have misheard her. "What?" I ask.

"I asked, how do you feel knowing Selva provided you with this opportunity—with the scholarship money?"

I blink at her, feeling a river of sweat sliding down my neck. The air has been wrung from my lungs, a desert in its place. I swallow, listening as my heart pulses against my eardrums, a low *thump thump thump*, like timpani keeping time.

"They what?" I ask, trying not to stutter.

Cristina sits up and smiles with media training I'm beginning to wish I had. "I'm sure it felt wonderful—it's very generous of them to have started a scholarship organization to help students like you." She pulls one of the gift bags from the floor, opens it to reveal my certificate and a T-shirt. She unfolds it, holding it against her chest. It reads: *Selva Shows That Communities Care.*

It's then I realize what is happening.

A rendition of what had happened at Thanksgiving, then again at Christmas. A community event to attempt to conceal all this company had been doing, now culminated in the largest public relations move I could have never thought of, their final checkmate.

It was perfectly timed. Right after the strike, and likely before the warehouse would be built beside the school. Mayor Warner had not announced an official decision, but she no longer needed to. Sitting there, her eyes burning into my skin, I realize it has always been decided. It's why she let us win: Julio and I were the perfect eclipse.

Two students who were passionately standing up against the harm they had caused the community being sent to school on their dime. There was nothing we could do to corner them; they had cornered us.

I keep staring at the shirt in Cristina's hands the way I'd stared at Julio's shirt in the lobby, trying to calm myself down.

I blink at the words curved against the fabric, screen-printed to look like a smile. To me, they reminded me of the sliced oranges my grandpa passed down every celebration. I think of his work in the bracero camps, his cough. And I think of my pa's work, his cough.

I think of their home, a warehouse now bordering the backyard, and remember what it was like before it was built. Julio and I would sit and watch the livestock roaming in the field, observing as the neighbors dipped their branding die into vats of liquid nitrogen to freeze-brand their hides.

I wonder if that felt anything close to this. Because sitting here feels like the searing pain of someone stamping an iron against my chest, deciding who I belonged to. And when that sting settled, it was replaced with dull disappointment that we had won this scholarship for all the wrong reasons.

That, really, we had won nothing at all.

Cristina keeps looking at me, gently waving her hand against her lap, coaxing me to answer. Julio squeezes my knee, urging me to respond. The silence hasn't lasted more than a few seconds, but it feels like it has dragged on for hours. I know I need to say something, but when I open my mouth, nothing comes out. That bitter air from earlier has returned, stuffed into my throat. I feel like I can't breathe.

Julio finally cuts in for me. "We feel great about it. It's an honor."

Cristina smiles at the monitor and cuts to a commercial break.

Her face drops then, twisting into true concern. "Are you okay?" she asks me.

I jolt up. "I'm sorry," I blurt, unpinning the microphone from my blouse. "I can't do this."

I throw the microphone onto my seat and walk down the steps of the stage, toward the exit. I linger by the door, waiting for Julio to realize what's going on, waiting for him to follow me. But he doesn't. The commercial break ends and the segment begins, and Julio remains seated, pulls the Selva T-shirt over his head, and smiles into the camera.

Thirty-Three

I FEEL LIKE I AM AT THE BOTTOM OF AN HOURGLASS. Every second since I walked off the stage feels like grains of sand are falling over me, making it hard to breathe.

I sit outside the auditorium, poring over the contract I'd stuffed into my bag. I read and reread the terms and conditions, praying that I am somehow imagining all of this. But they're the same:

Winners agree to provide Sponsor with any requested information, photographs, or other materials necessary for the promotion and publicity in exchange for prize monies. Winners agree to the following promotional services: one news segment, one photoshoot, and one live press conference broadcasted via television where they will thank the Sponsor in prepared statements about the company's positive impact on their educational pursuits.

I sit there, the sobering reality seeping into me. I can't accept this money. I can't help Selva be absolved at a press conference—not after seeing what they had done to the city, what they were doing to the community, and what they had done to my family—to my pa.

I can't stand in front of a crowd and thank them for all they were giving me after they had taken so much.

But then I look at the final line of the conditions, hovering just above my mockingly large signature: *Prize subject to both parties; if one member forfeits, both parties will forfeit.*

If I don't accept this money, then Julio can't accept his money.

It no longer feels hard to breathe, but impossible. Air traps within my ribs, pinching and tight, worse when Julio walks out of the auditorium, still wearing the T-shirt from the news segment.

"Hey," he calls, hurrying toward me. He looks concerned. "Are you okay?"

I stand up and start for his truck.

"Paloma," he calls after me again. "I know this is messed up. But we need to talk to Carrie. She said we need to prepare a thank-you statement by Tuesday—"

I look up at the sky. Clouds smear against its width, like God's fingerprints against a canvas. "Julio," I respond, my tone weak. "Let's go."

The drive is silent.

It reminds me of when Julio picked me up from the jaripeo. But this quiet is different. After the jaripeo, there had been so much to tell him that I didn't know where to start. Today, silence clenches between us, like invisible hands wringing my throat.

I don't know how to explain what I'm about to do. Thoughts wind through my head: How is he going to react? How can I fix it? Can I fix it at all?

A guilty heat bubbles at the base of my stomach, rises to simmer in the hollow of my throat. The blistering promise of tears. It worsens when we pass by Baker's.

"Are you hungry?" Julio asks. He cups his hand over my knee, shakes it tenderly to comfort me. "We can stop and get you something."

The pain scorches against the inside of my neck. I flatten my lips and shake my head, staring out the window. Every block closer to Julio's house feels elastic, like concrete could curve endlessly around the earth. I somehow want it to end and somehow wish it were longer, just so I could have more time to prepare what to say.

I push myself to be hopeful, thinking of ways both of us come out of this unscathed. Maybe there is a possibility where I could deny the prize money, he could still afford tuition, and we could still be together.

But when he parks in his driveway, there's a sour pull in my gut wondering if there's any room for the word "us" left at all.

I see my pa's car and Yvette's car and his ma's car lined up against the street. I know they're all gathered inside, wondering what happened when the segment returned and I wasn't there. My pa had called me a few times while I sat and reread the contract, but I didn't pick up.

I scramble out of the truck, and Julio walks to meet me along the grass in the yard. The sun is setting, and his shadow is dark in its descent. I peer through the kitchen window behind him. His ma is standing by the stove for the first time in years, Yvette circling around her to help prepare dinner.

The sensor light turns on, and light puddles onto the porch. I stare at it, perfect and yellow, like a sun on cement. It's the brightest I've seen the house since his pa died, and it makes me feel awful.

I held it in during the news segment.

I held it in as I read the contract.

I held it in as Julio drove.

But when Julio looks at me and asks, "What's going on?"

I do it, I cry.

The simmering pain in my throat boils over, piercing out of me like the whistle of a teakettle.

Through my blurry vision, I can see the worry sweeping over Julio's skin. He grabs my hand, but I shake my head and pull away. He nervously adjusts his Davis hat—three times, like always.

I try not to look at it. I don't want to see his pa's initials as I deliver the news. I look up at the fronds of the palm trees above us instead, whipping wildly against the winds like a mass of feathers.

"Julio." I sniff. "I can't accept that money."

Julio blinks at me. His lashes look heavy, like they're striking with the weight of every flutter. "Why not?"

"I can't promote that company in exchange for the prize money. That's what all of this is." I gesture to his shirt. He stares down at the fabric. He pulls it off, embarrassed, balls it up, and tosses it into the bed of his truck. "Are you okay with that?" I ask.

He adjusts his pa's shirt and puffs his cheeks out. "I mean, no," he admits, "but if that's what I have to do to get the money, I can do that."

"But it's just not right," I continue. "We just did a whole project on how these people are ruining this community. I can't take their money."

"Well, we already signed a contract," he pushes. "And they won't just give the money to me—it has to be the both of us."

"There has to be a way out of it." I point to myself. "*I* can't accept it."

He looks at me, as if he's waiting for me to say something else—to change my mind. When I don't, he runs a hand over his face.

"Paloma," he says, his tone calm, as if he's preparing for what's coming next. "Let's just think about this together. That conference isn't until next Tuesday. And that's what you really wanted out of this, right? You get the publicity—"

"Tuesday?" I ask.

Julio nods.

I look up, shake my head. "Julio, that's when the city council meeting is. The mayor will probably approve the warehouse then and use us as a scapegoat. It's timed perfectly."

Another gust of wind blows, my tears drying against its force. He takes a breath, practicing patience. "We don't know that for sure. It could still be your opportunity to publicize—"

"Don't you get it?" I ask. "This is not publicity, this is a *scam*. And I can't do that. I need to get out of this contract."

"You need to get out of this contract," he clarifies, speaking slowly. "Even if it means I don't get my portion of the money—even if it means I can't go to Davis?"

I stare at him, unsure of how to tell him that yes, that's exactly what I am saying. The wind gusts around us, small tornadoes twirling across the dirt in the garden. His pa's garden.

Looking at them spin gives me motion sickness. I lean on the brick side of the house, feeling bile stir in my throat. Waves of guilt crash against me, eroding each of the hopes that had built inside of me for the last few months.

Julio squints at me. He tilts his head, like he doesn't recognize me, his mouth dropping slightly. "Are you being serious?"

I nod. "I'm sorry," I start. "I just think that—"

"You *cannot* be that selfish."

He begins pacing again, darting between the trunks of the trees in the front yard. He pushes his palms against his scalp, sending his hat tipping forward, the bill covering his eyes, then cradles his hands behind his head. He inhales deeply, his exhale funneled through flared nostrils, his lips flattened into a firm line.

"Julio, I don't think it's selfish," I argue. "I can't stand in front of our community and tell them that this company is giving and caring and philanthropic. Not after everything they've done." I pause. "You're okay with doing that?"

"If it means I get to go to school, yes."

I blink at him. "But it's not right," I repeat.

"Not right for *who*?" he asks. "You?"

"I don't think it's right, period."

I stand up and meet him along the path. Another gust of air sends Julio's hat bill flying up, and I see his eyes. I expect him to be angry. But it's worse. His eyes are teeming with tears.

"Please don't do this," he pleads. His voice is thin, frail with desperation. "I need to go to school. This is the only thing in the way of me going to school. I need that money to come back here and make things better."

"Well, what if we can figure something else out? I can help you apply to other—"

"What is there to figure out?" he asks. "It's one hundred *thousand* dollars. Where am I supposed to come up with something like that? I need to pay my first quarter of tuition soon. You can't do this." His voice cracks, and the tears overflow from his eyes, not even rolling onto his cheeks. Just falling straight down, where the wind picks them up, sweeping them into nothing.

"Julio, I'm *sorry*," I croak. "But I feel like this is completely immoral—"

"But this isn't just about *you*!" he shouts. "This is also about *me*. This isn't just about your values and morality, Paloma. You're doing this to *me*." He points to his chest, his finger striking against his sternum.

He paces again, the way he had all those evenings when we worked on the project. He turns to me, shaking his head. "And you know what? I guess that makes sense for someone like you."

I cock my head back. "What is that supposed to mean?"

"Paloma." He sighs. "You're *so* nearsighted. You don't listen to anything else anyone ever has to say about anything when you think you're right."

"That's not true," I respond, my brow furrowed.

"You can't even listen now!" he scoffs. "You did this to your ma, you did this to Ale, I can't believe I didn't think you would do it to me."

"Julio, that's different. My ma and Ale are wrong—"

"Are they?" Julio presses. "This issue is so much more complicated than what's right and what's wrong. No, I don't want to promote their company. But how else am I supposed to go to school if I don't have the money to enroll?"

I step toward him. "But I bet there are other scholarships or money—"

"For *you*. *I* didn't get any other scholarships, Paloma. Remember? I won *their* money. And now I can't take it, not because I didn't win it, but because *you're* in the way? Because you're above taking some photos and shaking some hands?"

"That's not fair. You know it's bigger than that," I tell him. "It's not that simple. These warehouses split my family up, ruined my dad's health."

He steps away from me. "*Your* family?" he spits. "You *choose* not to talk to your ma. Do you know what it's like to not have a choice in not being able to talk to your parent?" He looks at me. "They ruined *your* dad's health? My dad *died*."

When Julio collapsed onto the stage floor yesterday, he had cried in celebration. When he sits on the ground now, he cries in sorrow. He sits there on the pathway, his elbows pressed to his knees, his head tucked into his chest, and he sobs.

The sobs are breathy, atmospheric. They stutter out as he struggles for air. I crouch down, sitting on the ground beside him. The winds push against the leaves of the palm trees, air slanting through the fronds. It matches his cries, a weeping in the air.

I extend my arm, trying to reach out to him, but he pushes my hand away.

"My dad *died*," he repeats. He exhales, his cheeks puffing out, and wipes his face with the collar of his pa's vaquero shirt, the cotton damp. He takes off his UC Davis hat, stares at the initials stitched into its side.

Then he looks at me, shakes his head. His lashes are wet, clumped into mounds of triangles. There's a tenderness to his gaze, no matter how piercing the words out of his mouth are.

"Who are you to decide what would be right for me to do? You haven't been through that." He clenches his jaw, the bone tight. "My plan has *always* been to go to school, to learn, to come back and make this community better to honor what happened to my pa. And if I'm going to do it by taking money from Selva, that's fine by me. It's the least they could do after what they did to my family."

He looks at me the way he had at the beginning of this argument. Like he's waiting for me to change my mind. Seeing him like this makes me want to, but all I can do is shake my head.

"I'm so sorry," I say, blunting the edge of my voice, extending my hand to reach out to him again. He pulls away. "But, Julio, I really do think we can figure this out. I can help you find other scholar—"

"We?" he asks.

Then I know what's coming. That sour tug in my gut expelled from my body, now a reality. Salt stings my eyes.

"There is no 'we' anymore," he says. He wipes his eyes, adjusts his hat.

"Julio," I start, "don't do this."

He looks at me, agape. "Don't do this?" he echoes. "That's what I've been saying to *you*."

"So, that's it?" I ask. "This is over?"

Julio doesn't respond. He looks ahead, at the crooked posts in the fence that bend against the breeze.

I feel a pang in the center of my ribs, a cavity carved into my chest. Every passing breath pierces me with pain, like air funneling into its hollow space. So many rotations of emotion: the shock from the auditorium had faded, moving toward sadness, then to guilt. But now, it's anger. It pulses through me, familiar and warm.

It's the same sensation I'd felt the entire year he'd ignored me, that I'd tried to cling to when he initially asked to work together, when I feared that this would happen. Perhaps it had never been anger at all, but the pull of intuition, telling me this whole arrangement between us was too good to be true.

I feel so stupid to have agreed to all of this. For thinking I could play any role in helping this community, for thinking that this scholarship was legitimate, but mainly for thinking that everything Julio and I had built was real. It had all been a transaction to him, and it was all over.

"It is what I thought it was, right?" I ask. "You only wanted to talk to me so I could help you with this project. Now that it's not going the way you wanted, you're breaking up with me?"

"Paloma, that's not why I'm breaking up with you." He sighs, his shoulders slumping forward. "I wanted to do this project with you because I thought you were the only person who would really get it. Who would understand what this meant to me. But I was wrong. You don't understand me."

"But you told me you loved me," I say plainly. "Did you even mean it?" My tongue outpaces him before he can respond. "Or did you only say that because I helped you win this money?"

The entire time we'd been out here arguing, Julio looked angry, sad, disappointed. This is the first time he looks betrayed.

"You have no idea how I feel," he says, shaking his head.

I sit there and look at him, becoming his inverse. Waiting for him to change his mind. But he doesn't. I'm struck with déjà vu of that day two summers ago—me, standing here, asking to fix something. And Julio slamming a door in my face.

"Paloma," he says, "go home."

I stand there in the driveway, amid the new darkness of the night. The sunset had elapsed, like everything else between me and Julio—the scholarship, our friendship, us.

It makes it hard to look at him. So when I get into my car and turn the ignition, I keep my gaze low. But my headlights strike against his body. And I see it all clearly: his dark shadow stretching over the porch, Yvette opening the front door, hurrying to see what's happened.

My pa curves around her, watching as I back out of the driveway. I pull onto the road and don't turn around, not even when I hear him call out after me.

I drive forward, looking at the palm trees swaying against the breeze. A gust sends them slanting and snapping back into place, moving as if they, too, are waving me goodbye.

Thirty-Four

HEARTBREAK PUMMELS AGAINST MY BODY.

I can't bring myself to drive home. Somehow, I feel like being there would make it more real. My pa tries calling me a few times, but I let the phone ring, rattling against the cup holder.

It's when my ma calls that it all finally hits me—the culmination of all that was lost.

This really would be for our indefinite future, our new dance. My ma would never come home, and I would have to spend the rest of my life looking at her face on a phone screen instead of seeing her in our house.

I turn off my phone so that I don't have to think about it. I pull into the Save-a-Minit parking lot, looking at the lot that Julio had imagined as his garden.

I flick my high beams on, the lights illuminating the end of the lot, the end of a dream.

When I flick them off, I realize how alone I am—not even the moon is out for company. Without it, it feels like it had at the end of that summer, at the end of all seasons. Dark.

When I finally go home, I see my ma's car parked in the driveway. That flimsy bandage of celebration that had appeared after Julio and

I had won finally lifts. It had never been enough to mend reality, the true break of a bone beneath its surface.

When I enter the house, my pa immediately rushes toward me.

"Are you okay?" he asks.

I don't say anything. I don't nod. I don't shake my head. I just sit on his recliner, dizzy and defeated, and lean forward. I press my head between my knees, staring at the balding carpet.

"What happened?" my pa asks, gingerly placing a hand on my spine. "Julio didn't tell us anything. He just, uh—"

I hold a hand up, urging him to stop. I can't bring myself to hear more about it. "I can't accept the scholarship money," I explain, watching a tear fall onto the shag beneath me, turning the light brown dark.

"What do you mean?" my ma asks.

I lift my head, look at my pa as I explain it. "The scholarship is sponsored by Selva, and they want us to do publicity to promote the prize." I sniff. "I told Julio I couldn't do it, but they won't give him the money if I don't take it. But I *can't* take that money. So, he can't go to Davis." I pause, force the words out from the fence of my teeth. "And he just broke up with me."

My pa exhales, cheeks jutting out, a low whistle slanting from his lips. He sits beside me, his body teetering on the edge of the twin recliner.

"That's terrible," my ma says. "But, Paloma, it's a lot of money. Maybe you should consider it." Her voice is animated, encouraging.

"It's *wrong*," I say. "I can't take money from the same company that started the whole reason Julio and I did this project to begin with."

"It's complicated," she agrees, "but you and Julio both worked so hard—you deserve to take that money."

"Ma, it wasn't about the money for me. I got scholarships to go to

Riverside," I admit, somehow more defeated than before.

My ma looks at me, brows pointed together. "Then why would you even apply for it?" she asks.

I blink at our wood-paneled walls, at all the family photos nailed to them. There was one of my pa's side of the family, amassed in front of their house. It was old enough that it was patinated, old enough that the citrus trees were still behind them, old enough that the warehouse was not yet there.

A photo of my pa and Julio's pa at a Dodgers game.

A photo of me and my ma one Noche Buena.

And then an empty space, a missing piece, where my parents' wedding picture used to be. A nail stands in its place, like a shred of hope, as if waiting to be of use again.

"I wanted to win this project because I thought it would stop that warehouse by my school from being built. And I thought, maybe then, you'd see that there's hope here. And if there's hope here, in this city, maybe you'd see there was some hope left for this family and move back. But I was wrong." I shake my head. I wave a hand toward the window, at the city, then between our bodies, at us. "This city is going to waste and I am never going to have the family I wanted. And now Julio doesn't get to go to Davis, he doesn't get to build that garden, we're not going to be together."

I feel the tears from earlier again, rhythmically rising like the height of a wave. But I push them away. Anger was the easy safety net beside me, something that always promised to catch me before I fell into the jaws of grief.

"But you would encourage me to take the money, right?" I ask. "Immoral, but easy, right?"

"Paloma," my pa interrupts, "that's not fair."

"No," I scoff, then point a finger at my ma. "It's what she did. Just left when you were sick and I may have needed her around—convenient, right?"

I hold my breath like a grudge, waiting for her to take the bait—I'd taken my own. But she doesn't. She allows herself the release I had denied myself. She cries.

"Okay," my pa says, standing up. "Why don't we all just take some time to think? It's clearly been a hard day. You don't have to make any decisions right now."

I don't have it in me to say that the decision has already been made. It's there, in the nebulizer on the floor. In the trash can, filled with the inhalers that cut his paycheck in half. In the air all around us, veil thin and transparent, but somehow always felt.

And I want to say so, but my pa urges me to get some rest. I stand up, looking at the disappointment swelling in his eyes. But it doesn't look like he's disappointed in me, or in my ma.

Somehow, it looks like he's disappointed in himself.

And that's enough to make me drop it, to make me go.

I crawl into bed and watch the ceiling fan twirl above me. I think of how it spun before Julio and I kissed. I close my eyes so that I don't have to remember.

The neighbors behind us are having a party. Laughter and dancing and music crescendos between my ears—another chorus of celebration that I wish would quiet. I let the thump of the music lull me to sleep, the bass as dull and monotonous as the pulse of a bruise.

Thirty-Five

I DON'T LEAVE MY BED ALL OF SUNDAY.

Every memory from yesterday makes me feel sick with guilt.

My pa tries to come in to talk to me.

"Paloma," he calls, gently rapping his knuckles at my door. "I made you some breakfast before I go to work."

But I can't respond. I don't have the energy to.

It wasn't like this the first time Julio and I broke up—it was the reverse. Back then, my pa was too busy mourning the death of his own best friend to notice I was mourning the end of mine in a different way.

It was my ma who helped me. She lay in bed with me and made me food and took me to the swap meet. Then it was Ale, who hugged me and let me cry into her hair and gave me every pep talk at Nicho's.

This time, I'm alone.

I know my pa means well, but he won't know what to do. A breakup is what a mother and a best friend are for—I have neither.

So, I lie there, quiet and still, for hours.

I track the time that's passed by the sunlight in my bedroom.

When it begins to shadow, I call Nicho's to tell them I won't be in for my shift today. I wait for Maira to pick up, but she doesn't. Ale does.

I panic when I hear her voice, freeze.

"Paloma?" she asks.

I don't say anything.

"Are you okay?" She pauses. "I saw the news segment last night."

I've avoided crying all morning. My eyes are so swollen that any fresh tears just sting. But they come anyway. I move the receiver away from my mouth and try to cry quietly, like I had that day in the walk-in freezer, but Ale hears it.

"I'll be off in about an hour," she says. "I'll see you soon."

Ale lies at the foot of my bed. She props herself up on her elbows, picking from a bag of Japanese peanuts she'd brought from Nicho's.

"So, I was right," she deadpans. "He does love you."

I lift the cold spoons from my eyes. Ale forced me to put two spoons in the freezer and hold them against my lids to help with the swelling, but they're still so inflamed that my vision has narrowed. I fling the spoons onto my nightstand, the steel chiming against the tabletop.

"Well, not anymore." I blink at her. "He's never going to want to talk to me again."

She snorts. "*That's* not true."

"It is," I counter. "I'm in the wrong, right?"

She adjusts her posture, the mattress coils creaking beneath her. "Yes." She nods. "And no. You're definitely more in the wrong than Julio is, anyway."

"What am I supposed to do?" I ask her. "I can't take that money."

"Well, what are you going to do without it?" she asks. "How are you going to afford school?"

"I have other scholarships," I explain.

"You got them?"

I nod.

She nudges me gently. "I told you you would."

I smile, weakly. Her kindness makes me feel ashamed. When she first arrived, I told her she didn't have to be here, especially not after our fight. But she came inside and listened to me, like she had all of those work shifts. I recounted every searing part of last night. The more I remembered, the more it hurt.

I'm shocked she's still here after listening to everything—but she is. She leans against a bedpost and looks at me. "Did Julio get any other scholarships?" she asks.

"No."

"Did he get any aid?"

"Some grants," I explain. "But since he's moving across the state, it's not enough."

She purses her lips. "Well, it was just this K-FER interview, right? You can just take the money now?"

I shake my head. "There's a press conference next Tuesday, at the city council meeting. They want us to get onstage and thank them for everything that they've done for us and for the community."

There's a long lull of silence. Ale lets out a breath. "That's hard," she offers. "I'm so sorry. You're sure you don't want to?"

"Not like this," I say. "But there's just no winning."

She nods, understandingly. "It's like what happened with my pa."

"Yeah," I agree.

I look at the sunlight pouring through the grids of the window, coating the walls in perfect squares. I stare at the pattern of dark and light, thinking of how much it looks like the map Julio and I had made for this project.

Everything seemed so simple when we were working on it, so two-dimensional. But when I look at Ale, I see reality unravel in front of me, fully formed, fully fleshed.

"I'm sorry," I say to her, the overdue words sitting in the space between us. "I didn't get it back then."

Ale looks at me for a long while. Her almond-colored eyes shine with surprise. After a long beat of silence, she finally says, "Wow."

"What?"

She shakes her head. "I never thought you'd apologize to me for that. I don't think you've ever apologized to me for anything."

"I'm sorry," I repeat, swallowing. "And I'm sorry I made you feel stupid. You're not stupid. Honestly, maybe I'm the stupid one."

She glowers at me, the bend of her fake lashes curving over the hood of her eyes, grazing the tips of her brows.

"I mean it," I say, earnestly. "This is way more complicated than I thought—you understood that before I did."

"Paloma, you're definitely not *stupid.* You know a lot about this stuff. That's why it's hard to disagree with you. You're right a lot," she says, tilting her head. "Just not all the time."

I lie flat on my back, splaying my arms against the width of the mattress. "Doesn't seem like it."

"You are. All of those articles you wrote are true—my pa *hates* working for Selva," she admits.

"Really?" I ask, blinking at the ceiling.

"Yes," she says. "That's what I was trying to explain to you. But you didn't listen." She pauses for a while. "Honestly, you don't listen a lot."

I look up at her, my neck craning over the pillows. "I'm sorry," I repeat, wondering how many times I can say that phrase before it dissolves, loses meaning. "I feel like I keep saying that. But I really am. You're right—I've never had to make a sacrifice like that."

"You're going to have to now," she notes. "And I really wish you didn't because it's not easy. My pa did *not* want to sign that deal. That's what I was trying to explain to you," she says. "He's so miserable. But he's miserable with money—and sometimes you have to play the game."

"But I don't want to play the game," I say.

"And that's fine for you," she says, "because you can afford not to play it. But what about Julio?"

I stare at the shag carpet beneath us, so compressed it doesn't look like a carpet at all, but like soil beneath our feet. I feel tears roll down the sides of my face, seep into the pillows beneath me.

"What am I supposed to do?"

Ale moves closer to me, her hand on my shoulder. "There has to be a middle ground."

"There isn't. It says so in the contract."

She shakes her head. "No, I mean between you and Julio."

I sniff. "He's not going to want to see me."

"He loves you," she says, "even if this is what happened."

I shake my head. "I don't think that's true," I say. "I feel like he only said that because I helped him win."

"Wow," she snorts. "You *really* think that? Maybe you are stupid."

I don't respond. I had been avoiding thinking about it at all. Every memory of Julio felt like sucking air into that cavity in my chest.

"Paloma," Ale scolds, "you know that's not true."

I stare up at the ceiling fan—its eye a disc, its blades a bloom. I blink at it, realizing how empty that sounds saying it aloud.

"Yeah," I admit. "I do."

She squeezes my shoulder. "You two will get through it."

"How do you know that?"

"Because we did," she says.

And then she pulls me in the way she had that day in the walk-in freezer. Without warning or announcement, just because that is the kind of person she is. She wraps her arms around my torso tightly and reminds me that everything is going to be okay. I don't know if she's right, but holding her here, I allow myself to believe it for a second.

Thirty-Six

ON MONDAY, I BEG MY PA TO CALL THE SCHOOL AND tell them that I'm sick. I feel a little better after seeing Ale yesterday, but not well enough to see Julio.

I lie in bed, staring at the plant he'd given me for Christmas. It had sat on my windowsill since then, blooming like we had.

I close my eyes. It feels safer to be here—in the dark. But then I hear my phone buzz beside me.

I scramble to get it, hoping that it's Julio.

But it's not.

It's Carrie, who calls every few hours. I haven't picked up once.

I set my phone down and wait for it to stop ringing. Then I read the poorly transcribed voicemail script, sitting atop my ma's from last night. Despite me saying terrible things to her on Saturday, she had still called, promptly, at seven thirty.

I glimpse at the transcription of Carrie's message, wincing at the words: *Hi, Paloma. We've been trying to get in touch with you since Saturday's interview. We need to confirm your attendance at next Tuesday's press conference. If I don't hear from you by tomorrow, I'll assume you and Julio will be forfeiting the prize. Please call us as soon as you can.*

I roll onto my stomach and press my face into a pillow. I know I won't be taking the money, but I can't bring myself to pick up and tell her that. Every time I even think of the words to myself, I feel like my throat is tightening, enclosed by my guilt. How could I do this to him?

I begin daydreaming about the impossible alternative—standing on a stage and shaking some hands, then holding Julio's after. Maybe that concession would be easier than feeling this way, like someone has pierced a fishhook into my chest and is pulling me in and out of the water just to watch me flounder.

But I know I can't.

I turn onto my back, stare at the ceiling. The balloons my ma had brought to the scholarship presentation have sunken into themselves, the foil depressed at the center. I've watched them unceremoniously drag from one corner of the room to the other, looking as deflated as I felt.

I am so angry with her, and I still wish she were here. I knew she was the one person who could tell me I would be okay, who could lie here with me and hold me until I slept, like she had all those times my nose bled.

But I'll have to settle for something different. My pa knocks at my door again, this time entering with a bowl of sliced oranges. When he sees me crying, he sits at the foot of my bed, rubs my shoulder.

"Come on," he says, "get dressed."

We sit beneath the arch of the hangar.

I look up at it, wooden planks slanting above us in even lines, joining at the center like a steeple. And maybe that is what equestrian arenas were for me and my pa, a place of worship.

He had driven us to one of the few arenas left in the county, on the very edge of Plum Valley. He'd offered to take me to the equestrian center close to our house, near Baker's. But I shook my head immediately.

My pa looked at me. "You don't want to go?" he asked.

"It's a warehouse now," I blurted, which was the truth. But really, after Julio, it had become so much more. I didn't want to be around it—it was a symbol of the past in so many new ways.

We sit on the benches surrounding the ring, stiff as pews. The escaramuzas have finished practicing their synchronized routine for an upcoming tournament, and the charros enter in their place. They ride horseback, ringing lassos around a bull dummy before releasing a real one out onto the field. My pa and I watch it circle the arena, hooves steadily trotting over dirt.

"He's gotta be faster," my pa mumbles, jutting his chin toward the horse.

I know he's just trying to be lighthearted, but it doesn't work. Sitting here with him reminds me of all the times Julio and I would watch the livestock during family parties, listening to their gait and gallop.

The landslide of tears begins.

My pa scoots closer to me, pulls me into his chest. I inhale. Since he got fired, he no longer smells like a warehouse—he smells like he used to, a mixture seeped in a past that seemed to be vanishing: citrus trees and fresh air and the soil from where he'd sprung. I press my face into his shoulder, relishing the scent, my chest heaving.

"Pa." I sniff. "Am I doing the right thing?"

I pull away, wipe my eyes. After days of lying in bed, I just wanted someone to tell me what I needed to hear: that this whole situation was complicated, but that I was right.

I know my pa will solidly be on my side—he knew more about

Selva's corruption than anyone else, carrying it as evidence embedded in the contours of his body.

But my pa is silent.

He tips his vaquero hat forward, eyes shaded in its bill, watching the animals running against the red dirt.

"I don't know," he finally says. "If I were you, I'd at least have to think about it for a long time."

"You'd *think* about taking it?"

My pa pauses, and my tears stop. A gust of wind blows against my face, stinging against my skin like a slap. I look at him, at the map of worry lines cut into his forehead. The race has kicked up clouds of dirt, and he coughs behind the collar of his T-shirt.

That sound was all I thought about when I'd first found out about Selva sponsoring the project. The biggest reason to say no. But when my pa looks at me with confusion in his eyes, I no longer know what to think.

He sits up, then shrugs. "It's a life-changing amount of money. It would be for anyone, but especially for someone like Julio. Even if it is from Selva—I see where he's coming from."

"So, you would do it?"

He shrugs. "I don't know. Maybe." He sighs and rubs his hands together. They're so chafed that the skin whispers against itself, like the quiet grit of sandpaper. "And that should be enough to tell you how complicated this is."

I press the heels of my hands against my eyes, pushing until all I can see is the hazy blur of shapes.

"I'm sorry," he repeats, "but I don't know a lot about making a choice like this. I don't like risks—I like stability."

"That's not true," I argue, moving my hands back to my sides. "You were on *strike*, that's a huge risk."

"You're right," he agrees, "but I didn't do that alone. I was part of a union. You're making a decision alone here—I don't know anything about that. The only person I know who has ever made a challenging choice for herself is your mother."

"But she made the wrong choice," I note.

"She made a decision that would be best for her," he corrects.

"And it was selfish." I point to him, definitively. "*You're* not selfish."

He looks at me. "I don't think what she did was entirely selfish." He tilts his head. "And I don't think what I've done hasn't been selfish at all. I also made my own choices—I could've quit."

"But, Pa," I protest. "You were helping other people."

He nods. "Yes. And that had its own consequence as well. I don't agree with everything that your ma has done. A lot of it has been hurtful. But I did put a lot on her." He's quiet for a while, rubbing the toe of his boots into the floor beneath us. "I really regret that—she was eventually going to break." He pauses again, watches the charro round the ring. "Your ma has taught me a lot. It's one of the things I love most about her—but I still have a lot to learn."

"You still love her?" I ask my pa.

"Of course I do," he says. "We both made decisions and stood by them. Only mine will be looked at as heroic, but it doesn't mean hers wasn't important."

I blink at him, remembering the conversation I'd had with my ma the night she chose to move. Even then, even through her exhaustion, she was able to say what my pa was saying to me now.

"The people who don't understand the turmoil of her choice to move would consider your ma very selfish," he says, looking at me pointedly, "just like with you—if you don't take that money, people may say the same. But they're not seeing the human nature of you sitting here crying about making that decision."

"They're not the same thing," I say. "I'm not doing what she did."

"You're right," he says. "They're not the same thing. But they're more similar than you think."

I lean back, my hands digging into the bench beneath me, the wood splintering against my force.

I have always looked to my pa with admiration. For his dedication and his hard work and his righteousness. But when I look at him today, I admire his empathy the most. He had been hurt the most by my ma's departure, and he was still able to offer her the compassion I'd been denying her, and been denying myself.

I look back at the vaqueros. They circle the ring, leaning forward to loop their lassos around the bull. It sprints forward, and it's the first time I pray it can outrun its fate. Because perhaps that's what I'd been doing all this time, circling and circling, only to rope myself back to my own start.

The day has become dark. I lie in bed again, looking up at the balloons grazing against the ceiling, miniature blimps against a man-made sky. They had deflated more throughout the day, the foil surrendering into itself. But they were still there.

I pick up my phone. I wonder if I'll find similarity there, another example of something that has slowly collapsed with the passing of time. But my ma picks up immediately, like she'd been waiting for a call. She was still there, like they were—floating, despite it all.

Thirty-Seven

I ASK MY MA TO MEET ME AT TOM'S.

I sit in a booth, peering through the windows while I wait for her to arrive. The Jurupas are bold against the last bit of sunset. The ridge is ragged across the sky, burning into a shadow of its shape. It blends bit by bit with the dark, indistinguishable at first, and then I blink, and it's gone.

And there, taking its place in my view, is my ma. I watch her pull into the parking lot and park right beside my car. I don't know why, but it brings me a soft satisfaction.

When she steps out and gazes at the 99 Cent Store across the parking lot, I can feel her memory working the same way mine had all those months ago.

I rise when she enters the restaurant; it's so small that she doesn't have to look for me—I'm just right here.

Though we haven't seen much of each other in the last few months, I feel I've always been right here, right in her line of sight.

And then, it's like all those times my nose bled. When I look to her, awestruck and afraid, wondering what to do next.

But this time, I'm not sure what she'll do. When I called her, all I said was that I needed her to meet me here, that I needed to talk to her. She didn't ask any questions—she just said she was on her way.

I don't know if we'll do the dance of ducking and dodging, unaware of how to greet one another. If she'll give me the tone I've been anticipating for weeks, the I-told-you-so I'd been hearing for years. Or if she'll think this is too complicated to fix. If she'll just leave.

But instead, she looks at me with a depth in her eyes. An expression I think I'll only understand if I ever become a mother, if I ever have a fraction of myself in front of me.

And then she embraces me, as she had done all those times prior. Even when I start crying. Even when I feel my tears soak against her shirt like my blood used to. She presses me tighter, allowing me to release freely without any judgment, holding me just so I know that she's there.

We split an order of chili cheese fries.

My appetite has been worn by adrenaline, but my ma forces me to eat. I push the fries around the Styrofoam platter with a fork instead, watching while she thumbs through my Communities Care contract.

She squints at the minuscule print, looking at this contract just like she'd looked at coupon clippings, collection notices, budgeting spreadsheets at our kitchen table—trying to find a way to make it all work.

Then she sighs. Defeated.

"I'm so sorry," she says. "This is an awful position to be in. You're sure you don't want to take it?"

I shake my head. "I can't do it."

I half expect her to try to convince me otherwise, but she doesn't. She nods.

"You have enough scholarships to cover your tuition?" she asks.

I nod. "Yeah, staying local cuts the costs by a lot."

She pauses for a long while, then nods, thoughtfully. "I'm really proud of you."

I look down at my nails. My cuticles have become raw and bloody from biting, hangnails like thorns against my thumbs. "I'm not," I mutter.

"Why would you say that?"

"Because I still don't know what to do about this," I say, glancing at the packet between us. "Like, I'm not going to take it, but what is Julio supposed to do?"

Her eyes skip over the contract again. "Well, this can't be the end of it."

"What do you mean?"

"This can't be the end of the conversation with this organization," she says. "Have you considered asking them to renegotiate the terms of your winnings package?"

"No," I say, "they wouldn't want to talk to me."

She shrugs. "Maybe not. But it looks like they've picked you two as winners for a specific reason, and they probably don't want to lose that leverage. You should call and try to set up a meeting," she suggests.

"What would I even ask them, though?"

"Ask them if you can walk away from all of it but have Julio keep his share of the prize," she responds, as though it's that simple. But afterward, she adds, "Just understand that it will come with its own consequences."

"Like what?" I mumble.

She inhales. "Like, I can't imagine they'd let you keep the credit on the paper you wrote."

I look at her.

My ma cups her chin in her hand thoughtfully. "Would you be okay with that? Your writing is really important to you."

I pick up the contract and thumb through it quickly, the pages fanning my face, the words blurring like a flip-book animation. I remember all the years of working on the school paper, thinking it was all preparation for writing this, to publish this.

I sit there, my ma's words falling over me. They feel like lead on my skin. How heavy, I think, to have worked so hard and have nothing to show for it.

But maybe it wouldn't be nothing.

I look at my hands, at the curved lines in my palms, and think of Julio's hands. How they always felt like a map of this city. I sit back, looking beyond the windows. Save-a-Minit is a few blocks north.

Maybe I couldn't have the future I'd imagined. But if Julio got this money, maybe he still could.

"Yeah," I say, "I'm okay with that."

My ma sets her elbows along the table, presses her fingers against her temples. She looks as I'd seen her so many times, at the peak of frustration. But instead, she begins crying.

I pull a napkin from the dispenser and hand it to her. "What's wrong?" I ask.

"I was worried I was setting a very poor example for you when I moved home. I didn't want you to grow up and be so selfish," she explains.

"Ma," I say, watching as she dabs a napkin against her eyes, her mascara staining the cotton in perfect half-moons. "You aren't selfish."

She sniffs. "I think—"

"No. I get it now," I interrupt, and then I swallow. "I'm sorry."

"I'm sorry, too." She pauses. "I'm at least really happy to see how your pa has been such a good influence in your life."

"What do you mean?"

"I lead with my head, but your pa leads with his heart. And even though I wish he would've put our family first sometimes, it's one of the things I admire most about him. I'm glad he passed that on to you."

"Pa got something done, though," I argue, then gesture to the contract, splayed out on the table. "Most of this has become a waste."

"Paloma, it is not a waste." She shakes her head. "Your pa sacrificed so much to lead that strike, including our relationship. And, after all that, he still lost that job. But that wasn't the point of him doing it. Even though he no longer works there, there are so many people who are reaping the reward of his organizing. Things for them aren't perfect—but there is progress."

I swallow. "It just wasn't supposed to happen this way," I explain.

"The point was to get the writing out now."

She pauses. "I know, and I'm sorry. But *that's* why I'm so proud of you—sacrificing something isn't easy. You're giving up something so large for Julio's sake."

"You make it sound so noble," I mumble. I slump down, resting my face against the table, the lacquered top smooth and cool against my skin.

"It *is* noble."

I look up at her. "Then why do I feel so terrible?"

"Because, whether or not you're doing the right thing, it's hard." She blinks at me. "I don't think anyone else could have shown me how hard your dad's decision to put others before himself was better than you are right now."

"That's what he said about you," I say, spearing the tines of the fork into the platter, the Styrofoam squeaking lightly. "About needing to make a difficult choice when you moved. How come you guys couldn't see that when you were together?"

She muses. "The space has really helped, I think. It helps you look *at* things, not from them."

She stirs the straw of her drink against the cup, ice sloshing against the plastic. "And I'm sorry you felt like doing this was going to get me to decide to stay here." She clears her throat. "I was never going to stay," she admits.

I look up at her. "You would've never come back?"

She shakes her head. "My decision to move wasn't about that," she says. "I mean, the way things have changed here hasn't helped. But it has more to do with me and your pa. We're different people. It's what

I was trying to explain to you when I first told you I'd be moving." She sighs. "And the more I think about it, the more I feel like I should have moved sooner. Not because I don't want to be around you, but maybe because you could have avoided all of this," she says, gesturing to the stack of papers between us.

"It's fine," I say, sighing. "It was stupid to have even hoped."

"No, it wasn't." She squeezes my hand. "It never is."

My ma walks me to the parking lot, our bodies washed in the hazy purple glow of the 99 Cent Store sign. I look at my car, then look at hers. I don't want her to leave, but it's the first time I know not to ask her to stay—not because she wouldn't, but because I understand why she'd want to go.

But my ma checks the time, then looks at me. "The swap meet is still open," she says. "You want to come with me?"

And so we go.

Thirty-Eight

"SIT TALLER," MY PA SAYS, CORRECTING MY POSTURE with a palm on my back. "Square your shoulders."

"And make eye contact when you speak," my ma adds.

It's Wednesday, and I have a meeting with the Communities Care representatives in a few hours. After talking to my ma, my pa helped set up a negotiation meeting, something that, at this point, he'd done many times before.

My parents and I are in the living room, where they've been helping me prepare.

They've guided me through talking points, given me feedback, and corrected my cadence for the last hour. I read from the notes in my lap, but my pa shakes his head.

"Speak *up*," he insists. He places his hands on my shoulders, squeezing them gently while he looks me in the eye.

I blink at him. "But, Pa, what if they don't go for it?"

"*They* have something to lose—they picked you two for a reason." He turns on his heels, pacing the living room floor with determination. Watching him dart across the room reminds me of all those times I'd watch him and Julio's pa lead union meetings, their animated enthusiasm coursing through the room. My pa points to me. "*You* have the upper hand, don't get that confused."

He looks to my ma for affirmation, but she's already nodding behind him.

"Speak like you are proud of yourself," she pushes, then waves a hand between the both of them. "You should be—*we* are."

Despite all of their years of arguing, now that they're in front of me, they find an easy rhythm. No questions, no comments, they support me like they have never been apart. It reminds me that before they were my parents, they were friends, they were people.

My pa stands taller. "Remember, the rule with negotiations is that you always ask for the biggest thing, then settle. You may not get everything you want, but you will get something. Start by asking if you can walk away, but have Julio take the money. If they say no, turn the table, remind them it's their loss, not yours."

I nod, then read from my notes again. I try to stay focused, but it's difficult. It's bright out, noon filling the room. I stare at the shaft of light, my mind walking backward through its own crosswalks, toward the memory of Julio.

I saw him in the hall on Tuesday, when I finally returned to school. It was the first time I'd seen him since we broke up, and it was worse than it was the first time around.

The year his pa died, he never looked at me, never even turned my way. It was like I was invisible to him. But when he saw me this time, he looked right at me. I expected him to look angry, but he wasn't. It was worse—a look heavy with heartbreak.

Ale was beside me. She squeezed my hand when he rounded the corner and disappeared into a classroom.

"Are you going to tell him about your meeting tomorrow?"

I shook my head. "I don't know what they're going to say. I don't want to get his hopes up."

"You nervous?" Ale asked.

I nodded.

"It'll go great," she said, trying to encourage me.

But I don't feel like it's going to go great. I feel something tectonic shifting inside of me, nerves splitting me apart. It persists even when my pa finally claps, nodding with satisfaction.

"You've got it," he says. "You want us to drive you?"

I shake my head. "No, I can do it."

My ma walks me to my car. She'll be leaving, too—going back to Pasto Verde. As we say goodbye, she fixes the part in my hair, adjusts the collar of my blouse. And then she hugs me.

"I'll call tonight," she says. "Is seven thirty okay?"

I swallow. "That works."

"You're going to do great," she says. "I'm so proud of you."

I watch her get into her car and push onto the road. I look at the space left along the driveway. Instead of feeling empty, it feels like an opening, a portal for her return. I know she won't be here when I get home, but it's the first time I'm certain she will be coming back.

The Communities Care office is inside of one of Selva's corporate buildings. They're like Russian nesting dolls—different facets of the same mold.

The inside is as I had imagined it would be: cold, new, gray.

I sit in a waiting room, where maps of San Fermín are framed along the wall. They're similar to the one Julio and I had made together—a bird's-eye view of boxes, warehouses stacked beside homes.

This display reminds me of the one in the journalism room. Framed articles with words that would outlive me, preserved there behind the gloss of glass.

I think back to what my ma had said when we sat together at Tom's. Today would be a concession, but it didn't necessarily have to be a defeat.

I think of Julio and feel the elastic stretch of possibility. He had planted threads of hope amid a field of vacantness. He could always think bigger, see more than what was made in front of him.

I know Selva will erase my name from the research.

But sitting here, I don't feel that limit as an end. I follow in Julio's example, and allow myself to imagine—years from now, the day I can return to our research, the day someone will publish it, the day people will know what is happening here, the day that map will not be a map of boxes, but a map of homes, and parks, and gardens beside a liquor store.

This sacrifice was only a release before a return.

"Paloma?"

I open my eyes, and a quiet office clerk stands behind the chrome sheen of the front desk. The word echoes through the room, traveling like its namesake.

"Carrie's ready for you," she announces.

We walk together down a long corridor of offices and conference rooms. The walls are made entirely of glass, giving a transparent view to the same sparse arrangement of furniture.

I count fifteen empty rooms before I see Carrie.

She sits at the very end of a long conference table, a laptop open in front of her.

I sit at its opposite end, a sea of wood and paperwork and quiet between us.

"Thank you for joining us," she says, hardly looking at me. "We'll begin momentarily."

I nod, staring through the glass walls at the other empty offices, thinking of all the land they had taken for all this excess: rooms that weren't even in use.

A man enters, long legs loping around the table, a briefcase clutched in his fist. He speaks in some kind of iambic, every one of his consonants perfectly enunciated. He explains that his name is James, that he is a lawyer, and that he is here to review the terms of my contract with Communities Care.

Then he sits between me and Carrie. He opens his briefcase, pulls out a series of files, and cranes his head low.

I stare at the crown of his head. He's bald, and his gleaming scalp reflects everything around us—the paperweights, the filing cabinet, the potted plants.

I try to see if I can recognize them from the plants Julio showed me in his pa's garden. But the longer I look, I realize they're all made of plastic.

Carrie half shuts her laptop and looks at me. "Paloma, you said on the phone that you'd like to forfeit your prize money," she says. "Is that correct?"

I nod.

James pulls a pen from his suit pocket. "I'm not sure you'll be able to forfeit unless your partner is here willing to concede as well."

"I'm not asking for both of us to forfeit," I clarify. "I'm here to ask if *I* can forfeit alone so that Julio can just take the money."

James's head rises. He looks at me for the first time since he's entered the room, his eyes a shocking blue. "You only want to forfeit *your* prize money?" He points the tip of his pen at me.

I nod.

He scribbles something onto a pad of legal paper, then turns to Carrie. She runs her fingers through her short hair, leans forward. "Paloma, I don't understand," she says. "We're just asking you to prepare a thank-you statement and take a few photos. A lot of students would be eager to take this opportunity."

"I'm sorry," I say, "but I can't participate in the promotional materials."

James sets his elbows along the table. "The promotion of this prize is very important to our organization," he says. "The prize money is contingent upon your participation as well as the participation of your partner. It will bring attention to your academic merits and to the credibility of our organization."

"I understand." I nod. "And Julio can do all of the promotional proceedings in exchange for the prize money so that your organization can still fulfill that goal."

James hunches over again. "Unfortunately, that won't be possible." He shuffles through the stack of paper. "The contract clearly states that both of you need to partake in the promotion of the organization in order to receive the money. So, if you are relinquishing your portion of the prize money, your partner will also be forfeiting his winnings."

I swallow. "Sir, no one else at that presentation did research about warehousing." I exhale. "If you don't give this money to Julio, who is going to stand at that podium and thank this organization before this organization builds a warehouse beside a school?"

He blinks at me, his thin lips flat like a slackline.

I continue. "I can't be that person. But Julio has said he can be." I sit up. "I think it would be in this company's best interest to allow him to accept the prize—with or without my participation."

James looks over at Carrie, his eyes glossed over. "Fine," he sighs, exasperated. "If you are surrendering your prize money, we will also need to remove your name from all the project materials. Including your research."

"That's fine," I say, remembering what I'd thought in the waiting room: a temporary release before a return. *I can publish it in the future, I can publish it in the future, I can publish it in the future.* I repeat this to myself the way Julio had before we presented at the Communities Care fair, with the hopeful plea of prayer.

James pulls a thick packet of paper from his briefcase, glances at it, then slides it over to my end of the table. It's so mechanical, like he's done this thousands of times before. I leaf through it slowly, then look up at him.

"What is this?" I ask.

"A nondisclosure agreement," he says, simply.

A quietness crowds the room. So still and empty that I can hear the sizzle of a semitruck's brakes outside.

"You know a lot about this topic," James explains. "We understand that you're very passionate about this. However, your paper, though very thoroughly researched, presented an incriminating depiction of our company." He pauses, weaving his thick fingers together. "If you would like for your partner to take this money, we need to be assured you will not be slandering our company—be it verbally or in writing."

"Is it slander if it's true?" I ask. "Everything we wrote just proves—"

He holds a hand up, dismissively. "I'm not here to dispute or debate any of the claims made in your paper," he says. "I'm here to either verify you will be positively representing our company at Tuesday's press conference, or to confirm you are okay with being legally barred from speaking about our company ever again."

"Ever?" I echo.

"Correct," he says, pointing to the contract with the tip of his pen. "This nondisclosure agreement is indefinite. It will prohibit you from speaking or writing about our company in any manner, positively or negatively, for the foreseeable future."

James slides a pen across the table. It rolls slightly before stopping, halving the space between us. I blink at it, the Selva logo gleaming beneath the fluorescent lights above us.

I lean back in my seat, all that hope I'd allowed myself to feel in the lobby evaporating. This research would become another casualty of this company's greed—it would be buried like the bones of homes and parks and people they had taken with it. I could never write about it, I could never speak about it, I could never publish this for other people to understand the reality of what was happening. There would be no return. This was all going to be a release.

I look up. The afternoon light angles through the conference room windows, retreating to reveal our shadows.

"If I sign," I say, slowly, "will there be something in this that guarantees that Julio will receive the money?"

James nods, clears his throat gruffly. "I can draft up a clause before you leave today. As long as he's in agreement, he will receive the full winnings package."

I arc across the table, taking the pen by the barrel. I push the knob. The spring of the coil echoes through the room, the click like a gun cocking.

Spring is a violent season. It is always described as a revival after the death of winter. But to bloom is to burst, to grow is to ache.

There's a shift in the air after I leave the office. After days spent in bed, then days preparing for this meeting, I expected this moment to be different. I thought it would harmonize with trees lining the parking lot, lush with their rejoicing, with their rebirthing.

Instead, I sit in my car and feel grief. There, beyond the fence post, I can see the field where Julio and I had laid a few days ago. The bull is a blip among the sprawling scar of the horizon, as distant and small as I feel inside.

My hopes for the publication had been snuffed, and I felt the residual smoke curling inside of my body as its final embers burned.

But it feels right for this season and its promised duality: to arrive means that something had to have gone.

My publication had to go, but when I look at the blossoms of the trees, I think of Julio. Maybe we didn't have to meet that same end.

I lean back, wondering what to say to him. I asked Carrie if I could deliver the news to him directly—she said it'd be fine as long as he signed by tomorrow afternoon. So I have to see him by tonight. I imagined it would be simple, transactional: everything is fixed, here is the money.

But looking at that bull in the distance, my mind races to prepare a script for everything else.

It reminds me of the day I drove to see him after his pa's funeral. Back then, I'd practiced what I was going to say the entire time I sat in the Baker's drive-through line, speaking to an imagined version of him in the passenger's seat.

Today, I don't even know where to begin. How to explain that I still privately hoped our fate hung in the seasonal air around me—something that could be reborn.

I start the engine and follow the route I've memorized: off Merrill, onto Mango, six palm trees, one church, two lefts, and there was Julio's house.

There was Julio.

Thirty-Nine

JULIO STILL LOOKS AT ME LIKE HE USED TO. WHEN HE answers the door, his eyes are bright with luminosity, with love.

But the warmth fades quickly.

The sneak of his smile turns to stone, his face hardening, like he's remembered what happened. He doesn't invite me inside. Instead, he leans against the threshold of the door, crossing his arms over the width of his chest.

I can see a slice of the living room behind him. The couch cushions are sunken in, the way they used to be when his ma slept there. The indentation is wider this time, longer. By the even imprints on his cheeks, I can tell he'd been lying there the way she had all those times I visited.

He wears a wrinkled white T-shirt and a pair of basketball shorts. His Dodgers hat lopsided on his head, and I wonder where his Davis hat has gone.

He adjusts it when he looks at me.

I can tell he's been crying.

His face looks similar to the way it did the months after his pa passed—cheeks bloated, eyes inflamed.

"What?" he asks.

I'm quiet. Julio blinks at me, impatiently, the way I had when he first arrived at my doorstep to ask if we could work on this project together.

I swallow a mouthful of air. "I need to talk to you."

"About what?" he scoffs.

"I was just at one of the Selva offices," I explain. "I went to talk to the Communities Care organizers about me forfeiting the prize. You can take the money now."

He's silent. He looks surprised, but he tries to hide it. He pulls the brim of his hat low over his eyes and he steps away from the door. He shuts it behind him, then meets me on the porch.

"They need your signature by tomorrow," I continue, relief coursing through me. "Call Carrie to set up a time, and it'll just be yours."

The flame that had been snuffed out in the Selva offices flares inside of me, blazing with the hope that maybe we can work this out.

I smile at him, waiting for him to do the same. I thought he would be celebrating, if not just relieved. But he doesn't look relieved at all. He looks resentful. The smile on my face falls flat.

I blink at him, wondering if he's kidding.

But he isn't.

"Paloma," Julio asks, his brow furrowing. "Why didn't you tell me you were doing this? I've been panicking for days about Davis. I almost deferred my admission."

"I didn't want to get your hopes up," I explain, my tone soft. "In case it didn't work out."

He pauses thoughtfully. Then he paces.

He walks back and forth over the length of the driveway, just like he had right after our scholarship presentation. His body distorts in the residual gasoline that seeps from the tailpipe of my car. Our exchange had been so brief that it was still there, wafting warmly in the air between us.

"How did you get them to agree to that?" he asks, skeptically.

"They'll be removing me and my name from all of the materials we submitted for the scholarship."

He stops midstep. "Like, even the research? Your name won't be on the research?"

"Even the research." I nod.

He looks at me directly, his stare as firm as an arrow striking. "Why did you do that?"

I blink at him, confused. "So you can have the scholarship," I respond slowly, like we're both speaking in languages the other doesn't understand—like there's something I'm missing. "So you can go to Davis."

"Did you ever stop to think about how I would feel in any of this?" He snorts.

I scoff at him. "Of *course* I did. That's why I worked it out."

"No, I mean about these new conditions—I can't accept that money like this." He sighs. "*You* did a lot of this work. *You* wanted to get published. *You* did all of that writing. That's why I wanted to work with *you*. I can't take sole credit for that—that's not right."

I look away from him. I wish I could explain how all of this felt—how signing that NDA sent the sharp blade of sacrifice piercing through my body.

I blink at the horizon beyond us, thinking back to all the citrus fields that were once here. My grandfather picking fruit, my pa picketing near a shipment gate. All of us working for something, all of us robbed.

My ma had said that giving up the publication was noble—I wish I would've prepared for how much it would really hurt. The entire drive here, I thought telling Julio he was able to take the money would relieve the pain. Instead, his anger pours salt in the wound.

"Julio, the publication doesn't matter to me anymore," I lie. "Plus, me getting credit in this publication is not nearly as important as you going to Davis. Call them and sign the contract."

"But you've been wanting to get published in that journal for forever," he says. "It feels wrong that my name would be printed, and not yours. It doesn't make sense that you wouldn't want it anymore—"

"I gave it up for *you*," I interrupt. My voice is louder than I expect it to be, a scraping rumble in the hollow of my throat. "I obviously didn't want to do their publicity stunt but I went there to fix this for *you*." I point at him. "You need this money, right?"

At that, he's quiet.

"Please," I urge, "just take it."

I wait for him to say something, but he doesn't. He shakes his head, looks at the ceiling of sky. The thumbnail edge of a moon hangs against the atmosphere—waning, like everything else between us.

"Paloma, it feels *wrong*. Now I either don't get the money or I have to take credit for work I didn't do? All because you don't want to do this anymore?" he argues. His finger cuts through the air, points directly at me. "I can't believe you would put me in this position."

We're quiet, stuck in a standstill. While he waits for my response, I retreat. I sit on the porch steps and look up toward the sky. Clouds ascend and angle upward, like a staircase to nothing. It mirrors exactly how I feel inside, climbing and climbing to no avail. I had tried to find a way out of this, but a new turn of the maze presented itself each time.

"Julio," I say, "I tried my best."

I want to say something more, but there's nothing else to tell him. I sit there quietly, wondering how I could have done better.

Julio trudges toward his truck, sits on the lip of its bumper. His feet dangle midair, sneakers kicking against the atmosphere. He slumps forward, the posture of defeat.

"I'm sorry," he says. "I know that probably wasn't easy for you. I really appreciate you getting that set up for me. I'm just mad." He swallows, then looks above. A vulture orbits overhead, its wings looping large ovals over us. It cycles the way the ceiling fan had before our first kiss, the sun dawdling behind it.

Finally, Julio looks back at me. "That's not true," he says. Then he shrugs. "I guess I'm sad."

I blink at him. First my opposite, now my mirror. I understood perfectly—how simple it was to avoid the true gravity of sadness, free-falling into anger instead. I had been doing it for months. It was always easier to have somebody to blame than to have somebody to lose.

"Me too," I say.

"It just wasn't supposed to happen like this." He sighs. The accusation has left his voice, replaced by the break of grief. "It was never supposed to *just* be mine—it was supposed to be *ours*. *We* were supposed to do this. Together."

"But it isn't ours. Nothing is ours anymore." I pause. "Right?"

He looks up at me. I see the answer from beneath the shade of his hat, his eyes reflective and wet.

I look away. Maybe he still needed to decide whether he'd accept this new contract, but the decision about us had already been made.

There would be no more blossoming, no opportunity at rebirth, despite the green of the season around us.

Whatever flame of hope that had reignited within me extinguishes again. This time, it does not leave the curl of smoke. It leaves the incineration of a wildfire's seething blaze—ashes to ashes, dust to dust.

I know those waves of grief that had arisen in my bedroom would arrive again. But right now, I feel how I felt after we first saw Mayor Warner at the jurors table a few days ago, the impending feeling that something was decided, no matter how deeply I hoped it wouldn't be—numb.

This really is over.

Which is why when I step forward to sit beside him, I sit on the opposite end of the bumper. The distance between us was much larger than what could be seen from here to there. And it would only grow wider when the school year ended, when he moved up north, when I stayed here, when we went back to how things were the year his pa died, when we stopped talking. It was so large it could never be measured—maybe never even crossed.

"Julio, you need to do what's best and what's right for you," I say. "It's what I'm doing. What we all have to do."

"Yeah," he says, quietly, "I guess that's all that's left."

When he turns to look back at me, I can see the sadness in him has gone. But it's replaced with something worse—something similar to the soft awe he had when we first began speaking again, stained with something different. Something sorry. A stare that no longer held summer in it, but in its place held the memory of every passing season.

Even this one, as we both feel it find its end.

Forty

MY PA CIRCLES THE CITY HALL PARKING LOT. HE'S BEEN trying to find an open spot for the last five minutes, but the lot is brimming with cars. Some of them are double-parked, some are on the crosswalk, some are in the bus zone. Squeezed between them are throngs of people waiting for the doors of the chamber to open.

The crowd for tonight's city council meeting is larger than it was a few months ago, when I came with Julio. Tonight, residents have not only gathered to hear the decision, but to see Julio speak at the press conference.

Mayor Warner had publicized it in her Mayor Monday segment last night.

My pa and I watched the evening report, the TV on in front of us, its hazy blue light flickering over his nebulizer mask.

"Please join us for our weekly city council meeting tomorrow evening," she announced. "We have pushed the meeting time to six to celebrate one of our youth who has won a significant scholarship through Selva's Communities Care organization. Join us in listening to his speech and celebrating all Selva is doing for the youth here in San Fermín."

The segment is how I found out Julio had accepted the money. He didn't tell me, because we haven't spoken at all since I was in his driveway last week.

As I went through the motions of our breakup, I never went through the stage of denial: every time I passed him in class or in the hallway, I knew it was over.

It was May, and I was relieved school would end soon just so I could remove myself from its agonizingly slow pace. I figured it would be easier that way. Once we graduated and Julio moved to Davis, I would not have to be confronted with what happened between us.

That was the justification I shared with Ale when she asked if I'd be attending the press conference.

"I don't think I can see him," I said.

We were closing at Nicho's, where we'd be working together all summer and through our first year of college. With the strike over, her pa was able to solidify his role as floor manager. Her ma went back to taking care of the triplets, which allowed Ale to go to community college next fall. I went with her to Chaffey last week to help her enroll, looking at the soccer field, where her future was seeded beneath its manicured grass.

We mopped the floor together, her on the front side of the store, me on the back. We met in the middle. Ale knelt down, wrung out our mops, then leaned her weight against their handles.

"You see him all the time at school," she retorted.

"Yes," I agreed. "And it's awful."

"Is this about the publication?" she asked.

The *Young Scholars Journal* had come out that week. A stack of them sat near the door of the journalism room. I had taken one and toted it around in my backpack for days, but I hadn't even opened it yet. I stared at it the entire shift, trying to will myself to read it, but I felt like I couldn't.

Ale caught me looking. She pulled it from the pocket, spread it over the register screen, and stood beside me, reading it with me.

It was brief—our ten-page paper distilled to a few paragraphs.

But more than distilled, it was deceitful.

The article did not specify that we had researched the negative impacts of the warehouse industry. It did not specify that we discovered that the particulate matter warehouses caused was directly linked to lung cancer. It did not specify that we found that residents who were exposed to distribution centers had a lower life-expectancy rate.

All it said was that Julio had reported on "an environmental issue," had won a prize, and would be going to UC Davis this fall.

I closed the cover, pushed it away from me. "What bullshit."

"I know," Ale said. "But I still think you should go see Julio at the conference. I'll go with you."

I looked at her.

"It's a big moment for him. You'd regret not going," she coaxed. "I know you're mad, but think about it."

I didn't correct her.

The most complicated thing about all of this was that I could not be upset with Julio if I tried. And I knew somewhere, deep within me, he couldn't be upset with me either. The looks in the hallway were not vivid with anger or resentment. They were not vivid at all.

If anything, they were hazy—the natural fade of seeing someone you once knew obscuring against a room, against memory. Enough to know they were there, but no longer enough to have anything left to do about it.

I figured that is how I could participate here—on the periphery.

My pa finally finds a spot. He pulls in, yanks the parking brake, then stares out through the windshield to observe the crowd. "A lot of people tonight," he notes.

I glimpse ahead at the swarm, then slump back in my seat. I wish I weren't here. I don't want to confront Julio, but I also don't want to confront the futility of my own hope.

All of these people were awaiting a decision that I still feel is my fault. I couldn't get the warehouse construction to stop, and I feel so stupid that I hadn't known better than to try.

I gaze at the mass, swallow the air pressing against my throat. My pa squeezes my shoulder. "Whatever the mayor decides, it has nothing to do with your project."

I want to believe him.

But when I step out of the parking lot and into the sea of bodies, I see a haze hanging low against the atmosphere. Maybe the mayor's decision would have nothing to do with the project, but it would have something to do with me. And my pa. And every other person who is in this crowd. And every person who could not be in this crowd because they are at home, at work. All of us would be forced to sit with the consequences, to breathe in this sky.

I squeeze into the mass, feeling the same heartbeat of impatience I'd felt a few months ago pulsing through it. But this time, it's mixed with something different. I look at their faces, expressions similar to the ones Julio and I had when we sat in the field after we won: a mix of eagerness and hope.

I feel the urge to tell them what is going to happen, to shield them from the fate of disappointment I'd felt the last few days. This was a fraudulent celebration preceding a monumental betrayal.

But I don't. Hope is an indulgence—it's a beautiful thing to savor while you have it.

We walk up toward the building, find my ma near the bike racks. She drove the hour from Pasto Verde to be here for me.

"Are you okay?" she asks.

I shrug in response.

She embraces me, and I breathe in the smell of fried masa clinging to her hair. The three of us walk into the lobby. I see Ale standing with her pa near the soda vending machine and elbow my way to meet her.

We stand on opposite sides of the machine, separated by the glowing, rounded door. Out of habit, Ale stands closer to her pa, I stand closer to mine, trying to pad the discomfort the way we had in the living room all those months ago.

But today, it isn't uncomfortable. It isn't peaceful either. It's even, accepting. No hands posed to point fingers, only outstretched to shake. After our pas greet one another, Ale looks at me.

"You ready?" she asks.

I shrug. "This isn't really something you can be ready for."

She smirks, then squeezes my hand.

As I wait for the chamber to open, I think of the way Julio swept me through the crowd. I think of him when the doors open. I think of him when I sit where we'd sat a few months ago.

I look for him everywhere.

I don't know why.

If I saw him, we'd still sit on opposite sides of the room, like we'd been doing in science class, separated by something larger than a crowd. When I finally see him walking onstage with Mayor Warner, I hold my breath, all of the atmosphere held in the elastic span of my lungs.

He wears the suit he'd seen at Ontario Mills. It perfectly matches his UC Davis hat. The pearlescent buttons gleam against the stage lights. A trimming from his pa's garden pokes out from his blazer's pocket.

Mayor Warner introduces him after the crowd has settled. "Thank you for gathering before our city council meeting to celebrate the accomplishments of Julio Ramos, the winner of the inaugural Communities Care scholarship. Julio researched the impact of warehouses in our community."

Her words slither through my mind, just as vague and deceiving as the publication had been.

She waves for Julio to take her place at the podium. He walks toward it amid lush applause, then nervously examines the crowd, the way I had a few minutes ago. I wonder who he's looking for—his ma and Yvette are standing behind him.

But then he looks at me, and it feels like time has stopped.

My heart kicks in my chest, trilling against the xylophone of my rib cage. Air packs in the hollow spaces, painful and tight. His lips are parted, but nothing comes out. He stands there, frozen and blinking at me, the way he had when he first arrived at my doorstep a few months ago.

When Ale had convinced me to come, I wondered how I would feel watching him accept the prize.

I anticipated being sad—mourning the impossibility of this situation that had ruptured our relationship, our friendship.

I even expected to be kind of angry—so much sacrifice, with little to show for it.

But I look at Señora Ramos behind him, light with relief knowing her son had accomplished something so large; at Yvette, watching her brother make a sacrifice for the legacy of their father; and at Julio, surrendering his pride for the potential of his community.

I'm surprised by my tears, by my pride.

He looks surprised, too—then concerned, once he notices me crying. I wipe my face and nod at the papers spread over the podium—urging him to go on, telling him it's okay.

He exhales, then begins reading.

"Thank you, Mayor Warner, for this introduction. My name is Julio Ramos, the recipient of the Communities Care scholarship." He swallows a lump in his throat. "I'm here to thank the generous sponsor of the Communities Care organization, Selva, for the contributions they are making toward my educational pursuits." He pauses, his jaw clenched. "Their giving nature and humanitarianism has allowed me to attend UC Davis on a full ride to study plant sciences, something my father would have loved."

He looks at my pa, whose eyes shine glossy and wet. "My father was a hard worker, but he was also a gardener, a friend, and a parent. He sacrificed a lot for this community, and I hope the sacrifices I have made to be here will help me honor his legacy while I'm at UC Davis.

I know he would have done a lot more for this community had he been given more time. Thank you."

Julio doesn't look at me again. He poses with the winner's check, takes a photo with the mayor, and ducks offstage. Then he obscures his face with his hat. When Mayor Warner approaches the podium, the room squeezes with anticipation. But Julio doesn't stir.

He knows what's coming, too.

"Thank you, Julio, for acknowledging all of the positive work Selva is doing in our community. With that, I have an important update regarding the notice of filing beside San Fermín High School." She clears her throat. "Seeing that Selva is providing students in our community with enriching academic opportunities, and pushing them to fulfill their collegiate pursuits, I am happy to announce that our council has voted privately and has decided that the lot beside San Fermín High School will become a Selva logistics center."

The room deflates and inflates all at once.

Community members slump into the posture of exhaustion, then rise into the position of defense.

She talks over the heckles in the crowd, presenting the same *more more more* like currency. I can't will myself to listen.

Seeing Julio had made that hope I had lost feel firm. Hearing Mayor Warner makes it futile again.

The guilt from earlier has returned, a gnawing ulcer against the lining of my stomach, acidic and sharp.

My parents decide to stick around to listen to the end of the meeting, but I tell them I'll be waiting outside.

"You want me to come with you?" Ale asks.

"No," I say, "I need to be alone for a bit."

I sit on the fountain beside the parking lot, watching the water cycle. I don't know why I expect something in it to change—it never does. It pools at the fountain's base, funnels into the pipes, only to erupt again.

I stir a finger into the depth of the water, watching it ripple, when I see Yvette crossing in front of me. I haven't seen her since I was pulling out of their driveway the day after our TV interview.

"Hey," she calls, walking closer. Her car keys are hooked against her fingers, clinking in the evening winds. "Are you coming tonight? We're having a barbecue at the house to celebrate when this is finished."

"Julio didn't tell you?" I ask. "We broke up."

She nods. "I know."

I blink at her. "You still want me to come?" I ask.

"Of course," she responds. "You're half the reason he even got it."

"I'm the main reason he hardly got it," I correct. "I made all of this so complicated for him."

"That isn't your fault," she says, dismissively.

I look back at the stream of water, watching it surrender into itself. "Yes, it is."

"What?" She cocks her head back. "Of course it isn't."

I wait for her to say more. But she's mimicking me, looking at me expectantly. I hear the fountain's water rushing around us, lazily pittering into the tile base.

But I leave it there—because I do think that.

I think it is my fault.

"Paloma," she says, sitting beside me. "Do you really think that?"

"Yes," I affirm, confused. "You don't?"

"Of course not. You didn't decide any of this."

"I did, though," I say. "*I* didn't take that money. *I* thought—"

"You didn't know they were sponsoring it, right?" she interrupts.

"No." I shrug. "But I don't know. I feel like I could have prevented all of this from happening. With Julio and with the warehouse."

"*You* could have prevented it?" She gawks. "Paloma, *they* shouldn't be doing it. They put you two in an impossible situation to try to distract people from what they're doing." She outstretches an arm to gesture to city hall. Her shadow falls dark against the tile, zigzagging against the grout.

I look at her, unconvinced.

She shakes her head. "The only people who could have prevented any of it are the people who planned it. They are responsible for a lot of people's grief, including mine and Julio's and yours. What more could you have done?" she asks.

I don't respond, because I don't know how to answer. Instead, I lean back slightly, curling my fingers over the edge of the fountain, the grout imprinting against my palms. I look out at the horizon, studying the clouds held in the arms of trees.

"I spent such a long time blaming myself after my pa died," she says. I look at her, remembering her expression that day we sat together in the church hallway—grief-stricken, guilty.

But today, her expression lifts into something light, hopeful. She looks at the expanse of the sky, her eyes traveling to find pockets of blue between the gray. "When Julio talked to me a few months ago, it helped. But what really made me forgive myself was when you would come in for appointments with your dad."

Her tears reflect the deep blue above us, two thin rivers rounding over the lengths of her cheeks.

She wipes her face. "It reminded me of when I would take my pa in for appointments. You kept asking me if there was anything more that you could do, and it was the first time I realized that there was nothing more that *I* could have done. Seeing you there was the first time since my pa died that I remembered I wasn't just a medical assistant—I was a daughter."

Yvette sniffs. "And then I read your report. I'd never seen anything laid out like that, with data and maps and interviews. I'm so disappointed they didn't publish it the way you wrote it, but it makes sense why they wouldn't—it shows such a clear antagonist."

I look at her. "But what was the point of even writing it if they cut all of that stuff out? It was supposed to help people."

"It helped *me*. It helped me understand that I did all that I could." She pauses, looks at me. "Paloma, you're *smart*. If you were able to get to the root of this issue in your paper, I hope you can get to it here as well. None of this is your fault. We are not our jobs, or our choices, or our decisions," she says. "We're just people."

The string in my spine that holds me in place every time I'm around her snaps. But it doesn't snap with sadness, it breaks with something different. The ache of forgiveness, for my ma, for Ale, for Julio, and for myself.

I wilt, pressing my elbows to my knees as I cry. And Yvette does what I've seen her do all of my life to Julio. What she did with her pa, through his life and his death. What she even did with mine, when she nursed him through appointment after appointment.

She slides on the ledge and comes close to me, cradling me while I cry. She wraps her arm around me. I curl into her, bend my neck against her shoulder. She holds me until the tears stop coming, until the meeting is officially finished, until a crowd of disappointed people exit through the plaza.

I glance up then, and Yvette squeezes me one last time. She stands, extends a hand to help me up.

We walk toward the parking lot together, splitting off near the doors. I find my parents up ahead, by the tower holding the city seal midair. My ma hugs me goodbye, and I join my pa in his truck.

When we pull onto the road, I see Julio's truck trekking beside us. I glimpse at him from the periphery. His face is washed pale pink, illuminated by the stoplight up ahead, a glowing red disc against the sky like the stamp of a summer sun.

He inches forward into the intersection, craning his neck left to check for traffic. And in that moment, our eyes meet.

I think he's going to be the one to leave first. But when the light turns green, my pa pulls forward. He turns the corner, and I watch Julio's truck sit there, despite the honks blaring behind him. Finally, Julio pulls forward and onto the road. I watch him pass the remnants of the old equestrian arena, his truck lost amid the stalks of grass and memory.

Summer

Forty-One

THE FIRST THING TO COME WERE THE WALLS—THEY came in May.

By June, there was a roof.

And now, in August, there is the paint.

I haven't driven by the school since graduation a few months ago. I didn't realize that would be the last time I would see the field intact—even the Phil the Farmer statue had been taken, rehoused near the horseshoe driveway of the school.

My car idles near the spot where Ale and I had eaten lunch all of those years. The view ahead was gone, replaced by gray walls lapping against the sky. In a few weeks, a ribbon will be tied over the entrance of the parking lot for a ribbon-cutting ceremony. Another red line dividing the north and south part of town.

I roll down my window to try to look around the walls, but I can't. The acidic smell of paint invades the car. It's familiar—acetone hanging in the air, thicker in the warm sigh of the summertime. I look at the painters circling around it, laying their brushes against the molding, and think of my pa and Julio's pa.

I look at that gray color, now matching every other warehouse lining the street by our school, and wonder what it's called—what Julio and I would name it.

I almost think of asking him when I drive into the lot. He asked me to meet him here—in the field by the equestrian center.

When he called to invite me yesterday, I hesitated. I hadn't been there since we won the scholarship, when he first told me he loved me. It seemed like too sentimental of a place to say goodbye to him before he left for Davis next week.

"The bull is still there," he said. "I promise."

And he's right. When I step out of the car, I see it, brown and spotted against the grass. Julio bends beside it, pulling weeds from its base. They're dry and yellow, like the ripe underside of a melon.

The stalks are so tall that they brush against my calves, whispering beneath each of my footsteps. Julio turns around when he hears me approaching. He bundles the weeds in his hand and throws them against the dirt. Then he looks at me.

His gaze makes math of my memory, an abacus sliding stills in my brain.

"Hey," he says, "thank you for coming."

I nod, pulling loose strands of hair behind my ears. "Of course."

There's a long pause. I begin to imagine how this conversation will go, a thought that has run through my mind since he called. I hadn't seen him since the press conference, and we hadn't spoken all summer.

Julio had gone to a summer bridge program at UC Davis. At least, that's what Yvette had explained when I took my pa in for a checkup.

I'd spent the summer working at Nicho's and taking a class at Chaffey with Ale.

The more time that passed since Julio left, the more he had become a memory.

But now, when he invites me to sit beside him on the bumper of his truck, it all becomes real again. All those days spent in his truck, all those nights spent in this field.

I look at him, his skin baked dark from the second side of the summer, his Davis hat high on his head.

"I wanted to talk to you before I moved," he starts, "to apologize."

"Apologize?" I ask. "For what?"

He blinks out at the expanse in front of us and puffs his cheeks out. "After the press conference, my pa's family stopped talking to me."

"What?" I ask, eyebrows rising. "Why?"

He shrugs. "They feel really betrayed that I decided to take that money," he explains. "They said it was like accepting blood money." He laughs a little, the trill like a wind chime. Then he's quiet. "They said that my pa would have been really disappointed in me."

I scoff. "Julio, they don't know that. They don't know anything."

"Yeah," he says, softly. "Neither did I."

He looks ahead. The semitrucks circle in the warehouse lot, the cargo snaking behind them. "When I accepted that money, I wondered if I did the right thing—for the community, first. Then for us," he admits. "When I enrolled at Davis, I was really sure I made the right choice. And then my pa's family said that, and I felt so gutted."

He clears his throat. "My ma and Yvette really defended me. While they were talking to them, they said a lot of what I'd said to you." He pauses. "And then I realized there was no way to win. If I didn't take that money, I wouldn't be able to go to Davis, and I'd lose. I took the money, and people think I'm like a sellout, so I lose."

"But that wasn't your fault," I say.

"I know," he says, gently. "But it wasn't your fault either."

He turns to me. His eyes are covered by the bill of his hat, but he moves it higher so I can see them. His pupils still dilate when he sees me, the black disc broadening against the brown. "I'm really sorry for what I said to you about it. It was an impossible situation to be in—for both of us. I didn't see that then."

I watch the remaining grass sway against the base of the mountain range, green lapping against the gold.

"I didn't either," I say. "Ale and my mom really helped—but so did Yvette."

He nods. "She tried to tell me, too. I wasn't ready to listen. I tried to explain that to my pa's family—if this was so impossible, the least I can do is go to school and come back and try to rectify some of it." He exhales. "And maybe one garden isn't going to do much, but it's a start."

"It's more than just a start—it's going to do a lot," I say, thinking of what he said the day we sat in the Save-a-Minit lot. "Things grow if you let them."

He smiles a little, then he shrugs. "I don't know if I'll even be able to do it," he says. "Yvette was in charge of watering my pa's plants while I was gone, but she's not really good at stuff like that. Two died already."

I laugh a little, and he smiles, relieved to hear it.

"Well, I'll be around," I tell him. "I can water them for you while you're gone."

"You remember how to take care of them?" he asks.

"Of course I do," I say, knocking my knee against his. "You taught me."

We're quiet for a moment. "Honestly, I wanted to talk to you earlier. But I was really mad at you—not even just about the scholarship," he admits. The wind sweeps between us, the hem of his T-shirt curling up in the breeze. "Do you remember what you said after we did the K-FER interview?"

I look at the sunset blazing in the horizon, imagining the chest of the city breathing deep beneath the trees in the parking lot. I raise my eyebrows. "I said a lot of things."

He half-smiles. "You asked me if I only told you that I loved you because we'd won. That really hurt my feelings." He blinks at me. "I've loved you my whole life. I always will."

We look at one another for a while. Then he offers me his hand. It's different from all those times he offered it to me while we were together. Today it feels like the last unification before a separation, the tangle of knuckles in a cat's cradle before it's pulled taut.

Julio and I lie in his truck bed. With his free hand, he points up at the clouds, his finger slicing against the air. It strikes differently than I'd imagined it would. It isn't accusatory, it isn't pointed at me, but instead is directed to the sky—gentle, observant, like the hand of a clock. Marking the time of today, of the future, of all that was still to come for both of us, and for everyone beneath it.

It points to the theater of shapes spread against the atmosphere. They morph in the air, one shape dissipating into another with the rock of the breeze.

I think of that Taurus constellation, its stars hidden somewhere against the sunlight. Bull horns once, then a wishbone, then a fork in the road. We were mirrored at its base, supine beneath the stretch of the sky one last time before inevitably splitting off.

The clouds shift until they're gone, revealing the sky beneath them—limitless, sweeping.

He asks me to name that color of blue, and I look at it for a moment. So wide and encompassing, and somehow small enough that it felt like it could only exist here, above us.

We release our hands.

I'm not sure if this is the last time we'll ever hold them, or if today is a day where we open them to something bigger. Even if it is to hold the expanse of the sky, something the two of us can share, holding it in the absence of each other.

This sky is heavy enough to keep our hands full. Weighing with hope—a blue so promised, perhaps only we would grow to know its name.

Author's Note

DR. DAVID WILLIAMS STATES THAT THE MOST POWERful predictor of a person's health and life expectancy is not their genetic makeup, but their zip code (Curtis, 9).

I learned this fact when I was twenty-seven years old.

By then, I had a bachelor's degree from UC Santa Cruz and a master's degree from UC Berkeley. I was, by some stretches of the imagination, an educated person. Still, I did not learn this until I was twenty-seven.

In some ways, it's embarrassing that I did not know this until then. In other ways, it is amazing that I now know it at all.

The first seed of this book was planted my junior year of college. I was taking a class called Urban Education, during which my professor assigned us a reading about my hometown of Oakland, California. The article discussed how water fountains in Oakland schools, some of which I had drunk from as a child, were found to have been contaminated with lead for decades.[1]

I stared at my peers while we discussed it. For many of them, it was

1. I read this article in 2016. A new outbreak was found as of 2024 and is currently under investigation.

a reality only to be theorized, a solemnity to be imagined. For me, it was a spiral of panic—a realization that I had been exposed to poison, that my family had been exposed to poison, that children today were being exposed to poison.

When I first began my research for this book, I dusted off the reader from that class. By then, it had sat on my bookshelf for nearly eight years. I had only written one note in the margins of the article: *Do they want us to die?*

I am not sure I have the answer to that question.

But what I have grown to learn through my own time in academia, in reading, and in research is that the racism in urban planning, the process of developing a city's infrastructure, is never coincidental. The location of city dumps, the location of highways, and the location of warehouses are always strategically planned.

I got the idea for this book in the summer of 2022.

I was spending a significant amount of time in the Inland Empire in that chapter of my life. The previous year, the Fontana City Council had announced that a warehouse would be built beside Jurupa Hills High School.

Following this announcement, a group of community members banded together to advocate against the warehouse's construction, forming the South Fontana Concerned Citizens Coalition. One of its founding members, Elizabeth Sena, was the primary inspiration for this book and is quoted in its epigraph. Elizabeth, along with many other community members, cited traffic concerns, hazardous air pollution, and student safety as their main reasons to stand against the construction of the warehouse.

Despite the group's advocacy and a lawsuit led by Attorney General Rob Bonta, in the spring of 2022, the city council approved the warehouse. It offered some minor mitigation to ease the impact on the neighboring community,[2] and it was built shortly thereafter.

I'd heard murmurings about warehouses in the area for a few years, but this case caught my attention the most. As an educator and a public education advocate, I found the building of the warehouse to be doubly alarming, not only for the physical ramifications it would have for the children attending this school, but for its symbolic consequences as well.

Symbolic curriculum—artifacts used to push morale in schools—is often used to positively influence students in their learning environments. Geneva Gay writes that it is most commonly seen in public displays that encompass the advertising space of schools, like posters, bulletin boards, and murals (Gay, 108). It often helps shape the neuroplasticity of children's brains—if a student sees a poster that says that they can achieve anything they set their mind to, with enough time looking at the image, they may eventually believe this to be true.

When I initially had the idea for this book, I wondered about the inverse of this. If students are constantly surrounded by factories,

---

2. Concessions included buffer zones, air purifiers, and ordinances around new warehouse construction. While some machinery now must be zero-emission, diesel trucks can continue passing through the community uninhibited. Many activists I spoke to felt as though this ordinance was a Band-Aid over a massive wound, as not much has changed since the lawsuit. In her undergraduate thesis, Chanah Haigh writes aptly, "The city doesn't seem to have learned anything from this lawsuit or the subsequent ordinance put in place. . . . [Developers want] to put an even bigger warehouse on the same block with no discouragement" (Haigh, 43).

distribution facilities, and warehouses, how would this inevitably affect their psyches? How are they not to believe that this is an inescapable facet of their futures? And how could people in power be okay with this?

Warehouses do not sprout from soil.

Their locations are designated by a committee of people voted into office. These people then make choices—to flagrantly place factories, distribution centers, and freight loading zones near the homes, parks, and schools of vulnerable populations. Though this phenomenon is not new and has spanned the country and beyond,[3] it is blatant in the Inland Empire.

Driven to the area for its affordable land costs and proximity to shipment ports, distribution centers have risen to amass over one billion square feet of the region. Although these centers have provided many residents with employment, most of these jobs are outsourced via temporary labor agencies (Allen, 38), which leaves workers with precarious schedules, poor working conditions, and little to no benefits.

These warehouses have been found to produce six hundred thousand truck trips per day, which produce about fifty million pounds of carbon dioxide (Newton). This, along with the region's specific geography, has resulted in some of the worst air quality in the country.

> "Particulate matter generated by diesel engines at intermodal facilities, coupled with pollution blowing eastwards from Central Los Angeles exacerbated the already-poor air quality in the Inland area. By 2001, for example, the South Coast Air Quality

---

3. I highly recommend looking up the warehousing in Nueva Esperanza, Tijuana.

Management District found that Mira Loma Village, a low-income Latino community in Riverside County had the highest levels of particulate pollution in the nation." (Sarathy, 257)

Diesel particulate matter (DPM) is incredibly small. With its microscopic size, it has the ability to stay in the air much longer than other particulate matter. Not only is DPM directly linked to respiratory health issues, it also carries the potential to affect cardiovascular and autoimmune health. Approximately 70 percent of cancer risk in Southern California can be directly linked to diesel particulate matter alone (Haigh, 26).

Penny Newman, founder of the Center for Community Action and Environmental Justice (CCAEJ) in Jurupa Valley, once stated, "Children born in San Bernardino or Riverside county will be exposed to as many carcinogens in the first 12 days of their life as most people are in 70 years" (Allison, 181).

But who specifically is breathing in this air?

Latino residents make up 80–90 percent of the community in South Fontana, the area where Jurupa Hills High School is located (Haigh, 6) and the area that inspired this novel.

In a heartbreaking parallel, this community similarly exceeds the 80th–90th percentile of DPM in the air. Northern Fontana has fewer warehouses, and has a DMP rate that ranks as low as the 20th percentile (Haigh, 27).[4]

---

4. Latino residents also make up 80 percent of warehouse workers in the region, 40 percent of which are immigrants (Allen, 40). I want to stress that air quality affects all residents, and is not specific to this ethnic group. Inversely, in midwestern logistic centers, Black Americans are the group most represented in this workforce (Reese, 103).

When I began writing this book, that sole warehouse sat beside the school. By the time of this book's publication, three additional warehouses were approved to surround the campus (Victoria).

These decisions have not come without resistance. Local activists and organizers frequently voice their concerns regarding such egregious approvals, but local governments are dismissive, to put it kindly.

Public comments at city council meetings should be a place where community members can speak on their concerns. However, some activists suspect that decisions about warehouse construction are made surreptitiously, and that the public comment periods are largely for show (Haigh, 42).

> "At a public hearing I attended, one woman gave public comments about how she, as an adult, had been diagnosed with asthma. Another spoke about her young son waking up to a bloody pillow, from nosebleeds every morning. . . . The council was, except for one member, completely uninterested in their commentary, with the Mayor scrolling on her phone during anti warehouse public comments, before voting in favor of warehouse development." (Haigh, 40)

I'm asked frequently why I write for children.

There are many answers to that question. At my core, I believe young readers should have access to books that entertain them just as much as they teach them and challenge them.

But the more I've thought about it, the more I've realized that it's really because I am afraid.

I learned about contaminated water in Oakland from the ivory tower of a university, a place that, for many people, is completely inaccessible. I don't want readers to have to walk down a pathway similar to mine to learn about harm in their own communities.

Apart from the test scores required to get into college, many of which (including the SAT and ACT) have been found to be based on eugenics and racist practices (Rosales and Walker), even if students jump through all of those hoops successfully, there still comes the question of paying for university.

Financing tuition is one of the largest barriers that most Black and Latino students will face when attempting to go to a university (Baum, 208; Baum and Flores, 187). It is one of the main reasons why I wrote this book—to tell the story of young people who do not aspire to *go* to university, but to *pay* for university.

Many of these students cannot attend college not because they are not intelligent, but because myriad systems have worked to make it impossible for them to afford it. It's an easy domino effect: no money, no school; no school, no language; no language, no power.

I worry that students will not know they are working against the weight of oppression because they simply do not have the language to identify it as such. Particularly in our current political climate, where access to these topics is being erased, even in the expensive confines of academia. Language is the first key to identify a problem as a problem, and the portal to linking these problems to other histories.

But what is most fascinating about this for me is that this is not just about identifying oppression—it's about the potential of discovering personal history. I spent a summer of undergrad taking a Latin

American studies class. I remember sitting in a classroom on the west side of campus, sweating in the un-air-conditioned heat, taking notes on the Bracero Program.

The Bracero Program was a program that was started during World War II. Mexican men were given permission to cross the US border to work in agricultural fields in exchange for money and remittances to send back to México. The program centered on Mexican men specifically, using racist pseudoscience that determined they were biologically suited for field work, as they were too intellectually inferior, specifically compared to white men, to perform other forms of labor (Saucedo, 553).

Subsequently, participants in the program were picked not only based on their perceived physical aptitude, but on their appearance of docility—someone who looked like they would not fight or talk back.

A representative of an agricultural committee went so far as to state, "[T]here never was a more docile animal in the world than the Mexican" (Saucedo, 549).

Despite its positive depiction in media (Oliva, 152), the program rarely, if ever, gave what it promised. Braceros were often paid little to no wages, ate spoiled food, and were forcibly sprayed with pesticides.[5]

While braceros commonly faced backlash from white residents,

---

5. Braceros were not the first Mexicans to face such barbaric treatment. In the early twentieth century, Mexicans were often subjected to medical inspections along the border. Many were forcibly bathed and deloused because of their perceived uncleanliness. This process included fumigation using Zyklon B, which is poisonous to humans. German firms later mass-produced Zyklon B; Nazis would utilize it in the gas chambers of the Holocaust (Romo, 240). These practices were, however, met with resistance. In 1917, one young woman by the name of Carmelita Torres refused to be deloused and began the Bath Riots (Khanmalek, 335). She was only seventeen, and reminds me of the strength young women have in the face of adversity and oppression.

they also faced criticism from other documented Mexicans in the United States. Because braceros were often used as strikebreakers during major unionization attempts, like the United Farm Workers movement, they were met with harassment and slurs, being called "wetbacks" and "illegals" even by notable civil rights leaders like César Chávez (Saldana).[6]

My grandfather was a bracero.

He was often forced to break strikes to be able to send remittances back to México for my mother and her family. His history reminds me of the nuance and complications around strike culture, and helped form the arc for Ale's family. Someone trying to get by while stuck between a pendulous dichotomy: a right and a wrong side; with this strike or against it.

There are obviously many differences between the Bracero Program and the warehousing industry. However, when I did my research to draft this book, I was boggled by the parallels:[7] the promise of a positive work environment only to be left with deception, abuse, and health ramifications, specifically as they relate to the respiratory system. In the same region where many Mexican men picked fruit to send across the country, many Latino people are presently packaging same-day delivery shipments.

But I wouldn't have known any of that if I had not sat in that specific classroom, on that specific day, taking notes on that specific lecture.

---

6. In fact, Chávez went on to organize an "Illegals Campaign" to help identify undocumented workers and assist in their deportation. Chávez holds a very complicated legacy, to say the least.

7. Some of these parallels do include the temporary labor agencies, which I touched on earlier. Nicholas Allen writes, "One could argue that the structure of employment in the Inland Empire never really changed when the region's economy changed from the agricultural to goods movement; the only difference is the workers are now indoors" (38).

And although I am grateful to have garnered this knowledge, I am so resentful.

I don't think any person should have to learn about their history, their oppression, their victory, within the confines of an institution that many of them will eventually be indebted to.

Although I believe that this educational access should be free, that higher education opportunities should be free, that there should be no such thing as FAFSA or scholarship foundations because learning should be free, that is not the world we live in, nor one I can bring about on my own.

Until then, I tell stories.

My goal with writing this book was to provide young readers with an entryway to these complex issues in a way that felt accessible and to ask: What *else* happens when a warehouse is built in a community?

Paloma's character was formed when I wondered how such a macroscopic choice affects a person on a microscopic level. The decision to build warehouses in her community does not just affect the air quality or the health of her loved ones, but significantly alters her family life, her friendships, and her relationships. They build over the memories of jaripeos,[8] splinter her already-strained relationship with her mother, and lead her to lose her first love.

But I also wanted to open a portal for them to learn about allostatic

---

8. Many people are attempting to conserve the equestrian lifestyle that is being jeopardized by this environmental discrimination. Though the organizers I had a chance to speak to are not based in the IE, they faced similar marginalization in their community of Avocado Heights when a battery-recycling plant pushed to expand its operations and threatened their historic and agrarian lifestyle, and when the Los Angeles City Council posed a rodeo ban on the community (Molina).

load, and the Whitehall study of health, and how redlining has created mass health disparities among marginalized communities. If you are a reader who already knew about the warehousing industry and the information outlined above, I hope this book has affirmed your knowledge. And if not, I hope this book has inspired you to question, to wonder, and always, always, always to learn more—I certainly did.

In many ways, I am now those students in my Urban Education class—imagining an oppression I have never faced directly.

In order to write this book, I read research article after research article, attended conferences, and interviewed community members on an experience I will never understand. I wrote most of it in the comfort of my home in the Bay Area, which boasts some of the cleanest air quality in all of California. I do not suffer from any respiratory health conditions, particularly not by way of my living situation. I have the privilege of indulging in research that I fictionalized for the sake of art instead of living in it.

My acknowledgments section will encompass this further, but I want to say clearly that I am an outsider to these issues. I believe wholeheartedly that the most important work, and work that should be most championed, is the work of local activists, organizers, and community members in the Inland Empire, many of whom helped me through the process of writing this story. To those of you: thank you. I hope this book serves as a testament to the work you have done, the resiliency of your community, and the hope that is rooted beneath it.

Bibliography

Works Cited (Author's Note)

Allen, Nicholas. "Exploring the Inland Empire: Life, Work, and Injustice in Southern California's Retail Fortress." *New Labor Forum* 19, no. 2 (2010): 36–43. www.jstor.org/stable/25701485.

Allison, Juliann Emmons. "What Happens When Amazon Comes to Town?: Environmental Impacts, Local Economies, and Resistance in Inland Southern California." In *The Cost of Free Shipping*, edited by Jake Alimahomed-Wilson. Pluto Press, 2020. www.jstor.org/stable/j.ctv16zjhcj.18.

Baum, Sandy. " Student Debt: The Unique Circumstances of African American Students." In *Race and Ethnicity in Higher Education: A Status Report*. American Council on Education. www.equityinhighered.org/resources/ideas-and-insights/student-debt-the-unique-circumstances-of-african-american-students/.

Baum, Sandy, and Stella M. Flores. "Higher Education and Children in Immigrant Families." *Future Child* 21, no. 1 (2011): 171–93.

CBS San Francisco. "Community Demands End to Lead

Contamination in Oakland Schools." CBS News, November 1, 2017. Accessed May 7, 2025. www.cbsnews.com/sanfrancisco/news/community-demands-end-lead-contamination-oakland-schools/.

Curtis, John. "On campus." *Yale Medicine: Alumni Bulletin of the School of Medicine* 45–47 (2011–2013): 9. archive.org/details/yalemedicinealum4547yale/page/n157/mode/2up.

Gay, Geneva. "Preparing for Culturally Responsive Teaching." *Journal of Teacher Education* 53, no. 2 (2002): 106–16. Accessed April 2025. www.design.iastate.edu/imgFolder/files/Culturally_Responsive_Teaching_Geneva_Gay.pdf.

Haigh, Chanah. "Concrete Everywhere: A Project-Based Analysis of the Unequal Distribution of Warehouses in Fontana." Scholarship @ Claremont, 2023. Accessed May 6, 2025. scholarship.claremont.edu/scripps_theses/2040/.

Khanmalek, Tala. "'Wild Tongues Can't Be Tamed': Rumor, Racialized Sexuality, and the 1917 Bath Riots in the US-Mexico Borderlands." NIH.gov, 2021. Accessed May 7, 2025. pmc.ncbi.nlm.nih.gov/articles/PMC8211937/pdf/41276_2021_Article_324.pdf.

Molina, Alejandra. "The Avocado Heights Vaquer@s and the Preservation of a Lifestyle." *Los Angeles Times*, July 9, 2023. www.latimes.com/delos/story/2023-07-09/avocado-heights-vaquer-s-and-a-preservation-of-a-lifestyle.

Newton, Jim. "California Warehouse Boom Comes with Health, Environmental Costs for Inland Empire Residents." CalMatters, January 26, 2023. Updated August 1, 2024. Accessed January 29,

2023. calmatters.org/commentary/2023/01/inland-empire-california-warehouse-development/.

Oliva, Alejandra. *Rivermouth: A Chronicle of Language, Faith, and Migration*. Astra Publishing House, 2023.

Reese, Ellen. "Gender, Race, and Amazon Warehouse Labor in the United States." In *The Cost of Free Shipping*, edited by Jake Alimahomed-Wilson. Pluto Press, 2020. https://doi.org/10.2307/j.ctv16zjhcj.13.

Romo, David Dorado. *Ringside Seat to a Revolution*. Cinco Puntos Press, 2005.

Rosales, John, and Tim Walker. "The Racist Beginnings of Standardized Testing." neaToday, March 20, 2021. Accessed October 10, 2025. www.nea.org/nea-today/all-news-articles/racist-beginnings-standardized-testing.

Saldana, Sean. "The Complicated Legacy of César Chávez." KUT News, October 17, 2022. www.kut.org/texasstandard/2022-10-17/cesar-chavez-complicated-legacy-united-farm-workers-immigration.

Sarathy, Brinda. "Legacies of Environmental Justice in Inland Southern California." *Race, Gender & Class* 20, nos. 3/4 (2013): 254–68. www.jstor.org/stable/43496944.

Saucedo, Leticia. "Anglo Views of Mexican Labor: Shaping the Law of Temporary Work Through Masculinities Narratives." *Nevada Law Journal* 13, no. 2 (2013): 547–63.

Victoria, Anthony. "Fontana Approves Three Warehouses Next to Jurupa Hills High School." KVCR, November 16, 2023. Accessed February 21, 2024. www.kvcrnews.org/2023-11-16

/fontana-approves-three-warehouses-next-to-jurupa-hills-high-school.

Williams, D. R., and Chiquita Collins. "Racial Residential Segregation: A Fundamental Cause of Racial Disparities in Health." *Public Health Reports* 116, no. 5 (2001): 404–16. www.ncbi.nlm.nih.gov/pmc/articles/PMC1497358/pdf.

References

AirNow Interactive Map. Environmental Protection Agency. Accessed June 2023. gispub.epa.gov/airnow/.

A People's History of the Inland Empire Digital Archive. Accessed May 6, 2025. omeka.ucr.edu/collections/s/peopleshistoryie/page/welcome.

"Bracero Program Exhibit Captures Inland Empire Connection." *Daily Bulletin*, September 26, 2011. Accessed May 6, 2025. www.dailybulletin.com/2011/09/26/bracero-program-exhibit-captures-inland-empire-connection/.

Chen, Shanshan, and Nicky Milne, dirs. *Earth Focus*. Season 4, episode 3, "Fighting for Air." PBS SoCal. Accessed August 20, 2024. www.pbssocal.org/shows/earth-focus/episodes/fighting-for-air.

Cheney, Matt. "Fontana." History and Social Justice. June 10, 2021. Accessed May 6, 2025. justice.tougaloo.edu/sundowntown/fontana-ca/.

Durazo, Fernanda. *Vaquero on Empty Plot of Land on Linden Ave and Santa Ana Ave Looking South/East*, 2023. Accessed July 2023. fernandadurazo.com.

Esquivel, Paloma. "When Your House Is Surrounded by Massive Warehouses." *Los Angeles Times*, October 27, 2019. www.latimes .com/california/story/2019-10-27/fontana-california-warehouses -inland-empire-pollution.

Figueroa, Sofia, dir. *The Warehouse Empire*. KVCR | PBS, 2024. Accessed May 6, 2025. pbs.org/show/the-warehouse-empire/.

Grajeda, Andre. "El Paso Border Practices Influence the Holocaust | The Texas Story Project." Bullock Museum. www.thestoryoftexas.com /discover/texas-story-project/el-paso-holocaust-influence.

Ladson-Billings, Gloria. "The Social Funding of Race: The Role of Schooling." *Peabody Journal of Education* 93, no. 1 (2018): 90–105. https://doi.org/10.1080/0161956x.2017.1403182.

López del Río, Celia, and Karla López del Río. "California's Inland Empire: Harbinger of the New Multiracial Suburb." The Future of Cities, January 13, 2023. www.thefutureofcities.org/californias -inland-empire-harbinger-of-the-new-multiracial-suburb/.

Los Angeles Times. "How Online Shopping Is Polluting California's Inland Empire." *Los Angeles Times*, November 18, 2021. YouTube video, 8:27. www.youtube.com/watch?v=oqmqVCp1634.

Man in Front of Orchard Holds Sign "Remove Bracero Strikebreakers" in Santa Cruz, California. 1956 to 1971, photograph. California Revealed. Accessed December 2023. californiarevealed.org /do/c7ca4811-42d8-415b-86eb-14a7852b3293#page/1.

Medina, Ernest "Jimmy." "Ernest 'Jimmy' Medina Interview." A People's History of the Inland Empire Digital Archive. July 20, 2000. Accessed March 2024. omeka.ucr.edu/collections/s/peopleshistoryie /item/28342#?c=&m=&s=&cv=.

Nadel, Leonard. *Bracero Workers Being Fumigated in Hidalgo Processing Center.* 1956, photograph. National Library of Medicine. Accessed February 2024. www.nlm.nih.gov/exhibition/outsideinside/collection-detail.html?imgid=25&imgName=OB12511-md.

Nelson, Shelby. "Settlement Reached with City of Fontana Over Warehouse Environmental Issues." KTL 5, April 18, 2022. YouTube video, 3:06. Accessed May 6, 2025. www.youtube.com/watch?v=hTiVYErxHFU.

Phillips, Susan A., and Michael C. McCarthy. "Warehouse CITY—an Open Data Product for Evaluating Warehouse Land-Use in Southern California." *Environment and Planning B: Urban Analytics and City Science* 51, no. 8 (2024): 1965–73. https://doi.org/10.1177/23998083241262553.

Reddy, Ajitha. "The Eugenic Origins of IQ Testing: Implications for Post-Atkins Litigation." *DePaul Law Review* 57, no. 3 (2008): 667–77. via.library.depaul.edu/cgi/viewcontent.cgi?article=1270&context=law-review.

Singh, Maanvi, and Aliya Uteuova. "Revealed: How Warehouses Took Over Southern California 'Like a Slow Death.'" *The Guardian*, December 29, 2022. www.theguardian.com/us-news/2022/dec/29/e-commerce-warehouses-amazon-ups-fedex-california-pollution.

Solon, Olivia, and April Glaser. "'Treated Like Sacrifices': Families Breathe Toxic Fumes from California's Warehouse Hub." NBC News, April 27, 2021. www.nbcnews.com/tech/tech-news/treated

-sacrifices-families-breathe-toxic-fumes-california-s-warehouse-hub-n1265420.

Stephens, Edward K. H., Henry M. Marshall, Venessa Chin, and Kwun M. Fong. "Air Pollution and Lung Cancer—a New Era." *Respirology* 28, no. 4 (2023): 313–15. https://doi.org/10.1111/resp.14464.

Tejada-Vera, B., B. Bastian, E. Arias, L. A. Escobedo, B. Salant. "Life Expectancy Estimates by U.S. Census Tract, 2010–2015." National Center for Health Statistics. 2020. www.cdc.gov/nchs/data-visualization/life-expectancy/index.html.

Acknowledgments

IF YOU READ MY DEBUT NOVEL, YOU KNOW HOW I FEEL about acknowledgments sections. To this day, they remain my favorite part of any book—both to read and to write. As the months and years have passed since my debut, many people have written to me or approached me at book events to discuss my first acknowledgments section. Unbeknownst to myself, I have created large shoes to fill. But it is my honor to fill them.

Jen, the summer my second book was due was the same summer I called you and told you I was scrapping that idea and starting over with a brand-new novel. Thank you for not freaking out, for believing in this ambitious concept, and for always pushing for this book to be better.

Elizabeth, thank you for your support when I pivoted to this story. Your feedback and mentorship have been invaluable in this process.

Rosemary, thank you for all you do at Quill Tree and in children's publishing. It is always an honor to work alongside you!

Shona, thank you for your careful eye in this copyedit.

Andrea, thank you for your thorough sensitivity read and for the attention you have given this book!

Alberto, Alberto, Alberto. You are owed one of those impactful, special, last-page-of-the-acknowledgments-section nods. But you're here at the beginning, because meeting many of the people beneath it may have been impossible without you. In the panic of not knowing who to talk to first to get my research started, you started this daisy chain of connection, and got me up on my feet, like you frequently do. Thank you for that, but thank you, especially, for that time you were sitting on my couch, listening to me worry about how writing this book would make many people think I was crazy, and saying, "When have you ever cared what people thought about you? You're really gonna start *now*? Who has the book contract here? Just you." I love you!

Enith, your experience as a medical assistant and an older sister to a younger brother was clearly not lost on me. Yvette's character is not you, but she wouldn't exist without you. Thank you for picking up the phone every time I had a question about scrubs or oximeters or urgent care shifts.

Liz. Where do I start? Thank you for not thinking I was insane when I flew down to San Bernardino to ambush you at a conference when you wouldn't answer my emails. Thank you for the many, many hours you spent on the phone with me while I wrote this book. I know the advocacy you have for your community has inspired so many people; it has deeply inspired me. I hope you feel your legacy is honored here. Paloma would not exist without you.

Anna, thank you for hopping on the phone with me years back to discuss your work with the CCAEJ, among all else. Your honesty and vulnerability about what it's like to raise children in the IE really helped me understand a perspective I could have never imagined before. Thank you.

Shane, you were one of the first people who allowed me to interview them. Thank you for giving me your insight and for all the work you do with the CCAEJ.

Toni, thank you for taking the time to speak with me about your process of organizing—both in activism and in art, and in the ways the two reconcile. Attending the *Our Common Foe* exhibit laid the way for this book's progress—I still think about the installation including warehouse noise often.

Fernanda, I looked at your artwork every single day while I drafted this book. Every time someone came to my place, they were just as awestruck as I was the first time I saw it in the Little Gallery. Thank you for answering my many questions and letting me get insight into your artistic process. You are the archivist and artist of a generation.

James, thank you for sharing your insight with me about what it is like to work in a warehouse. Our conversation shaped the details for Paloma's pa. Thank you.

Toni, thank you for making me laugh for so many years and for letting me ask you questions about what it was like to grow up in Rancho. Thank you for keeping me sane the first time I met you at that conference and for being the only person who understood my weirdly specific internet references about the Cheetah Girls and tuna sandwiches dipped in fruit punch.

Dr. Claudia, thank you for answering my cold DM many

summers ago. Thank you for meeting with me in a coffee shop in Fremont to discuss your work, guerrilla farming, and school mascots.

Genevive, thank you for also answering my cold DM after I saw your TikTok about warehouses in Moreno Valley. Thank you for telling me about your father's work sharing his love for plants with his community. It was such a minor detail in the scope of our conversation, and it somehow formed the backbone to Julio's pa. Thank you.

Samuel, thank you for taking the time to discuss your work with the Avocado Heights Vaquer@s with me. The work you are doing to preserve the equestrian lifestyle of your community in the face of environmental injustice inspired so much of this story. That culture was absent from this book until our conversation, and later became such a foundational piece of it. Thank you for that insight.

Anthony, thank you for all you do for the Frontline Observer, and for taking the time to talk to me. Your specific insight about the responsibility of journalism really stuck with me, and found its way to this story.

Chanah, your undergraduate research paper about warehousing was one of my major pillars of research. Thank you for the depth of that research, for answering my emails, and for making the time for a call all the way from the Czech Republic, even with our nine-hour time difference.

Gem, thank you for discussing the Air I Breathe with me. That same air monitor study made its way to these pages! It was a small part of our conversation and a small detail in this book, but your anecdote about going to México to purchase inhalers really stayed with me. Thank you.

Sofia, thank you for your work through Come & See Media. I have rewatched your (now Emmy-winning!) documentary about warehousing in the IE a handful of times and am always awestruck by your attention to detail. Thanks for taking the time to talk to me—shout-out to John 1:46.

Angie, thank you for speaking to me about your work as an organizer and the passion and fervor you shared with me about the love you have for your community.

Nene, when I think about all the dominoes that had to fall for me to write this book, they really begin with you. Shout-out to UCSC orientation and Pomona and all the ugly graphics of mine you made better. You've pep-talked me more times than I can remember. I am so privileged to know you and have you in my life. I love you.

Thank you to Susan Phillips and Mike McCarthy for their work on the Warehouse City map and their panel at the CCAEJ conference, both of which helped me tremendously in writing this book.

Thank you to everyone who embraced my first book so warmly. Huge love to the American Library Association, the *LA Times* Book Prize Committee, the Junior Library Guild, and the American Booksellers Association. A specific shout-out to Erin of the Frugal Frigate in Redlands—what a serendipitous connection. I hope you enjoyed your Easter egg here.

Thank you to all the indie booksellers— shout-out to the folks at Mrs. Dalloway's.

Thank you to all the unions; I am privileged to be part of one.

Thank you to my Berkeley cohort and to Fergie for "Big Girls Don't Cry." Allia, I missed you last time. Thank you, Allia.

Thank you to Highway 138.

Thank you to the smell of warm dirt.

Thank you to the smell of México.

Thank you to Mexicans.

Thank you to bubble gum ice cream and to the way it stains my tongue blue.

Thank you to street vendors, always.

Thank you to Dr. Robert Bullard.

Thank you to Hazel M. Johnson.

Thank you to Pam Muñoz Ryan and *Esperanza renace*.

Thank you to my ecopoetry class in undergrad, which I begrudgingly took for a graduation requirement and it ended up changing my life.

Thank you to my Urban Education class and to Dr. Lashaw.

Thank you to academia for teaching me to love research.

Fuck you to academia for being so far removed from the real world and systematically inaccessible to the people who may benefit most from it.

THANK YOU TO JSTOR! JSTOR, I LOVE YOU.

Thank you to carpal tunnel braces, which literally held me together the summer my hands gave out mid-revision.

Thank you to the idiom "until the cows come home."

Thank you to reggaeton, my favorite SSRI.

Thank you to Leila, thank you for pushing for more romance in this book, even when it made me feel violently sick to my stomach.

Thank you for all those walks in the summer and for reminding me that maybe I am a little crazy, but mostly I am just a writer.

Thank you to Mo, who read perhaps too many drafts of this book, laughed at parts that were too dramatic, pushed at parts that were not dramatic enough, and fed me many beautiful things she baked in the process.

Thank you to Sharon, who makes sure I go to all of my dentist appointments, even when I do *not* want to. Big, big shout-out to Steve and all the ladies at Seaport Dental. RIP Buddy.

Thank you to Sonal, for letting me cry and cry and cry in her backyard that one August afternoon when I was frustrated with writing this book and everything else happening in my life. Thank you for pushing me to think critically and dive deeper in everything, always.

Thank you to Reena, for holding me up at work and in life.

Thank you to my sister, whose degrees in public health and health administration really came in handy here.

Thank you to Frank Ocean. For so many things, but today, for writing that bull and matador line in "Solo" that I, lamentably, could not add to my epigraph. But it's there in the spirit of this book.

Thank you to the Taurus and Orion constellations.

Thank you to Beyoncé. The *Cowboy Carter* album was the score I listened to while I revised this book, specifically that galloping rhythm in "II HANDS II HEAVEN."

Thank you to the Dictionary app, but a *bigger* thank-you to the thesaurus tab in that app. Shout-out shout-out shout-out to the thesaurus tab.

Thank you to the Shelly family, who took me to Nicho's the first time I visited.

Thank you to sports paraphernalia.

Thank you to dartboards.

Thank you to TV trays.

Thank you to colors that are verbs. Thank you to poetry, which taught me all colors can be verbs.

Thank you to Mo, my astrologist, for reminding me that I am not cosmically destined to doom. Thank you to all my air sign friends who remind me to take my life less seriously—big love to the Geminis.

Thank you to my car.

Thank you to all the music videos I watch on Sundays when I'm folding my laundry and changing my sheets.

Thank you to mechanical bulls and shipping containers—shout-out to Rosalía.

Thank you to coin-operated horses.

Thank you to jaripeos.

Thank you to hangars.

Thank you to Q-Tip for that quote about the sophomore jinx.

Thank you to Cristina. Some days, writing this book felt like the hardest thing in the entire world. But you made sure whatever air bike workout you had planned for me that week would somehow be harder.

Thank you to Karen, for spying all my comments on Jessica's videos when she was picking out what to wear to her next jaripeo.

Thank you to Rosa for reminding me, "It's not about *that*, it's about *this*," every time I felt a little lost on the intention of this book.

Thank you to Raha, who read so, so, so many drafts of this book, its chapters, and random lines I had questions about. Who was on call the weekend of the ALAs. Who watched me sit in a pupusería and draft several different maps for this book that were all scrapped. And who reminded me that I "write books for smart people." Become a copyeditor already!

Thank you to my students, who keep me grounded, open, and always humble.

Thank you to the triplets I taught, who drove me crazy for ten months, but who I love so much that I had to honor them in this book.

Thank you, thank you, thank you to patience and delayed gratification.

Thank you to my grandfather, who I thought of when writing Julio's pa, because I watched him paint houses and garden all through my childhood.

Thank you to all the Latina girls. I write for you first, always.

Thank you to everyone who told me writing this book was a bad idea.

Thank you to everyone who told me writing this book was my prerogative.

Thank you to my Madrina and all those road trips to Riverside to visit her.

Thank you to outlet malls for back-to-school shopping.

Thank you to Stater Bros., Edwards Cinemas, and Islands restaurants.

Thank you to artistry, for giving me something to do with the many loose ends of my life, and giving me the opportunity to tie them into something beautiful.

Thank you to the past and all it has brought to the present.

To those I missed, thank you.

To those coming, thank you.

And God. I am so profoundly grateful that you have given me what I have needed and not what I have wanted. My favorite poem is by Rainer Maria Rilke, and in it, he writes about holding God's hand. I'm holding yours tight for this one! Thank you.